AMARANTH

BOOK 1

DAVID M. SNOW

FLAME ARROW PUBLISHING

Amaranth (Amaranth #1)

Cover design by Damonza

Printed in Canada

First Printing: 2023

Legal Deposit: 2023

Published by Flame Arrow Publishing

ISBN 978-1-9903680-1-1

www.flamearrowpublishing.com

www.davidmsnow.com

To my parents
For making my dreams possible

1

SKYLER

EVERY BREATH IS AGONY AND THE WAIT, UNBEARABLE. FOR A moment, the man seems to be free of his illness, but at the last second, he gasps in a large gulp of air, as if he were about to drown.

Skyler monitors his patient's irregular vital signs closely.

The Fairies have been relentless with their victim this time. They are unpredictable, and especially cunning. They will now enrapture the man by luring him into their invisible realm. It's a one-way ticket. First, the Fairies induce dreams of a world where anything is possible, where the Flood never happened. The dreams are a little longer each time, and then the harrowing of hell begins.

There is no shame in being tempted. Even Skyler would like a second chance.

But fairies do not exist, of course.

The pungent stink of solvent wafting off the patient is Skyler's cue to prepare the procedure. Everything must be ready before the man slips to the other side. It's a swift process, only a few minutes, and every second is crucial.

Skyler leaves the man momentarily to gather what he needs

for the next step. He makes his way through cases of pharmaceuticals—mostly painkillers—to the back of the circular room, where sits a recessed cabinet. He holds his breath and drags open a large, heavy cabinet drawer, its worn metal screeching, where a dozen remaining spheres each lie on its cushion, asleep, waiting for a host. The missing spheres are already buzzing with life in the Archives. Skyler makes a mental note to hit up the warehouse of the Medical Bay soon and replenish his supply.

He smiles at the gentle coolness of transparent glass in his palm. This is a victory that will change the course of history.

He closes the drawer, taking care not to damage the remaining spheres. They are invaluable, the result of many years of research and heated debates with his mentor, Dr. Nazar.

Skyler walks back to the dying man as Mira scribbles a few notes. His colleague's skin is strikingly pale, her freckles almost invisible in the stinging overhead light that dissolves all color in its path. Delta Division should have taken care of the ward's poor lighting by now, but just as with every other request aboard the Ark, Skyler would have to be patient.

He fits the sphere into the depression that feeds into the encephalogram at the head of the bed: Its integrated touch screen lights up with interlocking curves. Skyler prepares the calibration by checking the signature of the host's brain activity: an array of unique frequencies, much like a fingerprint, that the system recognizes.

"I'm not sure I understand," Mira says to Skyler as she moves closer to the monitor, pen in hand.

"Make sure you adjust the sphere to the brain's maximum and minimum frequencies," he explains, pointing to numbers on the screen. "If you want any chance of encoding all their memories, be as accurate as possible. Averaging the data out won't do. You must scan all the data from the last twenty-four hours."

"The system's measurements aren't good?"

"It tends to leave out sudden variations. But even minor variation is important to storing all the memories. If the range of data is too wide, it introduces too much interference, making it impossible to tell one memory from another."

"Good to know."

A muffled moan draws their attention. The man is in critical condition.

"Get ready."

As always, the wait is unnerving, but also deeply sad. Even though they were trained to remain emotionally distant from their patients, Skyler can't help but feel a twinge of sadness for Francisco. The poor man has no one to spend his last moments with. No family to care for him.

When the Fairies do their work, though, the victim doesn't feel regret. Quite the opposite; it's all blank looks and blissful smiles; a hollow happiness towards death.

A long, hoarse sigh brings a sickening acrid smell. Francisco is no more.

"Now!" Skyler says firmly. He supervises Mira as she initiates the transfer.

Four minutes. It only takes four minutes to extract the entirety of someone's lived experiences. It doesn't seem long enough, but it can be done.

Sparks escape from the center of the awakening sphere. They become long, hair-like strands that diffuse into the water, twisting and entangling as they swirl counter-clockwise.

If only the many who died before Francisco could have had the same chance. The life experiences of every Archean are invaluable to those who will repopulate the Earth. Their ancestors fought to survive, but what has become of their joys, sorrows, fears—their stories? What made them human?

Forgotten. Every last one of them.

The swirling finally slows, and the emitted glow deepens, which means the transfer is complete. The sphere fills with a scarlet light, a hallmark to the disease's victory. It is the individual's electrical frequencies that determine the light's hue: a biological signature unique to each individual, one that cannot deceive. However, the Fairy Syndrome alters this signature, although no one knows why yet, but Skyler intends to find out. On his own, of course, since the Delta Division will never get involved—they have other priorities.

"Do you have any more questions?" he asks, dropping the still-warm sphere into a cushioned carrying case he's pulled from the cabinet.

"I think I'm okay," she replies, while she finishes jotting down some notes. "I just need to try by myself next time."

"You'll be all right," he says with an encouraging smile. "You've always been one of the most competent people here."

"Is this even worth it?" snaps a voice he wishes he hadn't heard. Chris. The son of the Paragon general of the Theta Division, Duke Kay. Top of their class, he was spoiled for choice; he could have joined the ranks of an army ready to answer to him at the drop of a hat, but instead, he makes their lives a living hell in Med Bay. No doubt his father couldn't handle him either.

"I mean, going to all this trouble for a bunch of average people who lead mind-numbing lives?" adds Chris, who crosses his arms, his perfect face warped by its usual sneer as he glares at him. Despite being in his early twenties, his cheeks are still as smooth as a child's, giving him a deceptively innocent look.

"And your life is more worthy?"

"My knowledge of modern medicine will be useful for future generations. As for him," says Chris, pointing at the dead patient with a disgusted look, "the Syndrome has already affected his brain beyond repair. Do you really want future generations to remember his bouts of madness? What's the point?"

"What if it's the key to saving us? All of us?" asks Skyler, his fingers clenching the box of Francisco's memories. Chris snorts with an amused half-smile.

"Don't take your dreams for granted. Just because Dr. Siria supports your ideas doesn't mean they'll make any difference."

"At least I'm trying to make sense of our work. For all of us." Chris gets close enough that his breath grazes Skyler's chin.

Skyler doesn't flinch. Chris has been the same ever since he can remember and Skyler avoids him as much as possible, ignores him even, but working together complicates things. Why does Chris go to such lengths? If he put as much work into caring for his patients as he does for himself, no one would have to work overtime.

A glint flashes through Chris's eyes. Is he enjoying himself?

"You're wasting your time," Duke's son scoffs. "This Syndrome is a fate that we must accept. It is a fair response to our sins."

Mira blinks and stares at each of them. Chris thinks he has the answer to everything—a trait he borrows from his father—but if anyone should spend more time in the sanctuary pondering his sins, it should be him. Has he ever actually been there? That would be a surprise. His family is not known for its piety. Even his own mother didn't have a proper funeral.

"How would you know?"

"It's not rocket science, Sky. You disappoint me. You really do. I thought you'd be more perceptive, but by the looks of it, sympathizing with these weaklings has affected you."

"I don't have to answer to you, so get out of my way. I've got work to do." Chris thinks, blocking Skyler's path, for a long while—so long, in fact, that Skyler considers pushing him out of his way. But then Chris steps over ever so slightly.

A missed opportunity. There will be more.

"Somehow, I understand Dr. Nazar," Chris says thoughtfully as Sky heads down the hall. "I would have given up too, just to avoid listening to your grumbling."

"Yeah, whatever," says Skyler, his back turned, ready to leave. Mira asks Chris to stop, but Skyler doesn't dwell. It's always the same with Chris. He's been opposed to this project from the beginning, arguing that the memory spheres should be for those who truly deserve them. Well, that's not for him to judge.

Everyone deserves a chance.

THE HARSH LIGHTING of Med Bay gives way to the dim light of the corridor, which mimics the amber glow of dusk—or at least dusk as it's described at the Academy. Skyler rubs his burning eyes, another telltale sign that the ship is contaminated by poorly filtered underwater oxygen. His father often complains about the problems with ventilation and high humidity that he and his colleagues in the Delta division, the Ark's largest division, have to deal with.

Skyler narrowly avoids a puddle as he enters the nearest elevator. The condensation beads lining the doors glow dimly in the evening light. He takes a seat among a few civilian Archeans, decked in Delta uniforms, chatting quietly. Deltas are found almost everywhere, given the considerable burden of maintaining the ship and its equipment. Skyler gently releases his grip from the case he has been carrying, his hands sore and fingers stiff from clutching it so tightly. He brushes over the numbered buttons on the elevator with his fingertips. Those for the dining room and cabins are faded, but number seven is clearly visible, shiny even. He presses it.

Chris's jab has dampened his spirits. If only Chris could stop making his life insufferable... He lost Skyler's trust in the past and his snarky remarks only make it worse.

The metallic creaking of the elevator is not exactly reassuring, but life on a century-old Ark isn't without its flaws.

He becomes aware of a baby near him crying, a bitter reminder of how uncertain their future is. Not only might this shabby elevator never make it to the top, but they might never make it out of the ship alive.

Upon reaching the seventh floor, Skyler follows the hallway towards two large glass doors and crosses two Paragon agents on silent patrol, their electric batons in plain sight, who pay little attention to him. He is asked to identify himself by a computer-generated voice and scans the wristband he's worn since birth. He's immediately granted access and the doors slide open, emitting a cool breeze that gives him shivers.

Welcome to the Archives of Humanity. May you be granted salvation.

If only it were that easy. Machines have an uncanny ability to take words intended to be comforting and render them meaningless.

The lobby of the highly protected Archives flaunts a swarm of surveillance cameras and concealed doors. There is a sacred feel to this place that houses everything the Archeans know about their ancestors' world. It bathes in a diffused light with a simple corridor leading to a spacious circular room, where an equally spacious and circular reception desk marks center stage. The other employees do not notice him, apart from the young girl who usually prepares his Nave. They exchange a smile, but nothing more.

The Nave is blinking at him, but he's already used up all the time allotted to him this month. Taking in the fragments of the lost world in these private cabins can be an intoxicating experience. Limiting their time is a silly rule, since hardly anyone comes here, but the Naves are few and should be available to all authorized personnel.

Skyler walks closer to the dark, slightly raised granite counter lit by a bluish backlight against a dark background which is not what you would expect for a place like the Archives. It contains no physical books, since most of them were washed away. Those that were digitized before the Flood remain in servers stored here while the rest is lost forever.

Dr. Siria is not here, but, knowing her, she can't be too far.

He crosses the large room and slips through the dark hall that leads to a seemingly invisible corridor; due to some optical illusion, black on black, it perfectly deceives prying eyes. A faint light at the end is all that guides him as he passes through.

A smell of newly heated plastic wafts through the air of the room specially equipped for his memory spheres project. The spheres are stored and decoded here. For now, there's nothing too impressive, just a terminal and a repository that collects the spheres, which can reveal the memories of past existences. At least that's what Nathan claims, the Delta engineer breaking protocol to help them.

"So soon?" Dr. Siria greets him, her gaze shifting from the terminal screen to the box. "Had I known there would be so many, I would have reconsidered your request."

"Should I just stop everything now?" he replies defensively, Chris's jab still hurting.

"Don't take it the wrong way," she laughs as he opens the box over the receptacle.

The threads within the sphere spin lazily, casting a glowing waltz of reddish light that dances on the walls of the dark room. Dr. Siria stares yearningly at the sphere, mesmerized, and moves in to take a closer look.

"I would have better prepared, that's all. It is a great privilege to add these to the collection." The glow casts curious shadows on the face of Valentina Siria, the only doctor daring enough to support his project from the beginning. Although Sky likes his mentor, Dr. Nazar has been skeptical, and Dr. Siria had to convince him by assuming all the risk.

"At least these people won't be forgotten," he says, reluctantly leaving the fragile globe in the care of his patron, who places it into the receptacle which swallows the sphere whole.

The room loses the warm glow that gave it life and only the cold remains.

"We will soon have to make sure our efforts are not in vain," adds Skyler, breaking the contemplative silence that had settled. "Though how we might do so eludes me."

"We must not lose hope," she answers, a faint smile on her lips. "If our ancestors had given in to despair, we wouldn't be together here today discussing this."

How much longer will they have to hang on to hope? Repopulating is unlikely at this time, and the memory spheres are still in their infancy. Not to mention the resilience of the Syndrome taking hold.

How can you defeat an enemy that does not exist?

2

EMILY

Fiona Reyes. The fresh case that adds to the dozens of prisoners being held for crimes that range from stealing food from the dining hall to corruption. But her situation is special.

Fiona Reyes is a Maverick.

She didn't come alone. There was this other guy with her, Milo. No last name: You don't need one when you're a Maverick. It's a waste of time. Even if he had one, no one would remember it. But this Reyes has something just as interesting as her last name: her arrogance. The report said she struggled with and spat on the officers handling her case that she was missing that bewildered look so characteristic of other Mavericks who were caught in the last few years.

Emily walks down the main corridor to the cell block, two steaming coffees in her hands. She takes a right into a secluded passage. The only door here is ajar and Emily steps inside. The office is empty, but it doesn't matter. Yasmina seemed troubled this morning in her email about Reyes. Catching Mavericks always does that to her. Emily puts one cup down on the workstation. Caffeine should help Yasmina get through this one; maybe even calm her down.

Emily walks back out of the office and heads towards the cells, which are sealed off by a heavy double door that could literally withstand anything. Her own wristband doesn't even allow her in.

"It must have been a long night," Emily says. She hands the second cup of black coffee to the guard, who takes a sip. His pallid face brightens up a little. He suddenly looks younger.

"Good luck with this one," Ludo tells her. "It wasn't easy to shut her up." His hair and eyebrows are almost white, though he is too young to go gray. Is it because of some trauma he had in his childhood? Despite the white hair, his skin has a dark tint that sucks all his colors into an impenetrable clump. He is hard to read, but not impossible. Right now, he's pissed, most likely because of this Reyes.

"You didn't give her too much tranquilizer?" she asks, raising her eyebrows.

"Only what she needs." He has a sneer hanging on his lips, his eyes sparkling.

"Look," she adds, seeing that he doesn't approve. "It's difficult to interrogate someone who's high." He grunts his consent, then lets her into what they call the Hall of the Forgotten.

Ludo clams up when he feels threatened. The last time, he didn't speak to her again for an entire week. But they have to work together, so his cooperation is vital. Not so long ago, he drugged a prisoner to the point of forgetting his own name. Ludo's methods are questionable because they encroach on Emily's interrogations. Writing up a satisfactory prisoner psychological profile is no small feat. And submitting a botched report … it's better not to think about it.

Emily's steps echo over the buzzing sound of the overhead ducts. A firm step. It is paramount to be in complete control of yourself, just in case. She must work without the protection of a guard to minimize interference with the analysis. She couldn't focus properly otherwise. An impassive attitude works wonders with inmates who think they can coax her out; they come up against a wall even stronger than the cell that confines them.

A screen buzzes up as Emily halts in front of cell number twenty-four: She lays a hand on it. The prisoner had her long, black hair turned to the surveillance camera. Will she pounce like a rabid animal?

A beep signals the scanner has read her wristband and Emily enters the cell.

The sound of the door as it closes seems to suck the air out of the cell along with it. A muffled thud replaces the buzzing sound from earlier. The young prisoner bursts into a throaty laugh. A chill runs down Emily's spine.

"They're already sending one of their elite agents," says Fiona Reyes, facing the opposite wall. "They sure aren't wasting any time." Reyes stares at the unadorned wall, the same drab walls that line the entire interior of the ship, metal plates interlocked in a lifeless maze. These cells look every bit like the Bates cabin, minus the clutter. They are oppressive. Even more so when ... no, don't think about it.

Emily swallows hard. Her throat stiffens dangerously, her lungs short of breath.

She hates this place.

"No, they aren't. And the sooner you talk, the sooner this will be over," she says, swallowing a gulp of air.

"I'm not saying anything if I can't see Milo." That prisoner with no last name? So they can work out an escape plan?

"You're in no position to negotiate anything." Reyes looks back at Emily, arms folded. She is stone-faced.

"You want to know where the other Mavericks are, right?" says Reyes casually.

"Obviously."

"If I tell you, can I see Milo?" She's so persistent ... is he her boyfriend or something? Why give in so soon? Not so clever for a Maverick.

"Is that all you want?"

"If that's what it'll take to get some peace in here, why not? It's not like it's a secret to anyone." Reyes stares back at her. Her sunken cheeks exaggerate her prominent cheekbones.

"So where are they?"

"You gotta promise you'll bring me to him."

"Fine," says Emily matter-of-factly. "If that'll get you to talk." Too easy. What's going on in her head? If only Emily knew Reyes's color, she could make a guess about her true intentions. Come on, focus, Emily.

"Everywhere," says Reyes. Emily slowly circles the prisoner who watches her. The colors are quiet today.

Reyes eyeballs her. Can she hear what Emily is hearing?

"They're everywhere," Reyes repeats, hands on her hips. "There's your answer. Now I want to see Milo."

"You're lying," says Emily, coming to a stop. The air ripples around the inmate, her throaty laughter bouncing against the gray walls of the cell. Some variations are taking shape, coming off her dark hair, some kind of feeling. A little more, and the color of her aura will show itself.

Emily walks around the prisoner again.

"And how can you be so sure?" Reyes asks out of sheer bravado. "You know nothing about me."

"Enough to know that you wouldn't give up that kind of information so easily." Reyes's hesitation reveals dancing pink edges around her dark hair.

"That's not the answer you want, but I don't want to waste my time with you," Reyes insists with a falsely smug look.

"How great is that? Me neither," retorts Emily as she heads for the door. "Now you know what to expect for my next visit."

"Hey, wait!" Reyes's dismay is palpable.

An awful chill runs down Emily's spine. For a second, her body is not her own. Her skin is blinding white, and freckles ravage her forearms. Her hair lengthens, burning her shoulders, a luminous shine that could be mistaken for fire. No! She's not giving in now.

"Sorry, I'm on a pretty tight schedule," says Emily in a softer voice.

"You promised I could see Milo," Reyes yells. A concealed dread is burrowing in her eyes. That is how prisoners feel around Emily.

Her mouth is pasty and her face is numb.

"I didn't promise anything," Emily says, staring straight into her eyes. The echo of her own words sounds oddly familiar.

Emily turns away to step out of the cell. She doesn't see the blow coming and she is thrown against the opposite wall. Blinded by rage, Fiona has her in a choke hold. Emily backs up hard and wedges her attacker against the wall. Fiona tightens her hold, but Emily headbutts her enough to loosen her fingers. Emily grabs the arm pressing against her throat and hurls Fiona to the ground. In an instant, Reyes is incapacitated, face down, her arm locked behind her back.

"Don't you ever touch me again," warns Emily in a whisper.

"Go to hell!" spits Reyes.

"Nothing's stopping me from finishing you off right here and now. So, answer my question. Where are the Mavericks hiding?"

"I … told you … already," sputters Reyes under the weight of the foot on her back.

"If that's what you want…" Fiona cries out in pain as Emily jerks her back up hard. She throws her back into the cell and seals the door immediately. Her muscles remain stiff as she tries to calm herself down with Reyes's laugh still buzzing in her head.

Inexplicable tremors shake through her body. She sits against the wall to collect herself. Ludo cannot see her like this, or he will report it to Yasmina. The last person to upset on this Ark.

The weight of Reyes' mangled body in her hands ... *by* her hands ... lingers. Her own safety had been put at risk. Nothing else could have saved her.

Emily rubs her wet cheeks with the back of her hand. Now's not the time.

SHE WALKS BACK down the Hall of the Forgotten and tries to clear her mind. A surprise attack is always unnerving. Given Reyes's resistance during her capture, it was almost obvious that she would try something. This is not the first time this has happened. Reyes didn't stand a chance.

Why can't her muscles relax?

She lets out a sigh. Hot, burning muscles.

Her nails dig into her palms, and she slows her pace as she nears the gate. She glances at cell number twenty-four.

The Mavericks... They must be well organized to stay off the radar and elude the watchful eye of the Paragon. Yet, it is surprising that they are still alive after all these years shut off in the lower levels. But since the Incident, combing through those parts has become more than an issue. What if...?

Ludo looks surprised to see her back so soon. He gulps down the rest of his large coffee.

"Cut down her rations for two days," says Emily without stopping.

He doesn't reply. Ludo's gaze follows her gesture to wipe the corner of her lips where blood is beading. Suddenly, she can make out Fiona Reyes's aura: pink. But not just any pink: the same shade some flowers that used to grow on Earth had ... but not anymore, of course, since everything flooded over. Reyes's color, difficult to perceive, is now clear. Clear enough, at least, to know exactly what kind of person she is.

She was not lying.

On her way to the elevator, Emily waves her wristband and moves through a circular machine that detects any objects she may have on her. All these procedures are such a pain.

Sometimes, she wonders who the actual prisoners are.

3

SKYLER

Skyler fills the pot with water and places it gently on one side of the old-fashioned table anchored in the unadorned wall. The light-pink flowers liven up his parents' neglected cabin. It looks like a crude metal nest that could well have sunk to the bottom of the sea with the rest of the former cities.

His parents never repaired the loose cabinets in the tiny kitchen area, nor replaced the stained and damaged fabric on the sofa. The only object of appeal in their home is the century-old Goldberg family boarding pass, proudly showcased, larger-than-life, on a particularly prominent wall. Lacking is a port-hole on to the depths of the ocean, and with it, a breath of free-dom. But these cabins are prized. Perhaps, when Skyler becomes a full-fledged doctor, he'll be able to get one.

He glances at the chrysanthemums with admiration, their outer petals in bloom, gradually revealing the inside of their cocoon. Their grassy aroma is soothing. This breakfast will be a little different from the others.

He rubs his burning eyes and finishes setting the table. It was a long night. The Fairy Syndrome is gaining momentum, and *someone* has to take care of all these new patients. Chris is entirely unreliable; he would much rather leave patients to their fate.

In the living room, his mother is mesmerized by the computer screen. She is unrecognizable: Her hair is short, her posture slumped, her shoulders hunched, her skin chalky. Not to mention her recent tendency to hold herself in a constant embrace.

She takes notice of him as if she knew he was watching. Skyler's throat knots. Murielle's eyes no longer have the same brightness. Back then, they glowed with motherly love. Now, there is an abyss of pain, in which she has taken refuge for the last five years.

Skyler calls her over for the dinner he has prepared—a privilege for prominent families, who are sometimes able to get a hold of ingredients to cook at home—and sits before a hot plate of fish, steam rising from it. It's not ideal, but there isn't much choice. He can't afford to be picky on a ship that has to feed nearly two thousand survivors. This is a necessary sacrifice.

Murielle doesn't seem to have heard him by the way she continues to stare at the still screen. Skyler feels as if he no longer exists in her eyes, but that's a burden he has to bear. He can only blame himself for his mother's grief.

He picks at his plate but has no appetite. Is it the lack of sleep? Or having to accept this new reality? Murielle stares blankly, as if looking for something … or someone. The way her eyes jerk back and forth is unnerving. Her symptoms are misleading, but she isn't suffering from the Syndrome; Otherwise she would be dead by now. Victims only survive a few weeks after their diagnosis. She resists all known treatments, and in such a situation, one can only hope that time is kind to her.

Or that she forgives him.

Instead, Skyler shoulders the silent judgment of his absent father, who expects his son to take responsibility for his mother's day-to-day care. Dylan works most of the time, and rarely comes home. Only when necessary.

The aroma from the untouched meals is fading.

"Mom, you should come eat," he repeats. She does not reply, as if reciting a quiet mantra, far from reality. Finally, she wearily pulls away from the family photographs on the screen and drags her feet towards the table. Her features are drawn, telltale of severe insomnia. She sits reluctantly across from him, the lump in Skyler's throat ever more present. Every time she sets her intense gaze on him, the awkwardness of the moment—a constant reminder of his guilt—deepens.

Murielle finally picks up the fork that has been clinking against her plate. She scrapes and crumbles, scrapes, and nibbles at her fish silently. Her silence stretches. Skyler's ears are ringing, deafened by the continuous clinking sound. He swallows hard and his food rolls in his mouth.

His mother noisily eats a bean and glances at him with a searching look that compels him to clean his plate. Food is valuable aboard. Wasting would not be wise.

The constant clattering of metal and china makes him choke on his food. Murielle stares wildly at the chrysanthemums.

"Why did you put them on the table?"

"I thought you'd like them," he replies, gently putting down his fork. "Aren't they beautiful?"

Murielle's face, pink like the flowers, is quickly shadowed over by a color far more somber. Her stare pulls away from the flowers and bores into him, anger mixed with sadness replacing the dull glare of her eyes.

"Do you even know what this is?" she asks, her voice bordering on hysteria.

"Mom, I..."

"Do not ever call me *mom* again! You did it on purpose!" Her accusation pierces through to his gut. Tension numbs his body.

"I swear, I had no idea! You have to believe me!" She clutches her chest and sobs. He springs to his feet and rushes towards the medicine cabinet in the bathroom. He grabs a tablet, rushes back to the table, and drops the whitish capsule in Murielle's hand. Between two hiccups, she brings it to her trembling lips and swallows.

He grabs the flowers, and they wilt in his hand as he chucks them into the garbage. A few seconds is enough for his mother to calm down. Obviously, the medicine hasn't kicked in yet, but at least she now has the impression that everything is under control.

She wipes her cheeks with the back of her hand and lies on the decrepit sofa. She has slipped into her abyss. Is that a smile he sees on her face?

This attack has passed, but for how long?

HE WAKES UP, nauseous, drowning in the rancid smell of his childhood bedroom, cluttered with trinkets his brother Allen hoarded as a teenager. Skyler must have dozed off after dinner without realizing.

The top-bunk mattress is exactly as he remembers it: small and uncomfortable, wedged into the corner where the wall and the ceiling meet. Allen hated heights, but Skyler always felt pleasantly light higher up. The nightlight that their father's friend retrieved from one of their hunts casts lazy spinning stars on the walls. Everything remains unchanged. When he closes his eyes, Skyler can almost hear Allen snoring, or even the gibberish he would mumble in his sleep.

Skyler pulls himself out of the thin, damp sheet, and hits his head on the ceiling. He rubs his head, swallowing the instinct to swear. He jumps down from the bed, squats, and opens Allen's drawer. A wave of nostalgia washes over him at the sight of artifacts from their past: notebooks of every size filled with notes beyond margins, superhero figurines whose names have been forgotten, the remote-controlled plane they so often played with in the corridors of the Ark. The left wing of the plane is broken now, its missing plastic piece lying at the bottom of the drawer. That unfortunate accident happened during an air race. Chris had convinced his father that he needed a plane too. He couldn't stand not having something that Allen or Skyler had. Of course, being Duke Kay's son, he wanted to win at all costs, but Allen was the competitive type. Faced with his inevitable defeat, Chris pinned Allen's plane at the last turn, and the hit against the wall severed the left wing. Chris did not feel guilty about it. Since then, Allen had kept his toy plane hidden away.

Murielle is moaning. Skyler shuts the drawer and goes to sit by her side in the living room.

He should have stayed awake to make sure the medication had relieved her pain. In the early months of her depression, the painkillers were not enough. At that time, Dylan had no choice but to take care of her himself. Murielle's screams haunted their nights, and Skyler could not sleep much. That was a long and difficult period of their lives. A relapse could happen any moment, and he should stay by her side after she takes her medication.

She seems all right, though. Her breathing has slowed and become regular. Her moaning must be about some dream she's having.

A lingering smell of fish prompts him to pull out a lemon-scented candle and place it on the small kitchen table where the flowers of their suffering had been. The Ark's resources are limited, though the hunts sometimes turn out fruitful. This candle, for example, was well preserved in an aluminum can. Water nibbles away at most unwrapped items, especially organic ones, but some hold up well.

Skyler lights the candle, unfazed by the clicking sound of the lock. Dylan is back.

"I'm home." The flame flickers as his father walks by and Murielle wakes up at the same time with a moan.

Skyler goes over to the kitchen sink to scrub the pan and notices his father's comings and goings in the minute that follows: Dylan puts down his briefcase on the dining table and walks up to his wife; he embraces her, and they kiss. He goes into the tiny bedroom, takes off his ashen Delta uniform, and puts on a bathrobe before heading to the shower. And he does all that as if the last twenty-four hours had never happened. Completely indifferent. But why should he worry about anything, anyway?

"The ocean currents are still unstable," Dylan says, taking on his expert voice. "And so, the next hunt will have to wait. The storms are multiplying, for a change." As if to prove him right, the Ark pitches ever so slightly, not quite enough for the candle slip to the ground.

Skyler does not reply. He does not want to talk to the oceanographer. Dylan will slip into quasi-father mode after his shower; that is, if he doesn't have any last-minute reports to hand in the next day, of course. Dylan does not follow him either. No wonder he never cared for Skyler's silence.

Ever since his teenage years, Murielle has harped on about how Skyler takes after Dylan. She is wrong. Now that Skyler is an adult, only differences exist between them; Dylan's hair is fairer than Skyler's, his muscles have disappeared over the years, and he shaves his beard down to the skin. If his mother was of sound mind, she would argue that Skyler is a workaholic just like his father. Skyler is not sure whether Dylan should be proud of this when it means neglecting his own family.

In the other corner of the living room, Dylan empties his briefcase and spreads his files out on the desk. Then he locks himself in the bathroom, a luxury on the Ark.

No "hello." No "how are you doing?" No "thank you for

taking care of your mother." Apparently, that goes without saying.

Fatigue hits Skyler hard, and he's tempted to duck out while his dad is in the shower. But he was so careless this afternoon…

Murielle groans on the sofa, back in limbo. He can't leave her until Dylan is done, which means he will have to face him again. Worse even: talk to him. Their conversations are purely functional. Despite his semblance of calm around his son, Skyler knows his father blames him for what happened.

The feeling is mutual.

Skyler chisels at the burned fish skin twice as hard. A bead of sweat strikes his forearm, yet he keeps scrubbing harder.

Dylan could have tried to be a proper father: he could have spent time with his children. But he's always been too busy. Even through hardship, Skyler had to fend for himself to show to Dylan that he didn't need him.

The stubborn skin finally lifts off the pan when Dylan, freshly washed, comes out of the bedroom in civilian clothing. He walks to his workspace and stops to kiss Murielle on the cheek. He turns to Skyler, with a questioning look.

"Your mother is boiling." What? Skyler drops the pan and checks himself by feeling her forehead with his wrist. "Last time I checked she wasn't feverish." Worry wells in his throat.

"What did she have for dinner?"

"Seriously, what is there to eat?" Dylan raises an eyebrow and Skyler adds more quietly, "It might be related to her meltdown today."

"What happened? She hasn't had one in a long time," his father asks, frowning. Dylan's naivety is baffling. Murielle's condition is far from improving: An episode is always lurking. They have become more frequent and unpredictable. She hardly eats or sleeps unless she's medicated.

But of course, his father is never around. He doesn't know what she's going through.

"So?" Dylan says, arms crossed.

"Now you care?" Sweat is pooling on Murielle's forehead, and she is shaking like a leaf. Skyler feels her pulse. Too quick. She might have caught a virus. The original filtration system struggles to filter this dirty air. Despite regular maintenance, nothing can replace the fresh air of the surface.

"We need to get her temperature down," Skyler says, pressing on his mother's cheeks. Seeing his father doing nothing to help, he shouts, "Dylan!"

This lack of action is exasperating. Dylan snaps out of it, fetches a wet hand towel, and hands it over to Skyler. Does he think that because Skyler is a doctor, he should take care of everything? It's not like Dylan doesn't know what to do.

His father watches him intently while he walks over to his desk to work. Skyler focuses his attention on massaging one of her pressure points, the one between the eyebrows. He cannot muster the energy to engage with Dylan anymore.

His mother's skin has become thin, and he doesn't dare press too hard for fear it will crack. Murielle wakes up, her eyes open wide.

"Mom, are you feeling any better?"

"Don't worry about me," she replies with glassy eyes. "I need to go to the bathroom." He rids her of the towel and helps her get up. Once she is safely inside, she convinces him to leave her by herself. He complies and sits at the table, his mouth dry.

Hot wax pools around the flame, which flickers every time he breathes out. Skyler's eyelids are heavy, but the harsh sound of coughing coming from the bathroom startles him. He cracks open the door and finds his mother kneeling at the toilet bowl. He asks if she's all right. She moans her assent.

Fatigue is setting in quickly, and he knows he won't be able to stand much longer. He turns to Dylan.

"Can you take care of Mom for once?" he says sharply. His

father isn't listening, too engrossed in his oh-so-essential work. "Dylan, she needs you!"

"Don't worry. Everything will be fine," Dylan replies in a distracted voice. His favorite words to shut him up.

"No, it will not," he retorts, walking up to him. "Her condition has been worsening. I cannot take care of her by myself."

"You're overreacting, Sky. She'll get over it. You should know that by now."

"You don't get it. You don't get it at all! She's withering away and you're never here for her." Dylan finally looks at him. His face is placid.

"Sky…"

"No, let me do the talking. The person she needs most right now is you! Not me. It's time you realized that!"

"Sky!" He doesn't want to listen anymore. Dylan's all about his work. He doesn't give a damn about his family. Is he trying to seek revenge for what happened?

Skyler storms towards the door, seething. Dylan calls out to him, but he pretends not to hear. Skyler finally freezes when his father barks, "Do you really want to know why your mother is like this?"

The words echo threateningly. Is this when he blames him? Remind him who broke their family apart? Caused his mother's depression?

Skyler walks out.

THE NIGHT before feels like a hazy dream to Skyler as he wakes. A quick glance at the clock tells him he only slept for four hours. His work uniform is sticky on his skin, and the bed is still made.

He sighs.

Work hasn't let up since the day Skyler started at Med Bay,

right after graduation. He expected to be busy, but the rapid increase in the number of cases related to the Syndrome has complicated things. Staff can't keep up with the surge of patients. And since he cannot count on Chris to help, Skyler has to do all the dirty work. If Chris took his work more seriously instead of wasting his time flaying the memory spheres ... but wouldn't *that* be too much to ask. Chris only listens to himself. He's so Duke Kay's son.

Skyler leaves the comfort of his pillow and the dimness of the artificial light. His cabin is not as big as his parents', but it's enough for him. Yet, they owe this luxury to the ticket inherited from the Goldbergs: A piece of paper that determined their fate based on an unjust system.

The Goldbergs's background is exemplary: His great-great-grand-mother was a surgeon, his grandfather a scientist, and now, his father is an oceanographer and his mother a nurse, at least she was, before her illness. Skyler hopes he can become a full-fledged doctor, a chance many don't get. He does not believe that dividing Archeans by their family background is pragmatic, given their precarious situation. They should strive for solidarity.

In contrast, he doesn't feel guilty for taking advantage of his family's privilege, since the new generation must settle for the bare minimum: a compulsory step. He doesn't complain about his small cabin; since his work at Med Bay takes up most of his day, he doesn't have the luxury of spending much time in his cabin. The tight space also keeps him from feeling lonely. There is actually no space left. Just his bed and a simple desk with his computer hooked up to the core system of the Ark. As for the bathroom, he shares it with the other passengers on the floor. No kitchenette either. The canteen has everything they need anyway, and it allows him to get out of his head.

He takes a shower in the common area, which is a few steps from his cabin. He wastes no time—the hot water is metered.

No more than three and a half minutes. He puts on civilian clothes and hurries back home. He fills a large glass of water and takes a sip. Next to his bed, he turns on an artificial light, warmer than the others, then sprinkles just the right amount of water on the lilies, irises, and chrysanthemums that he planted several weeks ago. The composted soil soaks the water in and turns black. With a bit of luck, young shoots will soon start to show.

It's a shame he had to throw out the pink mums. They took a long time to bloom, and more than one try. He read in the Archives how their ancestors tended their gardens before the Flood, and he tried to replicate it. It was no easy task, but he learned from his terrible mistakes: Too much water and the plants drown, especially if they are still sprouts; they need fertilizer with good irrigation. That had been the most troublesome part: How would he find the soil he needed? His frequent visits to the Gardens of Humankind and a bit of trial-and-error have finally rewarded him with a few chrysanthemums.

He's likely the only one who grows plants as a hobby around here, but it's the best way to get the patients who flood the ward, day and night, out of his mind.

Plus, the Ark is sorely lacking wildlife. The Archeans are doomed to sail through the depths of the Great Ocean, without ever having the chance to know what life on earth is like. Does it make sense to give it up, though? When it comes time to repopulate, Skyler will be ready and get down to work, carry out, and teach them. It all started with the seeds he stole from the Deltas, who grow all the Ark's fruit and vegetables in its greenhouses. Now it is up to him to make his lilies and irises grow in these less-than-ideal conditions.

He examines them, but no stalks yet. He might have to review his ways. No one said it would be easy.

Once the soil is moist, he gulps down the rest of his water

and sits at his computer desk. He gets lost in the screensaver he found in the Archives.

A sea of skyscrapers reflecting the last rays of the setting sun. The buildings are the remains of a once-thriving metropolis, now under water for over a century. Sometimes, the Ark comes across them, and a team of diver pillages the remnants in search of anything useful. Life in those cities feels mysterious: There were so many things to do and probably not enough time to do it all.

Instead, Skyler is one of one thousand seven hundred and fifty-two passengers, according to the latest official report, a feat which can be ascribed to the best scientists of the time. Skyler is a fifth-generation survivor—a feat in and of itself—but they remain far from repopulating Earth. The Great Ocean isn't showing any sign that its waters are receding. And Dylan says it won't be anytime soon. The Archeans gave up ages ago. They accept their reality as a fatality, just like the patients that Skyler's been treating ever since he started working at Med Bay.

As for him, he remains optimistic. Even if he never has the chance to be among the settlers, he wants to absorb as much information as possible so that he's ready to play his part when the time comes, and to help his future kids in the process.

He quickly checks his messages; most are the usual announcements the crew makes. A quarterly simulation reminder? Time flies so fast; it feels like last quarter was just a week ago.

A jingle is followed by a video message invite that takes up the whole screen. He accepts and Emily's face appears.

"How much longer were you planning on ducking out like this? None of your excuses forgive what you did. How could you leave me in the lurch all this time? I've been wandering the halls of this cursed ship day and night looking for you. If you keep it up, I'm gonna know more about my prisoners than you will. Anyway, I'd better see you at La Orilla Friday night. With all the trouble I went through to get a

reservation, you'll pay dearly if you don't show. You'll regret it, trust me."

He smiles. His best friend has shown him more than once that she always gets what she wants, no matter what. He hasn't given her the attention she deserves lately. It'll be nice to be in her company.

Skyler does a quick search on how to take care of lilies and irises, but once he realizes how late it is, he puts his computer in sleep mode. He sits on the edge of his bed and puts on his work uniform, which features the Greek letter Omega, a remnant from yet another lost civilization.

While buttoning up his dark blue smock, his eyes catch the frame on his nightstand. He was fourteen at the time, and they had spent a beautiful family day having a picnic at the Gardens of Humankind.

With his brother.

The family photo is torn where Allen should be. It would be a perfect picture were it not for that missing piece. But their family will never be the same, just like this photo. He could paste it back together, but the tear is a scar that even time won't heal. No matter what Dylan promises.

Skyler would like to believe those promises. He really would.

But he knows all too well that nothing will ever be the same.

Not ever.

4

EMILY

"Emily Bates. I have a reservation for two."

The young lady taps quickly at her computer in fancy clothes at the entrance of the only restaurant on the Ark. Emily's heart pounds in her chest at the same rate.

A cool draft tickles her naked shoulders. She hasn't had a chance since graduation to wear this dress; her brand new metallic blue purse goes with it perfectly. A shiver runs down her spine. Tonight, she's not just Bates. She is *Ms.* Bates.

"Bates, was it?" The hiss of her name numbs her eardrums. Instinctively, Emily looks around. No one seems to have heard. Good. The young lady with the amber-colored aura drums her fingers on her elbow, as if getting ready to scold a child who accidentally made a mess. Emily tenses. What if they don't let her in? What if she isn't good enough for this swanky restaurant?

Emily fakes a casual smile and nods. "Is there a problem?"

Amber—as Emily has decided to call the girl—looks at her puzzled, then checks the screen again, her eyes bouncing. After a moment, Amber starts and starts again before saying restlessly, "Let me find out whether your table is ready. I'll be right back." She slips behind a molded door camouflaged into the wall, leaving Emily in the lurch.

Other people are sat waiting as well, but Emily has pins and needles in her legs. She paces across the lavish lobby, the sound of her heels muffled by the crimson carpeting. This must be the only place on the whole ship where carpeting is allowed. Isn't this going against safety rules? The desperate need of noble families to stand out. How charming. The carpeting, the paintings adorning the corridor of *La Orilla*…

The famous founding family—the ingenious Stella, her husband, her daughter—stand gloating, their greatest creation, the Ark, towering in the background. Right next to them is a biblical scene, straight out of the Last Supper, complete with Messiah. Certainly not original works. Replicas.

Art is a great escape on the Ark.

Emily rubs her aching fingers, marks still very much present in her now calloused skin. Suddenly, it doesn't seem so long ago that she spent her nights scribbling furiously until she could no longer hold a pencil. She learned the hard way to steady her mind while the world around her spins out of control. She would never show off in public like this. Never! These paintings —some would even call them works of art—are nothing but the fanatical cries of prisoners trapped on a ship sailing endlessly across a phantom planet.

"Amber" sure is taking her time! And Sky? He hasn't turned up yet either, after all the trouble she went through to get this illegal reservation. Amber is no fool. The Bateses are not regulars here. Since Mom was convicted for treason, the mere mention of the name Bates raises eyebrows and suspicions.

"A little prayer of redemption?"

Emily turns on her heel. A young girl with a violet aura, a basket dangling on her arm, is handing cards out to those waiting. "Violet" is draped in an ample tunic with flared sleeves, braced with ideology to assault anyone she encounters.

The customers don't seem to mind. That they are all Believers goes without saying. Violet makes the sign of the cross after each card given. Since when do priestesses campaign around the ship? Mom had always been wary of them. She didn't subscribe to their dubious methods. She had gone her own way, helping those in need, always willing to lend a hand or an ear. Mom should have been the one and only priestess in the Sanctuary. People looked up to her. She inspired them to believe in a better future. Now people like Violet take her place.

Violet scans for her next target. Her eyes meet Emily's, and she moves towards her. Please, no. Not now. Amber! Where is she?!

Too late. Emily opens her mouth, ready to bite back, but Violet beats her to it.

"It's a beautiful painting! … Or not. … It depends," she says in a soft, confident voice as she stops in front of the biblical scene. "Strange for a restaurant, don't you think?" This girl, not much older than Emily herself, worships a spiteful god, and Emily wonders if this is a test of her faith.

Violet doesn't wait for a reply, "You'd think we'd have learned from our sins over time, but these places continue to exist, to tempt us."

Emily stares at her for a moment. If Violet is talking about the restaurant, well, sucks to be her! Dinner at *La Orilla* every night would be divine. Sure beats eating reheated dining hall leftovers in her dingy family cabin.

Violet seems absorbed in the painting for a moment, then looks away and gives Emily a smile, not bothered in the least by her silence.

"Ms. Bates," Amber coos in a silky voice. "Please follow me." A smile creeps across Emily's lips. She's not going to miss this Believer conversation—with a priestess, no less! Emily floats away after Amber, her unexpected savior, without even a glance back. What a disturbing encounter! What did the priestess expect her to say?

The sweet scent of the dining room brings her back to the present, reminding her to enjoy the moment. She drools with envy at each passing dish as they flutter from table to table; the impromptu meeting just a moment earlier is forgotten. The only other time she has enjoyed a moment of fantasy like this was during her graduation ceremony. But this one is better! Around her, large windows, draped in heavy, elegant fabrics, line the dining room. Three elaborate chandeliers plunge the space into a glowing red twilight. Waiters waltz among the dozens of scattered tables balancing trays filled with foods that should be forbidden on this ship. To top it all off, a pianist, accompanied by a charming violinist, plays cheerful notes that linger over the diners' hushed chatter.

Amber points to a table placed against one of the large fake windows, a bit far in the back, but with a decent view of the musicians. She pulls a chair out and Emily, placing her purse on the table, settles in with a sigh of satisfaction. She catches herself smiling as she takes in her surroundings. Gone—at least for tonight—are the days when the Bateses were denied these privileges. Sometimes knowing the right people is enough to skirt the rules.

"Call me Cohen," says a dark-haired man with a jade aura, wearing a suit that shows off his slender stature. "I'll be your server for the evening. An aperitif to start?" He lights a candle and places it at the center of the table. He serves her his most delicious, dazzling smile.

"Sparkling wine?" she asks in a small voice, her taste buds shivering impatiently.

"Of course. Will someone be joining you this evening?"

"Yes. There will be two of us." Cohen's aura twitches. Disappointment?

"A friend," she adds, her cheeks warm. He gives her a keen

look before leaving. Cohen seems very nice. His arms are strangely skillful at balancing the various glasses on his tray as he glides around.

"Here you go, Ms. Bates ... and for your friend," he tells her, gracefully setting down two full flutes, the foam to the brim. Is he laughing at her, or does he take her seriously? The way his aura trills is off-putting.

"Thank you, Cohen."

"I'll come back for your order, Ms. Bates?" She nods. This evening is in honor of Emily and Skyler's friendship. Cohen is better off not learning the Bates's dark reality. He'd lose any interest as soon as he found out.

He gives her a courtly bow as he leaves, and Emily puts the flute to her lips. Generous bubbles wriggle on her tongue, and the sublime liquid swirls in her mouth. A taste this divine should not be reserved for only a handful of families. Why does ancestry condemn poor souls like her? It all would have changed had her father ascended to the title of Paragon Commander. But it was that damned Duke Kay, who was given the honor, automatically entitling his family to this kind of life, otherwise impossible to get. An unfairly missed opportunity, but tonight it doesn't matter. Emily sips her success.

The light music mixes with her joyful mood, and she takes advantage of the moment to observe the other diners. A rowdy group from the Paragon is whooping with delight. At first glance, Duke doesn't seem to be among them. She can't turn around to make sure, as some might recognize her as Jeremy Bates's daughter. Across the room, Mira, the redhead, sits with her father, Horacio Torres. Another prestigious family, a line of scientists who have revolutionized hydroponic greenhouses. Of course, the Torreses get special treatment!

"Emily?" Sky crosses the room under the supervision of Amber, who smooths the tips of her straight hair. He is short of breath, his face pink with effort.

"It's about time," says Emily, repressing a smile.

"I missed you too," he replies with a smirk, true to himself. He has rolled up the sleeves of his slightly unbuttoned shirt, and has even left a bit of stubble, which looks darker than usual in the dim lighting. His appearance speaks for itself: He has been working all day. The low density of his aura confirms it.

"What would I do without you Sky?" she adds, hugging him in a friendly embrace. "These prisoners are driving me crazy."

"Are they giving you a hard time? I thought you were stronger than that."

"You know it's the other way around. They don't stand a chance." She snorts. Reyes. She may be a challenge in the foreseeable future, but nothing that will compromise her evening with Sky.

"But hey, enough about work," Emily says as they both sit, she in her beautiful velvety chair. "I haven't gone out of my way to get a reservation at *La Orilla* just to ruin it."

"You should have asked me." True. Skyler is a Goldberg, another of the great families. He doesn't look like one, though. No extravagances or fake smiles. Even Amber doesn't seem to have recognized him when he got here. Sky takes a sip from his flute and sighs with satisfaction.

"I wanted to surprise you," she explains. "You know the food in the dining hall makes me nauseous, especially the fish. I swear, sometimes I feel like the smell clings to my skin, even after I've showered. Tonight is my detox. If I had to wait for you to make reservations for me, I'd be dead already."

"You haven't changed one bit! Though I'm sure not here to straighten you out," he replies, taking another sip of the champagne.

"Even time can't get the better of me." She stopped keeping track of all the pointless arguments he's saved her from. Good thing their Academy days are over. Since Mom's death, innocent young Emily, ready to embark on the worst tirades, has taken her leave.

Cohen is back and sneaks glances at Sky, who looks at the menu carefully without noticing. Emily holds back a laugh and looks over the offerings as well. It's all equally enticing. After a heart-wrenching process of elimination, she settles on a vegetarian meal. All those years' worth of fish smell soaked into her skin need to be purged.

Their waiter comes back wielding a bottle of white wine.

"You trying to get me drunk?" Emily chuckles. "Wine might not be the best idea."

"Shouldn't we make the most of it?" he replies while throwing a glance at Cohen from the corner of his eye.

"What exactly does that mean?"

"Look at me," he says, pointing at himself. "I work tirelessly instead of looking for a partner. You don't want that."

As Cohen comes back with the soup course (a hearty corn chowder), Sky's sharp features jump out at her. He looks older … more mature? The last time they saw each other was … at her little sister's birthday?

"I didn't know you'd gone for a beard," she teases him as he is mindlessly stroking his chin. He stops short.

"Age is wearing on me."

"Says the twenty-year-old. It's not a bad thing. It looks good on you!" He doesn't have his usual energy. Things at the clinic probably aren't easy on him.

Medicine. Better to die than to do that kind of work.

"Let us take a moment to savor this fishless delight," she says, closing her eyes and breathing in the aroma of the soup. "Come on, I'm not kidding. Close your eyes." Emily opens one eye to peek at Sky and catches him watching her. They both burst out laughing.

"To all the fish saved from an unjust death during this meal…"

"Really?" he asks her with a half-smile that she senses rather than sees. He gives a little roll of the eyes and sighs. "You're impossible, Emy."

"Just let me finish," she says in earnest. "Let our sacrifice be witness to our good will. Amen."

"Since when do you pray before eating?" Her eyes burst open at the pop of a newly uncorked bottle of champagne. The Paragon officers behind her sure are having a blast.

"Don't look so surprised," she says. "Be grateful. To quote you: *According to the Archives, the survivors of the Flood will repent for millennia for the actions of their careless forebearers.* We have to get used to it, especially if it is our mission.

"Do you really believe in divine punishment?" says Sky, stumped.

"That's not the question."

"What's the question, then?"

"I'll tell you when you stop judging me. Maybe by dessert?"

"Why wait so long?" The edges of his aura become impatient, but he can wait a little longer.

"I just want to enjoy our moment. Right here and now. We'll talk about it later." They finish their soup and Cohen, like a vulture, swaps their bowls for plates full of creamy pasta with asparagus. Not the most exotic of meals, but it will do just fine. As long as there's no fish in it.

After two bites, Emily excuses herself. She puts the napkin back onto the table, grabs her purse and heads towards the lobby. The chill outside the dining room gives her a shiver, and she rubs her shoulders. She steps quickly into the bathroom. Her short hair has come a little loose, but a few touch-ups are enough to put it back in place.

Violet is stationed at the entrance, relentless.

"You again?" asks Emily. The long brown-haired priestess just smiles and waves her basket of rainbow-colored prayer cards.

"People need hope at any hour of the day," Violet replies. "Even at night. Especially at night."

"Sorry, I'm not…"

"A Believer? You don't have to be when you're fighting a common battle."

"What do you mean?" Violet laughs, then collects herself.

"By the way, Emily, you can call me Dinah." Dinah…? None of the major families come to mind. Nor any of the young people she met at the Academy. The Ark isn't that big when you think about it. Dinah's parents should have called her Violet, with an aura like that. Violet it is.

"I don't think we've met…"

"No, we haven't. Surprising considering, we live on the same ship. But your mother was well known to the Farrells at the Sanctuary," says Dinah—aka—Violet as she crosses herself. Emily grabs hold of her purse and snaps it shut. And to think this was supposed to be *her* night.

"Well, I have to go," says Emily in a strangled voice. "Maybe some other time."

"Maybe."

Emily quickens her pace to blend back into the cacophony of *La Orilla*'s dining room.

At the table, she catches Amber cradling a bouquet of roses, chatting with Sky. Emily slows her pace to a halt next to her seat.

"I'm sure she'd like that," says Amber, smoothing her hair with her free hand.

"I don't want it," Emily cuts her off as she sits, her cheeks on fire. Amber's fake smile freezes, but Sky isn't fazed.

"I'll take two," he says in his ever-sweet voice. Well, what does that mean exactly?

Sky offers his bracelet and Amber scans it quickly. She hands him two roses, then teeters to the next table and repeats the performance.

"To our friendship," Sky says casually, offering her a rose. "Now it's your turn. Smell it." Emily sniffs the rose, then puts it down. The scent is subtle, probably spoiled by the sparkling wine. "You know how scarce flowers are," he continues, twirling one between his fingers. "We should treasure them while they're still around."

"You're a true romantic, Sky," says Emily, softening.

"Too bad no one gets to see it. These days, all my affection goes to my garden. But, who knows, I might get lucky!"

"Amber was a prime candidate."

"Amber?" Sky cannot see auras.

"The girl who sold you the roses," she elaborates.

"Oh," he says plainly. "You think?" Emily rolls her eyes.

"You're too picky." They carry on with their meal and the tinkling of their utensils blends in with the rushing piano notes. The violinist has withdrawn for a well-deserved break. She's played several solos since they arrived.

Emily finishes her dish and her stomach settles. If someone had told her a few weeks ago she would be eating this much, she wouldn't have believed it.

"Maybe next time I could cook up something for you instead," says Sky, now drinking a glass of white wine. "This restaurant isn't what it used to be." Sky has probably had every *plat du jour* twice over.

Has life been plotting to keep her away from delights such as these? On what grounds? None, other than a pathetic ticket bought over a century ago. Justice in all its glory.

"You'll have to take some time off," replies Emily after a bite of especially heavenly cheese. "They give you too much work."

"Tell Chris that."

"Who says it's his fault? He's not the only person you work with. Complain to Dr. Nazar. He is your mentor, isn't he?"

There's major tension between Sky and Chris, but Sky can be stubborn too. She really doesn't want to be the go-between.

"If you saw the things that he does to hurt me, you wouldn't be so quick to defend him."

"It's all about perspective. See, I have this new convict who thought she could get the better of me. I beat her at her own game. Now, she probably thinks I'm the biggest bitch on the Ark. And when I give her what she wants, her opinion of me will change yet again."

"What's that got to do with Chris?" he asks with his head tilted.

"Look, I remember ever since school there's been no love lost between you guys. You should open yourself up to new opportunities."

"The only thing I see is that he's a narcissist, and he enjoys making my life a living hell. After all these years, he's still the same. Because of him my project on the memory spheres almost didn't go through."

"Did you think for a moment that he might have wanted to start a dialogue?"

"Yeah, well, it didn't work. And even if he was genuine, he's wasting his time."

"Give him a break. We were kids back then."

"You know how I feel about that." He closes in on himself and his troubled gray eyes detail the contents of his plate. His complexion is too pale. Emily sighs inwardly so as not to add fuel to the fire. Sky has always been difficult to read: Turquoise shades that swing from one extreme to the other, revealing nothing more about his state of mind. A real walking mystery. But what makes him truly unique is his dedication, his sincerity. He is far from perfect, but he gives so much of himself to others that he forgets himself.

A waltz takes over the fading notes of the piano. She laughs and finishes her glass, Sky glaring at her, astonished. "I'm not sure I want to know why you're laughing out loud," he says flatly.

"You know as well as I do," she says, dabbing her eyes. "Looks like you still haven't learned your lesson." Emily drinks the rest of her wine, and as if by magic, Cohen appears to gracefully fill their glasses, slightly overflowing the rim. Did Cohen just give her a wink? Maybe not. The wine is playing tricks on her. "To that unforgettable graduation," Emily says, holding back a giggle, her glass raised.

"If you say so." He takes a sip. "What was his name again?"

"Leander. Geez, you can't even remember the names of your own co-workers."

"Don't you try and avoid it. That was quite the night! Poor guy, having to put up with a bully like you."

"Hey!" She smacks him with her napkin. "He needed to loosen up a little, and I gave him a moment he'll never forget. He might have waited another twenty years before making up his mind. I wonder if he's going to bring himself to reveal his feelings to Mira once and for all."

"Not anytime soon. Not with the trauma you've inflicted on him." She glares at him, takes a gulp, and slams down her glass, spilling some wine on the table and bringing a smile to Sky's face.

"I would like to remind you that you are the one responsible for that night's tragic end."

"Who, me? You must be mistaking me for someone else."

"Right. You'd had too much to drink. Though I clearly remember having to step in."

"What are you talking about?" he says, spinning his glass. So, Skyler Goldberg doesn't remember how the evening ended. Yet, he didn't dare show his face for the next three days. She drinks the rest of her wine, sustaining Sky's worried gaze. A feeling of triumph overwhelms her. "You should have told me you invited me here to torture me. I would've sat this one out."

"Not torture. Just having a good time with my best friend."

"Come on, shoot," he insists, finishing his glass too, under the ever-sweet melody of the piano. "I want to know." Emily refrains, as Cohen comes to rid them of their plates and serve dessert: a chocolate cake like she's never seen before. She takes a bite under Sky's watchful, waiting gaze. She closes her eyes. The velvety cake melts in her mouth and draws her into another world.

"At first you thought Chris had asked Leander to seduce me that night," she says with her mouth full.

"And what did I do?" he asks, clearing his throat.

"You wanted to settle the score with Chris and started a fight. It wasn't pretty, but I broke it up. It was the first time I've seen you take any action. I was proud of you if it makes you feel any better."

"No wonder he won't leave me alone," he says in a strained voice.

"Don't take it that way. You were drinking like most people. Chris doesn't blame you. And now you're an official member of my fan club."

"I don't know if that's such a good thing. The Bully Club."

"Say that again and you're dead," she scolds, earning her a smile. "Look at it this way: No one will dare to bother you again."

"Except Chris."

"Who knows? Maybe he just wants to be closer to the winners. You had a clear advantage over him if I remember correctly. You must have impressed him. Nobody expected that from you. I was immediately blamed for bringing out that side of you."

"I'm glad those days are over." And these days? Their new responsibilities have driven them apart. They see each other barely once a month.

The whole restaurant sings Happy Birthday along with the piano and violin. Sky and Emily sing along too, turning towards the birthday boy—none other than Horacio, Mira's father.

Leander approaches, Amber and Cohen at his side, carrying a cake topped with dozens of candles. Mira tenderly embraces her father, who has tears in his eyes. Once all the candles are blown out, the restaurant bursts in applause and the rest of the evening unravels in a more festive atmosphere, the violinist playing with renewed energy.

"Promise me that from now on, Sky," Emily says with shining eyes, "you will come and eat with me at the canteen. Otherwise, I'm going to make your life miserable by spreading rumors about your barbarous brawl. Even your patients will be suspicious of you."

"Don't even think about it."

"Promise me, then."

"All right," he says, clinking his cup against Emily's, one last time. Despite her apparent sobriety, she has a little trouble standing up. Cohen clears the table and wishes them a good night. He watches them with a look that is envious yet shaded by sadness.

Sky collects their roses, and they leave the restaurant together, giggling, arm-in-arm. He sees her back to her cabin, and they hug briefly on the doorstep. Maybe things could go back to the way they were.

"You left this on the table." Sky hands Emily her purse. She definitely doesn't have that feminine impulse. Sky leaves, and Emily falls into bed, sleepy. She rubs her eyes with greasy fingers. Mascara. Can't sleep with makeup on.

She rolls to the side, sticks her hand in her purse and fumbles for a handkerchief. She pulls out a small card instead.

A prayer of redemption.

5

SKYLER

A SHARP KNOCK, THEN TWO, AND FINALLY THREE. THEIR SPECIAL code. Ever since the Incident, when Paragon officers raided the dormitories, hunting down stowaways, Mrs. Farrell has been cautious. The officers didn't go about it in the most ... gentle way. Under the guise of birth control, the members of the Paragon believe they must use whatever means necessary to enforce safety and order on the ship. This includes physical aggression, magnetic handcuffs, and especially the dreaded taser: an arm-length stick fully capable of leaving lasting burns on raw skin. A kind of rebel branding system, indicating the crimes they must repent for.

Skyler knocks again under the watch of the surveillance cameras. Still no answer. Hopefully, Mrs. Farrell hasn't fallen asleep. It wouldn't be the first time. He grabs his Med Bay key card. When the lock clicks, he opens the door and announces himself.

The pungent smell of sage turns his stomach. He holds his breath and takes a quick look inside, only to realize she's not there. Mrs. Farrell's belongings are strewn everywhere; burned incense sticks lie on the furniture; her clothes are scattered, sheets crumpled on top of them. Even plates, utensils, and a powdery substance that looks like flour clutter her large kitchen counter. This is not in the least surprising. It's Mrs. Farrell, after all.

Elaine Farrell is a well-known patient at Med Bay. She is the last of the second generation of survivors. Commander Hawk invited her to take part in the consultations before they were held behind closed doors; he attaches particular importance to the Farrells, who played a crucial role during the Departure.

The survivors of the Flood faced almost certain death as they attempted to reach the Ark stored on the mountainside. The weather was severe and the rain torrential. There was a terrible accident within the convoy they were in. Abram Farrell and his family stayed behind to rescue the one hundred and thirty-seven survivors. Other families that had escaped from their vehicles unharmed had taken refuge in the ship. They threatened to leave without those still trapped in the debris. Against all odds, the Farrell children, Tomas and Claire, snuck onboard and convinced the Commander to keep the doors open, which was an enormous risk to take. Exposed to the full force of the weather, the Ark could have gotten stranded and never make it to sea. However, the Farrells believed that humans should not abandon each other, that every life mattered. To make a new beginning, they had to stand together. God's wrath was proof enough that they needed to change. Abram, his wife Hannah, and their children, Tomas and Claire, became the first heroes of the Flood. In fact, if it weren't for them, Skyler wouldn't be here today. Augustus and Silvia Goldberg, his great-great-grandparents, were among those rescued by the Farrells.

Skyler closes the door behind him, and it locks immediately. If Elaine is not in her room, there is only one place she can be.

In theory, Mrs. Farrell's physical condition does not allow her to travel long distances but convincing her of that is like arguing with a wall. Skyler doesn't get into that pointless debate; he leaves that to Chris.

Skyler starts to walk down the corridor, but a pair of Paragon officers—a medium-sized, brown-skinned man and a young woman with long braids—stops him. They ask him to identify himself. Skyler obeys without question. Agent Miles, his name shining on the badge dangling around his neck, steps up under the scrutinizing gaze of his partner, Agent Auberon. He stretches to scan Skyler's wristband to confirm he can be on this floor. Miles's uniform sleeve rides up to reveal ink on his forearm, something fairly rare on the ship. Allen had also had a strange fascination with tattoos.

After an agonizing minute, Agent Miles and Agent Auberon release him. Skyler doesn't linger and heads straight for the elevator at the far end of the lengthy hallway. It takes him at least five minutes to get there, walking at a brisk pace. His face is sticky with sweat. It's hard to imagine that at her age, Mrs. Farrell could be so adamant. She should have mellowed over time, but Elaine Farrell isn't the type.

He reaches the Sanctuary of Humankind, a spacious shrine whose walls are lined with thousands of fine golden inscriptions: the names of survivors of the Flood who have perished since the Departure. The sanctuary is large enough to accommodate a hundred Believers at a time. Long metal benches are gathered by the dozens on either side of the aisle leading to the wide altar. The sign of three intertwined fish, symbolizing birth, life, and death in an eternal wheel, overlooks the main room. It is the ichthys, the crest of the primordial religion, that dates back to the first biblical Flood.

Incense burns in every corner, and Skyler clears his throat. He scans the room for Mrs. Farrell. It's not time for mass, but some Believers are praying together in the pews, their hands clasped, and their foreheads pressed together. Others are kneeling on cushions in front of the inscriptions representing the deceased.

"Skyler!" Jacinta, his mother's best friend, grabs the pew to get up, her arms wide as if trying not to tip over. Her toothless smile is as he remembers it. Skyler represses a shy laugh and looks around cautiously. No one seems to care, except for an old man sitting nearby, muttering something to himself.

"Never thought I'd see *you* here," she adds in a shrill voice. "I haven't seen you in so long!" She motions to pinch his cheek but holds back at the last moment. Her haircut frames her egg-shaped face, and her baggy clothes look like a nightgown. When he was younger, Skyler could always count on her to bring him a pair of handmade socks, which he always ended up giving away because he had too many. No matter because Jacinta's supply of cotton was endless. She spent all her breaks at the clinic knitting. Jacinta was like an aunt to him when she used to pay regular visits to his parents.

"Yes, it's been a while," he replied coughing, his throat sore from the smoke of the incense.

"What brings you here? To my knowledge, the Goldbergs have never been devout believers. Well, Murielle … actually, I haven't even seen your mother in … far too long for me to remember." She squeaks and sways from one foot to the other, her hands hugging her belly—not too big yet—as if it was about to drop and roll down the aisle.

She grabs Skyler's shoulder, and resumes with a stern look, "But tell me, there's been no misfortune among the Goldbergs, has there? Ever since your brother … your mother … well, you know what I mean. I often reach out to Murielle, but … she doesn't talk much. I wouldn't forgive her if she kept me in the dark about something as important as the death of—"

"I'm here for work, Jazz," Skyler interrupts, out of breath. Jacinta's face lights up and she resumes her usual, comfortable posture: hands on her hips, belly out.

"Did Dr. Nazar send you on an errand? He never changes. He's so overwhelmed. I wonder why he insists on taking care of all the new recruits instead of entrusting them to Dr. Zanya, who really could do more to help him. Poor little thing. Nazar has such a brave heart!"

"What about you, Jazz? Your usual visit to the sanctuary?"

"Oh, you know me," she says absently, stroking her belly. "I came to pray for the baby, as usual. But ever since I had my little one... I just can't seem to find time." Every pregnancy is an event. Of course, he had heard about it at Med Bay. Fortune hasn't always smiled on Jacinta, but she's determined to enact her right to bear two children.

"Is it a boy or a girl this time?"

"We don't know yet. Chris told us the baby is not in a good position to tell." And yet it's quite simple with blood tests. Why didn't Chris offer that?

"But it doesn't matter," she adds with a confident look on her face. "Nathan and I chose to let life take its course. That's the most important thing the Flood has taught us: to accept our new reality. To stop fighting something that's bigger than us."

"I understand." Something stirs inside him, but he ignores it.

"Don't tell Nathan I said that," she whispers. "We had another argument about it recently. You know how on edge he can be. Especially now. Did you know it's the anniversary of his cousin's death? He doesn't want to admit it, but it's obvious that it still affects him." Skyler follows Jacinta's gaze and sees Nathan, the engineer who helped develop the memory spheres, kneeling before the inscriptions. He rises from his cushion to wave his wristband over one of the electronic lanterns, igniting a bluish light. A hologram face of the deceased emerges lifelike from the electric flame.

The squirt of antiseptic gel startles him. Jacinta frantically rubs her hands up to her forearms.

"But tell me, how is Murielle?" she asks, pouring on more gel. "If only you knew how much I miss her. The energy at the clinic has changed so much since she left."

"She's still undergoing treatment," he replies, his throat tightening.

"No improvement? Are her seizures still so … violent?" Skyler nods and looks away.

"Do you want some?" she asks, shaking the bottle of antiseptic.

"No, I'm fine, thanks."

"It's for the baby," she says, as if feeling the need to justify herself. "Well, I think he's done now. Give your mom a kiss from me." Once Jacinta reaches Nathan, Skyler sighs and walks down the center aisle, scanning the surroundings. Mrs. Farrell can't be very far.

"I was wondering when you were going to get here," an old woman with a rounded back, kneeling in front of the altar, calls out to him. "Any longer and I was going to have to remind you not to leave me out cold like that fool did."

"Don't worry. I won't let anyone else take care of you. I learned my lesson last time." Skyler had the misfortune of taking some time off to finish the memory spheres project and, of course, Chris covered for him.

"Had I been in charge of this Ark, I never would have let him in, trust me," she says. "The Flood wasn't all bad, as everyone here seems to believe. It had a cleansing power. It takes a major disaster to wake up even the stupidest among us." Skyler represses a smile. He likes her.

She rises to her feet as if untouched by time and moves towards the two cast-granite basins near the altar. She grabs a bowl, fills it with water, and raises it to her forehead. Then she pours its contents into the left basin. Slowly. The hollow sound of the water echoes throughout the shrine. Once she is done, she turns towards him, a goofy look on her face. Her silver hair contrasts sharply with that of the other believers.

"I feel liberated, don't you?" she says with a sigh. If it's the smell of incense and the dull hum of the ship that's liberating, he'll pass.

"I should come back here more often, like I used to," she continues, joining him, her gaze mesmerized by the ceiling as if seeing it for the first time. "At some point, you have to step down, even if it breaks your heart."

"Your grandchildren?"

"Yes." Mrs. Farrell is convinced she has two grandchildren who look after the sanctuary in her absence. Skyler has never met them, though he rarely comes here. With Mrs. Farrell's dementia worsening, it's hard to tell what's real and what's not. It wasn't easy for her to leave this place, where, when she wasn't consulting with the crew, she used to spend most of her time.

She tells him how her grandchildren do what all Archeans should be doing: helping each other to survive.

"The Farrells have been the exception to the rule from the beginning," she continues. "If it weren't for them, you probably wouldn't be here, and neither would most of the people on this doomed ship. They saw through the lies and beyond the fake smiles. They believed everyone deserves redemption. And what are we left with? A lack of humanism. This shrine should be full to bursting every day that the good Lord gives us. No one will get off this Ark as long as we persist in perpetuating human error."

Although her speech is difficult to follow, only someone with her life experience can draw those kinds of conclusions. Skyler doesn't claim to understand, but he hopes to learn from her wisdom.

"My grandchildren will be here to put us back on the right track. And you'll be there to help them, won't you?"

"I'll do my best," he says, trying to imagine what they look like.

"You're a good boy," she adds, patting his arm with her free hand. "You remind me of my little Philip. Or big, it depends." She laughs at a joke known only to her.

She slips her arm into Skyler's, who leads her to a hidden anteroom. As he helps her sit, she adds,

"Why can't the other Archeans be more like you? I swear you have Farrell blood running through your veins. Not that the Goldbergs aren't a good family, but you know what I mean."

"I'll take that as a compliment, even if I don't think I live up to it."

"Stop with the modesty. I know a pure soul when I see one. I'll tell my grandchildren to take good care of you once I'm gone. Because let's face it, my time is coming."

"Until now, you've beaten all the odds. You might see the next Commander in your lifetime."

"I'd rather not live that long. It was always the same thing: They would ask for my opinion, then they would do whatever they wanted anyway. I was only ever asked to keep up appearances. I did everything in my power to keep this Ark alive, but my influence was limited. Shaking up the old ways has never been a good strategy. Although age is not a determining factor, as you may have noticed; there will always be bullheaded people." She takes in a deep breath with sudden nostalgia. "I know you don't want to listen to a crazy old woman's ramblings anymore. But... I remember you talking about those memory balls."

"Memory spheres, yes."

"And they work? You told me that a ball ... sorry, a sphere ... can capture my memories."

"It can. The tests we've run at the Archives are conclusive so far."

"Well, my boy, if there's one thing I'd like, it's to have my own sphere. Who knows? It might open some eyes. A picture is worth a thousand words, as they say." Skyler pulls out the tablet with Mrs. Farrell's medical records on it.

"I'll do my best," he says, noting it down. "Ready for a routine test?"

"I know how it works, sweetie," she says, blowing into the tube connected to the tablet. "You know what that other rascal did? He made me blow ten times! Ten times, I tell you. Any more and I would have fainted." Skyler holds back a laugh.

"Would you like to report it to Dr. Nazar?"

"Gladly," she says proudly. "I'll be long dead before a Kay shouts at me again!"

"And how's your leg?"

"Oh, that…" She rolls up the bottom of her pants and reveals a purplish hematoma that covers a large part of her knee.

"I'll ask Dr. Nazar to prescribe you some blood thinners," he says, taking a picture with the tablet. "Try to walk around to keep the blood from pooling." He helps her up, and she slips her arm into his again.

"How old are you again? Sixteen?"

"Twenty."

"Worse. Time's running out. A handsome boy like you can't stay single forever." They exit the sanctuary, then walk through the corridor to the elevator, the humid, incense-free air finally letting Skyler breathe properly. Mrs. Farrell gives him some crafty advice on how to seduce a girl on the Ark worthy of him, ideally a believer. He knows what she's getting at; her granddaughter is single too. Before he can think of a way out of a blind date, Elaine stops, forcing him to stop too.

"Where are we going? I hope you're not dragging me to the clinic. I'm fine."

"We're going back to your cabin, Mrs. Farrell. I'll help tidy up while you rest."

"My dear boy, I tell you I'm doing very well. Come here. Let's go to the park instead. That's much better." She steps into the elevator and hits the button for the park with a proud, mocking smile.

Skyler follows her with heartache. He's going to miss her.

6

EMILY

THE SCREEN GLOWS IN THE DIM LIGHT OF THE BATES FAMILY cabin. Her empty stomach churns at the bright display of words. She lets out a sigh.

EMILY,

I thought I made it very clear that Prisoner 590 is our top priority. Commander Hawk was adamant about it. We must bring the growing Maverick threat under control as soon as possible. We wouldn't want to disappoint the Commander, would we?

Your last report was a disappointment. You are my agent! Need I remind you that Zeta Division is responsible for the security of this ship? Our prisoners are far from innocent and harmless. They conspire and undermine our already precarious lives. Remember that I stuck my neck out to grant you the title of Agent, regardless of the Bates's questionable reputation. And for what? Don't make me regret it, Emily. Mavericks are all over this Ark. That's a fact! We might as well make a public announcement welcoming them to the ship! Your next report had better be exemplary, or I will have no choice but to intervene.

Ludo told me you cut off prisoner 590's rations, and I know I was not wrong to put my hopes in you. Remember our shared vision. I am sure your mother would agree.

Yasmina Mirza, Chief Warden, Zeta Division.

Emily closes her eyes for a moment. Is Yasmina right to condemn her for her first interrogation with Reyes?

"Emy, what are you doing? I need your help," Gabrielle calls out as she emerges from the smaller room. Her younger sister, almost dressed, pulls her other arm through her uniform top and drops her bag by the door. Emily turns the screen off and picks up what's left of her mirror.

"Gimme a minute," Emily answers, dusting shadow over one of her closed lids. Her mirror's rough surface blurs her reflection. But when you're a Bates, you settle for the absolute minimum. Dark violet shadow now clouds her eyes. Good. But these bangs? Just wrong. She rummages through the wall-mounted storage drawer that's now crammed with mismatched objects. A few random trinkets drop to the floor as she fishes a tube out from the bottom. Great. She spreads some gel—or gelatinous water, more like it—through her unruly fringe and gets it to fall smoothly to one side.

Satisfied, Emily wipes her hands on her ragged old black pants and bends to pick up what fell, returning each object to its proper mess. When her hands find a notebook on the floor, she freezes. Curiosity wins and she opens it.

Her old sketchbook! It's full. Pages and pages of portraits. Many of them are of Mom. There are also some of Dad, Sky, Gabrielle, Chris, and even a few of prisoners. Each subject is represented in simple colors, contrasted with shades of gray—her signature style. Some even have auras. Auras first appeared for her when she started drawing in her teens. When was the last time she drew? Two years ago? Three? She's gripped by a feeling of emptiness.

"My hair isn't gonna comb itself! I can't see anything in here," Gabrielle, upset, is standing next to her, brush in hand. "What are you doing?"

Emily snaps the notebook shut and throws it among the drawer's clutter.

"Nothing," she says, grabbing the brush. "Stand still!" Emily struggles to untangle the mass of hair her sister has cascading as far as her backside. Gabrielle hasn't cut her hair since she was twelve. Long hair like this is so high maintenance, though! And way too girly. Same for lipstick. And foundation. All right, all right … some mascara, once in a while, is fine. But that's it. Mom sure loved it, though. Maybe Gabrielle wants to capture part of Mom by keeping this epic mane. Or maybe Dad wants to see that part of his wife alive in her younger sister. Maybe that's why he doesn't force Gabrielle to chop off all her hair.

"How was last night?" her sister asks in a honeyed voice.

"What about it?"

"Well, it's not every night you go to a restaurant with a boy," she adds, crossing her arms with her index finger raised.

"Stop implying things. For the record, I was with Sky. We hadn't seen each other for a while."

"Oh. Well, in that case," she continues, disappointed. "How was the restaurant?"

"Imagine your twelfth birthday dinner. With your best friends Brian and Laura? But with way more people. No wait, better yet, with all the food the canteen has ever had, and more."

"Oh my God," she whispers in a small voice.

"And finally, a duet of musicians playing piano and violin."

Gabrielle turns around, her eyes wide and her mouth hanging open.

"You can't be serious. You can't be serious!" Gabrielle has always loved the piano; Mom used to listen to it over and over while cleaning their cabin.

"I told you to sit still," says Emily with a repressed smile.

"Are you ever going to take me along? Please, pretty please..."

"Maybe." Gabrielle grumbles, picks up her brush, and mumbles a "thank you for my hair."

Now free, Emily can kneel, hands clasped, in front of her favorite photograph near the front door: the one of Mom. In this photo, she is unaware of the fate that awaits her; you can read her soul in her serene gaze. She has a womanliness Emily did not inherit: She has darker long hair, and she's wearing earrings and a glittering dress. She looks so happy.

Emily feels Gabrielle kneeling beside her.

Mom left them almost eight years ago, but sometimes they can sense her presence, like now. An impression, similar to an aura. Mom said she could see auras and use them to read and guide people. She always says this was their one true mission on the Ark. She was right. Shortly after her death, auras showed themselves to Emily and that's when she learned her true mission: to restore a sense of justice—a justice denied to Mom when they sentenced her to death.

Once their ritual is complete, Emily sighs with relief. Mom hasn't disappeared. She is here, somewhere, guiding her with these vibrant colors. Her guidance will help her face the inmates who know no justice.

She gets up, followed by Gabrielle, who grabs her school bag as they walk out of the cabin without a word. A flurry of solid-colored uniforms masses at the elevators. The corridor is busy with adults on their way to work and children heading to the Academy. Gabrielle hugs her when it's time to part. Emily kisses her forehead and then makes her way to the dining hall through the stairwell.

Yasmina's message bubbles into her mind and her insides tighten. Today's gonna be a long day. It won't be easy to meet her boss's demands. Three days without rations leaves prisoners in a bad mood, which means digging out information on the Mavericks will be no small task.

The buzz echoing through the multi-storied skylight, mixed with hundreds of melting auras is dizzying. The way the colors muddle in the crowd makes it hard to tell them apart, and it gives her an intense headache. As long as she ignores the auras, she can handle it.

The smell of bread and coffee wafts in; the smart vending machines are lined up against the walls. Emily spots a line that'll do over in the back. There's nothing worse than the ages-long waits in the long lines of the dining hall. Within two minutes she's holding her wristband up to the reader and a choice of snacks pops up on the screen. A protein bar will do the trick since her stomach is still upset. She sighs at the mind-boggling line for coffee and decides to go without. Anyway, she's already used up her three coffees for the week. She's not going to beg someone; they'll be more than happy to remind her about it the following week.

Emily reaches the prison within a ten-minute walk. Yasmina's words chime like a bell: *Your next report had better be exemplary, or I will have no choice but to intervene.* Yasmina meddling would be the absolute worst thing that could happen. Losing her job is the least of her worries.

Relic hunting would have been so much better! That had been her dream, once upon a time. Leading underwater expeditions to uncover sunken treasures. Sure, there are all kinds of spoils down there, but swimming somewhere as large as the Great Ocean, maybe even encountering underwater creatures, must be such a thrilling experience. Something the prison could never offer. It must be an adrenaline that rushes through your veins and energizes you like no other. Mad stories about the hunts spread like wildfire at the Academy. Sky, Chris, and Allen had even set up their own hunts aboard the ship. Nothing on the Ark could match the real hunts, though, so they had to wing it.

Her longing fades as she skirts around the atrium to reach the secured passageway. She waves her wristband over the reader, and the door slides open. She rushes in and towards another well-concealed elevator. The surveillance camera's watchful eye stares back at her as she bites into her protein bar. It scratches the roof of her mouth, but she doesn't flinch. The Paragon filters these recordings under the command of Duke Kay. Funny, it could have been Emily's father instead!

The Bateses would have been leading a decent life now. No stupid rules about enjoying *La Orilla* in good company, or about how to get paper, books, other stuff, which are now impossible to get without jumping through a million invented hoops. But life chose a different fate for their family. Mom…

The elevator slows its descent into the Prison of the Forgotten, a place no one but Zeta division members can find. Added protection against breakouts. She passes through the "best part," the Peeper, that infamous cylinder that sees through everything, especially clothes. An incredible invention in the name of security.

As you approach, the cloying smell of madness oozes out. The main hall is austere, with its bare walls and sealed door leading to the cells. The air gets warmer here than in any other part of the ship, and wearing light clothing is a must.

Ludo is pacing, talking to himself. Emily slows down to cast an anxious glance at him. His silver aura flickers when he notices her, meaning she's made him feel self-conscious. Being here full-time sure breeds its fair share of oddities.

She greets him as if nothing ever happened, then inquires

about Reyes.

"She was raving mad that night after your visit," Ludo replies, rubbing his neck. "It won't be easy to coax anything out of her."

"Did you cut off her food rations like I asked?"

"Yes, and she has cooled down a bit since then. She must think that if she behaves, we'll have mercy on her."

"Perfect. Anything else?"

"Yasmina was being very pushy about it all." Great, just what she needs. A sweet reminder that Yasmina has the power to reassign her to any despicable position of her choosing. The Bates's inferior status doesn't require her to keep Emily, but Yasmina compromised by suggesting that, given their shared vision, they would work well together. Mildly consoling compared to Ludo's crappy job.

"She won't break easily," says Emily with a dismissive look as she tosses her wrapper into a compost garbage disposal. "Reyes, that is."

"The Paragon is preparing a purge of the lower levels and this information would be timely," he tells her with his arms folded. "The last convoy was a failure they simply can't afford to repeat."

This problem should have been dealt with long before the Ark's lower levels were sealed off, four years ago after the Incident. The Ark hit a high-caliber piece of debris—most likely the remains of a drowned skyscraper—which flooded the lower floors. While repairing the breach, they discovered the Mavericks, stowaways who cut themselves off from the rest of the passengers, eluding the scrutiny of the Paragon. How else could they have kept off the radar for so long but by taking advantage of some loophole in the security system? That probability is far from reassuring. And yet, the Paragon launched an expedition to sweep the lower floors. Apparently, they underestimated the Mavericks, who still took over part of the Ark unnoticed.

"I'll see what I can do," she says, pursing her lips. "Tell Yasmina I need a little more time."

"She said she'll be taking a spin through today, and that she'll take care of it herself if you can't pull it off." Awesome. Even Ludo knows. Why can't Yasmina keep her messages to herself?

Ludo steals a glance towards Yasmina's office, and his silver aura wavers again. Did Yasmina overpower Ludo's unflappable sense of cool?

"If I'm gone more than an hour, come and get me," says Emily as she heads for the main gate. Ludo gives her a questioning look. "Simple precaution. I lose track of time when I start working."

"I sure wouldn't want to be her," he says, revealing a few teeth in approval. He unlocks the heavy door that leads to the cells.

Emily steps into the stinking corridor of the Forgotten. Not only is it hot, but the air ducts in this section are in abysmal condition—relics of the damage caused by the Incident. Of course, Yasmina could ask to have them repaired, but she has other priorities. Prisoners have no pressing needs, and her staff certainly don't matter.

Reyes needs help. Who knows what she has gone through with the other Mavericks in the Ark's depths? Even if Yasmina sees her as Prisoner 590, she is still a human being in trouble. If only justice on the Ark were different, Emily could get information in a less drastic way. Or simply guide people, like Mom did. People rarely recover from a stint in this damn prison. Why does it have to be this way?

The inmates aren't just misfits who have violated the ship's code of conduct. Many sway between reality and fiction, trapped in their minds. They are a danger not only to others, but to themselves.

This is the case with Reyes's cellmates. Clarissa Reed and Alexander Griffin ambushed a group of divers returning from a hunt, convinced they were coated in a lethal substance. Reed and Griffin grabbed whatever they could get their hands on and then went after the divers, claiming they had trespassed upon the forbidden territories ruled by the Fairies. Luckily, the Paragon found a way to knock them both out. Emily tried drawing up their psychological profiles, but she couldn't. They refused to drink water; keeping them alive was a challenge.

Their auras are elusive, typical of people with real problems. They suffer from something for which there is no cure. Until there is, here they stay, where they can do no harm.

Emily walks unannounced into Reyes's cell, where she finds her curled up in a corner. Her hair is greasy, and she's barefoot, still wearing the same grimy clothes as last time. The thin sheets of her small bed are crumpled up, pillow among them, on the dirty floor. Animosity flares up in Reyes's eyes when she sees Emily. Her rosy aura gives way to an erratic scarlet red.

"I know what you're thinking," says Emily, getting close enough to smell that her prisoner needs a really good shower.

"Pathetic!" Reyes spits with more vigor than she has. "You thought starving me half to death would make me talk? Well, go to hell."

"I'm here to give you what you want."

"My freedom? My dignity?" says the prisoner, clenching her jaw, her gaze murderous. Her voice is hoarse, her throat beyond dry from dehydration. A sight to behold.

"It's up to you," says Emily, crossing her arms.

"And then what?"

"Come and see for yourself," says Emily, crouching down. Reyes recoils and slams into the wall.

"Get out of my face."

"You wouldn't want to keep Milo waiting, would you?" Emily replies in her softest voice. "He can't wait to see you."

Reyes's lips quiver. She curses. Then silence settles in and the seconds tick away. She struggles to get up, most likely ravaged by sharp stomach cramps from the way she's squirming.

"You disgust me," the Maverick snarls. Emily takes her without a word to a well-lit common room where food and water await them on one table. This is standard procedure when prisoners have their rations cut off. Nobody would want to be responsible for any deaths here in the prison. Not that anyone would mind. Except Yasmina. She has her moments.

Once, Alexander Griffin was carving images into his cell wall and around common areas, where he was allowed on occasion. It was found out he was hiding a spoon, and they tried to confiscate it. Of course, he did not comply. He conjured up the so-called Fairies to come to his aid. He threw himself at Iris, a former co-worker, and strangled her with superhuman strength, causing irreparable damage to her throat. The poor girl. She never spoke again. As a result of the incident, she resigned, traumatized. In theory, Yasmina can deviate from normal procedures, and she usually does in special cases. Anything goes for the Chief Warden. But, strangely enough, she didn't at that time. Since then, Griffin remains in his own world, defined by the four walls of his cell.

Such a situation is rare and killing Griffin would have been pointless. Living with a death on your conscience is the worst kind of poison. An insurmountable offense.

"Wait for me here," says Emily, about to close the door.

"Hey!" Reyes holds the door open with startling strength. "I'm not an idiot. What's your game?"

"I know you'll never trust me, but I'm just doing my job." Emily swallows a snarky remark. "I'll be right back." She closes the door and leaves the prisoner alone in the common room. She feels a tinging along the back of her neck, and a sigh escapes her throat. What she wouldn't give to avoid playing the hypocrite like this.

She crosses the hallway and branches off to the right. Prisoner 591 should be over this way.

Milo is cross-legged on his bed, meditating, his aura in shades of orange. He doesn't seem to have heard her come in, and she clears her throat, unsure, afraid to startle him. Quiet inmates are a rare sight.

He opens the long lashes that surround his large blue eyes. His skin is pale and freckled. If he wasn't one of her prisoners, she'd find him very handsome. She asks him to follow her, and he does so willingly. Thank God, someone who listens!

A few moments later, Emily returns with a frail and silent Milo. She leaves them a moment to talk to each other. Leaning against the adjacent wall, she listens to their conversation via the video surveillance screen. They don't need words to talk. There are sobs, a long embrace. Emily looks away, her stomach churning.

She sighs.

Once she's sure their plates are empty, she goes in.

"What do you want?" Reyes asks, standing up, using one voice for her and her boyfriend. Reyes has regained her strength; her aura is more settled and vibrant.

"I came to warn you," Emily says, unimpressed. No matter what she says, it's too soon for Reyes to trust her unless she is honest with her. Or sound like it. "The Paragon is launching an assault on your community soon. No one will be spared."

"Why are you telling me this?" Reyes's tone is full of doubt. She gestures, "What about all this? What do you want, praise?"

"No, but there is still a way to avoid bloodshed."

"I'm not telling you anything." She crosses her arms.

"As you wish. You should know that there is the possibility for far worse than these little interrogations of mine."

"They aren't in any danger."

"How can you be so sure? Aren't you and your boyfriend here?" They exchange an indecipherable look. Milo avoids her gaze by shutting himself off.

Why do they insist on thinking they're safe? Reyes's answer during the first interrogation, that the Mavericks are everywhere, comes to mind. Is it necessary to take what Reyes says at face value?

"I'll take over, Emily," calls Yasmina, who comes in, flanked by Ludo. What is she doing here? What about her interrogation? Yasmina adds with a weary voice, "You can bring prisoner 591 back to his cell. I don't need him."

"Don't touch him!" shouts Reyes, beside herself with anger.

"We can talk about it in my office." Yasmina beckons to Ludo, who steps out of the darkness. Reyes has no time to struggle, the sedative already spreading through her body.

Ludo is used to subduing prisoners. After all, he is the one who saved Iris from certain death. He carries Reyes out of the common room.

"I *can* count on you to take care of prisoner 591, can't I?" Emily nods at this, biting her tongue. Her boss opens her mouth to say something else, but changes her mind at the last moment, a satisfied smile on her face. Her aura pulses with excitement.

Yasmina disappears into the darkness of the corridor.

Milo's stare is blank. Emily has almost forgotten he was standing there. She moves closer to reactivate his restraints and her eyes settle on the drawings etched in the table. The scratches are deep, hurried, the work of several weeks. Winged beings surround a man—Griffin?—with trees similar to those in the Gardens of Humankind and a profile of a smeared city. Where does he get these images, these … visions? A chill runs down Emily's spine, and she hurries Milo away. Far away.

Once Milo is back in his cell, Emily steps out and pushes the strange drawings out of her mind. Yasmina. Emily can't help but feel sorry for Reyes. For Milo, too.

No one knows what happens to those who enter Yasmina's office.

7

EMILY

HER FINGERS ARE SORE. EMILY HASN'T HELD A PENCIL IN A LONG time, yet she continues to furiously sketch the facial features imprinted in her mind. The muscles in her hands guide her through: They remember how to add the right amount of pressure to the gradations, to the shadows under the eyes, the profile of the jaw, giving the cheekbones salience, the skin texture. Each curve and line are revealing. They evoke the invisible story hidden beneath the face. They aren't words, but impressions, fleeting images.

Underneath this face is a tough childhood. Perhaps he craves isolation, a need to be with oneself. And what about the placid, stripped-down calm? It's a way to make peace with an inescapable present. Could it be related to his captivity? To his girlfriend Fiona?

Emily feels a chaotic web of confusion.

Something's missing ... maybe his eyes are too dull? The corner of his mouth too stiff? The lines of his jaw too dull? Milo is self-contained. What is he hiding under his distant airs?

The tip of her pencil catches on the outline of his eyes, as if to pierce them. She goes back to his mouth and opens his lips, a secret hanging within them. Milo's aura has a powerful energy, pulsating vibrant yellows and oranges. Something's off. Because of the prison? Because of Emily?

The only way to find out is to spend more time with him. Not because Yasmina asked her to, but because she wants to. Fiona Reyes may be a lost cause, but that doesn't mean she should give up entirely. Milo is her chance to make up for it.

Emily sets aside her sketchbook and watches her sister, who's awkwardly positioned across the small sofa, reading a storybook, where magic becomes reality in a land far, far away from this miserable cabin.

To think that Gabrielle still reads that story! This must be the hundredth time. The book itself is priceless, and that she even got her hands on it was a major stroke of luck. The rumors about the Raven, a black-market dealer, were far too tempting not to pursue. Gabrielle's eleventh birthday was coming up, and she deserved a unique gift. The Raven's timely appearance could only mean one thing: He was meant to help her. Their messages were all electronic and strictly confidential, and within a couple of days, they had agreed on a place to trade. The payment was another story, though. The only currency she had access to were the tranquilizers Ludo and Yasmina use on inmates. A few missing packages would only prevent more abuse. In the end, Ludo restrained himself until the next supply came in. Lucky for her, no one noticed what she had done.

There's a knock at the door.

Emily gets up and sneaks around the storage cabinets. She creaks open the door to reveal Chris, his hands shoved in the pockets of his ward uniform, a childlike look on his face.

"You remembered!" she says, letting him in. He smells of hair wax and mint shower gel. His dull, ash blond hair is carefully smoothed back, his chin beardless, as if he was going to an interview and not her home.

"I thought things would be less boring if I came over," he

replies with the shadow of a smile, catching Gabrielle as she throws herself in his arms to welcome him.

"Easy there..." says Emily, with a hand on her sister's shoulder.

"Would you have leave to play later, My Lord?" asks Gabrielle in a pleading voice. "We must reclaim my kingdom."

"Later," Emily answers for him. "Finish up your reading first."

"Listen to your sister, My Princess," Chris says in a solemn voice, taking a bow. Every Saturday it's the same thing; Dad has to work for the Paragon, so Gabrielle needs a chaperone. Emily is grateful for the extra company.

Gabrielle resumes her reading and Emily offers Chris a drink, who takes a seat at the kitchen table. He glances sideways at the still-open sketchbook and picks it up.

"Have you gone back to drawing?" he asks her, frowning. "Nice sketch. Your new lover? One lucky guy." Emily snatches back the notebook and shoves it into the drawer above her head.

"Stop your nonsense, would you?" she says, turning back to the whistling kettle.

"Don't get all shy with me, Emy," he says, apparently no offense taken. "There's nothing wrong with enjoying your time off." She ignores his teasing and adds dried tea leaves to two stainless steel cups. She pours over boiling water, and smoke swirls up like an awkward dancer. She gingerly places the cups on the table.

It's Emily who finally breaks the tension. "You have the look of someone who has something special to say." Chris's aura is gold and ever-changing today, bursting with light.

Chris raises an eager eyebrow. "I dream of the day I surprise you. At least once." He leans back in his chair. "You spend too much time with those goddamn prisoners. You could do so much more instead."

"Drop it," Emily says, brushing off his words with a wave of her hand. "I'm not interested in your father's dictatorship."

"And yet, you have everything you need to stand up to him." Chris gives her his best smile, his teeth glimmering.

"Don't you try to change my mind. You're wasting your time. Just tell me what you're getting at." He clears his voice and fakes a pretentious, pompous look that makes her eyes roll every time. She sips her tea to check if it's brewed.

"I have the honor of announcing that as of today, I will be addressed throughout the ship as Officer Kay. Laurene Milcah, Second Officer, and advisor to Commander Hawk, has chosen me as her Potential."

"Really? You?" Emily feigns surprise. "Oh yes, I forget myself. Forgive me. Duke Kay's son. No doubt your father played a part in your appointment?"

"You offend me," he replies with a hand on his chest. "Do you not recognize my natural talent? Officer Milcah does."

"It's not like you need to be reminded." Emily takes a good, relaxing swig. "I thought you always enjoyed being a doctor; though it's minor consolation for the senior position in the Paragon you never got, simply because your father didn't want you around."

"I'm over it. That was a long time ago."

"We only graduated two years ago."

"Treating hopeless patients won't make any difference, mind you."

"These people trust you," says Emily in a firmer tone as she recalls what Sky told her the other night. "Even if the treatment doesn't work, you can still offer them some support. It's an important role that you should be proud of."

"It's just not me. You know that." Of course, he has always longed for more. His grades at the Academy made everyone green with envy. His new position is a golden opportunity for him.

"When are you going to show me your special cabin?" Emily drinks more tea to chase the strange dryness that has settled in her knotted throat.

"I haven't accepted yet. I'd rather tell you about it first. See what you think." A transfer. Better conditions. A new cabin. Access to every area of the Ark.

But what does her opinion matter to him? If that's the path he wants to take, nothing wrong with it. He may have finally nailed down his one true calling after all.

"Accept. With that new status, you can take me anywhere."

"I should have known you'd want to take advantage of my privileges," he says, mischievous. "And what do I get in return?"

"Precious advice from me, and you won't even need to be my prisoner." He snorts with a false smile and Emily stifles a laugh as she finishes her tea. She gets up to refill the hot water and glances at the table. Chris hasn't touched his cup. Something is bothering him.

"Have you talked to Sky?" His tone is serious.

"Yes." She runs the hot water softly. "Why do you ask?"

"Nothing." He brings the cup to his lips. The history between those two is strange. They've been around each other for years, they even work together, but they can't talk to each other. And yet, Chris always asks about Sky when he visits.

"You guys will have to talk sometime," she says, feeling her way.

"Then tell Sky to stop messing around. He's always giving me a hard time."

"Isn't that what *you* do best?" she says, arching her eyebrow.

"Who? Me? You must be thinking of someone else."

"Chris, stop pretending you're innocent in all this."

"I'm done, My Lord!" shouts Gabrielle, indifferent to their conversation. "I summon you to an Emergency Council against the invaders." He reaches out to Gabrielle, skillfully avoiding the matter entirely, as if the discussion never happened. Typical.

Gabrielle gets her comforter, which is now wrapped around her neck like a cape. She has dressed up a stick with pieces of plastic she put together, which she uses as a scepter. What if Gabrielle was dressed up like this during an interrogation? Her sister could disarm anyone; even Reyes would have no choice but to bow before the fearsome Gabrielle.

If only Reyes had cooperated. She had her chance and decided otherwise. Emily bites her lip and dumps out the rest of her tea. She feels full all of a sudden.

Gabrielle raises her head with a confidence that would make their mother proud. "First, I must test your allegiance to Your Princess, My Lord."

"Yes, Your Majesty," replies Chris, who now dons his own cape, along with a belt embellished with foil, and a dummy sword sheathed at his side.

"Do you pledge on your head and blood your allegiance to me until your dying breath?" she asks, resting the pommel of her scepter on his right shoulder.

"Yes, Your Majesty."

"Should you believe my decisions foolish, you will leave them unchallenged?" She shifts the scepter to his right shoulder.

"Never shall I dare do such a thing. No more faithful a servant has ever lived, my princess."

"And to this you swear?" she stresses, the pommel now placed on his lowered head.

"On my life, my princess," he says with exaggerated flair. Gabrielle has a satisfied look on her face, and Emily bursts out laughing. Her sister is a Bates through and through.

"Good," says Gabrielle, brandishing a small, scribbled chart. "I have work for you, My Lord. And please. Just call me Your Majesty." Emily holds back a chuckle when she sees Chris, who has to give up his smugness to answer her sister's beck and call. He looks like he could start a happy family.

SHE HASN'T HEARD from Reyes for two days now. What exactly did Yasmina do to her?

Cutting a prisoner's rations is never straightforward. There has to be another way to get her to talk. A more effective way. A less radical, perhaps gentler approach?

But then what? Reyes would think she could get away with anything. Trying to manipulate her, even.

Emily lets out an annoyed sigh.

She stands up, knees reddened, her prayer to her mother complete. Mom's piercing eyes are a reminder of Emily's mission to guide others.

Emily rushes out into the hallway alone, since Gabrielle left earlier this morning when her friends Brian and Laura picked her up. Still a little out of it, Emily surrenders to the uniformed mass, letting it carry her to the dining hall.

Her sketch of Milo evokes inexplicable thoughts in her. She is just doing her job: interpreting the prisoners' psyche. When she receives special requests, she fulfills them. Her opinion doesn't matter.

And yet...

What if the Mavericks exist in large numbers, in a community even? Reyes was not listed in the database of registered Archeans. She could be the result of an unreported pregnancy. It wouldn't be unheard of. But the way she talked about the Mavericks suggests something much more ... significant. She said they were everywhere. What if there's a connection to Griffin's drawings?

Only Milo can tell her more.

She puts that thought on hold, standing in one of the endless dining hall lines. She squints at the wild brightness of the artificial skylight. In the deepest abyss of the Great Ocean, this is as close to the sun as it gets.

When her turn comes, Emily takes a breath and holds her wristband up to the automatic meal dispenser—a Delta Division special design—which whirrs immediately to life.

"What would you like for breakfast, Emily?" asks a soft, electronic female voice. The voice is supposed to be calming. It has the opposite effect on her, strangely enough.

"Like you don't know," she says, annoyed. "I've ordered at least seven thousand breakfasts since we've known each other, and it's not like the choices are getting any better."

"Out of respect for your decision-making power, my algorithm does not register passenger preference."

"Why waste my time talking to a machine that doesn't think for itself? I'll say it again: Next time, unless you have actual options, don't ask me what I want."

"You may choose between traditional oatmeal and modern-day oatmeal."

"Are those supposed to be two different options?" An irresistible urge to laugh overwhelms her. Machines should never have been given the ability to speak.

"Delta Division does everything in its power to deliver you unique flavors."

"I see that clearly now."

"Will that be modern-day oatmeal?"

"Oatmeal." The machine spits out a heap looking more like vomit than oatmeal, and Emily suppresses a gag. A perk of being a Bates. All her ancestors could afford was Economy, which was enough to save the Bates line, but not enough for proper nutrition. Her father always says they got a chance that billions of humans did not. But at what cost?

Emily grabs the bowl and a metal spoon and sits at her usual table, further away from the skylight. She stabs her spoon into the sticky, shapeless mass. She peeks around at the others' plates with interest. Far cry from *La Orilla*.

She is not the only victim of this culinary disaster, though there are some who fare better this morning. A distant scent of coffee and waffles reaches her. What she wouldn't give to feel a bit of sugar melt in her mouth.

"May I?" asks Sky, beaming, tray in hand.

"Since when do you have to ask?" she replies with a smile, her heart lighter. "I was wondering when you'd decide to work less so we could eat together like we used to."

"Not that I haven't tried. There's always work to be done." He distributes his plates and utensils according to an order only he understands. "Here, I figured you'd want some." He hands her a plate of waffles, an egg in the middle. Emily's eyes must have betrayed her because he looks amused.

"You're a lifesaver. I missed you so much, you know that?"

"I knew you'd be happy." He takes a bite. "Anyway, prisoners still giving you a hard time?"

"It's been worse," she says, to avoid talking about Reyes. "If you could hurry up and find a miracle cure that sends these fairies packing, my job would be a whole lot easier."

"Talk to Chris. He knows more than I do. Right now, I'm just on damage control."

A bowl breaks against the ground and a resonating silence settles. An unappetizing splash of infamous oatmeal clings in misshapen clumps to the metallic floor. Two kids laugh at the little girl they pushed down, kicking her spilled oatmeal back at her. The girl's face is red with humiliation. Emily clenches her fists. Don't these bastards have anything better to do?

Sky gets up and talks with the girl. She nods, holding back tears as she fumbles to wipe herself clean with the lapel of her sweater. Her face lights up when Sky gives her his plate, while all Emily can do is struggle off the urge to tell off those little brats.

Sky sits back down at their table. "That was nice of you," she says, "but now what are you going to eat?" She knows full well that Sky's higher family status means nothing when it comes to food. No one gets seconds.

"I wasn't that hungry anyway," he replies, crossing his arms. "Don't worry about me. All that matters is that the girl gets to eat." He glances in her direction with a smile.

"Kids will be kids," mutters Emily. "You'd think that over the generations they'd learn, but it's just a constant replay. It's like stupidity is in our genes."

"Don't be so harsh."

"Are you defending them now? It was a kid just like that who used to give you such a hard time—or have you forgotten?" A furtive glance passes through Sky's eyes, but he doesn't react the way she'd hoped.

"That's not what I'm saying, it's just part of their development." His bright blue shifts to a duller shade. "They have to test limits."

"At others' expense? They'll just end up in court and who's going to have to deal with them then? Better to weed out the troublemakers now."

"Is that really the answer? They're just going to do it again. Personally, I would take a more passive, less … direct approach."

"By taking away their favorite oatmeal?" she says wryly, spoon in hand.

"There has to be another way." Their opinions have always clashed, and letting the conversation go in this direction can get tricky.

"Want some modern-day oatmeal?" she says, moving on.

"I'll pass." Emily takes advantage of the silence that slips between them to finish off the waffles. What would Sky's portrait look like? Since graduation, his features have changed; his face is squarer, the hair of his beard thicker, his shoulders prouder, and his pale complexion now reveals delicate, once-hidden freckles. His eyes are as blue as ever, their vivid glow now fleeting.

Sky's silence is unnerving, and his aura reveals nothing more. It's ironic that she can't read him. They've known each other for years, but Sky keeps his secrets in a vault locked tighter than the Ark's prison.

The waffles wolfed down to the last crumb, Emily stares at her bowl for a few seconds, then stands. What remains of the modern-day oatmeal is definitely not part of her plans this morning. She doesn't want to spoil the divine sweetness that lingers on her tongue.

"I have to go to the prison," says Emily to break the silence. "I'll see you for dinner?"

"If I don't have to work overtime, why not?" They say good-bye, but Sky has shut himself off. It wasn't a good idea to remind him of his teenage years. His family isn't very close-knit, which couldn't have been easy for him. Whenever she visited him at his parents' house, his conversations with them were always very pragmatic. He never talks about them either. Not to mention Allen's death, which was a tough blow for everyone, though that was several years ago.

Emily throws the half-full bowl into one of the dining hall's garbage cans with irrepressible joy. She leaves the hustle and bustle and retreats into the darkness of the Ark's corridors, thinking up a way to approach Milo. He won't be easy to win over. He'll want to bargain for his safety, something Emily can't promise.

She tries to slip in behind a small group before the elevator doors close but fails awkwardly. The doors close on her hip and the alarm goes off. Emily exchanges an embarrassed smile with the young family, the little boy staring at her. She turns and grumbles, rubbing her side as she presses frantically to shut the elevator doors.

Just as they finally close, a shrill sound can be heard coming from the other side. There's an exchange of worried looks;

probably the doors got blocked one too many times. The whole Ark is going to fall apart soon at this rate!

But as the elevator goes up, Emily suddenly realizes those were screams.

8

SKYLER

THE SHRIEKS OF HORROR ARE BLOODCURDLING, AND ADRENALINE courses through his veins. Skyler doesn't remember getting up, but there he stands, staring up through the ten-story skylight at a young woman. She's about to jump.

They are here. The Fairies. An unseen enemy that eludes them all. The odds are against him, but if there's the slightest chance of dissuading her...

An overload of adrenaline surges through his legs, propelling him towards the nearest corridor. Can he get to her before she falls to her death?

The thought haunts him as he rushes to the elevators. He hits the call button, cursing at the damn machine to hurry. He steadies himself against the ramp to catch his breath, watching the slow climb of the floor indicator, his pulse pounding triple time in his ears.

It's too late. Like last time, it's going to be too late.

His throat tightens. His memories threaten to flood back. His fingers twist on the metal of the now damp railing.

He's not the same person he was then. He can prevent a tragic ending this time.

The elevator drags to a halt. Tenth floor.

With each stride, the ground shifts under his feet. It's like gravity has just given up. He's floating.

He pushes forward, scanning his surroundings to locate the woman: Her pale frame is to his left. She is sitting on the railing, back to him, arms raised as if about to take flight. Damn it!

He doesn't know her, but a harrowing thought overwhelms him: What if it's his mother? The woman turns and stares back at him.

Will she jump? What are the Fairies telling her?

The woman is only a few years older than he is; her face is ravaged with pain. Her lips move, but her mumbling makes little sense. He steps closer, alert. Below them, two Paragon agents have arrived to see to the ruckus.

What's he supposed to do to help her? Skyler might as well join the petrified crowd. It wouldn't make any difference. Below, people cover their mouths, holding in screams out of fear of what they might trigger.

Skyler clenches his teeth and searches what he learned in his classes, but the solution shuns him. He is disgusted by his helplessness.

"No," he says, as if the word itself held some tangible power.

"You can't stop me. It's too late now." She drops her arms, sobbing. "They told me this day would come sooner or later."

"There is another way." Another way to what? To talk to the damned Fairies? For all he knows, they don't even exist! The fantasy world has been playing inside her head for weeks, if not months. The only way to reason with her now is through a logic he does not possess. Patients in the final stages have shown similar symptoms, but their cases were similarly unique. The Syndrome mirrors the psyche of its victim and speaks directly to the mind of its host, tampering with its networks. The patient's brain becomes its own enemy. The only certainty is that the Fairies always win.

She grips the railing, her knuckles bleached, to get a better look at him. "You don't even know who I am. You don't know ... what I must endure." Her stare hardens.

"I know they whisper to you," he replies in a calm, confident voice. "They're here. Right now." Are they watching them, laughing at his poor attempt? They could be hanging out and playing with him for all he knows. They are invisible.

The young woman looks just like Murielle. She has short dirty hair, a lighter red than his mother's. There are bald patches where chunks have been pulled out, probably during one of her fits of madness. Her features are drawn, her complexion pale ... death has already set in.

The woman, poised, lets go of the barrier. The tips of her feet embrace the emptiness above the dining hall, brushing the fine line that separates life from death. Skyler holds in a gasp, afraid of taking one more breath upon punishment of watching her fall.

How can he get her back?

He slowly moves closer, keeping eye contact. "My name is Skyler. What's your name?"

A tear rolls down the woman's cheek. Her eyes soften and she stares off to her left at something that isn't there.

"What does it matter?" she says, slightly angry, in a strangled voice. "I'm worthless. I'm no one." Skyler suddenly remembers something from medical school. In fact, it's something he shouldn't do: Pretend to understand what the victim is going through.

"Why do you say that?" He takes one more step towards her. "It matters to me. Your name. Who you are."

"I had to betray my name all my life. A name that has no meaning anymore. They're willing to give me the chance I never had to be somebody. Do you know what it's like to deny your own existence? To hide from yourself?" Families? Their status on the Ark? Even though Skyler isn't sure what she's getting at, he silently lets her imaginary friends distract her. She responds to them by chanting in a curious language, and he closes the distance between them.

"What do they say to you?" he asks, now closer, motionless.

"They protect me from you," she says, shifting her attention back to him. "They have wrapped me in a bubble that's going to take me to their heavenly kingdom where everything is possible." She pauses as she peers at that same empty spot to her left, her mouth half-open. There's a flash of hesitation. "They ask if you want to come with me. With us."

"And what do they offer?" His muscles tense.

"You don't have to lie to yourself. Come and join us. They won't offer you this chance again." The Fairies got him.

His breathing quickens. They're not real. The Syndrome will kill her unless he does something. "I work at Med Bay. I can help you."

She turns her ear to her imaginary friends. "They feel sorry for you. For missing your chance. They can't guarantee your safety from now on."

"Can you ignore them for a second? Look me in the eye." What's he doing here? What the hell was he thinking coming all the way up here? Did he think he was some kind of superhero? That she was just going to follow him? This isn't a child's story. There are no happy endings here.

After a long time, she almost lets go of the guardrail to meet him, but instead she lets out a childlike laugh. "Nothing can ever change. Not for me. Not for you. Not here."

"Let me prove you wrong."

"You don't have that power. We're both stuck on this ship. The difference is, I have a chance to escape, and you don't."

"Take my hand," he says, reaching out to her. She hesitates.

"What's the point of living, if only to deny that you exist?" She consults the Fairy on her left, and a strange smell of wet earth fills Skyler's nose. A mysterious gleam shines in her eyes.

"I am a bad memory everyone would rather forget."

"I will remember you," he replies, his hand still outstretched. At that, she returns from a faraway land, and a smile floats across her lips.

"My name is Clarissa." She spreads her arms and lets herself drop.

Skyler lunges after her, catching his stomach on the railing and knocking the wind out of himself. He gets a hand around her ankle and is pulled downward. He manages to hook the barrier with his feet.

Damn!

Horrific screams erupt from the dining hall. He can't hold on much longer. His arms are quickly losing strength. How's he going to pull her up?

Someone is going to die because of him.

Clarissa hovers above a crowd of distant black dots. Skyler feels her bare foot slipping through his fingers, and then, nothing. For a split second, he ceases to exist.

The body does not fall. Is it floating?

No. Another hand is holding it. But whose?

"If you want to save her, it's now or never," a female voice calls out to him. "I can't hold on much longer." He hurries to grab the other foot. They pull with all their strength until Clarissa tips over to their side. Then, they release her to the ground, both out of breath.

The newcomer at his side must be the same age as him. She is wearing a bandana, her long brown hair in beaded braids that frame her face.

"I'm sorry," she says, looking away. He stares at her, puzzled.

Clarissa.

Clarissa's body.

Lifeless.

Skyler's trembling hand finds the artery in her neck. Nothing. He closes his eyes to focus, but still nothing. No pulse in her wrist either. He listens for breath in her rib cage.

Silence. The Fairies win again.

Every day for the past five years it's the same thing: one failure after another, one life after another that he's not able to save. That first time he met death, it took Allen and his innocence along with him. His brother ….

Pain grips his chest in front of Clarissa's lifeless body. Guilt sinks its teeth deep into him. He could have, should have, reasoned with her, dropped the veil of her illusions. True, there is no treatment for the Syndrome, but he could have tried *something* at least. A thousand times over Skyler replayed the day Allen succumbed to his fantasies, wondering what he could have said to snap him out of his madness.

Allen didn't have the Syndrome, not that Skyler knew of. Fairies are only the manifestation of a weakness humans carry. A flaw they use to further anchor themselves. Allen, on the other hand, submitted to his own obsession.

And now Skyler has to live with the constant reminder of his hopelessness. Allen, Clarissa, and all the other names will live on in the sanctuary only.

Another candle will be lit tonight.

What's the point of being a doctor if he can't save a single patient's life? He's just a bystander doomed to watch the same ending over and over again.

Skyler grits his teeth. This has to change.

"There was nothing you could do." The stranger crouches down next to the body, arms crossed. "She was already lost."

"The Ark wouldn't even exist if people thought that way."

"Hope … pushes us to commit acts otherwise impossible." She gets up and the marbles holding her braids knock against each other. "Though even hope has its limits."

"Why did you help me then?"

"To save you from yourself," she says, sternly. Skyler raises an eyebrow, unsure what to think. She claims to know him, but they only just met. She has no idea what the last few years have done to him. No one knows how the repercussions of his actions have wrecked his parents.

This is a burden he must carry alone.

The stranger's words hang in the air, drowned out by the sound of hurried boots against metal. The Paragon.

"Come on!" she urges, grabbing his hand with a surprisingly powerful grip.

"Why leave?" he says as they hurtle down the opposite corridor. "We did nothing wrong."

"You think they're going to bother to question you? They'll think you're infected, like her, and they'll want to conduct their own experiments."

"That doesn't make any sense. Performing biopsies is Omega Division's job."

"They make the rules," she says in an emphatic tone. "This way." Skyler looks behind him to be sure they aren't being followed. They wouldn't go so far as to think them responsible for Clarissa's death. Would they?

THE GIRL with the braids releases his hand when they reach where the usual cold lighting of the tenth floor gives way to a fiery glow: a new wing. The warmth of her skin lingers for a few more seconds; it feels foreign to Skyler. Has it really been so long since someone touched him?

Large doors slide open as they approach, and a breath of humid air unfurls around them. They pass through a decontamination airlock. They get sprayed down by a fine but persistent mist. Once that unpleasant process is over, they get to enter one of two places Skyler likes to spend his free time: The Gardens of Humankind.

Trees stretch several feet high toward an invisible ceiling. The heady smell of foliage and damp ground fills his lungs and invigorates him, chasing away the ghost of his past, be it only for a short while. He suppresses a silly smile, twitching the corners of his lips.

Skyler takes a deep breath as he steps onto the pathway, the girl with the braids a few feet ahead of him. Solace, connection to the land of old … on *this* ship. Hard to believe, but so necessary.

"I'll never tire of this place," says Skyler, spellbound by those tall trees that sweep the ground with their leafy foliage—their name escapes him. His limited knowledge of the chrysanthemums, lilies, and irises he grows comes from the Archives he has been combing through for the last couple of years.

Skyler runs his hand on the ridges of a tree trunk, which crumbles under his fingers. He smells one of the bright green leaves and the scent is so lush that he can almost feel the sap running down his throat. A welcome change from the horrible metallic tang of the Ark.

"I can't believe that none of this exists on the surface anymore," he muses as he gently feels the leaf in his palm and brushes it with his thumb.

"I never thought I'd ever be able to see this," she says, beside him. The echo of her voice fades into a sudden metallic creak chiming through the ship's hull. Skyler's feet are slipping out from under him. He casts a surprised glance at her; she's petrified.

Too late. He tips over and braces for impact.

The ground jolts and takes his breath along with it. Clattering noises rain down all around him. He rolls until a shrub finally stops him.

Once the Ark stabilizes, Skyler wrestles himself out of the bush. He twinges with sadness when he realizes the extent of the damage. Branches of every size litter the ground.

The shrub that saved him is riddled with crimson flower buds that tickle his nose with an earthy scent he has never smelled. Another flower to add to his list.

"Are you all right?" she asks, who comes up to him with a shaky step through the bush. "It was a close call." Skyler hopes his mother and Emily are okay. Med Bay and other public places have been equipped for this kind of event, the furniture fixed to the floor, things like that. Falling is still a real danger, though.

"I think I'm fine," he replies as he gets up, his back sore. "Just a few scratches." He'll recover quickly. The Gardens, however, will take much longer. Life is so fragile.

"I guess that's what Dylan meant," says Skyler, trying to explain what happened.

"Dylan?"

"My dad. He's an oceanographer. The ocean currents have been pretty strong lately." The girl with the braids nods silently and shuffles back to the main trail, as if lost in thought. He follows her.

They walk along, the rays of the artificial sun breaking through the sparse canopy, and a warmth spreads over his skin. They avoid the bits of branches that dot the path whenever they can, but sometimes they must climb over the larger ones.

"I've never seen you before," Skyler says to break the silence. "What do you do on the Ark?"

"You wouldn't believe me if I told you." She picks up a good-sized branch to use as a walking stick.

"Can you tell me your name at least?" She hesitates for a moment. Skyler starts to speak again when she answers,

"Tessa. Tessa Farrell." She must notice the surprise on his face because she retorts, "What?"

"I didn't think Elaine had grandchildren. You know, with her progressing dementia, you can't always take her word for it."

"So, you're the resident who takes care of her? Skyler Goldberg, right?"

"All good things, I hope?" Mrs. Farrell has a knack for mixing up people's identities. It may be a side effect of her dementia, but even in its early stages, two years ago, Dr. Nazar said she was already showing signs of prosopagnosia.

"I don't see her very often," she says, looking away. "Work always gets in the way."

"Can't all be good, then, if you're avoiding the question." He draws closer to the edge of the small woods overlooking a relatively untouched manmade plain. "Sometimes my co-worker Chris takes over, so if she's in a foul mood on those days, it might be because of him. She doesn't like him very much."

"Duke Kay's son, who took up medicine rather than follow in his father's footsteps?"

"I prefer the version of the story where it was his father who didn't want to have him around," he corrects, which earns him a smirk from Tessa. "How do you know about him?"

"It's part of my job." The only people who have access to the passenger registry either work for the crew, the prison, or …

"Well! The Paragon has a rogue member, it seems. I don't know if that should make me feel any better."

"There are different views within the Paragon. Duke doesn't always follow the orders of Command Officer Diana, and some officers have figured that out. So many people, so many opinions."

"Let's cut to the chase. Why did you bring me here?" he presses her in earnest.

"To warn you." She narrows the space between them, getting close enough for the salty scent of her skin to tantalize him. His body stiffens.

"About what exactly?" His heart drums along with his skepticism.

The pierce of her amber gaze pulls at something inside him.

Tessa knows more about him than she lets on. But isn't that what the Paragon does? Investigate people?

"Stay with your family tomorrow. They need you."

"What's going to happen to them?" he asks, cross.

"Remember Clarissa, her distress." The images hit him hard. Clarissa's face is replaced with Allen's, then with his mother's. She suffers from his brother's absence, and his father's indifference adds to her misery. Skyler must make amends.

He struggles with all his might to choke back the tears.

"Remember why you work so hard," adds Tessa, who offers him a look filled with empathy. "How things could have turned out differently." Her voice is soft and naturally lilting, and Skyler can't help but want to hear more of it. But something about her arouses his curiosity. Tessa has a face that lends itself to laughter but is veiled by a feeling he could recognize anywhere: a kind of deep melancholy. Why?

He has the troubling impression that Tessa understands him, that she shares the chains that hold him against his will. What if his mother awaits Clarissa's same tragic fate? The only way to avoid it is to deter the Fairies, who, if given the chance, will exploit Murielle's weaknesses to take her hostage.

"Don't forget who you are," Tessa whispers.

She moves away, the beads in her braids tinkling at slow and regular intervals. And then it all comes together. He's met Tessa before. Not so long ago.

***

THE SHIP'S lights have dimmed to mimic the earthly night. The dull ceilings have nothing to do with the starry sky they've heard so much about. A sky that stretches into infinity, each twinkle a gateway to a distant world, out of reach. A place far from the Ark and its bowels that have been digesting them for too long. Tonight, Skyler must settle for these four metal walls that strip him away of his freedom of dreaming for better days. Without the Fairies. Without his drowning mother.

Thankfully, Murielle wasn't hurt in the "seaquake," as Dylan calls them. The phrase came to Skyler's mind once he was back in the family cabin.

He spent the evening taking care of Murielle and eating her favorite salmon pasta with her. They also watched videos of old Earth and the billions of possibilities available to them had they been born in a different time. He didn't make her any promises. They're meant to be broken anyway. But deep down inside, he can imagine a way of harnessing humanity's second chance. With his family, by giving his mother back her former joy. Showing her that life has great things to offer, even if one of her sons will never return.

Tessa reminded Skyler that he belongs by his mother's side before anything else. He plans to send a query to Omega Division tomorrow to grant him full-time charge of his mother. He has shirked his responsibility, believing that caring for others would bring his brother back. All the while, he has neglected his own family.

Mom.

He must ask for forgiveness.

9

SKYLER

THE SWARTHY GIRL WHO WORKS IN THE ARCHIVES IS BRUSHING her long, jet-black hair while her eyes jump from one end of the screen to the other. She recognizes Skyler out of the corner of her eye and scans his wristband with her free hand, her usual shy smile hanging on her lips. Then she slides him a golden token with a number on it. Skyler mumbles an embarrassed thank you, but the girl is already back to her mindless brushing, her eyes riveted by something that is apparently a hundred times more interesting.

Skyler notes his assigned Nave and enters a sealed hallway that opens when he shows his wristband. The Naves are lined up next to each other, separated by frosted glass. Skyler takes a seat and is greeted by the familiar, soothing scent of lavender. The door locks, sucking the air out with it.

Total silence.

His ears are still ringing from it as he inserts the token into a recess on the arm of the recliner. The room starts to glow, and a circuit within the seat lights up. His name chimes, a screen appears announcing different menus, each obtainable by a simple hand gesture.

Clarissa Reed. The Syndrome's latest victim. Locating her in the registry was easy. When they met this morning, Emy told him that several prisoners who had tried to break out had similar symptoms to Clarissa's, though only a few had succeeded.

That conversation gave him an idea. If the Syndrome is widespread even in the prison, the Archives might contain traces of it. It's possible someone said something about it, it could have been recorded at some point in the Ark's history. Just a hunch, but worth a shot. There was a lot of research involved with the Memory Spheres Project, which is how the wealth of the Archives came to mind. The Archives' organization is not ideal, most recordings are poor quality, but they could hold small gems.

Skyler launches a search of Medical Bay's records. Some doctors from the first two generations published a medical journal monthly, but they abandoned the practice during the Furies, the Ark's Dark Age. Overpopulation had disastrous consequences: lack of food, shortage of oxygen, while several crucial parts of the ship had to be replaced. When Command regained control of the situation, stricter measures, such as birth control, were introduced to prevent another potentially fatal catastrophe.

Skyler sifts through the journal's publications. While trying to go back to the previous menu, he accidentally hits an author's name on her personal page. A list of her contributions appears, nothing special, but one word catches his attention. *Chronicles.*

Private recordings. This is very unusual. Normally, only official documents or a few videos from the old land would be classified. Nothing else.

Skyler taps on the first recording from 2089. An image fills the screen.

"Is it working? Hello? Good. It's strange for me to record myself. Luckily, I'm alone in my little office as you can see. My name is Ivanka Torres. I'm a resident here in the Med Bay of our infamous Ark. Future doctor! I can't believe it myself. But it won't be until I go through all the endless mock surgeries to get my official license. Whatever."

This Ivanka is as redheaded as Mira, but the blond blends in more. Her skin is so pale that her freckles stand out much more, especially in the typical fluorescent light of Med Bay.

"I thought it would be nice to keep a record of my experiences at work. The best way to prepare for an exam. I must be crazy. In fact, I don't know anyone else who does video diaries like this. Who would take the time to watch them, anyway? It's not like I'm famous for inventing a new drug. You must wonder what this Ivanka Torres has to share? That's okay. I'm also wondering that right now. Whether it's really worth it. How shall I put this? I don't know what's going on, but suspicious cases have been coming in. Nothing they taught us at the Academy. And I'm a good student. Of course, I asked my mentor, Dr. Taylor, and he got really quiet."

She freezes, her mouth gaping.

"Ah, what the hell is this?" She looks up at the ceiling. "Sorry. I must have taken over the worst office in Med Bay. The one no one wants because the pipes leak. Now, where was I? Oh, right! The suspicious cases. The patients are maniacal. Some die suddenly. It's beyond comprehension. I hope they won't ask about it in the examination. To be honest, that's the least of my worries right now. But what happens to them in the end? It's like people are going crazy on this Ark. Have they been cooped up for too long? Lack of sun exposure has adverse effects on mood, the nervous system and all, but hey, vitamin D supplements in the dining hall meals should do the trick. No. There has to be something else. I have a bad feeling about this. It's like…"

She lets out a scream as objects fly off her desk and crash to the floor. Her chair tips over and the camera wobbles to a halt.

A seaquake? The conditions on the Ark have never been easy.

The Nave offers Skyler to play the next two recordings. His heart pounding, he accepts. This time, Ivanka is in the thick of things. She is filming as she walks.

"I never thought I'd see this. One death after another. But worse is what happens before they die. Watch this."

There's screaming in the background.

"Patients are hysterical. Some are talking to themselves. They've all gone crazy! What can we do to help them, seriously? Even if you put them on life support, their nervous systems fail! Med Bay is overwhelmed, and that's on top of those who are dragged out of their cabins. We think it's an epidemic, but it doesn't make sense. I've been around countless infected patients and yet I have no symptoms."

Ivanka turns around.

"Stay down. You are sick. What the hell…? Help! Stop him!" Ivanka's voice chokes and the camera falls to the ground with a close-up of her feet.

A thud to Skyler's right startles him. Then the crackling of the intercom follows.

"Oh, Skyler! I did not want to frighten you," says Dr. Siria with her ever-astonished look.

"Yes," he says, still stunned by the last video. "What's going on?"

"Actually, when you have a moment, could you join me in the Sphere Room? I have something to show you."

"Okay. I'll be right there." Dr. Siria leaves. Skyler hurriedly puts the last video back on.

Ivanka is on a bed, probably the one in her cabin.

"How does this thing work again? Ah yes! That'll teach me for not using it all this time. I don't know why I keep making these recordings. My parents died of the mysterious disease, and I miss them terribly. As for myself, I survived. Barely."

She shows healed marks on her neck.

"The patient strangled me. It was Dr. Taylor who saved me. That event brought us very close. Now that I am officially a doctor, there will be no more misunderstandings since he and I are dating. But anyway. People avoid talking about this mysterious disease that killed nine hundred and fifty Archeans. It is a catastrophe. But we are recovering. We adapt. Our ancestors braved the Flood, after all. It must be in our genes! The future is murky, but life on the Ark is slowly returning to normal. With the help of the Paragon, the Deltas have cleaned up the mess from top to bottom and now my office at Med Bay is somewhat decent.

'What are you doing, honey?'

'Oh sorry! Just finishing something up. Give me a minute.'

Well then, I don't think I'll continue with these recordings. It's hard to be alone since I'm a full-time doctor and in love. Sorry to have wasted your time."

The video abruptly stops, and Skyler's mind goes into overdrive. Was it the Fairy Syndrome? Did it break out that soon?

He checks the date of the first recording. February 13, 2089. That's seventy years ago! Why would the Syndrome come back now? If it *was* the same thing, that is. But the similarities are too striking.

Skyler keeps digging in case he finds more videos from 2089. Nothing. Nada. The Archives contain mostly scanned books and images. Going through the other categories takes a lot of time, and even more to parse the profiles of all the authors who contributed to the medical journal. Depending on the results, he could spend hours on end searching.

He removes the embedded token, and the Nave goes to sleep. He exits the private hallway and quickly sets the coin down on the reception counter dotted with long black hair. No trace of the clerk. He doesn't wait for her and heads for the Sphere Room where Doctor Siria must be getting impatient.

But she is not here either, probably busy with something else.

Skyler gets closer to the pedestal and waves his wristband over it. The display lights up in a beautiful orchid blue, and the memory spheres rise on a rotating plate. So far, there are only three. Skyler encoded the very first one somewhat unexpectedly in a hunt that turned into a nightmare: Underwater debris snatched two members on one of their teams. Skyler chose the older of the two to better test the capabilities of his technology. Coming from a richer background, he was the ideal candidate. The procedure was a success and Skyler received the final green light for his project, and caught Dr. Siria's attention, among others.

The second attempt, on the other hand, was a failure: The sphere remained a dull gray. The calibration went wrong because he ran out of time. That's when he realized how important that little window of opportunity is. If brain activity is completely off, it is too late. This sphere contains only fragments that they can't decode. Skyler keeps it in case he can decipher it. One day perhaps.

Come to think of it, the first sphere was a fluke. All the best possible parameters were in place: The window of opportunity was open; the old man didn't have the Syndrome, and his brain was intact.

Skyler hasn't had time to check the third sphere yet, and now would be the perfect time to do so. He places his palm over the glowing globe, which rises: Francisco Rivera, forty-two years old. A longer description of his background in the Ark's community pops up, though the access would normally be restricted. Skyler had to get the Paragon's permission to access this information, which was as bad as arguing with Chris. Luckily, Emily's father's connections tipped the decision in his favor.

The strands of light hypnotize him. They are eerily reminiscent of the network of blood vessels in the human body. And if it weren't deep bright red, it could easily be a tree in the Gardens, with its branches multiplying in a complex tangle, some wider than others, and its heart-like center pulsing the energy it needs to its tiniest fibers. It's like a flower picked just before withering into oblivion, to overcome the test of time in its glass prison—its beauty, a timeless existence, scores of memories that the host may or may not have access to, beyond comprehension.

Skyler's heart races along with the sphere as he activates it for viewing.

He waits.

"Data corrupted."

His entire body goes ice cold. This can't be happening.

No explanation. The sphere, with its forbidden beauty, seems to give him a warning: Is he really willing to possess such a secret?

"Hey, Sky! Good to see you." A strong smell of oil wafts before Nathan, Jacinta's engineer husband, who strolls in with his typical smirk. Skyler doesn't show he's bothered by the stench and smiles back to Nathan, who pats him on the shoulder. His uniform is stained in more places than he can count.

"You couldn't have come at a better time," Skyler greets him, his brow furrowed. "I have a problem you could fix. Take a look at this." Skyler tries to view the sphere again, and the error message comes up.

"Mmm. I'm going to need some time. Was there anything freaky about this guy?"

"He died of the Syndrome." Nathan makes a face.

"That must explain part of the problem. Probably interference. Look, I'll work on it and get back to you."

"I can't thank you enough."

Nathan makes himself comfortable by leaning on the console, a smug look on his face.

"By the way, I have a little surprise for you," the engineer says, nodding towards the receptacle. "I am going to use this sphere to test one of my crazy ideas."

Skyler gives him a questioning look.

"You know that Jacinta and I are expecting a baby, a little girl in fact," Nathan adds distractedly. "When you told me we could know…"

Chris. Why can't people just do their jobs properly?

Nathan pauses, searching for the right words, then straightens up. "The memory spheres… If anything were to happen to me or Jacinta, I'd like our little girl to meet her parents, you know?"

Skyler nods. Nathan only ever talks about work. So, what exactly is he getting at?

"Besides, with the Syndrome so rampant, I thought, what if my little girl could meet her dad if something ever happened to me? Right now, the spheres only pull images out of our memory. When they work, that is." He scoffs while Skyler bites the inside of his cheek. If the first sphere worked, then the others can too—or the entire project will fall apart.

"But what if we could see the dead? My little girl could see her parents, no matter what. I've been working on that recently. You don't mind, do you?"

Seeing the dead? It's ambitious, even impossible considering the sketchy results, but if Nathan thinks he can pull it off…

"These memory spheres … no. This project is for all of us," Skyler says while rubbing the back of his neck. "To give us new possibilities." He shudders with excitement at the very thought. Sure, it would only be an imitation, probably an assortment of lights, but they would transcend their memories to make them … whole. Meeting loved ones again is a price many would be willing to pay, if only to find comfort. It could even be part of bereavement therapy, and the pain of separation would soon become nothing more than a fading memory.

Skyler's thoughts are racing through his head. "I trust you."

"I can't wait." Nathan rubs his hands, smiling like a child.

"Skyler," Dr. Siria calls out to him with a surprised look. "I don't mean to be a killjoy, but some people are here for you, and they don't look happy at all."

Skyler's heart sinks.

AGENT MILES, the one who questioned him after his visit to Mrs. Farrell's cabin, has been assigned to escort him.

No explanation. With the Paragon, better keep silent.

They walk through a vast corridor, lined by a large bay window with a breathtaking view of the far reaches of the Great Ocean. The sea salt-gorged air sticks to his skin. The exterior lights of the Ark are on, meaning that a team of divers is currently on the hunt. Natural sunlight barely filters through, and without this artificial light, they would see nothing. At least two dozen of the small Strahl vessels are glowing in the searchlight.

They make another turn, away from the bay window and into the heart of the Ark, where a familiar double door sits, the atrium.

Skyler's blood drains from his face. This is where criminals are summoned before being thrown in prison. What do they suspect him of?

They enter the atrium, a gigantic, blindingly white room with a ceiling so high it spans several floors, much like in the dining hall. There is an enormous crowd abuzz with conversation and excitement.

Something looks different: Hundreds of miniature naves that look like glass bubbles swarm the platforms. The agent leads him to one of them: Omega79.

"Next time, show up for the simulation yourself. We've got

bigger fish to fry," says agent Miles, who marches back to the entrance. It shuts immediately behind him.

The Nave welcomes Skyler and asks questions about the food he had in the last twenty-four hours—he forgot to eat lunch—and his sleep—too little. As soon as the electrodes lick his skull, the virtual assistant diagnoses high stress levels and rattles on the simulation procedure to calm him down.

Skyler leans back against the headrest with relief, the robotic voice barely a distant hum. The simulation had completely slipped his mind. The reminder must have been in the clutter of his emails. A simulation. Well, better than rotting in a cell over some misunderstanding.

"The purpose of the simulation is to prepare you for an emergency, measure your strengths and weaknesses, and ensure you are ready to repopulate when the time comes. Earth's climate can be arid and unpredictable. Although it is hard to imagine, you will face many hazards that will require all your skills."

Once every three months, each Archean must take this routine test, two or three hundred at a time. By stimulating certain areas of the brain known to trigger emotions and memories, the simulation proposes the architecture of the dream; the person's imagination fills in the rest to create the perfect illusion of an alternate reality, almost like a lucid dream. The results are compiled, so the program can learn from their experiences to target their strengths—to refine them—and weaknesses—to counter them. As expected, this was the Paragon's idea.

The reports are rather brief and are mostly used by the crew to devise repopulation plans. They don't believe it is necessary to reveal anything more. When Skyler was at the Academy, there were wild rumors about the simulation reports' actual use. Some thought the reports were how Paragon agents selected. Others said it was an excuse to implant chips in everyone, or, better yet, that our minds were already being controlled. As far as the adults were concerned, how the reports are used are of little interest. For lack of entertainment and nothing else, conspiracy theories have always been popular on the Ark. Skyler believes it's better to focus on concrete actions towards building the future, rather than dwelling on far-fetched stories. Obviously, there's a conflict of priorities happening.

"The simulation is the results of a collaboration between the Five Divisions," continues the ageless voice. "May you meet with success."

Relaxing music takes over and Skyler's throat clenches. He glances around to take his mind off what is to come. He spots Emily out of the corner of his eye, one row down the same section. Chris, Mira, and Leander are side by side.

Chris is speaking vehemently, but still looks smug. Mira, clinging to his arm, is annoyed; her face is flush with anger. The loud din in the atrium drowns out their conversation, but from the looks of it, the topic is motivated by jealousy.

Mira seems to have a crush on Chris, from what Skyler can discern. What could she possibly see in him? She's quiet and hard-working; Chris calls the shots as an excuse to flake out. Pathetic.

Emily is also watching from her Nave, the same thread of ideas probably running through her mind.

The virtual assistant tells Skyler his stress has been reduced to an acceptable level and the relaxing music stops. The lights dim and silence washes over the atrium.

With a confident gait, Laurene, the Ark's second-in-command, walks up the hexagon and takes a place at the center, next to another display of the iconic fish. Just like at the sanctuary, they are continuously jumping and splashing in ephemeral water. Another illusion.

Laurene's long brown hair falls along her blouse, giving her a certain presence. She has smooth skin, perfect teeth, and consistently exudes a timeless air.

Duke Kay follows, just off-key enough to stand out even more. He takes up most of the space, as if claiming the stage for himself. He oozes an insufferable arrogance. It obviously runs in the family.

Laurene's voice blares from the Nave's internal speaker system.

"Thank you all for coming to the quarterly simulation. The survival of our species depends on our ability to adapt. We have come a long way since the first generation of survivors. Since the Flood, we have braved ordeals no human before us ever faced."

Laurene takes a carefully thought-out pause as cries of joy erupt from all sides.

"Let us remember what has brought us here today. Why we are still alive, and why we will survive until we repopulate the Earth."

A solemn hush mutes the atrium. Skyler gets goosebumps at the thought of walking on ground, feeling rain on his skin, or sand running through his fingers, breathing in clean forest air, perhaps feeling the cold bite of wind. Not a figment of his imagination; life as it should be.

Duke takes over, under Laurene's interested look.

"This world has become hostile and merciless. It has destroyed the vestiges of our civilization, blasting relentless felt even here in the depths of the Great Ocean, yesterday's seaquake no exception. This world is a killer."

Duke scans the crowd to add an air of gravitas to his words.

"Each Division of the Ark works to defy our ill fate. To take back the reins from this raging world. Only by surviving and training can we overcome what this world hurls at us."

His tone is firm, his words heavy. He probes the crowd of the Nave with a hard look. Duke Kay is everything you would expect the leader of the Paragon to be. His spotless dark blue uniform. Calculated. His protruding cheekbones, his nose pointed like a blade positioned to slash through soft skin. A version of Chris, taken to the extreme. Someone best avoided.

"Those who died in the Flood had given in to loftiness and condescension, thinking that they were safe. That they were prepared. The weak lost. The strongest are here, now, more resilient than ever. We will not make the same mistake. Through this Simulation, a technology of unprecedented sophistication, we now adapt in real time, far faster than the imperfections of natural evolution allow. We will reclaim that which is rightfully ours."

Cheers rock through the atrium, but Skyler stays silent. Duke and Laurene exchange looks loaded with meaning, and she speaks up,

"The planet has cleansed us of our worst sin: Ignorance. It has given us an opportunity to start over. To learn. To *relearn*. But to do so, we have the test of time to pass. Over five generations have. And perhaps, future generations will continue to."

No. This ordeal has to be coming to an end. It just has to be.

"We have achieved a feat that even our ancestors could not have foreseen. We will not give up."

Clapping and whistling. They will be the ones to build the first city of the new era. Nothing can stop them now.

"For as long as we are out of danger, we can raise a new generation that doesn't have to suffer the same sacrifices we have to build a better future: In this future we will reconnect with our planet. Until then, we must strive, rally our forces, and achieve the impossible. Together."

Another round of applause. Laurene is in complete control of the situation and gives a satisfied smile. So does Skyler.

Outshone by Laurene, Duke steps down from the stage, meeting his agents stone-faced.

Laurene continues, "You must ready yourselves for tough times ahead. Whether or not you will pioneer the future yourselves, you must raise a new generation according to our values, our hopes, and our dreams."

She is silent for a moment and scans the room with a hard look that, for a split second, rivals Duke Kay's.

"May the strongest survive," she says, raising a hand. The Naves immediately light up in electric blue, giving the atrium an eerily similar atmosphere to the Archives.

The armchair Skyler is sitting in molds perfectly to his body, following his movements. A metal needle pricks his neck, and he clenches his fists as the liquid poisons his blood. His heartbeat thumps in his ears as the ice-cold substance spreads.

His vision blurs for a moment, and a slight panic gnaws at his gut.

This is unusual. He should fall into unconsciousness as soon as the injection is done. Untie him! Out of here, now!

Emily. Emily. Emily!

She swings her head from side to side. She can't see him.

He is choking.

10

SKYLER

SKYLER BLINKS AS THE ELECTRODES FALL OFF HIS SKULL. HE comes out of his Nave, holding the bubble's glass frame. His lethargy is disconcerting. What just happened?

"Congratulations to all of our candidates for completing their simulation," Laurene says from the hexagonal stage. "You may return to your quarters."

Is it over already? Skyler is feeling nauseous. It's strange that he doesn't remember anything.

He shuffles away from his Nave against the current of the crowd to find Emy, still in her seat. Whispers spread like wildfire through the Atrium.

"Do you remember anything?" he asks as he sticks his head in. Emy looks like she just came back from another world, frowning.

"It's normal to feel a little confused afterward," she says, reaching for Skyler's hand to pull herself out of the Nave, "but I gotta say, this time it's ... peculiar."

She shakes her head, rubs her eyes, and yawns loudly.

"I'm sure that—" His voice is muffled by the shrill scream of an alarm; Skyler covers his ears out of reflex.

The same robotic female voice as in the dining hall speaks in loops with stolid calm, "Attention. Please proceed to the emergency route… Attention…"

The atmosphere is getting tense, and the crowd begins to gather off in front of each of the six automatized exits. Confused, Skyler lets the closest group carry him away under the orange guide lights, Emily not far behind. Bodies are pressed together, and the inevitable smell of sweat mixes with fear.

Something is wrong. Where are they taking them?

Skyler walks the opposite way and goes past the window, the view now strikingly different: The water is cloudy, with a rustiness mixed through. The decaying remains of an underwater city?

Suddenly, through the din, something screeches like bending metal. He slows to match Emily's pace.

"Did you hear that?"

"What are you talking about?"

"It was a loud noise, as if…" Skyler doesn't have time to finish his sentence—a violent jolt throws him off balance; his jaw connects with the metal floor. He grunts with pain and climbs to his feet. Twice in two days. Just his luck.

Did the Ark hit something? If so, it must be one of those skyscrapers. So long as there's no breach…

He feels an ugly bump beginning to swell on his chin. Only superficial. Creepy cries of dread ring out, as a steady rhythmic tremor returns for about ten seconds. Emily clings to Skyler, who stumbles against the wall, dread seeping in as the realization hits: There is nowhere to take cover. There would be the Refuge, but it has been sealed indefinitely.

After the powerful tremor subsides, security guards bring the crowd back to order, shouting, "Calm down and proceed with the evacuation. This way."

They motion to the corridor that leads to a hatch, used only once during the Embarkment, more than a century ago. This is their only way out. It's sheer madness!

The crowd presses towards the great door, which grinds open. The gush of water that should pour in, doesn't. Instead, the scrape of metal against metal jolts through the hull of the Ark.

Skyler covers his eyes, blinded by the golden glow filtering through century-old dust particles. Why isn't the ship flooded?

The smell of wet earth. Earth?

Warm sunrays kiss his tingling skin. A beach? He follows the crowd outside, gaping. Sand like he's never seen before, its grains pale, more beautiful than in his wildest dreams.

He stalls with every step. He starts to sweat from the extra effort, but he doesn't care.

Skyler lets out a light-hearted laugh. Emily rolls her eyes. She must think he's stupid.

Wanting to feel the texture of the sand on his bare skin for the first time, Skyler begins to bend down, but gives in to the mob swarming around him. He has been hoping for this moment all his life. He can wait a little longer.

In front of them is the Ark, half-sunken, washed up on a piece of land like an oversized fossil of a behemoth. Skyler turns to take in a panoramic view of this foreign place.

Structures to his right startle him. Skyscrapers. A city.

Who lives here?

He moves closer, protecting his eyes with one hand from the dazzling sunlight. Nothing seems damaged by the tremor…

Emy breaks from the group to walk a little further down the beach, far enough that the Ark no longer masks the horizon.

"We made it," she says as he meets her with a clumsy gait, hindered by the sand. "This is what you have always wanted."

Skyler surveys the beach, and then beyond the line where the sea meets the broad skyline—it's as if it's unfolding in front of him. Actually, the sea seems awfully high, and the beach now extends much further out than when they arrived. How could that be?

"Emy, look over there," he says, pointing. "Don't you think something's strange?" She squints, makes a visor with her hand.

"You're right, something feels different." The water is receding rapidly.

Damn it!

"Emy, we have to get out of here fast."

"What?"

"Just do as I say! Just do it!"

Memories come flooding back. Footage from the Archives showing typical natural disasters suffered on the land. The tremor earlier was not caused by the ship running ashore, but by something much more terrible.

Near the Ark are two familiar figures chatting away. Dylan and Murielle. Skyler runs back to them on wobbly legs.

"Thank God you're all right," his mother says, her pale complexion glowing in the sun.

"You can't stay here!" Skyler shouts, panicked, to the Archeans gathered on the beach. "A tsunami is coming! Take cover!"

"Calm down son," says Dylan, glancing towards the ocean. His face freezes.

"You again!" shouts Agent Miles, marching towards their small group.

Skyler exchanges a look with his parents, then with Emy. Despite the guard's protests, he takes off running as fast as his body allows, Emy right on his heels, his parents running behind her. The city is their only chance.

The ground roars in a telltale fashion. As the tidal wave approaches, they clamber up the hill to reach the center of the city, Skyler looks over his shoulder to make sure his parents are still following. The wave is titanic, dozens of meters high, and killer—it looks like it could even wash the city away. They have to get higher. Much higher.

"We won't make it in time," Emy gasps. "Your mother can't keep up!"

Murielle tries to catch up with Dylan's help, their faces red from the effort. Skyler meets them.

"Come on! Hurry up! We don't have much time!" he says, running back and taking Murielle's hand.

"Don't slow down for us," Dylan pants.

"No way I'm leaving you behind," says Skyler as he helps his father pull Murielle forward. She hasn't moved this much in years and each step is harder than the last.

As the wave hits the ground, a heavy squall soaks them in seawater. The nearest skyscraper is about three hundred meters away and must be at least fifty stories high.

"In this building!" Skyler shouts while the wave swallows up the Ark and carries in its wake the people still on the beach. Some had started to run, but they are too late. Even the guards drown in the oncoming waves. Skyler tells himself to keep looking forward. Not back. Don't look back.

If death smells like anything, it's rotting fish. He feels nauseous.

Skyler is the first to break into the building, adrenaline coursing through his numbed limbs. He slips but catches himself as the wave breaks in with a deafening surge. Their screams echo through the empty halls as a deadly gust of wind shatters the windows and shakes the entirety of the concrete structure. Skyler's face drips with brine, stinging his eyes. He rubs them clean. Water is lapping up to his waist.

He spots a door leading to a staircase, but it's locked. Next to it, there's an elevator. Will it work? Skyler motions to Emily and his family.

By some miracle, the power is on, and the elevator doors slide open. Once crammed inside, they glimpse a lonely child drifting in the flooded lobby. His body bangs into a wall and bounces off like a doll, but he seems to be conscious at least.

Without hesitating, Dylan dives towards the boy, whose face is strikingly similar to Allen's, Skyler's brother.

Dylan grabs the boy and starts swimming back towards them, but a sudden swirl pulls him down.

"Dylan!!" More and more water rushes in. If they want to live, they can't hold the doors any longer. Dylan screams in pain as debris drifting through the flooded hall knock against him. He falters but doesn't let go of the boy. Blood pools around them. No!

When Dylan is only a few feet away, Skyler dives in, grabs him by the waist, and swims hard towards the elevator with his free arm. The current thrusts them forward, and they reach the others.

The doors screech shut, and they begin their slow climb, despite the continuous seep of water into the elevator. Finally, the water level drops, and they gain speed, the sound of their breathing filling the cramped space.

Murielle sobs at the sight of the gash on Dylan's leg. Emy covers the boy's eyes and whispers sweet words to comfort him. Skyler is out of breath, his strength failing, but manages to tear off a piece of his sweater to press against Dylan's wound to stop the bleeding. With each of Dylan's moans, Skyler winces.

They have their issues, sure, but Skyler is a doctor who values life more than anything else. He tightens the makeshift dressing.

The boy doesn't cry, despite their dire situation. He must be in shock, poor thing. Skyler would like to comfort him, like his own brother did at his age, but Emily is holding the child tight against her.

Suddenly the little one lets out a shriek as the elevator jolts them all to one side in sheer darkness. Panic. Soon the emergency light goes on.

Damn elevators!

They seem to be stuck on the forty-second floor. The doors open, but barely enough even to force them further. Murielle sobs silently, Emy hugs the little boy, who is trembling with fear. Helplessness gnaws at Skyler. A tsunami has trapped them in a skyscraper. Unbelievable. The Flood, more than a century trapped in an Ark, and they were not overcome. Two minutes on land, and a murderous wave nearly kills them.

Skyler grabs one of the doors and pulls as hard as he can.

"Let me help you," says Emy, leaving the boy in Murielle's care.

"On the count of three. One… two…" And they pull until the mechanism fails. The doors open onto a blindingly white corridor. Skyler tells the others to wait for him, but Emily objects, "You shouldn't go by yourself." He doesn't argue, and she comes along.

The hallway leads to a room as big as the hall on the first floor. In front of a window, standing against the light, is a man's silhouette.

11

EMILY

NOTHING SMELLS WORSE THAN BURNED FLESH. ESPECIALLY YOUR own mother's burned flesh. She's stabbed with an electric taser for every question she refuses to answer. Mom suppresses her cries as best she can. The identities of those she has guided must remain a secret. She has sworn to do so, sworn an unequivocal oath to protect one another.

The executioners revel in Mom's suffering, drinking from it as they torture her in the heart of the atrium. Worse are those who pack the bleachers to the rafters to watch. How is it so many come to witness such nefarious sadism? Is the Ark so boring that torture is now a prime attraction?

Emily feels the pain in her knees and wrists. At least she's not alone. Dad and Gabrielle are at her side under the accusing gaze of the Archeans. The onlookers' faces express sheer disgust. The Bates family is nothing but scum to them.

Emily knows what they are thinking, "Traitors! Wastes of space better served to a family of survivors worthy of this life. Worthy of this Ark!"

The last of the Bates bloodline is bound and gagged on their knees, waiting to be raised to the platform for judgment. Forced to watch the execution from the front row. Just a formality, some would say—in reality, their deaths are already written in blood.

Gabrielle shakes like a leaf, sobbing uncontrollably. The poor girl is only four years old, still in the prime of innocence, yet she must endure the most heinous side of humanity. She is not alone. Very young children are present in the crowd also, forced to be. The useless five-member committee of the Ark Divisions doesn't care about human lives or traumatizing children. Ludo is repeatedly tasing her mother on the hexagon of Great Justice. Right beside stands Yasmina—flaming hair, red-painted lips—barking orders. Is this what they call great justice?

A warmth spreads through Emily's head. Her body is too small, too weak, and too stiff to do anything. She shivers and her chest tightens and tightens and tightens.

No! She can't!

Her screams get trapped in her small throat. One hit. Another. Another.

They're wrong! Wrong! Mom didn't do it. They don't know anything. The Bateses have nothing to do with it.

They ignore Emily. Or they laugh at her.

Ludo grabs Mom by the throat under Yasmina's scrutinizing gaze, who then addresses the crowd, bogs them down in lies. Emily struggles, but the bonds are tight for the little girl that she is. Yasmina pronounces the sentence,

"For having close ties with the Mavericks, the Ark Committee sentences Tyna Bates to death."

Mom's arms and legs are tied. Ludo drags her like a dog to the other side of the platform where a strange circle is drawn on the tip of the hexagon. Then he spits on her. This is too much.

Emily retches and, still gagging, has to swallow the bile trapped in her mouth. Her throat burns, tears blur her vision.

Ludo's taser prods Mom to stand up straight. A glass

cylinder rises from the platform and traps her. Through the glass, terror contorts her face.

How could anyone design such an evil and cruel torture device? She's going to run out of air! Let her out!

Water pools steadily at Mom's feet, swirling in a continuous stream. A wild, animalistic force takes Emily over. Mom screams, but the rushing water muffles her cries. She is already submerged to the knees.

Dad, do something! Emily's look begs at him, but she doesn't meet his downcast eyes.

Gabrielle whimpers.

Help! Help!

Whisper. A voice? Who's there?

A searing headache. Nothing else.

Her restraints? Gone.

The chance she's been waiting for.

She removes her gag, unties her father and sister. The Bateses will rise.

Guards rush the platform. Mom!

Emily runs. Dad takes on three Paragon guards with ferocious rage.

A glance at her sister, Gabrielle. Is she grown up? An older version of her, maybe sixteen. An illusion? Her sister chips in, holding off two other guards with the same agility Emily had at her age. Years of fighting practice with Dad paying off. Defending the Bates family honor.

Mom is banging on the glass to break free and Emily lunges towards her, but she can't get enough momentum is this tight space. Mom's eyes bulge as the water swallows her nose. She thrusts her head back to suck in what little air she has left.

The sound of a loaded taser crackles through the air, followed by a wave of dread. No lethal bite, though. Ludo.

Emily leaps up and wrenches him hard, knocking him to the ground. She sidesteps him to strike with all her might and force against the glass prison. Again. And again. And again. Break, damn it!

There's panic on her mother's face.

"Mom! Mom, hold on!" Her voice is hoarse, her vision blurred. "Hold your breath! Just a little longer! I'll break through!"

Her arms tremble with fatigue and her legs are giving in under her weight. Suddenly she is pulled to the ground and her back arches in pain. Ludo stares down at her, his perfectly smooth white locks framing his ageless, clean-shaven face.

He nudges her threateningly with the tip of his taser, the eager embrace of its current resonating through Emily's rib cage. She kicks at an angle and makes a hasty roll. The taser crackles as it hits the ground, sparks flying. With her free foot, she kicks the back of Ludo's knee. Then, she uses her full weight to smash his head against the taser. She hits the ground, and pain begins to bloom in her elbow.

She glimpses Ludo's messed-up face, taking in a dizzying whiff of burning flesh. Satisfied, she grabs the taser and runs back to the glass cage. Mom's head is completely submerged, her hair wrapped around her body like a pall. Tiny bubbles still escape her mouth.

Emily takes a step back for momentum and runs against the glass with a shout. Break. You. Damn it! The glass starts to crack, but time's up. Mom's eyes go blank.

No way can Emily go through this again. "Mom!"

Emily ramps up and in two strikes, the glass shatters into pieces. Water pours at her feet and Mom collapses. Emily kneels, turns her onto her back, and removes pieces of glass from her chest. She applies rhythmic pressure with bloody fingers, trying to revive her mother.

Lifeless.

If the Creator exists, now would be the time to show himself! She cannot bear to lose Mom a second time.

One. Two. Three. Four. Five.

Emily is out of breath; her arms give out. She collapses against her mother and holds back sobs powerful enough to eat her alive. The pain is unbearable.

A splinter. A thorn. A stake.

Mom's body stirs. Emily steps aside, unbelieving. Mom manages to get up. She is not dead!

"Mom, Mom!" Emily pivots. "Dad! Gabrielle!"

They're gone. The platform's empty. The atrium's empty, and only a deadly silence remains. She calls her mother. No answer. Emily is the last of the Bates.

A voice. That voice again. A man?

At the bottom of the abandoned platform near the edge of the corridor looms the figure of a man walking away.

"Wait!"

The platform bursts into flames behind her, the fire spreading all around the hexagon. Quick! Emily jumps off the platform and breaks her fall in a roll. Her skin is fine, but the flames are spreading fast. She presses on into the corridor while a rush of heat licks her face.

The man is still in sight.

Run.

Run.

She breathes in each gulp of air faster than the last. The flashing corridor drags on and splits in two. The man forks to the right. Without hesitation, she charges forward. The distance between them shrinks. She's almost there. Almost.

She stretches out her hand and caresses long, water-smoothed hair. "Mom?"

Emily is thrust towards her mother, who slumps in front of her. The glass shards still buried in Emily's skin sink even deeper into her bruised hands. She winces in pain.

"Not so fast," whispers a familiar voice. Yasmina, taser in hand. It can't be!

Emily steps protectively in front of her mother, but a violent migraine overwhelms her. For a moment, the corridor goes dark.

Yasmina looks away, as if someone just called her name. The same look of surprise crosses Mom's face. What the hell is going on?

Emily screams, the pain crushing down on her brain. She tilts her head backwards to keep it from splitting open and closes her eyes to the blinding hallway lights.

Suddenly, the pain is paralyzingly acute. Everything goes white.

She knows she is not alone. Unable to move, she watches the man draw closer.

HE IS TALL AND IMPOSING, like a Paragon agent, his dark hair has brown highlights, his eyes are black as night. He pauses in front of her and frowns, then moves towards a bay window that swings open as he glides towards it. Thin face … high cheekbones … his features are vaguely familiar. Where has she seen him before?

As if time gave itself a kick start, Emily's body reacts. She steps forward, but a hand holds her back. What now?

"Emily!"

Sky. His face is sweaty. He looks older, his energy even more unsteady than usual. She has to blink away the flashes of light that distort him. Some kind of interference?

"I have to take care of something first," she says, trying to break free.

"Let me come with you," Sky insists. His voice breaks, like bad phone reception.

"I have to go alone. You wouldn't understand."

"Don't." He holds her gaze, his jaw tight. She breaks contact and crosses through the glass window and Sky's energy fades away. She's all alone now.

Once outside, a damp heat wraps around her. The man's pale silhouette is motionless, leaning against the wide balcony's railing to watch the blazing sunrays ricochet off the sparkling Great Ocean.

The Surface? How? The view is stunning. Large, white-washed buildings pile up like the toy blocks Gabrielle used to play with when she was little. The horizon is an endless blue, a shade lighter than the sea. The beach stretches for miles and miles——clear, fine, almost perfect sand, except for the beached Ark, its metal carcass ripped open. It is even more monstrous than they were told at the Academy.

Sweat runs down her forehead. The heat is stifling.

It's so unreal. Believing this place exists feels like lying to yourself. The cities of old have all been swallowed up, haven't they? That time has gone, the time of a forgotten generation. Yet across the disarming vastness, she feels the wind whip at her face.

She steps forward.

He has the look of someone with answers. They have already met. She tries to read him, but somehow, he has no aura.

"I'll get straight to the point," she says to break her bizarre gaze. "What is your connection with my mother, Tyna Bates?" He doesn't answer right away, but the corners of his lips tighten.

"How do you find the view?" A shadow of a tattoo runs down his arm. A large wave rolling up into his sleeve.

"Answer my question," she continues, gripping onto the ramp. "You knew her."

"According to the holy scriptures, it is paradise on earth, the Promised Land. A place that will be ours if we survive the Flood. It will be purged of all the atrocities we have committed. A second chance."

"I don't believe fiction, much less in utopian dreams." The

man's hollow cheeks make him look older than he certainly is. He wears an amused smile and lifts his head.

"Utopia implies it doesn't exist. Your mother believed otherwise." So, Mom was sentenced for believing in this nonsense? That's inconceivable! She wasn't stupid.

"What are you getting at? My mother would not have been lulled into a false hope. She knew it was only a matter of time before the Ark sank. She wanted to soothe the survivors so they could find eternal rest. Allow them to let go once and for all and accept their mortality, no longer in defiance of the Greater Will."

"Man has suffered enough for crimes they did not commit," he replied in a strained voice. "It is time to do ourselves justice and take back that which is rightfully ours."

"Did your god tell you this? Don't be so stupid; you'll fall for your own lies."

"What if I told you the paradise really exists?"

"Without proof, there's no point." His casual attitude is annoying. If he and Mom really knew each other, why didn't she ever mention him? Or did she?

She wipes her forehead. It's soaking wet.

"Your mother had proof, and so did the Brotherhood. But that's not the kind of information we've been allowed to share. Not until now."

"What did you do to her?" Doubt crawls under her skin.

"What did she do to us, you mean. She gave us a chance to start over." It doesn't make sense. And what *is* the Brotherhood? A group of enlightened people, wanting what exactly?

"My mother used to help the misguided," she says, recalling the times she used to tell her about her visits. "To help them find their true purpose and contribute to the greater good."

"And that's what she did. She made that day possible. The day when all survivors, regardless of their pasts, had equal opportunity to participate in the Grand Design; To take back the reins of our future; To refuse to allow the fate of all be decided according to the terms of a privileged few." His calm is unshakable. He has the seriousness of someone about to take decisive action.

Uneasiness creeps up in Emily's gut.

"The Ark was not an act of good faith. It never was," he adds, as he moves away from the railing to get closer to Emily. "From the very beginning, they have forbidden us from it. I'm not just talking about us; I'm talking about you too and more than half of the survivors on the Ark. How many privileges have you been denied just because of who you are: a Bates?"

The tiny cabin that Dad, she, and Gabrielle have to share. The elitist exclusivity of the restaurant *La Orilla*. Yasmina's condescension. Mom's execution.

The bitter taste of oatmeal fills her mouth.

No. Mom wouldn't have tolerated a group of rebels.

He goes on. "It's only a matter of time before they realize we are everywhere. That we have the same rights they do!" The same words Reyes uttered.

"You are a Maverick." She raises her voice. "You. The Brotherhood."

He turns away, the ink on his wave tattoo glistening in the sun. A faded blue.

"Mavericks, as you call them, have just as many rights as anyone else. The Brotherhood's mission is to give back what has always belonged to the Archeans. We have been lied to for far too long. We are on the same side."

"You doomed my mother." She's pacing back and forth, holding her head.

Were the things they said about Mom true? Mom betrayed her own family? The Ark? She would never do those things willingly. Unforeseen events or someone must have dragged her into it.

"I lost her because of you." Mom got caught up in something big. Too big. Utter madness!

Reyes, Milo, and all the other Mavericks. A threat from the inside. Why didn't Emily figure it out sooner?

"I wish it had turned out otherwise," whispers the Maverick. "Your mother would have wanted it differently." An icy liquid pours through her, the same unpleasant feeling from earlier. Her mouth no longer responds.

The Maverick's voice pulses in her head. "This message is for the Commander. The Brotherhood gives you seventy-two hours to reveal everything you know about the Promised Land and to prepare to repopulate Earth according to the resettlement plan."

He lets his words sink in while Emily's heart speeds up. Is that their true motive?

"If you don't comply with our ultimatum, the Brotherhood will take you out. You and all those who oppose us. For the greater good."

His eyes burn bright as he meets Emily's gaze before leaving the balcony, head down.

Were those tears?

12

EMILY

Emily has been mulling over this ever since the beginning of the Inspection. No one is allowed outside while the Paragon tries to locate the so-called Brotherhood. They are combing every floor, every cabin, every nook and cranny. No exceptions. What they want to know is whether any Archeans have been deliberately hiding Mavericks.

Why would anyone be stupid enough to do that? Helping stowaways? Unregistered stowaways?!

The cabin is stifling, especially since they can't leave, but, of course, Gabrielle had to wear her minty perfume that stinks of nasty cough syrup. A shower would do the trick, but the communal area is located outside their cabins, and therefore out of reach until further notice. Sweat and mint don't mix well at all.

Emily is lying on the bed she shares with her sister, who is engrossed in her storybook. Dragons and princesses in distress, her favorite kind of story. How lucky that she has an escape in such dark circumstances.

Emily rolls over on her side. It's tempting to sneak away if only for a breath of fresh air. It would be a good chance to investigate. The leader of the Brotherhood was involved in Mom's sentencing through a series of unfortunate events. What if Emily could prove her mother's innocence? This could restore the Bates's reputation and settle the score with those rebels.

The Mavericks are connected to the Brotherhood somehow. Their leader was clear on this when he gave his ultimatum. It might seem foolish to worry about a vision in a simulation, but everyone else has been talking about those seventy-two hours. Everyone experienced it in their own simulated reality and the Commander ordering an Inspection is no coincidence. Now, every Archean knows who the Mavericks are and the threat they represent.

The Mavericks' cause is delusional. They cannot face the obvious: The Ark is the only home they have left. Their attempts to give themselves some semblance of legitimacy not only jeopardize over a century's worth of effort, but they also downplay Mom's tragic sacrifice.

Emily contemplates her options. Reyes's threat was serious, but Yasmina has taken care of it for now. She can use Milo to track the Mavericks, though she doesn't have much time: The seventy-two-hour window has already been closed by twelve hours.

Gabrielle has been reading the same page for some time, probably worrying about Dad. Mom's death has left a constant, silent angst in the family. Ever since the Incident, Dad has been in the authorities' crosshairs. He is still alive only because they couldn't prove he knew Mom's secrets.

Gabrielle had been waiting anxiously for Dad when Emily got back. Usually Dad carried her sister over, but the Paragon ordered him to help them, so he had to leave her by herself. Every time something sketchy happens, they call him to duty—

to keep a close eye on him, of course. They must have questioned him about the hack in the simulation.

"Do we have anything to eat?" asks her sister weakly. "I'm starving."

"You ate my last energy bar." Emily shrugs. "You know how rationing works. We have to wait until the end of the Inspection to get something from the canteen."

Gabrielle whines but, like dignity, no more food will be coming the Bates's way anytime soon. Even so, a twelve-year-old girl should never have to starve.

"Tell me about your book," says Emily, straightening up her back, her legs bent. "It'll take your mind off things."

"I don't like this one." Gabrielle shuts the book and tosses it on the bed. She breathes a sigh of frustration.

Emily raises an eyebrow. "What's up?"

"The princess gets away, but the hero dies. Why didn't he live too?" Mother should have lived too.

"Not every story has a happy ending. Reality works the same way. That's why you have to fight for it."

How far is the Brotherhood willing to go to claim Command of the Ark? Sacrificing innocent people?

There must be a way to stay a step ahead. Get to Milo. Then what happens once Emily is in his cell? She lets out an annoyed sigh.

"Are princesses mean, too?" asks Gabrielle.

"What do you mean?"

"She's the one who killed him." Since when are children's stories so … gruesome? Emily doesn't remember ever reading anything like that. Then again, she's never been a big reader.

"Anyway, princesses don't exist," mumbles Emily, eyes closed. "Maybe read a different kind of book next time?"

She's startled awake by banging at the door. Dull, jerky, impatient thuds. Her body stiffens, the simulation still fresh in her bones. Mom about to drown, a fake Ludo stepping in. The Maverick, claiming Mom's death is his own salvation.

She groans, and, her heart beating frantically, gets up to open the door.

"Emily," whispers Chris, checking to see no one has been following him. He shuts the door.

"What are you doing here? Did you sneak out of your cabin?"

"Emily, I wanted to make sure you were okay. We didn't catch up after the simulation." He grips her shoulders. His touch is warm, pleasant, comforting, but the feeling isn't mutual. Chris has something on his mind.

"Don't worry about me," he says, as if reading her silent question. "All that matters is that you're okay."

"You sure everything's okay?" she asks, a little woozy. "I don't want you on my interrogation list."

"Just trust me. I might not be the model son my father hoped for, but he'd never let them." Funny that Duke Kay's conscience is intact enough not to treat his own son that way. Chris deserves so much better: a loving family, proud of whom he has become.

"How did you get past security?"

"Being second officer, Laurene's new protege, has its advantages," he says with a sparkling white smile.

"So, you accepted." She smiles back. This is a change for the best; it might even earn Duke's respect.

Out of her sleepy haze, Emily gets an idea. Her gaze travels from the door to Gabrielle. Time is of the essence. Chances like this don't come twice.

"Chris, I need your help," she says, taking both his hands.

"What kind of help? You know it wasn't easy to get here." He draws her close, and something stirs in her stomach. She swallows hard, tries to focus, fights the urge.

"I have something important to do," she says firmly. "I can't tell you what it is, but I need you to look after Gabrielle." He asks and asks, as if trying to break through her shell. She can't miss her chance to get to Milo and catch the Brotherhood in her own way.

"I don't know what I'm getting myself into, but I'm in, on one condition," he finally says.

"What condition?" A strange mixture of disappointment and relief overwhelms her.

"If you're not back within the hour, I'm coming to get you myself." She can't tell whether he's serious or being cute, but the offer is good enough for her. And she has no time to delude herself. As long as Mom's mission remains unfulfilled, Emily can't allow herself to think beyond the next sixty hours. They may well be their last.

Emily nods.

"WHAT ARE YOU DOING HERE?"

Ludo looks genuinely surprised. He looks ... alive. That's a first. Sometimes Emily wonders if he's enjoying life or just watching with no interest.

Sneaking through the maze of the Ark was challenging with the Paragon lurking around. Had it not been for her official uniform, she would have been stopped at her first turn. If Ludo doesn't let her in now, the whole thing could go horribly wrong. His aura is fluid, like water splashing on shower walls.

"It would take too long to explain," says Emily, tense. "I need to see the Maverick prisoner. You know, the one with Reyes."

"Can't." He gives her a hard look.

"Why 'Can't'? Do I need some kind of special authorization now?"

"That's not it. He's not here." Crap. Exactly what she needs, what after almost getting caught by the Paragon breaking out of her cabin.

"What do you mean, he's not here? Did Yasmina give him a taste of her special interrogation?"

"No." She peers at him. Since meeting the real culprit behind Mom's death, reality hasn't felt real at all. What about the bluish mark spoiling Ludo's otherwise smooth cheek?

"Your prisoner escaped," he adds, lowering his voice. "During the simulation." Another one? After Clarissa Reed, Milo broke out in the same week? Not a single prisoner has escaped before. There's one way out. One guard.

The prison is awfully quiet all of a sudden. Even Griffin's hoarse cries have faded. Yasmina must be furious. Where is she now?

Her office door is locked, and she hasn't sent any messages lately. She must be meeting with the Commander. This doesn't look good.

"What about Reyes? Have you seen her since her 'meeting' with Yasmina?"

"Gone too."

"You guard this prison. Tell me what happened," says Emily, on the verge of panic. "You'd better have a good explanation."

"Be careful what you say," he says, raising his voice. "I could say the same about you, dropping in here while everyone is on lockdown. Why are you here?"

Ludo's presence is oppressive. Picturing him holding the infamous electric taser doesn't seem so far removed from reality, all because of a damn simulation. Why did it have to be Ludo?? Don't panic. He could report it to Yasmina.

Emily crosses her arms. "I just need to check something."

"Is that all you're telling me?" His voice is deep, menacing.

"You know I could lose my job over a problem like this? If I can bring in any kind of culprit or suspect, to explain what happened, don't think I will hesitate."

"Threats? I don't play that." She holds his gaze without batting an eye. Ludo's energy says he is intent on doing whatever it takes to find the perpetrator. He tries to pierce through Emily, but she is too experienced to be easily swayed, even if he was Mom's tormentor earlier today.

"What were you expecting, coming here?" His tone is even.

"To finish off my work."

"You aren't on duty until the Inspection is over. Your work can wait."

"Listen," she says, closing the distance between them. "I don't tell you how to do your job. And, between you and me, it's no secret which of us does their job properly."

She clenches her teeth, ready to leave. If Milo has truly broken out, staying here is a waste of time.

"The rebels hacked the Ark's primary systems; they were in for five minutes," he drops to the ground suddenly. She freezes. Is he sick?

"The power was out for a while, long enough for them to take me by surprise. The locking system operates independently, so they must have disabled it manually while I was half conscious."

"How many were there?"

"There was a deafening bomb. They nailed me to the ground, and I couldn't see or hear anything." The Mavericks were here. Were the simulation and the ultimatum a decoy? Reyes and Milo must be key players. They'd caught other Mavericks in the past but have never seen an operation like this.

Milo's link to the Brotherhood is clear.

How do we find them now? And just how many are there, anyway? Lots. Too many. Especially if they know the Ark's systems well enough to escape the Paragon's control. They knew the outcome even before they gave their ultimatum.

Emily walks away, then right before going through the scanner, shouts to Ludo,

"I liked you better when you didn't speak."

13

SKYLER

"You seem fine, but we'll do a scan anyway."

His patient is a girl who was in his biology class at the Academy. She has a phobia of animals that manifested in the middle of class, when the instructor showed them a fairly well-designed three-dimensional bear, at least ten feet tall. Obviously, showing simulated land animals wreaked havoc on her mind. The marks on her arms are evidence of a recent panic attack; she scratched herself raw.

Since she arrived, the girl has been pretending not to recognize Skyler. This is common on the ship, so he does nothing to remind her. Hopefully, Archeans will stop treating each other like strangers once they reach the Promised Land.

She flutters her eyes open and moans in pain. Skyler examines her pupils with his ophthalmoscope, a small portable light. They are unusually dilated.

"For now, take these tablets whenever your migraines give you pain," he recommends, bottle in hand.

"How much longer will I have to put up with this?" she complains, pinching the bridge of her nose.

"I can't tell you until I get the results. Wait for me here."

Mira dimmed the lighting in the waiting room to avoid worsening the patient's sensitivity to light. She is arranging the files of the dozens of Archeans who have taken Med Bay by storm. Headaches, dizziness, nausea. This simulation was peculiar and brutal, but it is unclear whether it was changes made by the Paragon, or the Brotherhood hijacking that's responsible.

"Could you take care of the brain scans while I run the others through?" Skyler asks Mira.

"I'm on it," she answers, and leaves in a flash.

Skyler grabs the next set of files Mira prepared and flips through them. Is there anything they have in common, besides symptoms and having taken part in the simulation? Skyler doesn't have those symptoms, only the usual fatigue, nothing to worry about. Nothing unusual about Mira or Leander, either.

After the Inspection, over forty-seven people have come to Med Bay. They may already be in the first stage of the Syndrome, making them more vulnerable to neurological stimuli.

Skyler helps himself to a watered-down coffee gone cold. The waiting room is packed: Some are sitting on the floor, others are asleep. What if they truly were infected? The Ark can't afford to lose so many Archeans. Ivanka Torres's videos showed hysterical patients and utter chaos. If that is what the future holds...

Unless they find a cure. So far, the most plausible cause for the Syndrome remains being in such close contact for so long. Humans are not meant to be locked up for this amount of time. Biological weaknesses are bound to come through. Skyler hopes he's wrong, but only scans can confirm or disprove his suspicions.

Suddenly, the intercom buzzes; Skyler spills his entire cup of coffee on himself. He grunts.

"Attention. The Ark is about to circle round one of the

largest and most flourishing cities before the Flood. You can view its remains from the observatory. Hurry! Space is limited."

He puts down the empty cup and sighs at the thought of missing the show. Why now? Emily would have probably liked to go.

He fetches a washcloth to clean brownish stains on his uniform. As he walks, he sees Chris handing a clean, swaddled newborn baby to its mother lying on her upright bed. A baby powder smell hangs in the air and Skyler rummages through a housekeeping basket. He tries to block out the conversation between Chris and the mother but ends up eavesdropping anyway.

"I'm glad you took care of me," she said in a hoarse but calm voice. "Other moms won't be so lucky."

"Whoever comes after me will do the same," Chris replied smugly. "But thank you for the compliment." Since when does Chris Kay want out? Skyler catches him as soon as he walks away from the new mother.

"Did you quit?"

"I have my reasons." Chris motions to the nurses exchanging knowing glances to leave them alone. They scurry away.

"Anyway, you're in control here," Chris says. "You already fill in for me whenever I'm busy at the maternity wards."

"It's not the same thing. We're going to need more staff as the Syndrome spreads and…"

"Don't act like you care if I quit," replies Chris with a sad smile. The satisfaction Skyler would expect doesn't come. Instead, he is filled with emptiness. Chris lets them down right before the storm. How many victims will there be? Med Bay can't afford to lose anyone.

Even if Skyler has to put aside his differences with Chris.

"My priority is taking care of the Archeans," says Skyler pulling away. "Anything beyond that is none of my business."

"Don't lie to me, Sky. I see right through you." Chris's arm blocks the way. "You hate me." Here we go again.

"Why do you keep doing this?" hisses Skyler.

"Because. The feeling isn't mutual." Chris's features soften, as if, for once, he was trying to be honest. Are his feelings genuine, buried under a layer of arrogance? What next?

"Your memory lapses," Skyler says to snap out of this weird situation. "You know very well when it all started. I trusted you until I saw who you really are. Your trick game doesn't work with me. All you care about is your own interests. You don't care about other people."

"No matter what you think about me, you need to work this out on your own. You're taking the easy way out, putting all the blame on me. *You* decided."

"Stop lying to yourself." Still that smile.

"There's a party tonight," says Chris in a lighter tone. "To celebrate my resignation. You're invited."

"Wait, are you friendly now that you're leaving Med Bay?"

"I'd like you to come," Chris is dead serious. The last thing Skyler wants is to be part of Chris's social life.

"I'll think about it."

Chris motions to grab his shoulder, but Skyler skillfully avoids him.

"Don't touch me." Skyler slips away before Chris can say anything else.

Chris is acting weird today.

As soon as Skyler gets back to his ward, Mira hands him a tablet with his patient's latest brain scans. Shades of white and gray form electric patterns, each group identifiable by a different color. He reads the graph three times before his mind goes blank.

Chris. That bastard.

"Are you going?" Mira asks, bending over.

"What are you talking about?"

"I know your relationship with Chris is rocky, but ... he'd really like it if you went."

"Like he even cares. He never means what he says."

"He could surprise you." Mira doesn't talk much, usually. But, of course, she wants them to get along, since she spends most of her time with Chris.

"Every time I try to make things better here, he gets in my way. The memory spheres, helping the elderly, not to mention he's been taunting me since school."

"You work too much. Why don't you take the rest of the day off? I'll notify Dr. Nazar."

"I'm fine! I'm fine! He's the one with a problem." He must have raised his voice a bit because Mira is giving him a worried look.

"I know your mother needs you," she replies, staring at her feet. "Spend some time with her. I saw your request to take care of her full time." What's wrong with everyone here?

"Who gave you the right to go through my stuff?"

"I process applications before forwarding them to Dr. Nazar, remember?" Why does he have to justify himself for wanting to care for his mother?

The scan shows signs of inflammation similar to a concussion. That explains the symptoms, but not why not everyone who underwent the Simulation is affected.

Skyler shares his observations with Mira, who confirms with a nod.

"It's as if someone tampered with them," she thinks aloud. Yet the Deltas routinely inspect the Naves.

"Unless brain damage was present before the Simulation."

"What do you mean?"

"Don't you think this looks just like any of the scans of Syndrome patients?"

"You mean, they were already infected?" She mindlessly tucks a long lock of red hair behind her ear.

"Yes, and the electromagnetic variation worsened their condition, driving them out of the latent stage, most likely."

According to the few previous cases they've seen, there is (seems to be) a latent stage that lasts several months. Victims have reported acute fatigue, but that symptom alone doesn't allow for proper diagnosis. Since they are all living in isolation on the Ark, with a lack of natural light, and without a nutrient-rich diet, there are a multitude of other possible causes—depression, for example—potentially at play.

"Unlikely ...," Mira adds hesitantly. "How would the Syndrome have spread so quickly? We'll have to ask the Deltas for a detailed analysis."

"While we're waiting for the results, we're going to need reinforcements. Chris and Leander could help us administer preventive treatment."

For what it's worth. Surface-level healing will have to do for now.

"All right. I'll give them all an anti-inflammatory first."

"Good. And I'll try oxygen therapy to see if we can get better control of any internal pressure." Skyler begins to prepare a ventilator for his bedridden patient, but quickly realizes Mira hasn't budged.

"What's the matter?"

"Skyler, I want you to know..." She swallows hard, clearly uneasy. "I'm not judging, and please don't think everyone around Chris is against you. I know what you're going through is difficult, but at least let me——"

"No. You have no idea. You have no idea what it's like to care for a depressed mother, who will never forgive you."

That all came out at once. Shit.

Mira listens. Doesn't flinch.

"If you say so," she mumbles. Probably on her way to Chris.

The rest of the day flies by. No one bothers him, not even Mira. Although his patient continues to ignore him, he monitors her oxygen levels to see how responsive she is to the treatment.

Every once in a while, sharp images from his Simulation flood his brain, and he is pulled at by an irresistible urge to get *out* of this ship. He feels like he's drowning under the routine life on the Ark and the growing threat of this elusive Syndrome is getting to him. The next twenty-four hours are crucial. He will rid every one of these burdens once and for all.

He and the Brotherhood.

"Jazz?"

Skyler's skin is wet from the shower, and his sweater sticks to it. He has decided to stop by his parents' cabin to check on his mother.

"So, you're the one making my husband work so hard," Jazz says, closing the door behind her. Her hand rests on her swollen belly, which is further highlighted by her tight-fitting, light-pink dress.

"What are you trying to say?"

"I haven't seen him in a week. He couldn't stop talking about how delighted I'll be by these life-changing spheres. He tried to explain them to me, but I'll be honest, it all sounds like gibberish. How can he leave his pregnant wife high and dry like this?"

Skyler wipes his forehead with the cuff of his sleeve. Nathan is working really hard on this.

"I was feeling all lonely, so I came to see your lovely mother," Jacinta adds, standing legs wide, stroking her belly. "I've been thinking about it ever since our last conversation, and thought I'd drop by for a nice visit, you know."

"Mom must have been happy to see you." Murielle hasn't had visitors for a very long time, even though he pushes her to go out for a walk with him every week. Her contact with the outside world shriveled when she stopped working. Only Jazz takes the trouble to message now.

"We talked a lot," she says with a toothless smile. Skyler steps closer to the door, sensing the conversation might drag on. "I wouldn't if I were you," Jazz warns with a firm hand, joy gone. "She dozed off; she was particularly tired."

"Is Dylan there?" asks Skyler, furrowing his brow.

A tight smile. "Yes, he's looking after her."

In that case, best avoid another clash. Skyler doesn't have the heart to face him right now.

"You should get some rest as well. You look exhausted," Jacinta adds, stroking her own forearm tenderly. Then she pats his cheeks, and he sticks out his tongue, just like when he was younger.

"Dark circles at your age aren't a good sign."

"Not much I can do about it,"

Jacinta whispers in baby talk to her growing belly.

"See Angelique? It's Skyler! He works hard to keep us healthy and help you get out of here someday, doesn't he? And God knows I won't be complaining when that day comes." She leans back, one hand on her lower back. Then she suddenly starts rummaging through her tiny purse, as if she had forgotten something.

"My poor little Angelique," she whines. "Mommy has been careless. Please don't let the Creator hold a grudge against me." She hurriedly and profusely sprays her hands with antiseptic. Skyler stares at her for a moment, unsure.

"I just learned that bacteria travel through fabric at the speed of light. Isn't that right?"

"Well, you'd have to ask a Delta …,"

"That's what I was thinking. Better safe …," she smirks, waits expectantly.

"… Than sorry," he completes with a forced smile.

"That's what I always tell my patients." Jacinta drags him to the elevators. He lets her talk until she tires herself out.

"Skyler, are you sure you're okay?" offering him some gel, which he politely refuses. "You look exhausted! You should spend more time with your friends."

Luckily, the crowd around the elevator for Jazz gives Skyler a good excuse to take the stairs. Walking does him a lot of good, despite the smell of antiseptic filling his nose. On the way to his cabin, he replays his conversation with Jacinta in his head.

Jazz thinks he should see his friends more. He *has* neglected them for the past two years. Being isolated on a further ship is a deadly combination.

All right. Why not? Chris's party.

He cringes at the thought, but everyone will probably be there.... Why not go? Not for Chris, obviously. But Jazz is right; he can't keep working so hard. And, after their dinner, Emily did point out that he works too hard. And that was a fun night! Dylan can take care of Mom. Med Bay can give him a break.

Is he really talking himself into going?

14

EMILY

Sky mentioning going to Chris's party felt as if Gabrielle was shaving Emily's head. The answer: No. Way.

When she tried to talk some sense into him, he insisted on going, reminiscing the nice dinner at *La Orilla*. Has he finally decided to relax and enjoy life again?

This evening will be special for another reason: This party is illegal. It will be the perfect opportunity to find out who the organizers are. Yasmina would be happy to get her hands on this piece of information so they can be properly judged. If the organizers can sneak out of illegal parties as they please, where is the justice in all this? Also, it could quell Yasmina's anger over losing two prisoners in such a short time and help her think better of Emily.

Identifying the Mavericks may seem difficult at first glance, but they all have something in common: None of them are part of the official passenger registry. All it would take is a scanner from the Paragon.

Near the entrance of their cabin, Emily pulls one out of Dad's old drawer. It took her a full half hour today to locate it in all that clutter. It looks like an oversized metal pen whose tip connects to a wristband and… Voila! She rolls it up between her fingers before carefully pocketing it in her tight black pants.

Thanks Dad, though he is not aware of how he helped her out.

Emily picked dark hues to wear tonight. Her top is a dark purple, her favorite color. The idea is to blend in with the crowd in the dim lighting, and so the flashy dress from last time at the restaurant is out of the question.

Mom gives her a frozen smile, as if reading her mind.

"We don't have much time left to finish what you started. In twenty-four hours, everything could change. Tonight is the key to getting closer to them."

Mom nods. Wait, what?

Emily blinks, yet the photo is still. All this pent-up stress is really starting to get to her.

She shakes her head and quickly splashes her face with cold water from the sink, which gives her an unpleasant shiver. Using a hand towel, she wipes her face clean and tames her wild, unruly hair. Short hair can easily look too boyish, and adding some flair is a must to bewilder even the boldest man.

She glances at her lookalike in the small, ever-dirty portable mirror. The mauve shades shine mysteriously. This eye shadow is truly spellbinding. What would Mom say if she saw her?

She flicks her mirror away, but it shatters when the floor slips away from under her feet and she barely has time to reach for the corner of the table. She keeps her eyes closed until her dizziness clears. What is wrong with her?

What an idiot she is! She hasn't eaten all day.

She takes a deep breath and opens her eyes. She tiptoes to the cupboard, where she keeps some food from the canteen and snacks Sky gives her from time to time.

The cupboard is empty. The Inspection. Hopefully, there'll be something to eat at the party.

While Emily chugs a glass of water, someone knocks on the door. She wipes her mouth hurriedly and opens it.

"Are you going to prom or what?" she blurts when she sees Skyler, dressed up in a suit and bow tie, the same outfit he wore for their graduation ceremony.

Sky's cheeks turn pink, and he scrutinizes his outfit.

"That bad? I didn't know what to wear."

"You need to get out of the clinic more often."

"What do you mean?" he asks, confused. Eyes rolling, Emily comes out of the cabin, beckoning him to hurry.

"Just forget about what I said," she says, making sure the door is locked. "Are you coming?"

This late at night, the hallway is empty, except for the house-keeping clerk who drags a mop from one end to the other without ever feeling the need to rinse it. Disgusting.

They cross the hallway, carefully avoiding the wet trail left by the dirty mop, to get to the service elevators where Mira is waiting for them. She is wearing a green dress that stands out against her red hair.

"Well, I must be the only one who didn't understand the theme of the evening," grumbles Emily. "So much for going unnoticed!" she curses herself inwardly.

"There were no instructions on the subject," replies Mira the redhead, in her overly analytical, machine-like voice. "No one will notice."

So much the better, even if Emily's pride has to take a hit.

"I'm glad you changed your mind," adds Mira to Sky. "It'll be nice for everyone to see you in a different environment."

"Don't make him wish he'd never come out of his cave," says Emily, teasingly elbowing her.

"Keep on like this, Emy, and you will." Sky looks deceptively serious.

"You can't blame your best friend. What would you do

without me?" Mira lets out a shy laugh with her hands clasped around her waist.

"How's your father?" asks Emily to put her at ease, remembering the beautiful candlelight cake that Leander and Amber had brought them at the restaurant. "It was his birthday not so long ago, wasn't it?"

"Oh?" Mira blushes. She doesn't like being asked personal questions. She's too busy analyzing everything under her nose—the poor thing.

"Yes, it was his birthday. He's been … a little sick lately. It's not easy to deal with." Sky's aura ripples at that as they step into the sanitizer-filled elevator.

"You didn't tell me about it," he says worriedly. "You should have told me. I wouldn't have taken up so much of your time for the memory spheres."

"No, no, it's all right. The spheres are very … very interesting."

"The spheres?" asks Emily.

"You know the project I told you about at the Academy?"

"Oh, that! They weren't spheres then." No wonder he's been so busy lately. He has always been so dedicated. "Is it going well?"

"I hope so," he says, fiddling with his bow tie. "There have been a few problems, but Nathan the engineer seems to be on the right track to develop the full potential of the spheres."

"The full potential?" asks Mira, her eyes wide open. "What exactly do you mean?"

"Well, in his last message he said that the amount of information contained exceeds simple memories. There might be another layer of data buried."

"I don't want to be a party pooper, but where is this gathering?" Emily cuts them off as the elevator doors open. These overly technical discussions never interested her. That's why she never pursued a career in science.

Mira gets out first and beckons them to do the same. "You will see."

THEY CLIMB DOWN to the main floor and work their way to the dining hall, but then branch off into a nearby corridor. Emily's stomach rumbles with frustration, and she cannot help but look back with a stealthy, almost disappointed look.

They take the emergency stairs and sink into the bowels of the ship. Sky seems lost in thought as usual, but his energy shows that he is nostalgic. What can he possibly be keeping inside like this? This is something to work on once this whole Brotherhood thing is sorted out.

Back in the hallways, her vision has to adjust to the faint blue emergency lighting along the walls. She coughs at a strong ocean smell that fills her lungs.

The lower levels. So, this is what they look like. Two years ago, the Incident flooded this area, in the very spot where the search team disappeared. According to Dad, this should be the Mavericks' stronghold.

No one dares to speak out while Mira leads them deeper into a network of derelict corridors. Mold has infested every discernable nook and cranny. Large dark clumps glow in muted hues of blue. A slight buzz on the ground ripples through Emily's knees as they come to a stop.

"Here we are," says Mira in a clear voice. "We must show our wristbands at the door." Mira feels the wall looking for the reader, her eyes squinting in the darkness.

"Is it safe?" asks Sky, looking around him.

"You really should get out more often," Emily sighs, rolling her eyes.

"Didn't anyone suspect the Paragon could arrest us for breaking the law? This party is illegal."

"I don't see any officers around. Stop whining and—"

Emily shushes as she follows his gaze to the ceiling, where a red glow flashes at regular intervals. A surveillance camera.

Mira glances at it too, then casually says, "They are not operational. The wires have been severed. Look." The naked wires are hanging in a ray of bluish light. Just what they needed.

"Too late to run now." Emily winks at Sky, and he grunts while she suppresses a laugh.

Mira dabs at something on the wall, then waves her arm. Almost impossible to spot for anyone who has never been here is the eye of a reader. Mira doesn't look like it, but she is sharp-eyed.

Lower levels. Illegal party. Hidden reader. This setup is most definitely the work of the Mavericks.

See Mom? It will be over soon.

The invisible eye recognizes their wristbands one by one. Only when the three of them are done does the contraption in the wall slide quietly open to the din of music.

They step into some kind of vestibule with no light filtering through. There is something exciting about total darkness. Thanks to her sharp senses, Emily can feel Sky, who's a little nervous on her left. For fifteen seconds, some mechanism whirrs around them, shutting the entrance behind and slowly opening up to a dancing crowd. What kind of security system is this? Probably very sophisticated to slip under the Paragon's radar.

Emily's eardrums are buzzing with repetitive rhythmic music, toned down by a melodious male voice that rushes into the vestibule. Let the party begin!

"Over here," Mira mouths silently, her face lit by the strobe light.

It's a large abandoned warehouse, the ceiling higher than usual. Heavy crates are scattered around, and people dance to the beat of techno music. There must be more than a hundred people in this room alone. It's hard to believe they are under nearly a kilometer of water.

Sky's face lights up as soon as they mingle with the crowd. He's taking a liking to it.

Emily scans the crowd to see whether she recognizes anyone. Mira skitters off, and Emily puts off her search. Nearby, on a retrofitted stage, Chris is busy chatting with Leander, who spots them first. He leaves Chris hanging to greet them.

Emily laughs when she sees Chris also went for a tux. Sky's face is priceless.

"You've got some competition," says Emily in Sky's ear. He grunts, displeased.

Chris gives Emily a kiss on the cheek and Sky glares at him in defiance, a sharp contrast with his gentle face. Chris drives them a little further back, where the crates shelter them from the music.

"Not bad for a farewell party, don't you think?" Chris says as he takes a sip of a beer-like drink.

"Don't fool yourself into thinking that this party was thrown for you," retorts Sky, his serious air back in full force.

"True that, but why not take advantage of it, my lord?" Chris says, laughing in his shy and arrogant way.

Chris is awfully cute. After the Brotherhood, he will be her next mission to tackle. *Mom, I swear.*

"Relax." Mira hands a glass to Sky and another to Emily, the same drink Chris is sipping. It's velvety, a blend of beer with a dash of something sweet to drown out the bitterness.

They go closer to the stage where the party is in full swing, and Emily lets the music sweep her away. Sky stays close to her, turning his back on Chris.

It's so … strange. This kind of atmosphere is rare on the Ark. Some iconic songs are available on the common network, but after a while, you know them all by heart. However, this type of music, these regular beats, this guttural voice, as if possessed…

It's euphoric. Chris doesn't hesitate to grab her waist and let the flow of music guide their steps. He even gives her a taste of his beer now and then.

Before she knows it, Emily is sipping the third glass Chris offered. Sky isn't around, so she asks Leander, who tells her he has gone to get something else to drink.

Emily leans over one of the large crates to come to her senses. The alcohol gives her renewed energy for now, but on an empty stomach, it's never a winner. She feels almost as dizzy as she did at graduation when she and Sky had been drinking champagne. Good times, although the next morning had been a mess. According to the others, they had a lot of fun.

Well, so much for her potentially dangerous maiden look. Her reflexes are not at their best, anyway. She takes a bigger sip that tingles her nose.

Sky still hasn't come back, and Mira is busy ogling Chris. Leander joins Emily, who puts down her glass a little more forcefully than she first meant to.

"Hey, be careful," says Leander, who catches her glass just before it spills and splashes her feet.

"How long has it been?" she says, staring at Mira who wears her elegant dress with grace. She is not as stiff as she looks. She dances with Chris in a goofy way, an easy smile on his face.

Leander follows Emily's gaze, then says, "Does it show that much? I never had the courage to tell her."

"Are you kidding? She is leering at him."

"Oh, that! Yeah, I know. But I talked it over with Chris and he said he'd straighten it all out with her." Leander is frowning while shaking his head to himself.

"Okay, I don't think we're talking about the same thing."

"Forget what I said."

Emily smiles as she rewinds what he just said. "You love her, don't you? I can help you make it happen."

"I don't think that's a good idea. It has to come from her. When you push things, there's only—"

"It's pretty simple," cuts Emily with a sigh. "The sooner you tell her, the sooner she'll be yours."

Emily smirks as she thinks about what the future might hold for her. Lord Chris of the Bates family: She glances at him while he sings at the top of his lungs. They grew up together, but if something was going to happen between them, it would have by now. Emily pouts.

"Are *you* going to tell Chris that you love him?" retorts Leander, still spellbound by Mira.

"What are you talking about?" Her face feels warm all of a sudden. Where's her drink again? "I'm not that kind of girl," she adds before groping for her glass.

"Don't wait until Sky realizes that."

"What difference does it make? We're best friends. Nothing is ever going to happen between us."

"That's the point." His comment is left hanging, and he pulls her closer to the stage, at a safe distance from Chris and Mira. Emily must focus so she doesn't trip.

The lights go out and the atmosphere quickly shifts. The intoxicating music gives way to the fast beating of drums from the stage. Each beat sends a shiver down Emily's spine. Rain sticks and other instruments she has never heard before joining them, reviving an ancient tribe of Earth celebrating the power of the gods. They are on their territory, in their jungle, in the dead of the night.

Four dancers enter from the sides of the warehouse and wow the audience with their blazing flames that make the crowd ecstatic. Fiery rings swirl around, creating a truly hypnotic dance. The next moment, the dancers burst onto the stage with an acrobatic entrance and whip the air with flaming chains that hiss, with the drumbeats following their every move. The speed at which the tongues of fire waltz through the air is frightening: snakes ablaze. A reddish glow stains the frenzied crowd.

Sweat sticks to Emily's skin, the heat growing more and more overpowering with each breath blown by the beating chains. She almost feels as if she is back on that balcony during the simulation.

A final bare-chested dancer joins the group by making a dramatic somersault with a large, flaming stick that he twirls. The burning glow lights up his thick beard and gives him a wild look. He hits the ground, which flares up and sends sparks flying in all directions. The percussion becomes angrier, each blow beating throughout the warehouse. The bearded dancer performs a spin and breathes out a long blast of fire towards the ceiling, as if reaching out to the sky. Emily's skin cooks under the gust of warm air as the heat spills out in the room.

The fire's glow lights up a familiar face a few meters to her right. Emily takes advantage of the thunderous applause and Leander's distraction to sneak through the crowd.

His color does not lie: a yellow that defuses any hostile emotion—a magnetic sun. It's a wonder it had so little effect on Reyes.

Milo stands there, clapping, but Emily pulls him back hard and, when he meets her gaze, she gags him with her hand. He meekly follows her, knowing that resisting is pointless. She leads him away from the cheering crowd to a corner of the room concealed by several crates. Emily wrenches Milo's arm and presses his youthful face against the wall.

It's time for some answers.

She pulls the pen out of her pocket and presses the tip on Milo's wristband. It doesn't glow red as she had hoped. Is he in the passenger records?

"Where is the Brotherhood?" she asks in the hollow of his ear. "How did you escape?"

"You already know the answers," he says with unnerving calm. "Don't waste your time." Emily's body is pressed against his to make sure he can't wrench himself free. She can feel Milo's rapid heartbeat pounding against his rib cage.

"I'll be the judge of that. Tell me where I can find the leader of the Brotherhood."

"Even if you knew, it wouldn't make a damn bit of difference. He doesn't care about you or anything else." Mom's murderer doesn't care? Although it disgusts her, at least he won't stop her from coming to him.

"You haven't answered my question," she insists, tightening her grip. "Answer. Now."

"Or what? Are you going to kill me? Or take me back to your prison?" he scoffs, breathlessly. "That's the problem with all of you, it's your law and nothing else. You've lost your sense of humanity." Emily gives him some space so he can get his face off the wall. He stretches his neck to have a better look at her and licks his chapped lips.

"I'm not the one jeopardizing thousands of people and generations of effort to keep the survivors of the Flood alive," she says.

"What's the point of saving those who will persecute us once we get to the ground? I'd sooner die."

The certainty that shines in his eyes is truly admirable. A force ... as powerful as his aura claims. The last time she saw such determination was in Mom's eyes when she and Dad argued shortly before she was sentenced. Mom had insisted on going back to her proteges and taking the risk of exposing herself further, even though suspicions of her betrayal had already been raised. Dad did everything he could to hold her back, but there was nothing he could do. Mom had gone back to continue her work among the Mavericks like Milo. Did he know her? Probably not. He must have only been a kid at the time. But the other members of the Brotherhood…

"People like you will get us killed," she says more insistently. "Pursuing an illusory dream at the cost of others…"

Sacrificing lives for nothing—Mother was a beautiful, generous, and loving soul. And what did she get in return? A public execution.

"What the Brotherhood does is lie to itself and to all of us," she adds. Milo turns his body to face her, and she doesn't stop him. His gaze softens.

"Where is your leader?" she repeats, her drunkenness making her a little sluggish. "He came to me during the simulation, so I guess he doesn't mind if I know who he is."

"Neal knows what he's doing and there's nothing you can do to stop him. It's already too late."

"Then tell me where Reyes is." Powerful hands suddenly haul her back. Emily curses the alcohol for slowing her reflexes. Her neutralizing shot is a total failure and before she knows it, a blade presses against her throat.

Milo coughs while he catches his breath and Emily turns around to see the specimen of a man holding her captive. He is bare-chested, his cold sweat clinging to her. A dancer.

He tightens his grip on her and makes sure Milo is okay. Then he threatens Emily.

"Dan! It's all right. Just let her go."

"I don't need your help," she spits, still numb.

"No way," says Dan, the dancer. "She will alert the others. Turn around while I get rid of her."

"Is this really how you want to make things different? We promised we wouldn't stoop to their level. We must change now."

"Who says she won't hurt us?" Milo is looking right through her. Emily can't believe her life is in the hands of a bloodthirsty

Maverick. She hates to admit it, but she really screwed up on this one.

"She doesn't know." Dan and Milo exchange a glance that makes Emily regret not being able to read minds. Their auras reveal no more than their current emotions. Distrust. Anger. Anxiety. A contradiction typical of terrorists who are on the verge of destroying everything they know.

"By the way," says Milo as he draws closer to her, resolute. "Reyes is safe and nothing you can do will change that. Not after what she's been through."

"I gave her a choice." Emily can only imagine the torture Yasmina must have put her through. "All she had to do was talk."

Milo turns his back on her and for a second, his energy flickers. Emily doesn't see the blow to her temple coming.

Her ears ring and Milo's face freezes before her eyes. Sweaty and suffused with sadness.

For Emily.

15

SKYLER

"What made you change your mind?"

Chris's pupils are more dilated than usual, his lips still wet from the orange liquid he just swallowed for the umpteenth time. At this stage, it's almost methodical, sipping the bottle after each sentence.

"Don't get too excited," Skyler shouts over the music. "I didn't do it for you."

"Who did you do it for then?" For his own sanity. To live in peace and move on, so he doesn't have to remember that the only thing Chris cares about is himself and that he would drag in anyone foolish enough to believe his wise advice.

Skyler used to, but not anymore.

"What difference does it make?" says Skyler, stoic. "I'm here. That's what you wanted."

"Don't be so heartless," replies Chris, taking another sip. "I know that deep down, you're going to miss me."

"Don't make me wish I hadn't come." Skyler swiftly rids himself of his glass, put off by Chris, who is reeking of alcohol.

"Are you dwelling on the past again?" Chris staggers towards him: too close. "Do you think all the moments we shared ended when your brother killed himself?"

"You killed him," says Skyler in a hollow voice, his face numb. "If it wasn't for you, he wouldn't have died."

"It's easy to blame someone else when you can't stand your own mistake. Let's put the past behind us and start over. I don't want this night to be a reckoning." Their breathing quickens.

"I can't forget," drops Skyler, teeth clenched, the words burning in his mouth. "His death haunts me every day. That day destroyed my family. My life."

"Yeah, well…" Skyler stops Chris's jerky motion and pushes the bottle out of reach. Things will get out of hand quickly if he keeps drinking.

"You've had enough to drink now."

"If you say so, doctor," he says tauntingly. Chris is sweating profusely, deeply intoxicated. One more drop will get the better of him.

Should he trust Chris?

Skyler shouldn't be here. Coming to this party was a bad idea.

He walks away, ready to let Emy know he's leaving, but Chris catches up.

"There's something I've been wanting to tell you. Maybe this will help you understand." Skyler sighs loudly and wrests himself free.

"You have ten seconds."

"I just… I just…" And Chris collapses.

Shit. Just what he needed.

Skyler's instincts take over. He crouches down to make sure Chris is still breathing, then turns him over into a safe position. Chris is shivering, his body ready to expel the crap he's been drinking all night. Now they are going to spend the next few hours together. No kidding.

Somebody bumps into him, and Skyler barely manages not

to fall over and drag Chris with him. Skyler cusses the fool and then something catches his attention: a wave-shaped tattoo that runs down the man's arm.

Could that be…?

Mira and Leander are rubbing up against each other, and Skyler rushes to them. He asks them to take care of Chris and they give him a surprised look. Skyler doesn't give them time to react and goes after the tattooed man.

He shoves whoever stands in his way until he finally makes his way through the tight crowd, dancing along to the dizzying melody.

Is that him?

The distance between them shrinks, but Skyler stops dead in his tracks when a familiar voice calls out to him over the tribe song,

"Need help?" Their eyes meet.

"Tessa? What are you doing here?"

"I should ask you the same question. Let's go someplace quiet to talk." The crowd is pressing against them, and the tattooed man is nowhere to be seen.

Skyler follows Tessa on the double. Her outfit doesn't fit the Ark's standards: Her bandana wraps her head keeping her braids from spilling out, her top bares a shoulder, and her short-checkered skirt matches her black nylon stockings buried in dark leather boots. Is this really the Paragon's dress code?

They leave the din of the warehouse and exit through the sliding doors. The corridor is still empty, only a faint vibration in the background.

Once they climb the stairs, Skyler breaks the roaring silence that has set in. "Are you the lone wolf of the Paragon? Don't they ever follow you?" He clears his throat, his voice raspy after all the shouting. They head towards the observatory before she gives a reply.

"As I told you before, not all the members of the Paragon

support Duke Kay." She slows down and the beads in her braids rattle. "You heard what the Brotherhood intends to do. Duke takes it personally, and cocky as he is, he will never submit to the Mavericks. His pride depends on it."

Skyler says nothing. He wants to pry, but Tessa is a walking mystery.

She crosses her arms. "Do you doubt me, by any chance?"

"I have my reasons to be suspicious. Besides, we haven't known each other for long." She remains silent for a while. A puff of air that reminds him of the salty smell of the simulation catches him by surprise.

"I get it," she says in her melodious voice. "I could be very dangerous." Skyler blushes with embarrassment, and she lets out a giggle.

"That's not what I meant."

"Don't get me wrong," she says with a more serious look. "You seem to be a good guy. What you did with Clarissa…"

Skyler could not save her. A heroic act from the outside, but in the end, it didn't matter.

"You care about others," she insists wistfully.

"How can you be so sure?" Tessa opens the door to the largest bay window in the entire Ark. Gigantic beams of light flood the remains of a sunken metropolis in more than half a kilometer of water.

Welcome to the observatory, announces a genderless electronic voice. *Today, you can enjoy one of the ancient cities of the twenty-first century: Boston.*

The concrete structures extend for miles that even the lights cannot reach. The ship is moored at the city's edge at a safe distance from the tallest skyscrapers, whose upper floors barely pierce the ocean. From here, they are quite close to the surface, much closer than usual, given their proximity to a raised continental plate. This kind of stopover is very unusual, because of the risks. The Ark must be preparing for a large hunt to replenish its supplies.

Skyler reluctantly peels away from the view. Tessa's mind seems to wander once again. She looks unnerved. He waits a moment before speaking softly. "You look sad."

"You think so?" she answers without taking her eyes off the city. Tessa takes a deep breath and looks down. She runs a trembling hand through her braids and then crosses her arms as if she were cold.

"The Paragon has access to a wealth of information, including a list of those who were connected to the simulation. During the Inspection, we tallied those who were there in the hope to find a lead or an intruder in hiding. I came across your file and read a little about you. Only background information, nothing incriminating."

He nods silently, and she continues.

"We discovered that the system was hacked from the outside while the program itself had been altered. We suspect that the Deltas have been infiltrated."

"You did some research on me *before* we met," points out Skyler, who doesn't understand what she's getting at. "That day with Clarissa, you didn't come for her."

She plays with the ring on the pendant she's wearing. It's plain white gold.

Skyler presses her. "I'd like to believe you, but you have to tell me everything."

"You're wrong. I did my research *after* we met to find out whether I could trust you."

"Trust me?"

"Don't you think life has more to offer than this Ark? If the Brotherhood decided to strike now, it's no accident," she adds, uncrossing her arms. The dull walls that surround them seem to close in on them.

The Brotherhood vowed to rebuild civilization in the

Promised Land, a mythical place listed in the Bible. This land seems so close now, something Skyler never thought possible before the Brotherhood came along.

Tessa comes down from the observation deck and continues. "The Archeans wish to see the light of day. To live like the people before the Flood."

"Who wouldn't want that?" Serendipitous freedom.

"But Commander Hawk and his proteges are withholding crucial information from us including the Paragon though they should be neutral and serve the Archeans' interests."

"Is it really in their best interest?"

"Duke Kay supports Hawk claiming that we are not ready. But the question remains, when will be the right time?"

Circumstances force people to act, just like the Flood. No one was prepared to change, but they did the most sensible thing to do: adapt in order to survive.

"The Ark won't last forever," says Skyler, who follows her downstairs. "When its lifespan nears its end, there won't be enough people left to keep the Sacred Fire burning."

"This is just the tip of the iceberg," she whispers as she opens a secondary door. Tessa's expression sends an unpleasant shiver down Skyler's spine. He follows her.

The smell of old, wet metal is strong in the warehouse where the small vessels used to collect resources in underwater cities line up. There must be a hundred of them.

"Have you ever ridden in a Strahl?" Tessa asks while tapping away at a control panel.

"Why this question?"

"Because we're going for a ride." The pressurized door pops off and leaves an opening big enough for an average person.

"Isn't that illegal?" says Skyler annoyed as Tessa makes herself comfortable in her seat.

"Not with a member of the Paragon. Anyway, that shouldn't stop you from coming, after what you did tonight." Fine. He walks down on what looks like a dock, and Tessa looks satisfied. Skyler climbs into the Strahl, rocking under his weight. He holds on to the frame, and his heart rate picks up.

What exactly is he getting himself into with this girl?

There are only two seats in the Strahl, so Skyler sits in the co-driver's seat even though he has no idea how this thing works. Unfortunately, riding the Strahl isn't part of the Academy's program.

"Do you think the coastal city in my simulation exists?" he asks, trying to draw on his closest experience to expect what's in store for him in the next minute. Tessa steers awake the controls and glances at him furtively.

"The Brotherhood created the code with what they found in the Archives. Tonight is the real thing, though." Skyler straps on his safety harness after they whizz forward. The shaking is giving him a hard time, but Tessa seems too eager to slow down.

The hangar door opens just enough for their Strahl to slip through. Once in the antechamber, they are propelled out of the Ark almost instantaneously, and Skyler tightens his harness straps.

He clenches his hands on the armrests as he realizes it is his first time outside the Ark. The feeling is dizzying. Every centimeter of ocean he sees through the Strahl's large panoramic windowpane overtake him with new details he never noticed. Schools of fish push themselves out of their wake, bubbles cluster around them, and slither down the walls of their vehicle. And it only keeps getting better. Boston. Not one of those pristine underwater cities. They head straight for it until they reach the first skyscrapers.

"This is our reality and that of our forefathers," Tessa explains in a mysterious voice. "This is what awaits us if we don't act."

A world that was once alive. The roads are still visible, as evidenced by the spaces between the buildings. Their Strahl thrusts into the heap of concrete that has withstood the test of time. The Flood spared only a small part of the city, likely the most recent one.

Algae and an assortment of nameless objects line the seabed, altered by water. They don't look like anything he's ever seen. Hunters usually entrust their finds to the Sigmas, who then use the Archives to find out what the objects might be, and finally pass the information on to the Deltas, who reconstruct them. With all the mess on the seabed, hunters prioritize either what is useful or in mint condition. The list is not that long.

At the Academy, they showed them safes or bunkers where most things are salvageable. The hunts were originally random, but now they only locate those treasure troves which is a better use of time and effort.

The Strahl meanders past former public squares, perhaps even a huge central park which stretches for miles. How many families in this city could reach the Ark on time? How many passed away?

"The greatest challenge was not the Flood itself, but everything that came afterward," whispers Skyler worried the millions of corpses that lay beneath them could hear him.

All that suffering. A perpetual struggle.

"You remind me of someone," Tessa says.

"Someone good?" She giggles.

"Yes … but I don't know if I'll ever see him again." Tessa drums on the wheel, distracted.

"It's hard not to run into everyone on the Ark at some point," he says with Chris in mind.

"I wish you were right." The Strahl takes a sharp turn that leaves Skyler breathless. The fluttering becomes jerkier, and he's holding on as best he can.

"What do you think of the Brotherhood?" she asks suddenly. "The idea of going back to the ground?"

"It's true that we don't have much time left to make a move," he says quickly to avoid thinking about the buildings they brush past. "The Syndrome is growing and..."

"The Syndrome?" She frowns, puzzled and intrigued. The rushing sensation unnerves Skyler, who turns his gaze away to focus on Tessa.

"It's a neurological defect we have detected in the last few months, the same that caused Clarissa's problems. There is nothing we can do to stop it."

"An anomaly," she muses.

"Unless we find a cure, but that will take time."

She takes a moment to think. "Commander Hawk is getting ready to take out the Brotherhood. You know they were at the party, don't you? That could jeopardize the resettlement plans." Suddenly, the evidence hits him. To protect him.

"That's why you brought me here."

"I didn't want them to run into you. You can't mess with the Paragon." The Strahl arcs back to their home, which glows faintly.

"Whatever the Commander and the Paragon do, the Brotherhood will follow through its ultimatum. Those ready to return and divulge the truth will be granted access to the Promised Land."

Duke Kay's loyalties never made Skyler trustful. This is Chris's family, after all. But the Brotherhood...

Tessa's eyes meet his own, and he takes a deep breath. "What do I have to do?"

16

EMILY

Emily wakes up, spread out in an empty hallway on the lower levels. Alone.

Her headache is unbearable. She must leave this cursed place at all costs. If Milo or the bully is hanging around, she won't make it out. Normally, she could defend herself all right, but her body hurts like hell and her temple is painfully sensitive.

As if that wasn't enough, the damn Brotherhood will make a move in less than twenty-four hours.

The air reeks. Emily strides under the flashing light glinting off the puddles of tarred water in the winking darkness. With each step, a sharp twinge splits her brain. That will teach her for carrying out her own investigation. She wades through a layer of water fed by a jet that spurts out of nowhere. A breach? It should have been patched by now since the Incident happened years ago. How can the Mavericks live in such conditions? People like Milo!

The good news is that there is still a secured path because of the Incident, running from the upper levels to the Sacred Fire, the mechanical heart of the Ark. Once she finds this passage, the

Mavericks will be out of her way. Even better, she won't rot in here.

At the corner, the corridor is oddly similar to the dormitories on the upper levels. A row of ghostly gray doors with disabled magnetic readers and forgotten names are still visible on lackluster metal plates that have endured. The poor lighting makes her squint to make out the faded names: Taylor, Clark, Walker, Nelson, Parker, Rivera, Reed, Herrera, Graves, Shelton, Wolfe.

So many families lost. Names that survived the greatest catastrophe, only to disappear forever. Some of them probably moved to the upper levels, but none that she recognizes.

Does the Brotherhood really think they can bring them all back to the ground? Aren't all these deaths proof enough that they can barely survive? Every moment brings them closer to that fateful day.

At the end of the corridor, the emergency exit sign glows faintly and makes her heart leap. She picks up the pace while an obnoxious feeling grips her, as if forsaken ghosts were watching her, although there is obviously no one here. She slows down, as the feeling is getting stronger.

Fluttery, she glances behind. The pale light flickers, but no one else is here except for … a noise. A whisper? It's probably exhaustion.

She nears the exit, but then the whispers grow until they become voices. She huddles up against the nearby wall and listens in.

"Why are you standing up for her?" The voice is muffled, and Emily must shift back to hear more clearly.

"She is not a danger to us. Daniel has her under control." Emily frowns. She takes a split second to recognize Reyes talking to Milo. All her senses are sharp.

"It's obvious that she warned them," continues Reyes's familiar voice. Her raging footsteps ring out on the metallic floor. "How else do you think the Paragon pinpointed our location? As far as we know, she is the only one who recognized you."

"Isn't that what we wanted, anyway? To have a free party? Don't fall into their trap. That's what they want to push us around and bend us to their will. Our freedom began the day we hacked into their simulation."

"I know that. Don't take me for an idiot," she says in her typical arrogant tone, just like in the prison. "The ultimatum ends today, and we can move on to the next step."

Their voices slur, and Emily chokes down a curse. So close to knowing what they're up to.

Reyes survived Yasmina's interrogation. Worse, she is back with the Mavericks. That doesn't bode well. Besides, who knew Reyes could be so tame? Milo must be her weakness, her lover, maybe? Emily records this precious information and walks away. Now is not the time to fight, no matter how much she longs for it.

Milo. Why was he protecting her from Reyes? It doesn't make any sense. Emily tackled him, threatened him, and she was very unsparing with his girlfriend. Could he be any different from the other Mavericks? Yet her instinct has never misled her.

Emily runs to the emergency stairwell and up the stairs, the flow of her blood pounding in her aching head. Maybe she still has leverage after all.

***

SHE KNOCKS. No answer.

She knocks again. Still nothing.

Emily fishes out her key card and opens. A pleasant floral scent fills her lungs, and the artificial lights gradually come on.

Sky's night was not easy, judging by the trail of clothing to his bed.

Sky is sleeping curled up in a ball, snoring lightly with his back to Emily. A glance at the digital clock tells her it's almost noon. Well, so much for being an early riser.

"Are you going to sleep like this all day?" she says, bouncing on the bed. He moans, then looks at her bleary-eyed.

"What are you doing here? I don't remember giving you a key."

"Nothing can stop me." She swiftly strips off his blanket. "You should know that by now."

"Yeah." he grumbles, rubbing his eyes.

"Hurry. We need to talk."

"Give me at least five minutes." She lies on the bed and scans his room as he drags himself out of the cabin.

There is a mixture of colors on the left, and she rolls over to the side to get a better view. Flowers lie in a corner where a small set-up gives them the energy they need. When they went to the Gardens of Humankind, Sky would always stop to smell them. He probably took away a few of them. The roses he bought from that Amber who was flirting with him at the restaurant are also there, though they've lost their luster, their petals wrinkly. It's a shame.

The floral scent isn't as strong as when Emily walked in, but she brushes the roses with the tip of her nose and closes her eyes. Their sweet aroma soothes her for a few seconds before her mind nags again.

How is she supposed to deal with what happened with Milo the day before? Her thoughts are spinning at a dizzying pace.

"So, what's the matter?" Sky's voice has lost its lethargy. He smells like shower gel, the same as Chris.

"The Brotherhood," she says, snapping her eyes open. He freezes, a vague feeling of anxiety overwhelming him. Has he learned anything about them? Maybe last night? "Did I miss something?"

"Why are you interested in them?" he replies, a little stiff. He's building up his defenses. Typical of him when you touch a sensitive spot.

"Don't you want to know what a rebel group intends to do with our lives? Have you already forgotten about the simulation?"

"I didn't say that," he suddenly says more relaxed. "I just don't see what we can do about it."

"So, if I understand correctly, you prefer to leave our fate in the hands of the Commander."

"You woke me up just for that?" Just for that? Emily stares at him in shock. Sky's face is stony, and the narrow opening he showed thirty seconds ago is gone.

"You can't be serious," she answers as she gets up.

"Listen, Emy, I have loads of patients waiting. I don't have time to dwell on a group of terrorists who will probably get arrested in the next few hours." He avoids Emily's gaze and puts on his uniform.

"Where were you at the end of the evening?" she asks, raising her voice.

"I left." He stuffs a bag with jars of medicine. "I was tired."

"Tired enough to sleep late in the morning too? If we don't do anything, maybe you won't have any more patients, because we'll be dead, anyway!"

"Emy, you should..." He sighs and snaps his bag shut. "Just forget it."

"I should what?" She crosses her arms, her cheeks on fire. He peers at her with his blue eyes, clearly not taking her seriously.

"Stop being so fatalistic," he drops, looking uncomfortable.

Realistic. Not fatalistic.

"Now get out of my cabin, I have to go," he says, looking away, bag slung over his shoulder.

"I'm not going anywhere, Skyler Goldberg." Emily blocks his way with her arm, the door frame almost bending under her grip. "How long have you been hiding things from me?"

A mixture of anger and indignation gnaws at her stomach.

"What are you talking about?" he says flatly.

"That. Your attitude. I want to know what happened last night. I want to know now."

"Look, Emy, I'm…" he stammers. "I don't think that's a good idea. This whole thing is complicated. I don't even know where to start or what to think about it. I don't even know what you might think." He's always struggled to put his feelings into words. Maybe that's why he's so closed off. He simply avoids the subject. Less doubt, less pain; logical but sad.

"Trust me then," she says, softening her voice. "If you keep everything to yourself, we can't be best friends, can we?" She tries not to act like she would with a prisoner, but it's almost second nature. He is her best friend after all, but she means well. He needs her help, she knows that. She can feel it.

He sighs in annoyance and tosses his bag on the bed. Emily's muscles relax at the same time.

"It all started with the Syndrome. You know, those people who talk to the Fairies?" Emily frowns, unsure. He was honest, and not just about what happened the night before.

"Yes, we've already talked about it," she replies, recalling one of their conversations. "It's a problem we have at the prison, too. After a while you lose them. They hallucinate and talk to invisible people."

"Well, this is getting more and more serious. A few days ago, when you left the canteen after lunch, Clarissa died."

"Who is Clarissa? One of your patients?" The name sounds oddly familiar.

"No. This woman was ready to jump off the tenth floor to end her life. The Fairies urged her to join them."

"And what does this have to do with the Brotherhood?"

"They know. That's why they want to save us all. Soon enough, we'll all be infected."

"Hold on. Who told you this?" There's a sparkle in his eyes; it's obvious he knows a lot more. He spares her the details, and only reveals what he thinks is necessary.

How can he know so much?

The truth hits her as the glow in Sky's eyes fades. He looks almost scared when he sees she has understood.

"Did you talk to them? They tried to convince you to join their ranks!"

"Emy, calm down." She steps towards him, her senses numb with the danger they face.

"Don't make this mistake," she says, controlling her trembling voice, giving away her panic. "You don't want to betray your own family, your friends. Me!"

"I don't want to persuade you they are right and that their Promised Land exists," he says, weighing his words. "But you can see it in a different light. They have a plan to save us."

"By getting rid of the Commander?" she says, thinking of Chris, who is now part of the crew. "Of Commander Hawk? No one else has the knowledge or experience to control the Ark."

"You said it yourself: control. Haven't you ever wondered why they never said anything about the resettlement plans?"

"Because there aren't any, Sky! There never has and there never will! It's a utopia that gives people hope so they can go on living. Would you find the strength to live if you knew there was no way out of the Ark?" He doesn't answer to that though his aura is melting away. Mom would tell her to have better control of her emotions, but right now she doesn't care.

"Tessa told me about the repopulation plan a hundred years after the Flood. These are the scientists' prognoses: the time it will take for the waters to recede on some elevated areas. The one hundred years have passed for at least fifteen years now. What are we still doing here?"

"Who is Tessa?" reasons Emily. "I can't believe you've already fallen for one of their members."

"She's not from the Brotherhood," he insists, his features tense. "She's part of a Paragon group that doesn't support the current leadership or the plans they have for the Ark."

"A rebel group in this case. You could say it's the same thing. Rebels from the Paragon, the Mavericks, the Brotherhood!" He sighs, looking distraught. He can't really believe what he says! It's easy to believe what you want to hear, even if it's not the truth.

"You wanted me to be honest with you and that's what I'm doing," he says.

"That doesn't give you the right to be that naive and stupid, damn it!" she explodes.

Sky is livid.

"What they're saying borders on hysteria," says Emily, sweeping Sky's arguments aside. "That Tessa is one of those rebels! It's so obvious! How can you not see it?!"

"You're the one who's hysterical!" Sky's face has taken on a dewy hue that she's never seen. The Mavericks' utopian ideas have corrupted Sky's mind.

"I have work to do," he says dryly. He bolts away without letting her add anything.

Emily stands still, beaten, the cabin door still open. My God, what just happened?

Her hands are shaking, her breathing is shallow. She comes out of the cabin in silence, hoping to speak sense to him, but he is no longer there. She replays their conversation back and forth.

She covers her face and lets out a sigh. Maybe she went too far this time. She doesn't even remember everything she said. Will he forgive her?

But … but Sky can't just fall for the Brotherhood! Or that Tessa! How could things turn out this way?

What a nightmare.

Right. She's lost Sky for now, but not forever. There's still something that needs to be dealt with urgently. A personal matter.

Emily hurries to the elevator, then goes down to level three and heads for the atrium. Once at the entrance, she turns into the hidden corridor that leads to the prison and the magnetic eye scans her wristband. She walks through the damn detector and into the prison.

As soon as Ludo sees her, he perks up, but she doesn't give him time to talk.

"Do you want revenge?"

17

SKYLER

Skyler spits, but the metallic taste of water lingers on his tongue. He digs in a drawer for a lemon-flavored lozenge he adds to a glass of water, which turns a translucent yellow. He gives it to his mother, who drinks without batting an eye.

"Here you go. The water is foul."

"The same as usual," she replies, gulping her glass. "Sugar is not good for you, and your body will become addicted to it. That's what I used to tell my patients."

Murielle's eyes go blank, engrossed in her memories from the time she worked in the ward. If she recovers, she could go back to work and surround herself with her old friends like Jacinta. Dr. Nazar has agreed to let Skyler take care of his mother, but he remains on call for emergencies, such as for the memory spheres, when Mira is not on duty or for cases of the Syndrome. It's only a matter of time before Murielle regains her cheerfulness. She needs permanent care and progressive psychological support that will help her overcome her trauma. If Dylan were more present, her condition would have improved by now. However, he doesn't have his family at heart.

Sometimes he gives the impression that she died at the same time as Allen.

Skyler takes a sip and cringes. The aftertaste lingers, and he swallows hard to end his suffering. Pure water shouldn't taste that bad. Hopefully, this torture will end soon. Tessa said nothing can stop the resettlement.

"Mom, come on. We're going out today," says Skyler, packing a small bag with medicine, energy bars and flavored water. "It'll make you feel better."

"But Dylan will need me when he comes back," she protests. Skyler glances at the note his father left on the counter.

"He has important tests to do. He won't come back before the end of the day."

"You must be busy as well. Don't worry about me, I can take care of myself."

"I'll be fine."

Sometimes the sparkle of his mother's life fades away, the telltale sign of severe post-traumatic shock. When she learned of Allen's death, she lost consciousness and by the time she woke up, she had become a different person. Dr. Nazar's diagnosis at the time was favorable, but now he doesn't know if she will ever recover, though it doesn't mean much. Skyler's mother will be back to her old self, and together they will enjoy life on the ground. Skyler is sure of it.

He is walking along the bay window of the main floor with his mother by his side when a swarm of Strahls emerges from the Ark in swirls of bubbles to venture into the sunken remains of Boston. The freedom he felt during his ride with Tessa tantalizes him, and he feels giddy. Could it be because of what she asked him to do? He might have to share confidential data on the patients who took part in the memory spheres project, but if his contribution can help them reach the Promised Land…

Tessa deserves his trust. She works for the Paragon, who may theoretically access classified documents.

The stillness of the Gardens and the fresh smell of the greenery are invigorating, the floral fragrances intermingling in an enchanting aroma. They pass through the antechamber and sink into the woods to the sound of locusts, serene now that the seaquake damage has been cleaned up. The artificial light at this hour is an orange hue that mimics the setting sun on the surface and gives the impression of bathing in its rays.

"Remember when I used to bring you and Allen here every morning after work?" Murielle says as they cross the place where Skyler met Tessa a few days ago.

A moment of lucidity.

Skyler nods with a mixed sense of relief and melancholy.

"I don't remember feeling so happy since then," she continues. "My two boys together. I still don't know why you stopped talking to each other." Confusion, as if her mind had changed her memories, altering its own structure to hold back the pain. Reminding her now that Allen died could trigger an attack.

"It's complicated," he simply says. The sunlight flickers through the thick foliage.

"How's your brother? I know he's not the talkative type, but…" She lifts her index finger to her mouth as she does when she's thinking. "Oh, and now that I think about it, no one in the family talks much. You two take after your father. A real conundrum."

Dylan, who only ever cared about Allen. Those two agreed on pretty much everything. Maybe he thought Allen would follow in his footsteps, something Skyler had never been interested in. His mother was his inspiration.

Murielle's wan face lights up. Skyler would like to freeze this moment just to keep her in this state of awareness, but he has a job to do.

"Do you remember why we haven't heard from my brother for so long?" She squints as if the sun were too strong.

"He was so happy to finally graduate and focus on his future. He had so many plans."

"You know, he wasn't so much as happy."

"What do you mean?" She looks surprised.

"In fact, he was undecided. He couldn't choose between joining the Deltas' research center with Dad or leading his own hunting team."

"Did he? I always thought he'd do the same as your father. Dylan is so proud of that."

Allen was curious and questioned everything. Had he been hunting, he could have satiated his wanderlust while exploring a new piece of underwater wonderland. However, the research center was bound by constraints. He would either predict the ocean variations of an incoming storm or optimize the energy output using the ocean currents' kinetic motion for hours on end. That would have gone against his nature.

At the edge of the woods, Skyler continues. "What about Allen's graduation?"

"I don't know," she says with a grimace. "I have … a funny feeling when I think back on it. A kind of emptiness." Her brain goes into self-defense mode by short-circuiting her memories.

Allen died before he could graduate from the Academy.

"Put words on how you feel," he gently encourages her. "I can help you remember."

"It's like a part of me has been ripped out, and your face keeps coming back every time."

Abruptly, the brightness in her eyes changes, filling with anger.

"You killed him," she says in a harsh, trembling voice. She walks on while Skyler freezes up.

"You don't really mean that. That's not what happened."

"Don't try to deceive me," she says, cocking her head. "*They know.*"

His face drains. No.

"They remind me that you're my son's killer."

"That's not true."

"Quite the opposite. You gave him up to save yourself." Murielle's face is hard as stone, as if someone else is speaking for her. Allen's pleading voice repeats his name: Skyler. Skyler.

His brother falls to his death. His mother's lips move, but he can't hear her voice.

Listen to him.

Before he knows it, the wail reverts to the continuous buzzing of the locusts as if nothing ever happened. The artificial sun is gone, replaced by the electric lights that make the trail glow.

Skyler's breathing settles, but for a short time. Where is Murielle? He calls for her and spots movement outside the woods. He rushes over and breathes a sigh of relief. His mother is sitting on a rock and gazes.

What the hell just happened? That scream… He hadn't heard it since his nightmares when he was at the Academy. And how long has Murielle been sitting here all by herself?

Now that it's getting late, chances are Dylan's back.

The trip back is quiet, and Murielle doesn't mention his absence. They enter the cabin and, as expected, Dylan is working at his computer.

"I was wondering when you'd be back," Dylan says in a mindless voice. He glances at Skyler.

"Got a minute? I need to tell you something important."

"Not tonight," Skyler replies dryly. "Later." Dylan doesn't make a move to stop him when he walks out. Skyler needs to know what happened at the Gardens. To remember.

He climbs to the seventh floor, but instead of going to the

Gardens, he turns right into a dead end. He feels the wall's surface until he finds a loose tile, a narrow space invisible to the untrained eye. He pushes, and it drops with a thud.

Skyler crawls through the opening barely wide enough to slip sideways, while holding his breath. It leads into a dark, moldy maintenance route known as "the in between" that stretches for hundreds of meters under the flicker of a few small blue-white safety lights. This is where the piping, the electricity and everything else meet, the perfect place for Allen and him to spend their after-school evenings.

Allen found this place first, excited about exploring an unknown corner of the Ark, a forbidden territory. Luckily, the Paragon never caught them, or they would have been goners. Though it happened to Allen once.

Skyler walks along the in between. His foothold is steady, the darkness welcome and familiar despite the years. He climbs and sits on a pipe that connects to an even more complex system that spans several floors. The air is cooler here, and a shiver licks his skin. Water crashes through the pipes that crawl into the abyss and snake along the walls of the Ark like the veins of a slumbering giant.

This is where Skyler lost Allen forever. The light is so dim that the gaping hole seems dense, almost material. At least, that saved him from a horrifying sight: the dismembered body of his brother at the bottom of that hole.

It all happened so quickly. One of the pipes was leaking, and the surface was slippery. Skyler caught up with him at the last moment when his brother lost his footing.

"You came back, after all." Skyler jerks around and sees Chris. He didn't hear him coming.

"What are you doing here?"

"I kept coming after he died," Chris says as he approaches. He glances into the hole, hands on his hips. "Every day."

"You shouldn't be here." Skyler clenches his jaws.

"And yet here I am. I wasn't his brother like you, but we were friends whether you like it or not. You can't take that away from me."

"*Was*. Why did you follow me?" Another dead-end discussion.

"I was wondering what you could be doing around here at this hour, and I thought I'd check it out so you wouldn't do anything stupid."

"If there's anyone to watch, it's you. Not me." Chris bites back a comment, probably stepping on his pride, and sits next to Skyler, who looks away, put off.

"Thanks for last night," Chris tells him. "You came, and I ruined the evening. Too much to drink."

"Just doing my job."

"You could have watched me choke and do nothing. If you hated me so much, you would have." Like shoving him into that hole, right here, right now. But Skyler is not Chris; he respects himself.

"I'm not here to talk to you," Skyler says sheepishly. "Leave."

"I don't want your death on my conscience."

"You're imagining things." Skyler snorts. What madness is going through Chris's mind?

"I'm worried about you."

"I'm ready to move on. Forget about the past. See? I'm listening to your advice."

"About us?" says Chris, interested. He bends one leg and leans against it.

"Allen," says Skyler and his voice echoes under the tons of steel around them. "There's nothing I can do to bring him back, but I know that if you hadn't been there, he wouldn't be…"

"You would have joined him." His voice sounds alarming. "That day, I saved your life. I had to make a choice. You were slipping, and I caught you at the last second, though you were stubbornly trying to save your brother."

"You should have helped me instead of pulling me away from him. You did nothing to save him!" Skyler tempers his emotions that could overwhelm him any second. Chris's cheeks are flush and his breathing shallow.

"I didn't want to lose you too." Chris's voice breaks. "It would have been too much."

"You lost me anyway."

"There must be a good reason if you stayed, and he didn't."

"To forget what happened and pretend it never happened?" Chris falters at that.

"You were my best friend. Accepting your past is not denying it, Sky." Skyler flinches. "Listen to me. What do I need to do so you can forgive me?" Chris's eyes are pleading.

He's not himself. Why is Chris so desperate for forgiveness? A true friend wouldn't sacrifice the life of another. There shouldn't be a choice. Period.

"I don't know," Skyler mumbles, confused. "Just leave me alone."

"Fine." Chris gets up as a tear rolling down his cheek sparkles. He should have suffered when he sacrificed Allen. Not now.

"I won't bother you anymore," Chris says more firmly. "Skyler."

Skyler stares into the void while Chris's footsteps fade into nothing.

Long after Chris is gone, Skyler bids Allen farewell, promising to do everything in his power to help every person on this cursed Ark, including their mother, himself, even Chris.

And Emily. He misses her. For as long as he can remember, she can be hotheaded. As soon as he can sort out his own problems, he'll explain to her.

Feeling lighter, he pictures a map of the in between and its maze of corridors leading to the Archives of Humanity. Allen will protect him from the tragic end he met.

Allen will guide him.

18

EMILY

The ultimatum is over.

Emily picks up the pace, more determined than ever.

She has had time to think about everything that could happen, from taking hostages to a major central system failure. The Brotherhood is very capable of doing just that if what Ludo says is right. The inmates could never have escaped without the outage during the simulation. It could also explain how Clarissa Reed broke out.

Emily expected something more barbarous, like a riot, or an announcement about the Brotherhood taking command of the Ark. Not that Commander Hawk cannot manage the crisis, but the idea that they might collaborate with a rebel group is not a happy one.

But the funny thing is that nothing happened at all. No explosion, nor a word.

Mom used to talk about these disillusioned people broken from the inside. She said there wasn't much she could do for them, but that she had to try, anyway.

Emily is not her mother.

If their mission is to endanger the lives of thousands of

survivors from the greatest cataclysm, she will do whatever it takes to stop them. Not all causes are noble. How fair is it for those who do not share their delusion?

Their tactics remain unknown, but their silence can be the harbinger of something greater.

Emily wades into the familiar darkness of the prison and comes across a sealed door with no trace of Ludo. She waits under the few recessed lights that bathe the place in an electric blue, and paces back and forth, arms folded, while reviewing the various interrogation techniques she has learned over the months. Anything that might help her perform her makeshift plan.

Ludo takes about ten minutes to step out of Yasmina's office. He sports the faintest smile, noticeable only for the trained eye, a rip in his smooth-skinned face.

"How did you know?" he asks.

"You got what you wanted, didn't you?"

"I only managed to get my hands on the boy. He was in the lower hallway stripped from the surveillance cameras you mentioned. But the girl…" They should have been together, but now Reyes is actively working with the Brotherhood. If only Ludo had caught her instead of Milo… Yet, it would be surprising if Reyes left Milo here to rot, which means she'll try something soon.

"What did Yasmina say?" asks Emily.

"You know her. She gets on her high horse when it doesn't suit her, but when things go back to normal, she won't be grateful. She only thinks of herself."

"Did you tell her it was me?"

"No, I didn't." Emily sighs with relief. It's best not to arouse her suspicions. Yasmina could interrogate her to find out what she was doing at that free party. Sky and Chris could be in trouble because of this, and Emily wouldn't forgive herself.

Knowing that an inmate has as many chances of getting out of Yasmina's office as a fish to fly…

"That's what you wanted, isn't it?" asks Ludo, arching an eyebrow.

"Yes." He looks at her with an inquisitive look. He can tell that she knows more than she lets on.

"What do you want? I guess the information you gave me comes at a price."

"I'd like to talk to him," she replies, meeting his transparent gaze. "I need to check something."

"I negotiated to have a private session with him so he wouldn't try to run away again. I can cover for you this time, but it won't be long before she pays him a visit." He runs a hand through his fascinating ghostly white hair. He waves his wristband under the reader, which lights up instantly.

Without further ado, she walks towards the half-open door.

"Give me at least half an hour to enjoy him a little," Ludo coos. His sadistic needs are … quite special. Emily nods; the less she knows, the better.

Nothing has changed in the long corridor for the last two years. She was unyielding, though naive at the time, willing people to trust her, to entrust her with the most serious cases. She quickly moved from giving general therapy to interrogations where she had to manipulate relentlessly until she got what Yasmina wanted. Now that Emily has her trust, everything could go wrong if Yasmina found out why she came in after work hours.

The walls are bumped, and the metal dented in many places near Milo's cell. Only fists of steel could bend these walls or a heavy object at hand. She can almost hear Ludo's cries of rage when he realized they had tricked him after the breakout. He looks calm from the outside, but these people are the most dangerous. They are unpredictable, their limits fickle.

Milo is back in the cell where he was before his escape.

Emily checks the surveillance screen and sees Milo lying on his side in a poor condition. His purplish bruises glow a dark hue under the neon lights. Ludo has not been idle. What else could he want if he's already beaten him?

She goes in and Milo doesn't even look at her as he speaks in his tired, listless voice.

"She told me not to trust you and I was too stupid."

"You don't know me very well," says Emily defensively, quickly gauging him to see how she can pry the information she needs, a reflex learned through many therapies.

"I know enough to know that if I'm here, it's because of you." He takes a deep, labored breath as he turns sideways. "What do you want from me?"

"Tell me what is supposed to happen at the end of the Brotherhood's ultimatum." He laughs softly while holding his ribs, probably fractured.

"And why would I do that? So that you can harm them just like you did to me?"

"Reyes is still unharmed. I told them not to mind her, and that I had caught Dan, another member of the Brotherhood. I could change my mind and issue a special notice just for her."

"Leave her alone," he says with clenched teeth as he tries to get up.

"Easy. Tell me what they're doing."

"I don't know exactly. It depends." Emily quietly draws close to him and squats down to have a better look at him. Bruises stain his swollen cheeks, and they look at each other for a moment before she speaks again in a softer voice.

"What does it depend on?"

"Whether the Commander has decided to collaborate."

"I guess there must be a plan, regardless. A plan that ensures they get what they want."

"Yes, but..." He sighs in annoyance. He grunts as he

straightens up to better study her. "How can I make sure you will keep your word about Fiona?"

"You have to take my word for it."

"Too risky. If I find out you did anything to her, I'll spread the word that you're part of the Brotherhood."

"What?" she shouts, on her feet. "That's not even true."

"So what? If they have the slightest doubt, they'll check. You exposed yourself coming to our party. Everyone's name is recorded in a database and your name is in it." She remembers scanning her wristband and wishes she was six feet under. "Do you still want to know, or won't you dare take the risk?"

"I have nothing to lose. They won't believe you."

"One day, your stubbornness will cost you your life. Not that I mind, but if we have to lose everyone on this Ark before we go to the ground, it won't do any good."

"The last thing I want is to live with people like you. Like them." The bitter memory of the simulation haunts her. What if they're Mom's killers? Just the thought makes her feel sick to her stomach. It's worse than dying. She won't ignore their part in Mom's death; it will be her or them.

"I don't know if it has happened already, but—." He seems to search for his words, as if he can't believe what he is about to say. "—It should happen at the B-248. Tomorrow."

"What, exactly?" she retorts. What the hell does this code even mean?

"I told you I don't know. The information is carefully controlled, to avoid compromising everyone's release, to prevent someone like you from getting involved." Tomorrow. But when?

She gets up silently to go out, deep in her thoughts.

"The Brotherhood will save us all," he rasps. "If you care about your life and the lives of others, let them."

"That's entirely up to me." She opens the door and meets Ludo, leaning against the wall, impatient. Her heart skips a beat.

"You have company," she says, her voice faltering. Milo's face contorts when he sees Ludo taking Emily's place.

"Emily," Milo shouts with desperation. She doesn't hear what happens next because the door shuts with a thud. She feels numb. What has she done?

A tear rolls down her cheek.

"Emily?"

Her heart stops instantly. This voice has been fueling her nightmares since the simulation. Her vision blurs. No. No! Not now!

"Can you come to my office?" Emily swallows hard and swiftly dabs at her eyes. Smears of mascara coat her fingers. Damn it! She inhales, her nose still stuffy, then breathes out a hard blow before stepping into the half-open office.

Only the backlight is on, under the desk, and near the ceiling and floor. The screen Yasmina is tapping on lights up her face in a pristine white, the deep red of her hair a little darker than usual. She is wearing a tight-fitting navy-blue suit that hugs her ample curves. It's hard not to be dazzled; her aura is as rich as Chris's, golden intertwined tendrils.

"Emily?" asks the Chief Warden, interrupting her frantic drumming. "Sit." She obeys, while controlling the tremor in her hand. She is in no condition to handle her.

Yasmina feeds off the silence that settles between them to scrutinize her, her body posture upright. She looks like she is looking for something.

"How are you?" Yasmina meows, her voice as velvety as a sickly creamed coffee. "I'm worried about you."

"As well as I can be these days." Emily's voice is less assertive than usual. *Pull yourself together, for God's sake.*

Yasmina puts her palms on her desk, the ghost of a smile stretching her cheeks.

"There is no denying that the Brotherhood has caused an unprecedented crisis. However, there is no reason to worry. Commander Hawk has the situation under control. I am surprised that your father did not update you." What does she know about her father? She must know that he works for the Paragon, even though they have never spoken openly about it. Is he in danger? Has she unwittingly gotten him into trouble?

Yasmina's aura has disappeared. The glow of her eyes is indecipherable.

"Emily?" She swallows with difficulty. What's wrong with her? "What's the matter?"

She must look like a lunatic. Oh my God. Emily's clutching the armrests of her chair lest she sink through the floor.

She's not supposed to be in the prison. Yasmina knows that. She's a goner.

"Nothing," Emily says. "Nothing."

"Emily." Yasmina pronounces her name as if she owned it. She rolls it on her tongue in all the possible directions, to test it, to feel the limits that define it. Possessing every syllable, every sound, every expulsion of air, means absolute control. Emily has already lost.

Her name no longer belongs to herself.

"How is your work with prisoner 591 going?" Yasmina purrs after a beat. Milo's desperate cry of despair strains her throat, suffocates her even. She wants to scream.

"He started talking. Ludo is taking care of him."

"And what did he say?" Yasmina leans forward with cusped hands, her gaze hungry.

"B-248."

"Interesting," she says with a barely perceptible smirk. "Commander Hawk will be delighted."

"What does it mean? The code."

"It's not for us to know, Emily," Yasmina replies slowly, taking on a motherly air. "There are people who keep us safe. And we take care of their safety."

Her insides squeeze. If by safety she means locking Milo up and letting Ludo play with him... Terrifying images of horror creep into her mind.

Is this really what her work is all about? Destroying lives to ensure the safety of others?

"It's a good thing you helped Ludo find him," Yasmina adds in a lighter tone, as if unburdened. "We don't track down a Maverick every day, let alone one who escaped only a few days ago." Ludo, that bastard! He told her.

Yasmina leans forward. "Is there something you want to tell me?"

"Not right now," swallows Emily, her neck stiff, so stiff that she swears she will paralyze. "I'll make a report."

Her boss is stone-faced and waits a few seconds to recline in her chair.

"Don't forget to take over once Ludo is finished. It will be the perfect opportunity. When all hope has left them, they open up more easily." A sadistic glint flashes through her eyes.

Emily nods. She gets up, her legs wobbly, and tries hard not to run.

"Oh! Emily," meows Yasmina, who freezes her in her silent run. "Remember, I don't like liars."

IT IS DARK, as dark as it can be on a ship that follows the cycles of the sun on the surface. The dozens of candles glowing in the darkness offer unexpected comfort in the most unlikely place, the very antithesis of her beliefs.

Since Mom died, Emily has never set foot in the sanctuary,

but here she is now. Mom's fine inscription should be nearby. There she sees it, amidst golden letters. Tyna Bates.

Emily squats on the cushion to pray, and the tears flow freely. It's a good thing no one is here to see her in this sorry state.

But what has she become?

Milo. His face tense with terror. His pleading voice.

Ludo. His smug expression. The envy in his eyes.

Yasmina. Her feline slyness. Her silent threat.

It's all too much. Is Emily the one responsible for all this evil?

She didn't help Milo. She didn't stop Ludo. She did not report Yasmina. If Commander Hawk knew, he wouldn't accept these *methods*.

Why didn't she figure out what kind of trouble she was in before? This is no simple mess; It's a whole new level of mess.

A sob escapes from her throat.

She accepted all this without saying anything, without doing anything, a Bates, a traitor to humanity.

She gasps for air, drowning in her tears until her body is empty of all emotion.

Anesthetized.

When she finally feels a burning pain in her knees, Emily stands up, her legs wobbling. She waves her wristband in front of a candle that comes to life and glows a faint purple. Her chin trembles.

A crackling sound. Who is there?

Emily turns around sharply.

"I didn't want to disturb you," the girl with the prayer cards says carefully.

"What are you doing here?" says Emily in a stiff voice.

"I could ask you the same thing." Violet. The last person that she wants to see. Did she hear Emily crying, or worse, see her?

Emily quickly wipes her cheeks and sniffs. Now Violet must have her doubts.

"But I won't," Violet adds in a softer voice.

"I think I'd better go." Emily hurries towards the exit.

"Your mother was a remarkable woman." Emily slows her pace despite herself. "She left a deep impression on our community. Her unwavering determination and her belief that there is good in all of us is inspiring. Grandma used to tell us about it all the time when we were younger—that we need to will the gem buried deep within ourselves to clean it, polish it, make it shine with all our love and good will."

That metaphor was one Mom used all the time when she and Gabrielle were kids. Emily shifts, her irritation melting like sugar on her tongue.

"Mom never told me about it," she says with a quaver in her voice. "Your community. Not like this." Violet gives her a friendly smile.

"Everyone knew her. In a good way."

"If she was so good, why was she condemned?" Emily's painful memories are about to rise.

"When you stray from the light for too long, it is even more difficult to return. Our Ark has been submerged for generations. People have lost their way." Is this a way to justify their carelessness, their thirst for blood? Emily doesn't know what to think anymore.

"I'm so sorry, Emily," adds Violet, giving her a serious look. "No one should have to go through this." Her throat knots dangerously. Not again.

Emily casts her eyes down.

"But we all make mistakes," the priestess continues. Emily immediately thinks of Milo, violently, as if someone wanted to brand his face in her mind forever. She gave him up, and not just to anyone. *To Ludo.* She holds back a sob. Milo doesn't deserve this; he protected her from Dan, stood up for her against Reyes, and never resented her for being his girlfriend's persecutor.

Justice.

She snorts inwardly. Her justice is worthless. What would Mom say if she knew?

"But there's always tomorrow," Violet says in a more cheerful voice. "To make a difference." What if this crisis with the Brotherhood marked the end? There would be no tomorrow, no chance.

"Every moment counts," Emily lets out in a strangled voice.

"Yes. More than you can imagine." Every moment. Yes.

The same creaking sound from earlier echoes again. It's coming from that wicker basket Violet is holding, covered up with flowery fabric. Violet seems to understand her silent question because she says, "Oh! I brought some cupcakes. Would you like some?"

"No, no, it's okay." Her stomach is rumbling.

"I cooked them myself," she says proudly. "I use Grandma's kitchen occasionally. I even have tea in the back." Violet doesn't give her time to turn down the offer, and she rushes into the back room, to the right of the altar by the holy water basins.

Why not? There is nothing left to eat in their cabin anyway since they haven't restocked after the Inspection. Emily follows her, drained.

A smell of incense welcomes her, some herbs, though she can't tell which ones. Violet is busy boiling water, taking out small clinking plates and teacups. She sets everything on a wobbly table in front of which Emily sits, enjoying the warm silence while the water heats. Violet clears up some space on the table cluttered with old photos, and Emily shuts her eyes.

Once the tea is ready, a steaming cup dampens her face and a somewhat scorched cake with a white cream drizzle on top makes her mouth water. She takes a bite and sighs with relief. Before she knows it, she helps herself to another cupcake from the basket beside the table leg. Violet watches her while sipping tea.

Her second cupcake wolfed down, Violet says, "Some trials are more trying than others, but there is nothing the Creator did not design."

Emily fiddles with her warm mug. She's been collecting those trials since she was twelve. If only the Creator were the answer to her questions. But she is not a believer. He wouldn't want to waste his time with her, anyway.

"Violet, I…" The priestess frowns and Emily realizes her mistake. "Sorry, I mean, Dinah."

"Strange that you call me Violet. Your mother called me that too when we first met." Another connection to Mom. How could Mom have hidden her relationships with the people of the sanctuary?

"You can call me Violet, you know. I don't mind. I'm sure Grandma wouldn't have minded naming me after such a beautiful flower."

"You often talk about your grandmother. Your parents—"

"Carried off by the disease. Grandma raised us." Violet knows what losing a loved one means. Suddenly, her pretty girl's face looks different: more mature, less naive, less … religious.

Dozens of large frames are leaning against the wall. Paintings. They strangely remind her of those at *La Orilla*. "Do you paint?"

"I don't. My brother does."

"How long has it been?"

"As long as I can remember. He likes to reproduce certain images he finds in the Archives. Grandma would prefer that he paint only biblical scenes, but he just does whatever he likes."

On closer inspection, some of these paintings are not bad at all and should replace those at *La Orilla*. Violet's brother has a fascination for the founders, which are the subjects in most of his paintings. He also likes flowers, some she saw in the Gardens of Humankind. Portraits have this mysterious appeal, but how interesting it is to see other people bringing out the hidden beauty of entirely different subjects.

Keenly aware that she hasn't touched her tea yet, Emily takes a sip. The lingering sweet aftertaste piques her curiosity.

"This tea is good. I've never tasted anything like this in the dining hall."

"Oh, there isn't. Mr. Torres, one of our most fervent members, supplies us. May God save his soul."

"Is he not well?"

"He has been fighting this strange illness that keeps him from coming to pray. I insist on visiting him regularly. His family has long supported the sanctuary through generations. It is the least I can do." She pauses for a moment, thinking. "Sometimes I wonder what it will take to appease the Creator's anger."

She picks herself up, as if caught in the act. "I shouldn't question the Creator's Design. Forgive me, Emily. Don't tell my brother or Grandma, or else they'll make me recite the sermon for a week." Violet giggles and they exchange a knowing smile.

"It's getting late," Emily says as she slides her squeaky chair back. "Thank you for the tea and the cakes."

"May the Creator's ways enlighten you."

WHEN SHE GETS into the family cabin, her father is snoring, and her sister is fast asleep. Emily slips into her little bed in the corner of the bedroom they all share. She can't remember the last time she felt so drained.

For some reason, her eyes won't shut, so she gets up quietly and crawls to get her purse buried under the mattress. She rifles around and prays to find what she is looking for. Her mascara, her broken mirror … there.

Curious, she uses the computer screen to light up the prayer of redemption that Violet slipped into her purse that night at La Orilla.

Each person is a window to another world.

Emily repeats the phrase to herself, over and over again, until sleep drives her to bed. She falls asleep with the feeling that this is only the beginning.

19

SKYLER

Skyler presses on to Med Bay, while he runs a distracted hand through his messy hair. Two hours of sleep is not much. His foray into the in between lasted longer than he thought.

The night air reeks of putrefaction, so much that he wonders if he is still dreaming. Before reaching the corner of the corridor that leads to Med Bay, panicked voices shake him out of his daze. He picks up the pace.

Dozens of parents line up, holding the lifeless bodies of their children. Anxiety grips his chest. Not only children, but adults too. Damn it!

Dr. Nazar towers over the chaos and beckons Skyler to follow him as soon as their eyes cross. They rush into an empty office where Mira and Leander are waiting. The small room looks eerily similar to the one in Ivanka Torres's video: The furniture layout is identical, including the rust marks that run from the ceiling and drip down the walls.

Despite the fluorescent light, Dr. Nazar's tanned complexion glows.

"Skyler," he says. "Are the memory spheres ready?"

"Well, some problems persist and—"

"But the data is stored?"

"The engineer working on the project confirmed they are, though temporarily inaccessible. We must make some modifications to our decoders."

"There is no room for error," insists the doctor, frowning. "I have families here with their dead who want their memory spheres."

"Is there nothing we can do to save them?" asks Skyler, who feels the heat burning his face.

Mira and Leander listen to the exchange quietly lest they garner unwanted attention. Dr. Nazar and Skyler have had several run-ins over the project in the past, which Dr. Nazar felt was too risky. But now that they've got their finger in the pie…

"We can't save them anymore," Dr. Nazar adds firmly. "But we can offer moral support for their loved ones. With the recent events, we will end up with problems that will put us all in danger if we don't react effectively. People in psychological distress are capable of horrible things." He weighs his words enough to make Skyler shudder at the thought of what might happen.

"Even if we wanted to, we don't have enough beds," Mira chimes in, glancing knowingly at Skyler.

"What do you propose, Mira Torres, daughter of Horacio?" Dr. Nazar is a little too concerned about the reputation of Mira's family, which has solved several major problems on the Ark over the generations. How fair is that?

"I drew up a summary list of the key characteristics of the victims," she answers in her analytical tone as she hands over her tablet with both hands.

She must have done a good job. Mira spends her days either in Med Bay or the lab so much that she could be born in a test tube. The pressure to excel at science in her family has always been too great. Although she keeps her private life to herself, Leander slipped some details about it, since he spends time with her in the lab after work. Mira must have downloaded all the patients' details from the official registry they have access to and selected key characteristics to better compare them: age, occupation, background. Brilliant.

"What do you think?" asks the doctor, who looks up from the tablet. Mira is unfazed by his curt tone. She smooths out a red curl, deep in thought.

"There are two options. Either we prioritize those who have vital knowledge and a key role on the Ark, though that precludes children. The parents definitely won't like it. Or we do as we would for normal cases: first come, first served." Skyler winces at that.

Although revolutionary, the memory spheres are not equally valuable to everyone. On one hand, upon the recommendation of a doctor, they can help bereaved families cope with their loss. On the other hand, the spheres preserve knowledge, memories, and experiences to inspire future generations so that history can be told. Those are two very different goals.

Neither option is satisfactory. There must be a better way.

Skyler's indecision translates into a heavy silence, and Leander speaks up. "We could also do a quick neurological analysis."

Leander has their attention and continues, acutely aware of their mentor's expectations.

"We would figure out the extent of the damage and then prioritize those in better condition to guarantee the success of the procedure."

Interesting.

Leander wrings his hands nervously as he waits for the verdict.

"How long does a scan take?" Dr. Nazar muses.

"A minimum of fifteen minutes per patient is required," Mira replies apologetically.

"A few of them are brain-dead, but they are still being diagnosed. If that is the case, then they must have died only thirty to forty-five minutes ago," he says under his breath, his face stern.

The window of opportunity is still open. One hour, at most, to save as many as possible. Skyler seizes his chance.

"What if we converted the regular beds into two separate stations? One for the spheres and one for the scans. We don't need detailed scans, so we could use our older scanners that are still functional, but not as sophisticated." Dr. Nazar's quirky sideways smile throws Skyler off every time.

"It could be done."

"How are we going to handle the sphere stations?" asks Mira, puzzled. "We only have one, or two if we add the portable machine."

"Skyler should have an answer for that, right? They are your spheres after all." The attention is back on him, his cheeks burning.

Fortunately, he already thought about it. Since Allen's death, Skyler has imagined every possible way to use the memory spheres, as he tirelessly combed through the Archives. He made unexpected friendships with Mrs. Farrell, who recently offered him the support from the Sanctuary to make the spheres available to believers and during funeral services.

This is just a theory, but the machines' capability is higher than that required for a single transfer. By splitting the energy flow into two independent circuits, it would be more efficient.

He shares his thoughts with anticipation and, much to his surprise, his mentor lets go of his usual skepticism and gives his approval.

"Show Mira and Leander how to do it. There is not a second to lose."

Dr. Nazar even pats Skyler on the shoulder when he leaves the office.

SKYLER REPEATS the procedure for more than an hour until the transfer fails. The last two spheres are incomplete since brain death is irreversible; the patients' synapses have deactivated like old unusable hard drives.

Before Skyler gives in to his frustration, Mira says, "We did our best. We preserved twenty-three people out of sixty which is twice as many as we could have saved under normal circumstances."

The lifeless bodies are lined up further away as the sobs of the grieving families reach Skyler and Mira. The shock will be harder on the families who won't have a sphere, but hopefully they won't hold a grudge against them.

Leander comes in, looking serious, and the persistent crying fades into the background.

"I noticed something strange," Leander says while showing the scans on his tablet. "Doesn't that remind you of something?"

The Syndrome.

"We've never seen such a violent and sudden reaction," replies Skyler. "What changed? A mutation of the disease?"

"Possibly," Mira replies thoughtfully. "Hard to say, but the marker is very similar."

"How could this happen now for so many people?"

"Unless they were infected at the same time, with the same strain. However, I found nothing in their records that would point to some predisposition to the disease."

A hunch has been gnawing at Skyler for a while, but he doesn't want to be right. With everything Tessa said about the dissension among the Paragon, and the Brotherhood acting behind closed curtains, there could be a far more sinister explanation.

"Or maybe there was human intervention," Skyler says with disgust.

"Why would anyone do that?" Leander roars. "To children?"

"Mira, did you say they shared nothing in common?"

"Yes. Their ages and backgrounds are all different." Mira and Leander stare at Skyler. He must check something before sharing his budding hypothesis.

Meanwhile, the intercom drowns them in static. The Commander?

"Dear Archeans, we mourn our dead tonight," buzzes a familiar male voice.

It is not the Commander. Everyone in Med Bay stiffens, hushed, their eyes fixed on the ceiling as if witnessing a visitation.

"The Brotherhood gave an ultimatum to our leaders, who refused to respond. They would rather hunt us down and scare you into thinking that we are responsible for these deaths, but we are not. *They* are the ones to blame. Had they told the truth from the beginning, this carnage could have been avoided. Stepping down is the only fair solution for our future. This is our final warning. Join our cause and plan a return to the ground. Now."

Static drowns out the man's voice as panicked whispers and cries of anger spreads like wildfire.

"This is Commander Kevin Hawk." The authoritative voice blares out of the intercom. "I will never let the Archeans down. On my life. The Inspection is reinstated until further notice. No exceptions. You have thirty minutes before the doors shut. The Paragon will be deployed to ensure order and your safety."

Panic and chaos spread as the throng of mourning families rush out haphazardly. Some refuse to leave behind their loved ones who have just passed away.

"Can you secure the spheres?" Skyler shouts to Mira and Leander over the din.

"What are you going to do?" replies Mira, worried.

"I must check my theory before the Inspection." She nods silently.

"Be careful."

———

THE PARAGON FLOOR is swarming with guards preparing for the Inspection, and Skyler must hide several times to avoid being turned away before he can get the answers he needs.

Tessa knows more about the Syndrome than she lets on.

Skyler is near the entrance to the Paragon's headquarters and, as he suspected, there is no direct way to get in without getting caught.

Allen showed him a map of the Ark's maintenance routes, the in betweens, which are just about everywhere: a secret network. All Skyler has to do is to find the right one. A place like the Paragon's headquarters must have a tangle of passages as complex as in the Gardens.

Skyler feels the wall next to the main corridor. Usually, each passage is identified by a number. The problem is that if it hasn't been used before, it might be obstructed. Allen had cleared up the one in the Gardens, but he never mentioned specifically what other exits he might have used in the past or those that others might have found already. The Ark's maintenance teams may use some of them regularly, though Skyler and his brother never knew for certain.

The number 71 tells him he is on a wall connected to the network.

When he is almost at the end of the corridor that leads away from the headquarters, the second to last tile moves. His heart misses a beat. He looks around before stepping out, then securely puts the tile back to make sure no light filters in.

The hum of electricity pulses while it stinks of heated plastic. Skyler walks along the tube fixed on the ground until he sees an arrow pointing to the right. Whoever was here knew where to go. Probably.

As his mouth feels like it's filled with dust, a large X points to the exit tile. He slides it open and ends up in an empty locker room with the panels still ajar. He spots an opening and slips through, heart pounding. One false move and it's over.

In the hallway, he second-guesses himself for coming all the way here. It's one thing to infiltrate the Paragon's headquarters, but another to locate Tessa. She never mentioned where her cabin was.

Once the way is clear, Skyler heads for the staircase adorned with a symbol that looks like a bunk bed. As he starts climbing, someone calls him out. He flinches and can't decide whether he should run.

"What are you doing here?" Is this Tessa?

"I did what you asked," he says as he recovers his voice when he glimpses one of her braids. "I transferred the research documents to the address you gave me. What went wrong?"

Tessa pulls him back down in the opposite direction.

"Follow me," she whispers, tense.

"Why all these deaths?"

"We couldn't stop it." She cuffs him with a magnetic snap that baffles him. "Don't say anything. Makes it easier." Her glower is enough to talk him down as they walk into a hallway teeming with groups of two or four agents, too busy to spare them a glance.

"I'll walk you to your cabin, so you don't get in trouble," she says, her breath catching. "You'll be safer if you stay there."

"Tell me the Paragon is not conducting experiments on the Archeans."

"What are you talking about?"

"Sixty died of the Syndrome at the same time." Skyler forces her to stop and look him straight in the eye. "It's no coincidence."

"The Syndrome is a complex disease." She tightens her grip.

"Why does the Paragon know more than us at Med Bay? Do we have to stand by and watch these people die? Tell me what we're dealing with. Otherwise, I can't help."

"Keep it down." She halts just before bumping into a group of agents turning around the corner. An impressive Paragon guard sporting a star-shaped badge blocks the headquarters' exit.

"Is there a problem, Tessa?" he asks, hands clasped behind him.

His uniform shows his muscles as he reaches for a long weapon hung on his back: a weapon capable of neutralizing anyone and reserved for the highest ranks of the Paragon. Tessa instinctively clutches the holster of her pistol.

"No, everything is fine. This civilian looked suspicious, so I questioned him to see if he was conspiring with the enemy. His record and answers matched."

"Good. Since you'll be in the residential area, wait for Agent Miles. He should be there in seventeen minutes. You guys will team up for the Inspection."

"Shouldn't it be Agent Valdez?"

"Last-minute change. General Kay has decided to break from protocol. If the Paragon has a mole, the rebels won't see this one coming."

"I see." The guard nods in agreement, then stands out of the way. As they exit the bowels of headquarters, Skyler could swear the guard stared at them the whole way.

"So?" Skyler says once they're out of earshot. "I need answers."

"I warned you about those experiments when we first met." She walks at a steady pace. The deployment of Paragon agents aside, the ship's hallways sound hollow.

"What kind of experiments?"

"Anything to crack the perverse effects of the disease even if that means using subjects without their consent. Most of them don't make it out alive, anyway."

"The Paragon slaughters them." From what Chris said back

when they were best friends, Duke is corrupt, but *this* is beyond belief.

"Duke Kay. We must stop him. Now," Skyler presses. "We're going back to headquarters."

"Are you mad?"

"We can't let him!" What is the point of treating these people if they die the next day?

"You've done all you can for now," Tessa says to calm him down. "The Brotherhood is fighting against this, too, you know. We've been fighting the Paragon from within for a while now. This is bigger than you think."

"You mean I have to wait nicely at Med Bay until the bodies come by the dozen?"

"It will be over soon." They are caught up in a power play and he understands too little, just as he thought.

A countdown on the screens warns them that the Inspection will start in less than fifteen minutes.

"Next time you want to contact me, use this. I'll come find you." Tessa un-cuffs him and hands over a tracer barely bigger than his thumb. At the touch of his fingerprint, it buzzes up. Skyler is about to thank her, but she is already gone.

20

SKYLER

"SKYLER!" SLIGHTLY OLDER, THE TALL MAN WEARING A VEST HAS this serious, almost feisty look that the Archives' attendants give off. "You take care of my grandmother, Elaine Farrell, right? I'm Philip."

"What's going on?" Skyler replies as he was about to open the door of his cabin. Philip catches his breath, his face flush. His fingers are smeared with paint, and a few droplets are in the wrinkles on his forehead. He looks worried.

"Come see her. She doesn't have much time left." Skyler doesn't ask questions and follows him. The countdown ticks by as he races down the hall to the elevators: eleven minutes. It's going to be tight. He doesn't even have his equipment to make the transfer.

Mrs. Farrell's grandson frantically presses the call button of the elevator.

"They blocked the elevators for the Inspection," Skyler says. "Anyway, I must stop by Med Bay first."

"I'll go with you."

They run down the stairs as if their lives depended on it. Elaine... How did her health worsen so quickly? She was in great shape during her last examination. What could have happened in the meantime?

Philip waits at the entrance of the emptied Medical Bay while Skyler rushes to the spheres' cabinet. He grabs one of them and slips it into a cushioned box. After everything that's happened, it's a miracle there are some left. He takes along the portable transfer machine that no one put away, and the analyzer for a routine examination. The origin of Elaine's impending death is bizarre. Despite her illness, she should have lived for several months, years even.

From the entryway, Philip gazes at the box, mesmerized. Skyler asks for his help to carry it.

"We must hurry, or we won't be able to reach her in time," Skyler urges him. Philip nods and they break into a jog to the nearest stairwell, then climb the stairs two at a time. Eight floors up, the looping announcement reminds them to shut themselves in their cabins. Too late for that now.

With ringing ears, Skyler walks quickly to Mrs. Farrell's cabin while Philip struggles to keep up the pace. How far can this be?

Inside, the air is heavy under the dim lights, saturated with the same unpleasant smell as in Med Bay, as if death had seeped through the air ducts ready to smother its next victim. Skyler closes the bathroom door on the way and glimpses Mrs. Farrell lying in an awkward position. She moans as he shifts her arms and legs so she can breathe better.

"Philip… bring… Skyler. Your sister?" She coughs.

"I couldn't find her," replies Philip, who kneels and takes her hand. Skyler sets up the equipment on the nightstand while trying to figure out who they are talking about and then it hits him. Philip is Tessa's brother.

"She must have gone to the sanctuary to pray for your recovery," adds Philip apologetically.

"I was with her just before you found me," says Skyler, uneasy. "Had I known—"

"Really? I'll bring her back." Skyler puts a hand on his shoulder to stop him. This is when a family needs to come together to ease the grief over the loss of their loved one.

"It's too late now," says Skyler, who crosses Philip's bewildered look. "You'll have to break the news to her yourself. But with the sphere, you'll be able to live through the good times with Elaine again."

Philip's mouth twitches, a telltale sign of his conflicting emotions.

"The most important thing is that you are here to preserve her memories," Philip finally says, slumping into a chair beside the bed.

"It's the right thing to do. Elaine needs you." Philip turns to his grandmother, whose breathing is labored. Skyler connects the equipment to a power source while an eerie silence settles.

"How did this happen?" asks Skyler as he takes her vital signs with two electrodes.

"I came to check on her as usual, but she wasn't responding. I went in and found her moaning and coughing on the bathroom floor."

"Was there any blood?"

"Not that I noticed, no."

Her nasty leg bruise is still there, but it doesn't seem to have gotten any worse. As for her head … blood is clotting through her white hair. She must have fainted and fallen, which can often result in death among the elderly.

"Breathing …," she gasps. "Why … them … now?" Mrs. Farrell blinks with difficulty, in sheer pain.

"Let's see what's wrong," Skyler says with a sympathetic smile. He connects the analyzer to Mrs. Farrell's arm using a wristband, and the screen shows abnormal readings. Her nervous system is crashing as if it could no longer self-regulate.

Her fall might have precipitated the latent symptoms of her dementia. There might even be cerebral hemorrhaging.

"Is there any hope?" asks Philip eagerly.

"I'm sorry." The door clicks. The next few hours will be trying. Philip's distraught eyes meet his.

Skyler leaves the analyzer connected, which will give the signal to start the transfer.

"I can't … believe … that they would … dare," continues Mrs. Farrell, half-conscious. Is she lucid? It's hard to tell from the way her head sways from left to right.

Skyler leaves Mrs. Farrell alone with her grandson for her last moments. Her cabin is huge, and he finds a quieter place near the porthole overlooking the ocean. The glass under his palm is icy and numbs his fingertips, but he doesn't take his hand away.

This artificial layer is the only thing that separates them from the outside world, and yet it holds together. Losing a loved one as the Farrells will experience will be difficult, but not impossible to overcome.

Allen … after all these years, he must be all right wherever he is now. He's not coming back, though. There will never be a memory sphere of him to comfort Skyler in his lowest moments. This is a fact he must accept. Clinging to his own imperfect memories of an imperfect past they shared. Unspoken words… Skyler longed to go through these hardships with Allen by his side, to have someone in his family that he can fully trust, who understands what it's like to be born a Goldberg, to deal with their parents. Allen and Skyler would each have had children and in the distant future perhaps, built a house on the ground with their own new families who could share, cherish, and grow together. Dreams that will remain dreams, nestled in his mind, the only place where he is safe, despite the woes that afflict the Ark. At least he can visit this dream whenever he wants, and no one can ever take that away from him.

Mrs. Farrell's last exhale is distressingly deep. Skyler can almost feel her breath in his ear, although he is not in the same room.

The continuous beeping from the analyzer confirms that Elaine Farrell is no more.

Skyler walks in to check on her and a presence wraps around him, like the warm bedsheets he snuggles in at night, as if Elaine was not quite gone. He rubs his eyes as he tells Philip how to set the sphere onto the ring of the portable device. Bands showing the electrical variations of the brain now in latent mode are displayed: the window of opportunity. Skyler calibrates the magnetic pulse by selecting an optimal frequency range to synchronize the sphere to the brain signature and then activates the transfer.

Yellow filaments with a shade of orange crowd the sphere, eerily similar to the birth of a small sun. Sparks flash one after another to take on the shape of an expanding solar cloud, an electrical network mimicking the neurological connections in their pure state, but on a larger scale.

Skyler and Philip keep silent as Mrs. Farrell's existence is crystallized into the sphere.

Philip does not cry, but his stare is blank. Skyler didn't cry when Allen died either. Only rage blinded him, and Chris was there to answer it, followed by guilt that spread until it poisoned him. Now it's different. There are new opportunities to ease other people's suffering. What he couldn't do for Allen, perhaps he can do for the Archeans.

"Thank you for Grandma," says Philip, breaking the lethargy that had set in. "She really wanted to see you in her last moments. She couldn't stop talking about it."

Skyler has a sad smile. He could not prevent the inevitable.

"I'm sorry about your sister," says Skyler. "Sooner and—"

"You don't have to. My sister prayed so hard for Grandma to live longer." The image of Tessa kneeling in the sanctuary forces itself into his mind. What would his childhood have been like if he had grown up in a family so different from the Goldbergs?

"Treasure your grandmother's memory sphere."

"Count on me. I will store the sphere in the Archives and then hold a ceremony at the sanctuary as she always wanted as soon as the Inspection is lifted." Silence hangs with the thundering of boots outside the cabin door. Will the Brotherhood succeed in their plan? Does Philip know his sister supports a resistance group within the Paragon?

What if he is part of it, too? Maybe Skyler should ask him.

No. Philip would have known where Tessa was or what she was doing. Sharing the same blood does not mean sharing the same opinions or allegiances. Allen had opinions Skyler did not support. In fact, they too often argued over this.

"What do we do now?" asks Philip. Skyler sighs, then glances at the door.

"We wait."

21

EMILY

When she got to the B-248, she was too late.

Without Chris's help, she would never have been able to find this lonesome place: the waste disposal dock. Chris suspected that Milo's information referred to the Ark's coding system, which only shows on old maps found in the Archives. The research stole her invaluable time. It *had* seemed like a lure, though. What could such a place hide?

How naive of her.

There were dozens of people, not rebels, but Archeans, tied up by their feet, heads dangling above a gigantic basin used to clean the recovered waste from the ocean. A deadly silence hung over them as they looked sedated, just like in the prison, to control uncooperative inmates. But these people had not been convicted. They were Archeans, and innocents like Mom.

Suddenly, the cables they were attached to unwound; they dropped headfirst into the pool. Helmeted Paragon agents watched them drown. Some, tablet in hand, were manically tapping away, but no one took exception to the massacre taking place before their eyes. More armed Paragon agents were lined up to ensure that what looked like an experiment went smoothly.

Emily tried to see if she knew anyone but couldn't make out any faces in the crowd. Who were the real culprits?

The leader of the Brotherhood, Neal, who was in the simulation: It had to be him. How ironic that he wasn't even there. Such a coward, making others do his dirty work. Why did Milo want her to witness this? Milo didn't seem like the type of guy who would support this kind of massacre. If it wasn't the Brotherhood, then who?

She fled as quickly as possible, her mind branded with the twisted faces of the Archeans, drugged, terrified. It was a nightmare come true. She had no choice but to get out, or else she would have been in that pool next.

They were murderers.

Sky told her about the unusual death toll he dealt with last night. He also confided his doubts to her, but since the events at the B-248, anything goes.

What if the deaths Sky spoke of were related somehow? She feels nauseous just thinking about it. How could someone sacrifice his own people?

EMILY OUGHT to be babysitting Gabrielle, but it might be the other way around. Since Emily sat on the floor of the cabin's corner, her body refuses to move. The faces from earlier are playing on a loop in her mind. How long has it been since she returned? She couldn't say.

There must be some logical explanation.

Her eyes are wet, and she presses her fingers against her temples to relieve the tension that threatens to explode into a migraine. If only the events of the last few days could miraculously disappear from her memory.

It's too late. Her brain constricts under the ruthless light of the cabin.

"Turn off the lights," she croaks. Gabrielle complies without flinching, even if Emily's words sounded like an order.

The room plunges into darkness with a hush. Gabrielle's breathing is slow and regular, her head leaning against Emily's shoulder.

Do they know? The Paragon? Dad? A new Inspection started shortly after. Could it be...?

Eyes and cheeks burning, Emily loops a protective arm around her sister. What if Gabrielle had been in that pool? Emily prays that all those lost souls find rest.

But most importantly, she prays that her family will be strong enough.

A CLINKING sound snaps her out of her nightmares.

How long has she been asleep? A message on their screen is flashing, "The Inspection is over."

Did they stop the Brotherhood? She should feel relieved that it's over, but she can't shake off the unease.

A knock, and Gabrielle flies to open the door. Emily's legs are still weak and sleeping when she rises to greet their unexpected visitor, and she must sit at the table to come around. The light from the hallway tears through the darkness of the cabin and she squints at the figure standing.

Chris's face is somber. She can't decide whether it's because of the lighting.

"Hey, what's wrong?" he asks as he crouches down, worry in his voice. He lays a hand on her shoulder and strokes her gently.

"It's nothing," she replies, looking away. "A migraine." He probably doesn't believe her, but he doesn't show it.

"Come with me. There is something I want to show you," he says, holding out his hand.

"I can't leave Gabrielle alone." Emily glances at her sister on the bed with her book open.

Gabrielle looks so peaceful, oblivious to the dangers on the Ark, engrossed in her beloved stories of valiant knights who will never exist to keep her company while Emily worries herself sick. Emily wishes she could believe those stories, too.

"She's big enough now," Chris argues. "Aren't you, my princess?"

"I can take care of the castle while my queen is away," Gabrielle says, totally composed, without looking away from her book.

Emily smiles, the tension in her muscles easing a little.

"Can I count on you, my valiant knight, to protect her even if your life depends on it?"

"On my life, I swear it," he answers, smiling.

"Chris," whispers Emily. "It's not that simple."

"I helped you out last time and then there was the code. Do me the favor. Come on." Chris came to her rescue several times without her ever thanking him. If this can make him happy…

Though he offers his hand, she gets up by herself. Her moment of weakness is over.

"Can I trust you, Gabrielle?" asks Emily. "Don't come out until Daddy comes back. Don't open the door to anyone." Her sister nods in agreement and Emily reluctantly kisses her on the head.

"Are you going to tell me where you're taking me?"

"Surprise," Chris says with a hint of mystery as he shuts the door.

"I don't like surprises." He arches an eyebrow, and she rolls her eyes.

Some Paragon guards are lurking around but don't pay much attention to them. This is one of the perks of being accompanied by Chris, now one of the crew members. There aren't any civilians around, but the atmosphere is heavy. What happened during the Inspection? What about Dad?

Her head pulses as she walks, her headache nagging at her. She closes her eyes for a second and runs into Chris, who stopped dead in his tracks.

"What is it?" she whispers as he frowns at a group of soldiers walking by.

"Don't you think it's weird?"

"Besides the soldiers patrolling?"

"The Inspection is over now that the Brotherhood was arrested."

"Really?" Emily tries to hide her sudden interest, but this may be her chance to get even with Neal. "Where is the Brotherhood now?"

"I can't tell you. Let's hurry." They stop in front of a nondescript wall, and Chris makes an arcing motion with his wristband. The wall retracts as it becomes a door, and Chris steps inside. Emily hates not knowing where they are. Since B-248, her ignorance about her own home staggers her.

What is the Ark exactly?

They enter a circular hallway with a reinforced door, an exaggerated version of the prison's heavy door. Chris motions for her to wait and he stands on a circle drawn on the floor. Almost instantly, a full biometric analysis identifies him, then the circular door corks open as it depressurizes.

"Where the hell you are taking me?" she asks, anxiety creeping up.

"I want to introduce you to someone."

"Who is it?"

"You'll see. She has heard a lot about you." Emily hesitates and Chris slows down. "You trust me, don't you?"

"It's not you, it's just—"

"You didn't tell me what you saw in the B-248," he cuts her

off. "Or where you got that information from. I don't want to force you to tell me what happened, but if it affects our relationship, I need to know."

"Maybe I'll tell you one day, but not now. I can't. It has nothing to do with you."

He sighs, but Emily won't go through that again. She has to refocus first, let her wound heal to regain just enough strength to keep going.

"All right. Are you coming?" She follows him and shudders when the door repressurizes behind.

"Why is there a door like this here?"

"We are in the command area. In the event of a fatal break in the primary structure of the Ark, this section is detachable. It must be tightly sealed to withstand the water pressure, or else we would implode."

"There won't be enough room to hold everyone in here," she says thoughtfully. They round a corner that connects to the main command area. The lighting is brighter here, which doesn't help her headache, not to mention that horrible smell of heated plastic.

"We must make choices," Chris replies in an emotionless voice. Emily snorts.

"Should it surprise me that saving everyone isn't part of the emergency evacuation plan? We're hopeless."

"What would you do?"

"I don't know. It's a waste of time, I guess." Their footsteps echo, and the hustle and bustle from earlier is a distant memory. If someone told her they are alone in this world, she would believe it. Is this how escaping the Ark feels?

Emily wouldn't want guilt to eat away at her conscience.

"Is Skyler okay?" Chris asks abruptly.

"Why? Unless you guys talk, there's nothing to say."

"I worry about him."

"I don't think he'd be thrilled to know that. When was the last time you saw him? A week ago?"

"Less. But with everything that's been going on…"

Is Sky still angry with her? Their argument about the Brotherhood is still too recent. "He's fine, I'm sure." She hopes so. They reach a room where people are staring at screens that display a series of incoherent symbols. They're in the Command Center.

"What an honor to finally meet her," expresses a familiar-looking woman who glides to them. "I'm Chris's mentor."

"Second officer," says Emily, bowing her head slightly.

"Laurene will do," she replies with a fake smile framed by long bright hair that falls on her shoulders like a waterfall.

It must be her skin. It's too perfect, stretched where the wrinkles of aging should show. The technology that the command of this protected wing has access to is insane.

"I've never liked formal titles," adds Laurene, arms crossed in her too-tight suit—a fad gaining momentum it seems. "It deepens our differences and goes to the head of many who believe they are invincible." She pauses at that. "Why should we insist since we all share the same fate?" Her smile is almost mischievous.

A common destiny? It sounds more beautiful than it is.

"I wish I could say the same," says Emily, annoyed. "With such a safe Command Center…" Chris gives her an embarrassed look, and Emily leaves her sentence hanging, swallowing up her anger.

Laurene's prying eyes peer through Emily, who crosses her arms in turn, shivering. The second officer's oppressive azure-blue energy is stifling. Privileged as she is, she has never experienced what it's like to make sacrifices.

Besides, Laurene's speech at the simulation rang hollow. If family titles and reputations didn't matter, why discriminate against people through their wristbands?

Laurene keeps her composure.

"Choices must be made to ensure humanity's survival. But sometimes we have to make hard choices for the common good. Selecting the elements that can truly sustain our civilization. You will understand in due time."

"Once I pass my training," Chris completes, looking hopefully at Emily.

Laurene thinks she knows what's good for them from her gilded cage disconnected from reality. Her vision is disjointed, but is Emily a better judge? Laurene must certainly know what she is doing to hold such an important position. She is right below Diana in the chain of command, the second most important person on this ship after the Commander.

"What does it have to do with me?" says Emily, puzzled.

"You haven't talked to her yet?" Laurene asks Chris, genuinely surprised.

"I haven't had the chance." He turns to Emily, who is jittery. "Close family members can relocate here once the appointment is official. It's a way of thanking us for our full-time contribution since we can rarely take time off. We have to be ready no matter what."

"How many people know about this *privilege?*"

"Why does it matter?" he replies as if the question was senseless.

"You do not need to worry about anything," Laurene says with unwavering confidence. "We carefully monitor the comings and goings at the Command Center. As I'm sure you've learned from recent events, one can never be too careful. You, of all people, should know that. Those Mavericks you've been watching at the prison are a serious threat."

She's referring to Reyes's escape and how the Brotherhood involved mom in their scheming.

"You seem to know me pretty well," points out Emily. "I wish I could say the same about you."

"You will," replies Laurene, relaxed. "As soon as Agent Kay has completed the first phase of his training. It should not be long from what I have seen so far."

"Sorry to interrupt, but I need to have a word with you, Second Officer." An Alpha-uniformed man in his forties, his face framed by round glasses, whispers something to her. Laurene's expression remains emotionless.

"Excuse me, but I have to go," she says simply. Turning to Chris, she adds, "Why don't you give Emily a tour of the Command Center? I'm sure the Commander would love to meet her. He likes to get a first impression of our next residents before they move in." She walks away, her heels clicking on the metal. Chris puts a hand on Emily's shoulder with a satisfied smile on his lips.

"She likes you."

"Does it really matter?" Emily replies, unconvinced.

"She's on the committee that allows relocations, so yes, that's a good thing. Perhaps you would you like a guided tour?"

"Why not?" What could lie beyond these walls? She hates to admit it, but what if there is any truth to what the Brotherhood says?

The Command Center is exactly what you would expect: rows of computers, dozens of screens everywhere and a view of the vast underwater expanse with the remains of Boston still lurking. The Ark could meet the same fate one day. If the Archeans were to learn that the crew planned to abandon ship in an emergency, there would be anarchy. Emily's soul aches. As Violet said, people haven't seen the light for far too long and have lost their way.

What will become of them?

Everyone is too busy at their posts to notice their presence. Good. She appreciates Chris for thinking of her for this reloca-tion, but she can't just leave her dad and sister behind. Sky could take her place here, where he'd be a lot more useful. His ever-hopeful attitude might actually save them all.

Chris introduces her to Commander Hawk—Kevin to his friends. His deeply dark skin highlights his jutting cheekbones. He looks at her curiously, a discreet smile hanging on his lips. His hand finds Emily's shoulder, and she feels like shrinking. The Commander's eyes are the closest thing to what a starry sky must look like. There is something reassuring about him, like a father watching over his family.

"Welcome to our group. I hope to get to know you better."

"The feeling is mutual."

"I was told that you work at our prison?" Emily nods.

"It must be challenging," he says with a frown. "Here you'll be able to achieve your full potential. Something that can truly make you happy." Chris smiles at her.

"I'll do my best," she says, trying to conceal her surprise.

The Commander gives her a friendly smile this time and wishes them a pleasant visit. Although he holds the most important role in the Ark, he treats her like an actual person—not like a Bates, not a traitor.

She likes him.

A broody woman with hard features who goes by the name of Diana stands like a watchdog by his side. Either her epaulets, or the fact she is Chris's dad's boss make her look particularly unfriendly. Rumor has it that she's had an affair with Kevin, and some people are unhappy—including Duke Kay, who never liked her—though Chris highly doubts it. His father is convinced that they unfairly denied him the position of first officer because of that woman. Emily just blames it on jealousy.

Once the many introductions have been made with the entire main crew—whose names she can't remember—Chris gets ready to walk her back to her cabin, but then a male voice freezes him in his tracks.

"My own son can't be bothered to see me. I must have made

a horrible impression on you, boy. Or maybe you don't want me to meet your new girlfriend." Duke Kay is dressed in an unblemished uniform, bearing the golden symbol of the Paragon that is part of the Theta Division: the letter O streaked through, and a wing spread open. He smooths his graying bangs that fall limply to the side.

"Father," swallows Chris uncharacteristically.

"I think I know why you didn't want to introduce her," Duke sputters. "A Bates. Surprising how that one's still alive."

"Why are you taking pleasure in making our family's life impossible?" Emily retorts, stung to the core, her headache already forgotten. But who does he think he is?

"Emily, please," Chris whispers as he protects her with his arm in front of her.

"And she's got nerve. In the eye of our good old Creator, it doesn't make much difference. You live or you die." Grinning, he smooths the tip of his salt-and-pepper beard.

Emily deliberately bites her tongue. Breathe.

"Son, I understand you want a minor distraction, but choose wisely in the future. Now that you have a position with the Commander, it would be foolish to shoot yourself in the foot so early."

"Father, don't," Chris retorts in an even but forced tone. "It's not up to you to decide who I should be friends with."

"True," Kay says with that maddening nonchalance. "Your mother's blood is thick in your veins, even though she's no longer here to turn you against me. What a waste, though. You have so much potential. When I become the next Commander, things will change. For the better."

"Or the worse," Emily mutters through her teeth. Duke makes a small gasp. Did he hear her?

"Oh, my dear. This ship will see better days under my command and my dear son's. You may be mouthy, but you sure know how to leech off powerful people. Maybe that's what will save you in the end. Unless I get personally involved."

"Father, that's enough! Emily has done nothing wrong to you."

"You don't choose to be born into a family of traitors, do you? But that's the way nature is."

"Did you really have to gallivant here so you could harass her?" says Chris, whose aura twitches. "If that's the case, you should go back to the Command Center. I'll meet you there later. But leave her alone."

"Son, if you could show as much fervor in your work, and especially towards your father, this ship would already be on its way to the Promised Land."

Satisfied, Duke turns on his heels with his unbreakable grin hanging on his face. Despite all the atrocities he said in less than two minutes, Emily can't be bothered. She's used to it, anyway. But Chris protected her just like Milo defended her. Chris is so different from his father, the very proof that one's background does not define a person. She's a Bates, yes, but in her own way and not a traitor like others want to believe.

"I'm so sorry about what my dad said," Chris apologizes, squeezing Emily's arm affectionately.

"Don't worry about it. These days there's nothing that surprises me anymore. Thank you for not being like your father."

"Thank you for not getting involved in his game."

"I almost did, but… I'm tired."

"Your headache?"

"Yes, among other things." He doesn't ask any more questions, for which she thanks him inwardly. They return to Emily's cabin, her mind wandering while her neurons are whirring as an idea bubbles up. She decides to let her intuition guide her.

"You mentioned Sky earlier because you want him to move

to the Command Center?" she asks incredulously, as the idea seems so bizarre. A flash of embarrassment shadows Chris's face, then he laughs nervously.

"I get to choose two people. I thought you'd probably like it if he came too."

"And your father?"

"He's already got a secure spot, unfortunately. He is the least of my worries."

"I don't understand," she says, stopping in the middle of the hallway. "You sound like you're getting ready to run away from the Ark." He looks at her speechless and so is she, as realization dawns on her.

"Emily. I can't tell you more, but the Brotherhood has done more damage than you might think."

"What are you talking about?" Her emotions might burst any second, and she quells the anger that swells inside.

"I'm trying to protect you and Sky." She wants to argue over this, but the last few days have taken their toll on her. Chris has shown he would do anything to help her. She has to take his word for it.

"Don't do anything crazy until my next visit," he says, taking her by the shoulders. "Will you?"

"I can't promise you anything," she replies with a smirk.

22

SKYLER

SKYLER didn't remember the ARK could smell so good. Liberating. After a day spent with a corpse, he would never complain ever again about the air being too damp or cold.

The corridor is crowded with patrolling Paragon agents, some posted at strategic locations, others whispering in codes that make no sense. A team has taken over to deal with Mrs. Farrell's remains. Skyler had plenty of time to fill out a detailed report while they were confined. He really didn't feel like staying any longer than he had to.

As for her sphere, Philip promised to take it to the Archives and to tell his sister Tessa. If the rebel group of the Paragon failed, this will be a hard blow for her.

What is she doing right now? That night in the Strahl, she said they would expose the truth themselves if the Brotherhood were to fail. Maybe that's what's happening now; they are taking over as part of the plan.

Skyler longs to see his mother. He hasn't been able to watch over her the way he would have liked with all that happened recently. But there is something he must deal with first. Emily.

He knocks several times and waits patiently. After a while,

he listens for any sound coming from the inside, but there isn't. Maybe Emily is sleeping, or they called her back to the prison.

Disappointed, he heads for the elevators. Hopefully, she won't be angry with him again, though that wouldn't be like her at all.

Three Paragon agents are already inside the elevator and stop talking as soon as they see Skyler. Their behavior suggests that they could be part of the rebel group, but he prefers not to ask. His curiosity would expose him. Tessa will contact him, she said. He has to trust her.

In his parents' cabin, Murielle is dozing on the couch. The layout of the furniture, the stale smell, Dylan's stark absence and his mom's perpetual daze. Everything is in order.

He types a terse message that urges Emily to contact him and hits the send button. If she doesn't respond in the next few days, he'll go back to her. She tends not to check her messages often.

Skyler sits next to his mother, who is curled up on the couch armrest, her favorite spot. Her breathing is slow and steady, so he decides to hug her and close his eyes.

She is so small and frail in his arms. He broke her, too.

His mother could have been Mrs. Farrell, dying unexpectedly. Every moment counts.

He finds some comfort in Tessa's words: an opportunity to start over. The only hope that hasn't failed him yet.

No matter how the future unfolds, there will be no turning back.

23

EMILY

Had someone told her she would cook, Emily would have laughed herself to tears. That was before she got covered with flour while her sister and Violet laughed out loud.

It all started when Violet showed up, embarrassed to have asked around to find their cabin. She could have simply sent them an email, but Violet is anything but tech-savvy. Blushing, Violet invited them to have a girls' cooking day. Gabrielle couldn't stop begging to go, so Emily finally gave in. Yasmina didn't hound her since their meeting, so why couldn't Emily enjoy a well-deserved day off?

Violet's cabin is gigantic, the kind that could have been assigned to Duke Kay himself. It must be at least four times the size of the Bates's and even has proper windows!

Emily took in as many details as she could in every nook and cranny. The living room has comfy fabric chairs with warm lighting, and the master bedroom has a beautiful four-poster bed with sheets softer than a baby's skin. Plus, the mattress is at least twice as thick as all the Bates family mattresses combined. A strong but pleasant smell of incense similar to that of the sanctuary pervades the cabin, which is so much better than the perpetual humidity of the ship. Violet's cabin is in excellent condition, despite the sheer amount of half-open boxes piled up along the walls as if she had just moved in.

The private bathroom is even better. What a dream! Emily feels like a child again when she used to imagine the perfect home she would have loved to have.

"A school of fish!" squeaked Gabrielle, her hands pressed against the window. Multicolored, medium-sized fish danced under the ecstatic cries of her sister. When was the last time Gabrielle had been so happy?

The kitchen adjoins the entryway, and the converted living room has everything: a counter, two hotplates instead of one, an oven, and lots of utensils whose names Emily does not know.

Obviously, the Bates are not among the few families who can own a kitchen. A small pantry and a single hot plate for boiling water are enough since the dining hall is supposed to meet all their basic nutritional needs. In other words, a diet of oatmeal. But even if they had a kitchen as amazing as Violet's, the Bates don't have the contacts to get ingredients which are too valuable. They could get some, but Emily would have to get in touch with her black-market contact. This wouldn't be a good idea, especially now that Yasmina watches her every move.

Too busy examining Violet's home, the cloud of flour caught Emily by surprise. The culprit was no other than her sister, and Emily let out a noisy sneeze before joining in the laughter.

After cleaning her face, Emily puts on a small, patched apron —Philip's—that Violet lent her. As for Gabrielle, she puts on Grandmother Farrell's since she has a smaller frame.

"The secret to cooking is intention," Violet begins in a patient voice.

"Sounds like a game," Emily replies, crossing her arms. "You're not messing with me, are you?"

"Emy, this is very serious," her sister rebukes her.

"Why do you both want to cook today? Think about it for a

moment." Emily remembers the divine taste of the cupcakes from last time but chases away this selfish thought.

She wants to cook for Sky. Since their fight, their relationship hasn't been the same. A simple apology won't be enough this time, and this will be the perfect opportunity to ask for forgiveness. This isn't their first fight, but she's gone too far. Who is she to judge his acquaintances? Even if he joined the Brotherhood, it wouldn't make him *the* Brotherhood. He would still be her best friend. Her personal issues with Neal shouldn't jeopardize their friendship, which is definitely stronger than that. Their friendship is sacred.

"All right then," says Emily, uncrossing her arms. "I'm ready."

"Me too," adds her sister, raising her arm for effect.

"Here we go!" Violet is smiling as she passes along a list of ingredients and steps to follow. As they get to work, Emily rushes to the huge pantry, its shelves filled with a variety of foods she has never seen before.

"We are fortunate to have such a generous community of followers," Violet explains. "They donated all of these ingredients to us. It would go against our values to keep everything for ourselves, so we share our supplies whenever we get the chance."

People who donate, expecting nothing in return? That's a first.

Emily picks up a new bag of flour and comes across a cold compartment at the bottom where she finds butter and milk.

"Don't forget to add the amaranth seeds," Violet reminds her as she places her haul on the counter. Meanwhile, Violet takes over and shows Gabrielle how to prepare the mixture.

Emily goes back to the pantry and examines the first shelf with small, labeled containers.

Seeds, seeds … here. A container larger than the others is filled with strange dark seeds. She bites into one and winces.

"We must cook them first." Violet giggles. Emily's sister

parrots Violet, proud of herself, and Emily rolls her eyes. Gabrielle snorts.

"They put them in just about everything in the dining hall because of their nutritional value," Violet continues, taking a handful of the seeds Emily gives her.

"Even in the modern-day oatmeal?"

"That wouldn't surprise me. The taste is not strong at all when cooked, kind of like a nut. It would blend in easily with other flavors."

They take turns mixing under Violet's supervision. Once the mixture is smooth, Emily and her sister watch as Violet fills the small silicone molds that she lays on a metal plate.

Without her usual get-up, that dress with hanging sleeves, Violet doesn't look like a believer. She is slim, with long silky dark brown hair tied into a tail that frames her very pale round face.

When their turn comes to fill the molds, Gabrielle spills the mixture everywhere and Emily takes over. Her sister balks and Emily makes a face at her.

Violet puts their filled trays into the oven. Emily grabs a jar on the counter, filled with an orangish powder.

"What is this?" asks Emily as she smells the contents while dipping her finger into it before tasting. Hmm. Some kind of spicy sugar.

"Remember the tea from the other night? I added a hint of this spice."

"The secret ingredient," says Emily thoughtfully. Sky would love to try this tea, and so would Chris.

"Let's make some tea then, while the cakes are baking," suggests Violet, who puts a kettle to boil.

They sit at a nice table that looks on the portholes. With the dancing fish, this moment is close to what magic must be. Emily feels like a new breath of life is filling up her lungs.

"You're lucky to have such a great cabin," she says in a dreamy voice.

"Actually, it's Grandma's," replies Violet, whose aura ripples.

"Oh! Will she be back soon? It would be nice to meet her." Violet puts down the tinkling teapot. Then, she pours tea into their cups with a shaky hand and spills some.

"No, she…" Emily rushes to wipe up the boiling water dripping on the floor. "She … has met with the Creator." It takes Emily a second to understand Violet's words.

"I'm so sorry."

A wave of sadness overwhelms Violet, and her aura darkens. She sits with them and sips her tea in silence while Gabrielle gazes through the porthole.

Violet has a chance that few have. Emily's grandparents died when she was a baby. So few make it to sixty. At least Emily could grow up with her parents. She can't imagine what it would have been like had she never known her Mom or Dad.

"Where is your brother?" Emily thinks aloud. "Shouldn't he be with you, especially now?"

"He's with his new girlfriend from the Archives," she replies, slowly putting down her cup. "I don't blame him. I never committed myself to embrace my spiritual life fully."

Violet puts back one of her strands that has come loose from her ponytail.

"I knew this day would come. The day I would have to take over the sanctuary all by myself. Philip will be there to help me, of course, but I am the official priestess now."

She holds her head high as she says these last words. She is resilient, more so than Emily was when she lost her Mom, but there are things that can only be learned with time.

A heavenly smell fills the cabin and the oven chimes. Emily gets up first and races with Gabrielle to take out the cakes, using Violet's mittens so as not to burn herself.

The warm breath that escapes the oven takes Emily by surprise and she nearly drops the cakes. Gabrielle lets out an exaggerated laughter at her fringe rolled up against her forehead. Violet represses her laughter at once as Emily glowers at them.

They let the baked goods rest for a few minutes before transferring them to containers covered with plaid cloth.

"Something is missing," says Emily, who remembers seeing something lying around in the cold compartment. "There!"

She takes out a bowl and comes back for a spoon.

"The finishing touch," Emily says as she tries to get off the cream from the spoon by wiping it in different ways.

The result is terrible, but it doesn't matter. All three of them take a cake, clink them like wine glasses and taste their victory. Gabrielle squeals and gobbles hers up in five seconds while Emily enjoys the moment for at least twenty seconds. Once Violet finishes her silent prayer, she enjoys watching the two of them.

"This cream is divine," Emily says with Gabrielle nodding approvingly. "You'll have to teach me how to make it."

"It's a little embarrassing to say, but I do not know. Cohen, one of our followers, works at the Ark's restaurant and occasionally brings us leftovers."

The waiter with the jade aura. Violet blushes when she says his name.

"Cohen," teases Emily, wiping her mouth with a cloth napkin. "He's pretty cute."

"The Creator's ways are my priority," Violet breathes in a soft voice, hiding behind her serious face. "The sanctuary will take all my time now that—"

She grabs her wicker basket filled with pastries.

"These cakes will be my thanks to the community. We'll all gather tomorrow to honor Grandma's passage into the Creator's realm."

"Daddy will be happy with mine," says Gabrielle, proud to

have her own little basket. "Don't you dare give him any, Emy. Daddy will be pleased enough with mine."

"I have someone else in mind," she replies with a hint of mystery. Violet looks at her questioningly, while Gabrielle growls.

"Besides, my valiant knight must be waiting for me," adds Emily to Gabrielle. "See you later!"

"What?" her sister says, mouth agape.

Violet waves at Emily, who closes the door behind her.

SHE IS WAITING for the door to open while her mouth waters at the cakes' aroma. She would eat another, but it would spoil the surprise if he saw her face smeared with crumbs and cream.

Finally, a clicking sound! A tall blond man cracks the door ajar, as if trying to hide something inside. His eyes are rheumy with swollen dark circles. Sky's father.

He recognizes her, then casually says, "If you're looking for Sky, he's not here."

"Oh," she says awkwardly. "He wasn't in his cabin. Is he—"

"He didn't say. Sorry." Sky's father talks as if he didn't know her. Well, she hasn't come here in a while, but still.

"Did he seem … all right?"

"I don't know. I've barely seen him." He scratches his unkempt beard, as if it had bothered him, then adds, "Sorry Emily, I have to get back to my wife."

Sky's father shuts the door as quickly as he opened it, without giving her a second glance. Emily is stunned. The sharp ends of the basket dig into her palm. What the hell did she do to him?

Unless Sky told his father about their argument. He could have. His family might be mad at her, too. She lets out a sigh and turns on her heels.

All the more reason to settle this now. It would be a shame for their relationship to go down like it did between Sky and Chris. Their friendship is different, though. It wouldn't.

Truly.

Where can Sky be? At Medical Bay? It's worth a try.

She walks, basket in hand, and relaxes her grip. Her chafed right palm is warm, and she moves the basket in her other hand, relieved.

She stops abruptly when something strange tickles her nose. A strange smell. The cakes?

She sniffs her basket. No, it's not coming from there. Wisps of smoke? They wrap around her feet like broth.

And then a fiery breath blooms on her back, followed by a blow that thrusts her several meters forward. She hits the ground, which knocks the breath out of her while her basket flies off and crashes a little further, dumping out the cakes.

Her ears twitch, her vision blurs.

Cakes. Sky. No.

She tries to get up, moaning.

She sinks.

24

SKYLER

SKYLER IS ALONE, PRAYING TO A GOD HE HAS NEVER WANTED TO acknowledge.

Prayer is a big word. The Creator always hides himself, and he won't make an exception now. Even when humanity was in danger of dying out, he did not show up.

Skyler is waiting for a divine intervention, or for the Brotherhood to take over the ship. In both cases there is too much time to think.

Tessa has been ghosting him, and Emily never responded to his message.

But what exactly did he do wrong?

The thousands of names that shine around him with their unearthly glow are witnesses to his plight. They perished in the Flood either from disease, by accident, or even by choice. There are so many ways to leave this unforgivable world. And what is left of them? A burden is passed on from generation to generation, each time heavier to bear.

What exactly did he come here for?

The sanctuary is rather empty without Mrs. Farrell to take care of it. The basins under the great fish have not been changed for a long time, judging by the green moss that has built up at the bottom. Even the Believers seem to have fled like the plague, reducing this place to a pristine photograph, a reminder of what it once was. Until the Farrell grandchildren take over, this place is just a space between two times, two eras. A retreat.

Loneliness. Yes, that's what brought him here. Eventually, it hurts less. No admonitions, no painful memories, no guilt.

But some things remain, like helplessness. Should that surprise him?

A morbid thought flashes through his mind, but he suppresses it, pushes it away hoping it won't come back. He knows that it's still there somewhere, he can feel it, but he doesn't want to give in.

The embedded neon lights assault him, desperately trying to cleanse him from all these negative thoughts before he drowns, but even their power is not enough to warm him up. Only the sun can, and it is too far from here.

Skyler gets up to walk around the altar near the symbol mounted on the wall. The stained air has tarnished it and the golden crust is crumbling at the edges. Microscopic aggregates that have grown out of proportion dull its once gleaming sheen.

The door to the anteroom is open, and Skyler decides to check it out. The small bench that Elaine sometimes sat on for her daily check-ups is now just another one of those useless, cumbersome items discarded in a remote corner.

Something important is missing, though. The usual clutter is gone; the paintings are piled up in the back of the room, and Elaine Farrell's belongings have been thrown away. Smoother incense replaces the usual potent smell of sage, but he couldn't tell which plant it's made from. He'll have to ask Philip.

Skyler feels a twinge of sadness. This place won't ever be the same.

An oversized painting of a young woman that takes up the entire time-worn wall catches his attention. She wears a gray-shaded uniform, different from those of the Ark. She looks like she is carrying the burden of a harsh life, as evidenced by the furrows on her forehead that contrast with her young features. An original, perhaps a photograph has inspired the portrait. A strange halo of purplish-red shines on the woman's contours, giving her an almost spectral air. Why did they add this strange effect?

"You shouldn't stay here," Tessa says, restless. The echo of her voice buzzes in his ears and Skyler blinks at her blurry silhouette. Tessa must be here for the Brotherhood.

"Why?" His tone is terse, heavy with anger. Is that all she can say after taking so long to get in touch with him?

She arches her eyebrow. "I am dead serious." Why can't she say things clearly for once? The Brotherhood. Their plan. Everything.

"I guess I should take this as bad news. What's going on?"

"You ask too many questions." Skyler could swear he heard her voice quiver. "We don't have much time." Tessa turns away, ready to leave.

"I wouldn't usually say anything, but this is bad timing. I'm tired of being kept in the dark. Tell me what's going on." She hesitates, one foot outside the anteroom, her hand on the door frame. Skyler adds, in a shaky voice and clenched fists, "I need to know if we still have a chance."

Is it rage or sorrow, or both ... maybe even despair? He doesn't know, but one thing is certain, he is suffocating in this Ark. He must get out.

"Some unexpected problems came up, but nothing that can't be fixed," she says, tucking back one of her stray braids. "I've come to get you so we can get things moving unless you've changed your mind."

She stares at him, waiting for an answer. Should he feel relieved to know that the Brotherhood hasn't failed? Yet, the unease isn't going anywhere.

"What am I supposed to do?" Tessa's face lights up, her coconut scent heady. Her shy smile pulls him like a tug of war between heaven and earth. So close, yet so far.

"Follow me." Skyler does so, but as soon as Tessa reaches the entrance of the sanctuary, he bends over into a coughing fit, his throat burning.

He can't breathe.

His eyes well up with tears, and Tessa curses as she starts coughing uncontrollably. She pulls his arm towards the exit, but a bright light blinds them, followed by a shock wave so powerful that it pulls them apart.

Skyler's back buckles under the impact. He tries to gulp some air, his hand on his chest, but feels like he's drowning. His vision blurs … lack of oxygen … and the unbearable, burning smell makes him cough until he feels nauseous. Suspended particles shine under the bluish glow into a thick dust cloud.

A persistent whistle numbs his eardrums, and Skyler opens his mouth to crack them, to no avail. He breathes into his cusped hand and calls for Tessa, but his voice sounds hollow, barely a throb in his throat. Even if she answered, he probably couldn't hear her, and the cloud is too dense to see anything.

His body sore, he scans his surroundings and fans his arms to clear the dust that presses around him like a vice of white-hot metal and sulfur.

Tessa's face is glowing in an electric blue, leaning against the wall, slightly bent, her eyes sparkling under the recessed lights. Her chest is heaving.

"You're hurt," he says in a dull voice, searching for the source of her pain. "Let me take a look."

She groans as she tries to stand up and Skyler catches a dark stain gleaming on her pale gray uniform. The debris from the explosion gashed her flank down to her lower back.

"You're going to have to take your top off," he says seriously, his voice becoming clearer and louder. Tessa glances at him over her shoulder.

"Is it that bad?" she says, mockingly. "I wasn't referring to that when I said we should get things moving." A half-smile hangs on her lips and sweat beads around her mouth. Skyler suppresses a laugh that turns into a dry cough as he realizes the innuendo.

"From a professional standpoint, yes. I have to examine your wounds if you don't want it to get infected." She stares at him as if considering her options. "I work at Med Bay, remember?

"I know."

"So, trust me then." Skyler looks at her straight in the eye to show his good faith but can't seem to grasp what she's trying to tell him.

"It's not what you think," she says, looking down. Tessa winces as she struggles to lift her sweater halfway up her back. Once it's done, she pulls her braids over her shoulder.

"How about this?"

"I can work with that," says Skyler, who turns her body towards the light source.

Metal shards embedded in the flesh confirm his fears. She has a nasty hemorrhage that could fester if he doesn't give her proper treatment in a timely fashion.

"What am I thinking, then?" asks Skyler to distract her while peering at the wound.

"What?" she answers in a jerky voice. Tessa props her head against the wall while Skyler labors to locate the larger shards swimming in blood, lymph, and glistening chunks of flesh.

"You said it's not what I think. What am I thinking?"

"Do you really want to know?" Tessa glimpses his smirk. "All right. Don't get upset if I'm too direct."

Now that she is busy, Skyler extracts the smaller shards first to test her pain tolerance. Two good-sized pieces are driven deeper. It's a wonder she hasn't passed out yet.

"You are too young."

"What?" Taken aback, he loses his focus.

"It's a fact."

"You're barely older than me," he objects. He clenches his teeth at the snags of the metal digging into his fingers and the flesh fighting against his pulling.

"Don't take it the wrong way," she groans as he successfully pulls out a medium-sized piece from her back. "I have other … concerns."

Skyler brings back his attention to the two remaining shards. He wavers about removing them now. Even the healing gel they use at Med Bay for emergencies would not be enough to heal the two gashes. However, if he doesn't act now, they'll be stuck there. As soon as she walks, her lumbar spine will create friction: Either the pain will be unbearable, or the muscles won't contract properly, or both.

He must extract them.

"You'll get over it," she says, snapping him out of his daze.

"We both want to help the Brotherhood. I won't let my feelings get in the way."

"Then it's settled." Tessa shifts her weight to her other leg and frowns. "Why did you stop? Are you done? Because it still hurts like hell."

"We have a problem."

Skyler straightens up to loosen his muscles.

"I don't have any healing gel to remove the other fragments. Unless you have some, I can't keep going without risking your life."

"Why didn't you say so earlier?" she says without flinching while digging in the pocket of her uniform. "Here. Take this to disinfect."

Skyler frowns at the small tube whose symbols are indecipherable. Does the Paragon encrypt their information now?

"Where did you get this?"

"Does it matter?" Skyler doesn't press further and applies the ointment which liquefies in a few seconds to seep into the wound. What he sees then leaves him speechless.

The substance spreads quickly, as if guided by the wounds. An odd foam spreads to cover each cut, even though he has only used a tiny amount. Is this some advanced nanotechnology?

After carefully assessing the risks, Skyler works on the first piece, large enough for his thumb and forefinger to grab. Tessa lets out a scream and the sucking of flesh turns his gut, but he doesn't flinch. Blood is already oozing from where the shard was a minute ago. The relief he feels is enough to make him forget Tessa's moaning.

One more to go.

Eyes burning, he wipes his forehead while Tessa is shaking. With wobbling arms, she grabs the nearby bench smashed against the broken votive candles.

"Are you holding up?" he asks worriedly. "We can stop now while you recover. It's a heavy stress on your body, and you are losing a lot of blood."

Tessa's eyelids are half-closed, and cold sweat slides down her unusually pale skin.

"I can't move with this in my back," she slurs through chattering teeth. "Keep going." Her hands tighten around the bench, and she closes her eyes in anticipation of the pain to come. "Do it."

Skyler leans over and blocks out any thoughts that might affect his concentration. He imagines, just like at the Academy, that he is on land, a beach that runs along the vast ocean tufted with a few tropical trees. The rolling of the waves is continuous, hypnotic.

He is alone.

The last fragment is stuck in a particular angle. If he pulls it out the wrong way, he may create more damage. In fact, if he gets it wrong, he could paralyze her. The piece is lodged very close to the spine, which also explains why she can't move properly.

Skyler ensures the bleeding from the last wound has stopped with the special ointment as he vows to do his own investigation.

After analyzing how the fragment could have gotten in, he comes down to two possibilities. Either it entered upwards, and the tip grazed the nerves, or it sank into the muscle tissue during the fall. There's a strange curve in the metal flush with the wound, and flesh covers the rest. Short of a scan—or scratching and making it worse—he has no way of knowing.

He could also wait for help and avoid taking the risk.

The choice nags at him with the rolling of the waves. Roll in, roll out.

Skyler grabs the fragment and pulls it up. He feels some resistance.

Damn. The spine.

Skyler pulls towards the opposite side as he twists slowly upwards. The splinter tears off the wound as Tessa slumps against the wall.

She is unconscious. No!

Skyler turns her over on her side, his hands dripping in blood. He hastens to unscrew the tube which won't open. With slippery fingers, he tries four more times, until he takes off the lid for good. He squeezes most of the gel out and prays he didn't screw up. The ointment takes on liquid properties as the wound drinks hungrily. The blood flows so much Skyler wonders if it has not flushed the medicine out.

Tessa is still breathing. Her pulse seems fine.

No, she is too weak. He shouldn't have taken out the piece. Her fall probably damaged whatever was around.

She may be paralyzed.

The anguish petrifies him. His limbs refuse to move, and he cradles her as he finds comfort in the smell of her hair. He closes his eyes, hoping she will wake up.

———

His thoughts are still fuzzy when he wakes up. Tessa's head is resting on his thigh, and two of her braids are undone. He must have played with them while he was asleep.

That she is still not awake is worrisome. At least her pulse seems to have stabilized, although Skyler had to count three times to be sure.

The bleeding has stopped, but the wound tore sideways, which now looks more like a sore multicolored bruise peppered with dried blood. The ointment seems to have worked, but to what extent?

Skyler looks around. The dust particles have settled, and the jammed exit is in plain view. A pipe is leaking, and he is sitting in about an inch of water.

He is shivering. The temperature has also dropped.

He does not dare to move for fear of hurting Tessa further. As he waits in silence, he drives off the thoughts that she might never wake up. How are they going to survive this?

Time ticks by.

Tessa's eyes flutter open. When she realizes she was sleeping on Skyler's thigh, she sits up too quickly, which takes her breath away.

"Easy," says Skyler, who props her back for support.

"How long have I been unconscious?"

"I'm not sure. Part of the night, I guess."

Tessa's face is still a little pale, but she seems to have recovered. She rubs her eyes, then leans forward to stand up, but has to give up. She utters a complaint of pain mixed with frustration.

"You need more time before you use your back."

"The ointment is effective against superficial wounds within two hours," she says, looking at him as if to confirm her self-diagnosis. "Something I should know?"

"You lost consciousness during the extraction, so it's difficult to know the extent of the internal damage. The shard may have come into contact with your nervous system."

Skyler swallows hard, his mouth dry. The words struggling past his lips.

"You could eventually become paralyzed. If fragments are lodged and inflammation sets in, removing them will be difficult. We avoid playing in that area since the surgery itself is risky."

Tessa pulls up the bottom of her uniform and feels her wound with her free hand to see for herself. She could yell at him, but she doesn't.

"Use less next time," says Tessa calmly as she pulls down her top. "The ointment is hard to come by."

"I'm sorry," he says, his voice breaking.

"I couldn't stay like this." Tessa's warmth on his thigh has gone, replaced by the coldness spreading through the sanctuary that has become their tomb.

"Do you..." she begins as she shifts into a more comfortable position, the side of her shoulder pressed against the wall, her face facing his. "What do you think my chances are? Be honest."

Skyler throws his head back and stares at the oozing ceiling. The explosion blew out an entire section, damaging the piping. Cables are hanging loosely, and water is dripping.

"To tell you the truth, I have no idea. You have to go through a scan first. Tell me, what does this ointment do?" Tessa purses her lips.

"This is a nanotechnology that the Paragon uses to heal minor injuries before seeing a doctor."

"I mean, what exactly does this nanotechnology do? If I know how it works, maybe I could—"

"I don't think it can fix the nervous system," she cuts him off. "How long do I have to wait before I can get up?" Without the right tools, he can't decide, but he can do something to find out.

"While you're sitting, move your legs." Even if she says nothing, it is obvious that she is suffering.

"Does it hurt in your back?

"A little."

"Okay. We'll give it a try." Skyler stands up, silencing the unpleasant sensation of his wet pants sticking to his skin. He slips his arm under Tessa's shoulders and grips her tightly.

"Slowly," he breathes. Her movements are easier than he expected.

"It's all right, I think," she says with strain.

"Are you sure?"

"Yes. I can bear the pain."

"Now walk. Slowly. Lean on me first." She does relatively well, even without his help.

"At least I can stand up," she says, hobbling.

"For now. The more you walk, the worse the inflammation will get. You should limit your movements until I can examine you. If any splinters remain, it's only a matter of time before you break a fever."

"Yes, doctor. Now let's find a way out of here." How can she walk after this trauma? This ointment…

The Omega Division provides pharmaceuticals for the entire Ark, including Medical Bay. Why won't they let them have access to such an effective drug? It doesn't add up unless the Paragon has its own facilities. If Chris's father is anything like his son, nothing is impossible.

"We're stuck here." She surveys the obstructed exit, one hand against her back for support.

"Where did the explosion come from? The Brotherhood?" he asks.

"What makes you think I know?" Tessa scans the rubble. Why did she come to him right before the explosion?

"You wanted us to leave this place at all costs. You knew what was going to happen."

"Not exactly." She sits on a bench with a wince.

"What else do you know?"

"What I do know is that things just got a lot more complicated for us." Skyler sits beside her while keeping some distance.

Tessa is so shifty. She needs to open up to him. It might be the only way out of here, or at least make their time together more bearable.

"Why are you helping me?"

Skyler's question remains unanswered. He goes through the list of strangers that glow like some of those fluorescent fish who enjoy a midnight swim in the ocean. Elaine Farrell's name is there, though it has no special ornamentation, blending in with the other late Archeans. Clarissa Reed, the prisoner victim of the Syndrome, is also there and countless others. The cycle of life and death follows its course.

"Since Clarissa," he adds. "You told me I reminded you of someone."

"That's right."

"Is it someone you lost?" Her response is slow.

"Not yet." More hesitation. Does she not trust him?

"All these names … these are people who died, but their presence lingers," says Skyler, pointing to the shiny lettering. "My brother's here, too."

His name shines faintly. Although it is a good distance away, it glows clearly in his mind: Allen Goldberg.

"How long has it been?" she asks, her eyes transfixed on the thousands of dead.

"Enough that people would expect I have moved on." The sound of dripping water is constant, and a shiver runs through him.

"I can understand the feeling."

"I'm sorry," he says. "I shouldn't have mentioned this, especially with what just happened to your grandmother." Tessa gives him a curious look, then stares at the opposite wall where the golden fish glow with a dull sheen.

"Some people believe we must face reality and accept it as if it were as natural as eating or sleeping. In fact, it's more like trying to wake up and failing. You are trapped in your own sleep, in a dream you have no control over."

The echo of her voice fades and faces crowd Skyler's mind: Allen falling into nothingness, his mother losing her soul. Each time, he was the spectator of his life. The emptiness is still there and nothing he can do will change that.

"I shouldn't have insisted," apologizes Skyler, with a bitter taste in his mouth. Tessa nods with a sigh, her eyes wandering.

"I wasn't always like this, you know," she says as if split between two worlds. "I just hope I can get back to my old self."

Tessa takes a break and plays with one of her untied braids.

"Life's ordeals can help us grow," she muses as she stares at the damaged ends of her hair, then continues with renewed confidence. "That's why what the Brotherhood is doing for the Ark is so important. They want to give us all a second chance. Not just to rebuild our civilization, but to change for the better."

They still have the present. The Brotherhood has started something, opened a window of opportunity.

They are only the two of them, engulfed in a semi-darkness, in a room that gets colder by the hour. What is going on outside these walls?

"The Command Center," she says, looking serious again.

"They'll need all the manpower they can get to get the truth out."

"And if they didn't make it? What are we going to do? We don't even know what they want to do after, or their plan for—"

He feels so stupid. How could he not see clearly before?

"You know what they will reveal. You also know what happens next. Do you—"

"I coordinate the operation from the Paragon," she replies. "What will follow after the Brotherhood controls the Ark is what they promised during the simulation. Going back to the ground."

Tessa has the power to make it all possible again. Even if they fail, she can carry out their original plan.

Skyler kicks at the water flooding the sanctuary and watches the ripples spread.

"You know the coordinates where the mainland is," says Skyler, barely believing his own words. "You will be the one to lead the Ark."

"No."

Tessa grabs his hand.

"No matter what happens to the Brotherhood, I won't be alone. You will be there."

25

SKYLER

Tessa's body is against his, her breathing slow and regular.

They had to huddle together to keep warm since the temperature has dropped sharply. Right now, the only way out is from outside, but there hasn't been a soul around for hours. The damage must have affected several sections and prevented anyone from reaching them. There might even be other people trapped elsewhere.

Was this explosion orchestrated by the Paragon or the Brotherhood? Tessa seems to believe that the Brotherhood would not risk the Archeans' lives when their chief aim is to save them. That leaves the Paragon, whose members do not align with a common ideal. A lone wolf or an eccentric pack may have answered the Brotherhood's call in its own way. If that turns out to be the case, they might have to deal with them, too.

Skyler enjoyed imagining the reasons that could explain the blast, although he should find a solution to their urgent problem. Otherwise, they are doomed to certain death and everything else won't matter.

The problem is that the sanctuary does not open onto any

other section of the ship. It is secluded to allow the faithful to meditate in peace.

As he sinks into a semi-comatose state, too numb from the cold, he sees himself infiltrating the Paragon headquarters to find Tessa. He gets lost, runs, retraces his steps in the maze of in betweens.

Why the hell didn't he think of that before?

He's never ventured into the sanctuary, but according to the map Allen showed him, there are in betweens just about everywhere. You just have to find the entrance.

Tessa is still drowsy, but at least she's not shivering, and her pulse has finally settled. Searching for this hypothetical entrance means Skyler will have to leave her alone and put her at risk of developing hypothermia. Hypoglycemia, dehydration, and a slowing heart rate are all serious threats as well. They need to keep warm as much as possible, but finding a way out is worth a try.

Skyler first scrutinizes the walls for a gap, or some kind of contraption maintenance technicians use to access the massive piping over the ceiling that has been squirting at them for hours. What if it is in the passageway now blocked because of the debris? The piping would follow the main corridors, which means his idea is worthless. Skyler sighs, defeated.

Tessa is still sleeping, her head resting on the back of the bench. Her face is relaxed, her mouth ajar. Skyler puts an arm around her neck and rests his forehead on her shoulder, his eyes hot from fatigue.

His thoughts are jumbled, as if he were running a fever. Images come and go without making sense as he waltzes from one semiconscious state to another. The dripping of water is like a countdown, the thread that keeps his subconscious from drowning him.

He jerks awake and his arm falls on the still warm metal.

"Why?" shouts Tessa, standing by the altar. She holds on to

the back of the bench, her features drawn by her throbbing pain.

"Did something happen?" he mumbles, confused.

"I thought I made myself clear, but the second I'm asleep, you act like nothing happened."

"We have to keep warm," he says defensively. "You were even more vulnerable in your sleep. Just so you know, the temperature here has been dropping steadily. The explosion must have affected the ventilation system."

"You could have woken me up."

"I did what I had to do," he objects, leaning on the altar.

"Is this the doctor or the man speaking?" Tessa crosses her arms.

"The doctor."

"You didn't wake me up. Was that the doctor or the man?" Tessa's gaze is deep and wild.

"Don't get upset," Skyler says, uneasy, while she walks away.

Without a word, he walks to the altar and stumbles upon his reflection in one of the water-filled bowls that survived the explosion. His face looks so awful that he can hardly recognize himself. His reflection stares back at him, distorted by the ripples created by the low-frequency hum of the Ark. The bowl has a tube that comes out on the side and at the base. Something clicks in his mind.

He tries to move the altar, but it won't budge. Then, he moves back to get a better view.

"I think I found a way out," Skyler says. Tessa is gazing at a recessed doorway, unresponsive. "Is everything okay?

"What kind of exit?" she replies, sniffing.

"Come here."

"It's better be worth it." She limps to the altar, suppressing a wince with each step. Skyler is about to help her but refrains despite himself. She probably wouldn't let him.

"There's a pipe that goes into this floor, which means we can follow it," he explains once she is beside him.

"How do you plan to do this? Should I remind you we have nothing to breach metal?"

"No need when there is already a path." He points to a tile with a serial number.

"What does that mean?"

"This kind of code tells us which part of the maintenance corridor network this trapdoor is connected to. We'll use it to get out of here."

"And this trap door will open by itself?"

"We just need to turn it in the right direction. Nothing fancy." Skyler grabs the notch where the normal tiles meet around the hatch and pivots until it clicks. Then he pulls it open. He smiles and thanks Allen inwardly. Who says the dead can't help the living?

Skyler climbs down the slippery steps first, the water in the sanctuary flowing. Dim specks of light come to life as he splashes through the passageway. The piping fades into the darkness ahead, with only the glowing reflection shimmering on the floor and metal walls to guide him.

"Where does it lead to?" Tessa asks.

"We should end up in the main passageway."

"Can we reach the Command Center from here?"

"I'd need a map for that." The in betweens stretch for miles across a wide network. They could spend days going around in circles without ever reaching their destination.

Tessa thinks for a moment before saying, "Can you take us out into a hallway?"

"One thing I know is that these passages are interlinked. There should be more than one exit, though I don't know which one."

"We have only one chance to free the Ark," she stresses, and Skyler nods.

He leads the way into the depths of the in between. The relatively narrow hallway stretches to what appears to be a larger room where multiple pipes meet and the eerie resemblance to where Allen fell is striking. Skyler nearly loses his footing, water making the smooth surface treacherous. His mouth is so dry that he's almost tempted to drink the water that's oozing out of the walls. He resists though his throat contracts with discontent.

The main room stinks of sulfur, and Skyler covers his nose. Tessa wades in, slowed down by her injury.

"Now, where do we go?" she asks, peering at the intersection where a serial number identifies each of the corridors. Although Skyler is familiar with their use, their actual meaning escapes him.

"Any will do, I suppose," he decides, picking one path. "As long as we can get to an exit." She nods silently and follows him down a hallway wider than the one they came in through. A whiff of moisture and wet earth like the fertilizer Skyler keeps in his room washes over them. What little light they had flickers out. Skyler can't see a thing, not even his hands.

"Are you okay?" he asks Tessa.

"Right behind you. What do we do now? The power is out, even where we came from."

"The exit shouldn't be too far." Hopefully, she won't notice the waver in his voice. "Would you rather wait for the power to come back on?"

"No!" Her reaction is over the top, but he doesn't press on. The in betweens are not the most welcoming.

"Take my hand, so we don't lose each other," he says, feeling in her direction. Tessa squeezes his hand a little too hard as they step forward into complete darkness that feels unpleasantly solid. Skyler focuses on Tessa's hand to steady himself.

Gloomy metallic creaks ricochet as if a giant were rocking the Ark for fun. The ground rises and falls with each step and

Skyler fumbles along to lean onto the nearby wall, but his fingers can only grasp darkness.

Tessa squeezes hard when a jolt makes him lose his footing.

A seaquake?

He drags Tessa in his fall, expecting the impact. Skyler closes his eyes as they slide into the emptiness.

Shit.

26

EMILY

Her body hurts in more places than she can count.

Emily is lying on a small sofa, legs dangling over the armrest, a silky cushion under her head. Who brought her here?

She tries to roll onto her side, but the movement makes her wince in pain. Her ribs may be cracked. Great.

"Sky?" asks Emily with a twinge in her jaw. Her vision sharpens after a few seconds, but her confusion remains. She doesn't recognize this place, far more spacious than a cabin, especially the high ceilings. Less dirty, better ventilated, more … quiet.

"Where are we?" The air smells of solvent, and the well-preserved gray furniture is a far cry from her home.

"You are safe here." This voice sounds false. It's so quiet in this room without the usual vibration that rattles the Ark. Airtight.

Emily straightens up enough to see who is approaching. It's not Sky, but Chris. How did he find her?

There is a bed, a sofa, a small desk, a chair. Everything is simple but laid out differently than the cabins in the residential area. Chris's new cabin?

"You can't ignore me forever," he says, almost startling her.

"What are you talking about?" she answers, more confused, deep in her thoughts. She adds more to herself than to him, "I was in the hallway and then..."

The shrill sound of the explosion flashes back to her mind. What was she doing there? Why would Chris bring her here?

"The Brotherhood," he says, scanning her. "They've put their plan into action. The farther you get from them, the better."

"I can defend myself, you know."

"So why did I find you unconscious in a collapsed hallway? Trust me. You'd better stay here."

Suddenly, Emily makes out the thick door frames that allow for pressurization, and a bad feeling creeps up on her. Chris's new cabin, the one in the Command Center.

Chris is wearing a different uniform: A somewhat black suit that hugs his body to the neck, as if preparing for an underwater hunt.

"That was the plan all along, wasn't it? The escape..." Chris's features tense up. The tendrils of his energy are swelling, the typical pattern when he is upset.

Commander Hawk could have at least taken responsibility and protected the Ark with his life. Instead, he runs away with his crew. Underneath his sympathetic looks, he is anything but an honest man.

"How long has it been since we broke away from the ship?" Her voice is dull, dissonant.

"Why do you want to know?" he asks with a hint of suspicion. He draws closer, his mouth half-open as if the words were stuck in his throat.

"I have the right to know my fate. You did decide for me."

"Should I have just abandoned you, then? I did everything I could to—"

"Tell me you don't really support the Commander and his folly." Emily's body stiffens in anticipation. Chris is her friend.

They have known each other for as long as she can remember. He has been treating patients at Medical Bay for nearly two years. He is a good person. Chris can't be corrupt.

"It's more complicated than that." He rubs the back of his neck. "I meant well."

"Even our best intentions can meet a tragic end," she says bitterly. "Unless you put it into perspective, you can't pretend it will do much good." An unease that she has never felt between them before sets in. He looks away while she waits.

"Preparations are underway." Is that really what her honorable Chris has become? An accomplice of the Commander's foolishness?

Chris is about to leave the room, and she stands up, oblivious to the pain that grips her chest. Her voice quivers as she says, "Do you realize that desertion is a crime against humanity?"

He blinks, his angel-like face ever so charming and disgustingly innocent.

"Rest," he replies stiffly. "I have something important to do."

"That makes you a criminal, Chris! I know you. You're not like this. Get a hold of yourself!" Chris looks down, his upper lip trembling.

"Can't," he says as Emily's anxiety rises. "They have pressurized the exits already."

"They *will* have to depressurize sometime if anyone wants to get out of here alive!" She steps over the sofa to reach the door, but he blocks her way. Before he knows it, he is panting against the frame, unable to move. She feels a pang of sadness as the familiar smell of Chris stirs her.

"Don't you dare stop me," she hisses, fighting her inner voice telling her this is nonsense. "You can't confine me here while your group of cowards wants to leave the rest of humanity behind. I am not one of you. I am not a *criminal*."

"You can't stop them. Nor the Brotherhood, nor the Commander."

"We'll see about that." Dad. Gabrielle. Skyler. They need her. Together, they can stop this carnage.

"Wait!" he shouts, as she suddenly pulls away from him. "You don't know the danger you're putting us in!" But it is too late. Emily is already on her way to the escape pods, clearly marked on the evacuation plan posted on the walls. She walks briskly, then breaks into a run. The mere idea of having to stay with murderers makes her nauseous.

History is bound to repeat itself. At the time of the Embarkment, if it hadn't been for the Farrells, the two hundred passengers would never have made it onto the Ark. What is the point of teaching this legend if people don't care? How can you restore your faith in humanity when you witness such a crime?

She runs into a commonplace emergency stairwell, narrow, suffocating, too long. The door locks behind her to prevent survivors from turning back and she slows down to catch her breath. A large gas pipe juts out of the ceiling, running into the floor, with a row of dials that display different pressure readings. She grabs an emergency axe from its case and smashes the pressurizer. The dial goes off and gas hisses like an angry teapot. The alarm blares almost immediately. Good luck running away from the Ark now.

She runs down the last few steps, fueled by the bellowing alarm, and rushes into a room where a few dozen pods that look like miniature Strahls are lined up. When she slips into one of them, the controls automatically buzz awake.

Emily grabs both steering handles, a feeling she had missed. In her teens, when she was still pursuing the futile dream of becoming a relic hunter, Dad had given in and had sailed on a Strahl while pretending they went hunting together. There were some blissful days between father and daughter at a time when she was mourning Mom. There were times when life was making sense again.

The tiny Strahl splits the water at a frightening speed and the thrust nails Emily to the bottom of her seat. Past the small opening, the Great Ocean's arms reach out to embrace her.

The immensity of the Ark is overwhelming. Either end is invisible unless you get far enough to get a good view. The middle floors have hundreds and hundreds of glowing windows. At this depth, even sunlight can't filter, making everything so dark that the pod's headlights can barely pierce through.

This is their entire world. This ocean and this Ark only protected by layer upon layer of metal sheets pushing against billions of liters of water. The hands of criminals could soon shatter this world: the Brotherhood, the Commander. Chris.

She takes some time to configure her route to one of the main docks. First, secure the pod. Then … what comes next?

Adjust the internal pressure to avoid being squashed into oatmeal? Yes. Then, select the pre-recorded coordinates to engage in automatic mode. The coordinates? Where are they?

Emily navigates through the menus with impossible terms that stir the pain in her ribs. Dad always took care of this part. Emily should have had the official training of the Paragon, but Dad's teachings will have to do. She closes her eyes to visualize Dad's fingers tapping away. Down, right, left, and … the option should be in the upper right. There.

She lets out a sigh of relief when an electronic voice confirms her success, "Estimated time of arrival: ten minutes."

Her knuckles against the handles hurt, and she relaxes them. The Command Center is far behind, but are Dad and Gabrielle still alive? What about Sky?

A light from the Ark winks out. Again. Then they keep flickering out one after another. A power outage?

Emily docks her escape pod in the docks where hundreds of

Strahl sleep, then follows the corridor that leads to large port-holes blurred by the Observatory's bright lights. Why didn't these go out? Is the Ark damaged?

Her ears are still ringing from the sudden change in pressure. Fast-approaching footsteps? She flattens herself against the nearest wall and Paragon agents accompanied by absent-looking civilians pass by. Armed. Have the Archeans picked their side?

Emily makes her way to the residential area, carefully avoiding detection, her heart pounding. Once there, she stops. Metal shards litter the floor and water leaks from damaged pipes in the gutted walls. Part of the ceiling has collapsed, too. How could she survive this?

There's no way in. Gabrielle was with Violet, both out of reach. As for Dad, he was working. What should she do?

She glances around, thinking. Why was she here when the explosion occurred? Violet came to get her and Gabrielle, and then they went to Violet's cabin. No, her grandmother's. They cooked and…

Cakes. Sky!

Emily traces back her steps and takes the fire escape. She hurtles down one floor and lands in a corridor that looks abandoned. Medical Bay. She wanted to come here to find Sky, but as she is about to go inside, she hesitates. The Brotherhood could be here at any moment, or even the Paragon. Whom should she trust?

A shout comes in her direction. Her blood freezes, her limbs numb. Run!

She runs blindly, and the pain in her ribs takes her breath away. She climbs stairs at random, avoiding a horde of patrolling Paragon agents who respond with gunfire that is fortunately out of range, turns right into a corridor, and climbs a few more flights of stairs.

She is out of breath and leans against the wall out of the

stairwell. Her labored breathing is so loud she can't tell if they followed her. She holds it for a few seconds to listen.

Nothing, but she can't just stand in the hallway in plain sight. The humidity is heavy, and her lungs feel soaked.

A glance to the right: sliding doors. She enters.

Then, a spray squirts at her with a substance that makes her cough violently.

The Gardens of Humanity. She takes a deep, shaky breath to calm her coughing fit. The air-conditioning system must be damaged because the artificial climates no longer work. A haze shrouds the tropical vegetation, and she can hardly see anything. The humidity on the floor probably comes from here.

Fine droplets settle on her skin. Could Sky be here? At the Academy, whenever he had a bad day, they would meet in the Gardens after class.

She ventures inside until she can no longer see the entrance, now thick with fog. There isn't anyone here, or energy signature for that matter. Could stress be playing tricks on her?

Emily rubs her temples and closes her eyes, hoping that this damn headache will help her find Sky. A bluish glow is all she needs.

She sighs as she opens her eyes again. Nothing. This place is miles long, the entire length of the Ark.

She continues, trying to remember the exact spot where they would gather. The trees are gigantic, their tops lost in the mist. Emily hugs her ribs as she coughs at the strong smell of wet earth. A presence?

Someone grabs her from behind and constricts her forcefully.

He was prepared because he gags her. She twists her neck to see the face of her attacker.

He wears a wet suit and a gas mask.

THE DRIED straw creaks under her heavy body, a side effect of the crap her captor made her breathe. Her limbs are like cotton, and her wrists are tied in front of her, chafed by her bonds. She is so weak that she can only moan and roll onto her side.

This place looks like a warehouse, a modern version of a barn. It's dark, with only a few snatches of dusty light filtering through ventilation slits where slices of greenery intersect the metal slats. Are they still in the Gardens?

There are over fifty of them, crammed together like animals in a cage. No distinction of age or gender. Children, adults, elders. The only thing they have in common is their wretched outlook. This gas has even more perverse effects than making people lose consciousness for a couple of hours. It induces a state of weakness and vulnerability for over twenty-four hours, the time the body needs to flush out the toxins. It's the same gas they use on the Mavericks at the prison. Yasmina never wanted to listen to Emily's protests against its use during interrogations, since her boss wants only one thing: to break them.

Break the body to open the mind, she said.

A guard at the entrance finishes eating something that looks like a sandwich, and hunger gnaws at Emily's stomach, her throbbing headache worsening. With each heartbeat, the auras fade in and out of focus. The effects of the gas, however, affect her sixth sense as if a veil dampened Emily's vision.

She watches the peculiar colors of her cellmates for a while. Then, after everyone else has helped themselves, she notices the two large metal containers filled with water and food. Those who can walk put as much distance as possible between their neighbors who crawl to the troughs.

Emily shuts her eyes, the stench of the swill making her miss the damned modern-day oatmeal.

She goes without food, but she needs water. Her ribs are too painful to squat over the trough and she falls sideways. After recovering from her fall, she kneels before the dirty water filled with bits of straw and floating leaves. Emily closes her eyes, dips her tied hands to collect water and drinks. She sucks too fast, choking. A strange aftertaste lingers, but fades at the second sip. Dying of thirst is not part of her plans.

She curls up where she woke up earlier, her head against the wooden walls of her cell, her eyes burning. What fate awaits her?

27

EMILY

"It's you," says a voice in an accusatory tone.

A boy around her age lies down next to her. He fidgets for a moment, probably trying to find a somewhat comfortable position. The dry straw crinkles under his legs, which are much longer than Emily's. If they were standing side by side, her head would probably be level with his collarbone. He's such a nerd with that stubble and wavy hair.

"Me what?" she asks as she casts him a glance. They stare at each other for a few moments before he breaks the ice.

"My sister told me about you," he says, scratching the hairs on his cheek.

"Your sister? Who are you?"

"Philip."

"Oh, you're Violet's brother." He stares at her again. Of course, he doesn't know her nickname, but Violet's real name escapes Emily at the moment.

"Where is she?" she worries. Philip squints with a knowing look. Gabrielle was with Violet.

"Not here." She bites her lip. Philip's aura is blurry with light green or turquoise, she can't decide. "So, you see them too. I thought I was crazy."

Her mouth opens like a fish, and he lets out an awkward laugh.

"I would make the same face if someone said that. Sorry." He must be bluffing to get her to talk. They'd call her crazy if she admitted it, and she'd get a one-way ticket to prison. Worse, they'd make her share a cell with Griffin, the lunatic who scribbles fairies wherever he goes.

"What do you think I see?" she finally says.

"You know what I mean," he scoffs. "The way you were looking at me a second ago. And before I came to talk to you, you were watching everyone here, not really looking at them, but at something *around* them." He can't be serious. Some prisoners they share the barn with are listening with keen interest. What if the word gets out? She opts for a falsely disinterested silence.

"By the way, I don't know your name, but I might as well call you Scarlet."

"My name is Emily," she retorts.

"Scarlet. A bomb ready to explode any time." She gives him the evil eye.

"Emily."

"Scarlet."

"Leave me alone." Her tone is unapologetic, but it looks like it will take more to discourage him. As if rotting in that barn wasn't enough. Emily's mouth is dry, and she pretends to go for a drink. He doesn't hold her back. Good.

The water level has dropped enough that the bottom of the container reveals blackish clumps in the corners. While Emily imagines what she could do to the guards who are exchanging jokes as a distraction, she gulps three sips to quench her thirst. The aftertaste of mold, real or imagined, lingers until she lies down on the opposite side from where Philip is watching her.

She closes her eyes, hypnotized by the whispers carried by the humid breeze of the ventilation system.

"The Creator makes us see, not without consequence." She startles as she was about to doze off. The Creator? Of course, Philip is one of those zealous believers! As if she needed that. Violet is not the same, though, an exception that confirms the rule. These believers all have this arrogant and annoying air, as if they knew everything about everything. The Creator says this, the Creator says that.

"This Creator often speaks to you?" she taunts him, her eyes still closed.

"When I paint, when it is necessary. And now more than ever." He talks about the Creator as if he were alive, a person in his own right. It's the most ridiculous thing she's ever heard. The drugs must be coursing through his veins. Poor guy.

Philip's little nerdy eyes scrutinize her, expose her, and it's annoying. He won't make her swallow that he can read auras like she can, much less that he can read her mind.

To keep her mind busy, Emily fidgets with straw. How long will they stay here? And why are they keeping them in this filthy barn, like animals?

What she would give to be with Gabrielle and Dad.

She wipes away tears of rage and sighs loudly. She throws a handful of straw that falls limply, then brings her legs up. It can't end like this. They will release them as soon as the Ark is under control.

Philip dabs at the corner of his mouth with his Sigma uniform sleeve and, when he meets her eyes, he stalks her by sitting nearby without a word, and it unnerves Emily.

"I thought I was clear."

"It doesn't work like that," he replies, glancing towards the entrance swarming with Paragon guards. "For now, I suggest you relax."

"Is that you or the Creator speaking?"

"What does it matter?" Emily's heart drums in her chest against her knees. At least she's still alive.

"Do you paint?"

"No." Emily closes her eyes to make him stop, but Philip continues in a low voice.

"I would need special pigments to paint you. Let's see. Red amaranth would do the trick though a little dark. I would make it more vibrant with the sunflower, a fit candidate with its rich yellow, and a hint of cinnamon powder, of course, to add a more earthy hue. It would be a punchy painting, to say the least."

A painter? Her eyes snap open.

"So, you're the mystery artist who exhibits in public." The paintings at the entrance of *La Orilla* that are anything but authentic: the founders' family in front of the Ark, the biblical scene of *The Last Supper* and other characterless platitudes. Bland. Conformist.

"You don't like them," he says, matter-of-factly.

"I didn't say that," she sighs.

"You don't have to say it. I can see it clearly. You make it sound like you disapprove." People are whispering and pointing at them. Exactly what they needed.

"Quiet!" shouts a masked agent Emily did not see coming. The blow comes so quickly that she forgets to breathe. The hollow sound of the baton against Philip's shoulder echoes in her head while the agent threatens them again before returning to his post at the entrance, his knuckles white against his baton.

"You enjoy watching people suffer," Philip moans, rubbing his wound with a wince. "I knew it."

"What the hell are you talking about?" she whispers stiffly. She sits cross-legged to better look at him. Sweat rolls down his cheeks.

"You could have stopped it, but you didn't."

"My wrists are bound just like yours. I didn't see it coming either," She waves her hands under his nose.

"I thought you were trained for combat, ready to act in any situation. If your legs aren't tied, you should know what to do."

"If you're so good at guessing exactly what kind of person I am, then why don't you use that to your advantage against those guards?" He wipes the sweat oozing from his upper lip with his good shoulder. On the other side, the fabric of his sweater is stained a dark red.

"I am God's painter, remember?"

"And what exactly is that supposed to mean? That you are a martyr?" He does not answer. People glance at them, and she realizes she has raised her voice too high.

Too late. The same angry guard returns with reinforcements.

"What did I say?" This time, he doesn't go after Philip. It's Emily's turn. Their tormentor beats her and a metallic taste spreads in her mouth. Another guard holds her until the guy ends up gassing her when he is too out of breath to continue. She struggles as Philip watches idly. Emily cannot read any emotion on his face, nor in his aura.

EMILY WAKES up with a taste of dirt in her mouth. In fact, her face is covered with it. She dusts herself off with the back of her hand. With all the beating, she is lucky to be alive. Thanks to the gas that still numbs her, the pain is bearable. But for how long?

A section of the wall disappears to let two people come in, each wearing a gas mask, like her attacker. They drop an unconscious man and woman. The woman has a double aura, meaning she is carrying a child. How can they treat her like this? Once the guards are gone, Emily approaches the new prisoners to check their condition.

A dizzying smell of perspiration overwhelms her. The dazed pregnant woman has only bruises, but the man's condition is bad. His hair is slick with blood and his face is swollen, as if he had been in a fight. If Sky were here, he would know what to do.

The man's aura is faint, but strangely familiar. Emily's face drains.

Dylan, Sky's father.

The woman must be Murielle, Sky's mother. Wasn't she seriously ill?

But no doubt she is pregnant. Does Sky know?

Maybe that's why he spends a lot of time with her, but ... they've already had two children.

A third child is forbidden no matter what.

One by one the pieces fall into place. Sky had to know about the baby and tried to hide it as best he could. Being a doctor, he can do the follow-up care himself, but the risk he exposes himself to is unthinkable.

Sky's parents lie in plain sight. They can't stay like this. Where is Philip?

If he's not here, then what have they done to him? Why hasn't he done anything to help her? Maybe he colluded with the guards to gather information about her in exchange for her release. Is he really Violet's brother? If he was, he must have been willing to do anything to save himself.

Even though she is still very weak from the gas, Emily moves Sky's parents by herself, pushing awkwardly with her tied hands to give them some dignity. She then goes back and forth a few times to get them to drink. The process is painful; she places their heads at an angle to pour some water through their chapped lips. Murielle has the reflex to swallow despite being unconscious, but Dylan does not react.

Emily sits next to them, hoping one of them will wake up.

Where are you, Sky?

SKY'S PARENTS are still out when Emily wakes up. Murielle's belly heaves at regular intervals, but Dylan is gasping. This is probably not a good sign.

Philip is still not in sight, though she would appreciate his help for once. Smart ass as he is, he would know what to do. But she has probably guessed right, he colluded with the guards.

The only good news is that she is gradually regaining control of her body, though not all her energy. She needs proper food.

Inaudible whispers come from outside, and Emily walks around slumped bodies, seemingly lifeless. Their breathing is so shallow that they are no better than dead.

She crouches near the cracks welded into the wall and it reeks of rotting. Two men speak, "Release her right away."

"That's not what we're meant to be doing here," the second one says. "General Duke has been very clear about what to do with the survivors until the Brotherhood is out. This is his battleground now that the Commander is safe."

"My father doesn't care about civilians," says the first. "All he wants is to be in control. Let me through." Chris! It's Chris!

"He didn't say anything about you." Chris mumbles an incomprehensible expletive.

"If that's the way it is…" A static noise, then Chris resumes in the same imperious tone as his father Duke. "Second officer Laurene Milcah herself gave the order to come and get the girl. She is one of the proteges."

"Why didn't you say so instead of wasting my time?" The voices fade into nothing.

Did Chris follow her? How could this be? He wouldn't leave his cozy nest to save a poor girl who called him a criminal. Has he changed his mind? Maybe there's still hope.

She returns to Sky's parents. Murielle has woken up, pale as a ghost, and watches her as she sits. Murielle gives her a crooked smile.

"Violet…" she whispers. "Everywhere." Violet? Does she know her?

"What do you mean?"

"It is a mixture of blue and red." Sky's mother has gone mad. The gas is affecting her badly. The only time Emily saw this kind of reaction, the prisoner was already on medication and there was something wrong with his blood. How could Emily help her?

Sounds of commotion at the entrance draw her out of her thoughts. A white-masked man barges in—Chris, judging by his energy. A second follows, the same who brought Sky's parents earlier.

Chris stands in the doorway as if something was holding him back. The man who beat her up says something to Chris, then comes to find her. She does not resist, even if her body wants to arch. She must trust Chris.

Her tormentor doesn't beat her this time, even if his eyes shoot flames of contempt at her. Once close enough to Chris, Emily sets her feet firmly on the ground.

"I'm not leaving without them," she says, her finger pointing at Sky's parents. Murielle's head is resting on Dylan, and she is watching Emily.

"Look, I can't," Chris replies, his voice made hollow by the mask.

"So, you get to decide who lives? Right, you're experienced at that."

"Don't play that game, Emily." His aura shivers. "I chose you, even though you ran away and put us all in danger."

"*You* are playing a dangerous game. Do you realize they are Skyler's parents? If anything happens to them, you'll be held responsible for wiping out his entire family." Chris gives her a bewildered look.

"What happened to them?" Chris asks the executioner.

"They were trying to flee to the research center," he replies dryly. "We intercepted them on the way while we were sweeping the area."

"What did you do to him? He's still unconscious!" Emily growls.

"We neutralized a threat to public security."

"The threat is you, fool." The slap of her torturer leaves her speechless. She kicks him hard in the crotch in return, and the guard collapses. That'll teach him for his fooling around earlier. The heat of the slap spreads in Emily's cheek while the guard groans on the ground.

"Feels good," says Emily, stretching her jaw muscles.

"You shouldn't have," Chris scolds her, keeping a safe distance from her.

"The day I need a second father, I'll let you know. Take off my ties." He looks at her unmoving while her attacker tries to get up.

"Are you waiting for him to throw himself at me or what?" Chris gets moving and once freed, Emily takes the bonds off his hands.

"So much for karma," she says between clenched teeth. Chris raises an eyebrow.

She bends down next to the guard struggling to his feet and takes off his mask.

"A good breath of fresh air will do you some good," she whispers to him while she ties him up.

He shows no signs of resistance, already in a daze. His body will take some time to get used to the gas, although she'd rather have him knocked out.

She puts on a mask and breathes in clean air. In a few hours, she should regain her full strength. Then, Sky's mother lets out a bloodcurdling scream, her hands on her face. Dylan's aura has dispersed.

The people who were around move away in a disorderly fashion. Three guards flock in the opposite direction to see what is going on.

Chris stops a guard who barks orders to take Murielle out.

"Where are they taking her? Tell me they're taking her to safety." Emily asks.

"They will put her under observation, separately." Emily jostles past him.

"I told you their death would be on your conscience," she hisses without waiting for an answer. The guards don't pay her much attention as she storms out, too busy restoring order in the barn as some children began to cry.

Chris has his share of blame, but the guilt gnaws at Emily; she should have done something for Sky's parents. Anything.

It takes a while for Chris to meet her.

"Come on," he says curtly. "There is not much time left."

"Before what?" she answers breathlessly. "I'm not leaving here until I find Sky." Chris's mask hides his expression, but his voice is firm.

"I know where he is."

He walks away from the warehouse, and the mist swallows his aura.

28

SKYLER

THE SHOCK OF THE FALL, AND THE UNCOMFORTABLE POSITION Skyler is in with Tessa slumped over him, takes his breath away. He keeps his eyes closed until his head stops spinning.

Tessa's warm breath tickles his neck and sends an electric current down his spine. Despite the gun holster pushing against his stomach, he can't help but enjoy this closeness.

Skyler does not dare to move and opens his eyes to distract himself from his uncontrollable thoughts. Brightness pierces through an air duct and makes the place look like an old photo streaked by blotches of ink. A whitish smoke filters through the light, absorbed by the darkness.

"I can't move," Tessa whispers in a panicked voice. The vibration of her voice against his chest quickens his heart rate. Tessa stirs slightly. Her hair gets in Skyler's face, and he turns his head to keep it away from his mouth. He feels his cheeks catching fire. Fortunately, the lighting plays in his favor.

"It's probably the shock," he says seriously. Some fragments may have partially damaged her lumbar nerves, which makes the risk of paralysis real. How can he let himself be distracted by anything else when Tessa's condition is so worrying?

"Don't strain," he explains, trying to sound calm. "The more tension you add, the worse it will become."

Tessa shifts a little to steady herself, one hand on Skyler's chest and the other on the adjacent wall, blocking what little light is in his field of vision.

Any movement could be dangerous, but they don't really have a choice. Skyler reluctantly moves Tessa's hand from his chest to the floor, then wriggles backward to give her room. Once he has enough space and she's safe, he stands up.

"Damn!" he shouts, rubbing his head.

"What? What's going on? Did you see something?" Tessa's distraught voice surprises him because he can't imagine her shaking like a leaf. "Damn it answer!"

"I hit my head." She sighs loudly and mumbles something.

The ceiling is much lower than he thought, which means they must have fallen into one of the Ark's vents. It's hard to tell which one, though.

He blinks repeatedly to get used to the darkness and, once it's bearable, he asks, "I'm going to put you in a sitting position, leaning against the low wall. Just relax, okay?"

"Do I really have a choice?"

"Not really," he says, amused. Even though her face is bathed in darkness, he can tell she is smiling, too.

Skyler moves her gently, then once she's settled, he sits next to her, a hand's length away. This time he has the excuse of being in a tight space.

A flush of heat warms his face.

"I wonder what caused the outage," he muses aloud. "I thought generators would take over the ventilation system."

"The Brotherhood. Something happened." She sounds worried and shifts in a rustle of fabric. "It must have something to do with the explosion or the people who caused it."

"Dylan told me once that the Ark wouldn't survive without a functioning ventilation system."

"We will make it our priority when we are in charge." The idea of changing the course of history is appealing—that the Ark is not an end in itself, and he will do so alongside Tessa.

Skyler moves closer to the vent opening to see where they've landed. He squints, blinded by the white light. The fault seems localized unless the electrical system here is independent. If he had a map of the in betweens, he might guess where they are, but he'll have to settle for a visual scan.

He reaches through to feel the surface, his face pressed against the thin-edged metal blades digging into his skin.

"I know where we are," he says, not knowing whether he should be happy.

"And?"

"We are in the Gardens."

"Good. So, how do we get out?" Now that his vision has adjusted, he can make out the grass which is the wrong color. Further up, thick smoke engulfs the tree trunks to create some kind of fog.

"It's bad."

"Worse than being trapped in a hole?" she presses him.

"A seaquake, a power failure, and now this?" he says, distraught.

"Please." Tessa squeals, and he sighs, defeated.

"Actually, we have two problems. First, few people pass through here. We are in a forest."

"Aren't there people to maintain the place?"

"Normally, they would. But with this thick smoke, it's hard to tell. You can hardly see anything and inhaling it could be fatal."

"If it's smoke," she stresses. "Carbon dioxide would choke us, but we're at ground level, which helps."

Skyler can already imagine what is likely to happen. They will die in this hole, slowly. The metal blades are welded to the wall and even if someone were to find them, they couldn't help them from the outside.

What exactly is this smoke?

Skyler sits next to Tessa and shuts his eyes. Stress creeps into his veins, and a lump forms in his throat. He massages his numb cheeks.

His mother needs him. He can't let her down again.

When their ancestors faced the Flood, their fate was already sealed. Resilience was the only way to keep on living.

"I didn't come all this way to fail," Tessa mutters, her voice breaking. "I can't lose you."

She sniffs. He would like to embrace her, but something holds him back.

His thoughts are a jumble, and he momentarily forgets where he is and what they are doing here. Not so long ago, he was on a beach on the surface. They had made it.

His concentration escapes him, and his eyes can't focus. Stuck. Air vent.

"Zack." Tessa's voice is surreal, an echo.

He mumbles, confused, "What?"

"He will pay for what he did to you." Darkness flickers, blends, swirls, and reshapes continuously for eternity. Clouds, waves, wings.

As time passes, his body becomes heavier and more tired. He struggles to keep his eyes open while Tessa is already sleeping. He moves closer to her and puts his forehead against hers. Too hot as a ray of translucent light showers them. Tessa looks at him with glassy eyes, their faces so close to one another. The curtain of darkness parts so that Skyler can gaze at Tessa's melancholic beauty.

He breathes.

She exhales.

He inhales.

Tessa's mouth is plump, and Skyler swallows hard. He feels

her fever; they share it as energy flows between them. Skyler's body takes the lead, and his lips melt over Tessa's. He closes his eyes and breathes in relief. She moans softly as she returns his kiss in a mixture of pain and satisfaction. A whisper. That name again: Zack.

Feeling his limbs grow heavier and heavier, he drops to the cold ground that sticks to his now bare back. How did this happen? No strength to care.

Soon his legs rub against the metal warming under his feverish body.

It tastes so good. Coconut. The real thing, not the artificial flavor he knows.

The softness of her neck against his fingers. A shiver.

He tastes her skin, and each time it gets better. His moans are sometimes loud, but irregular as if he submerged his head in water and came out to catch his breath. Skyler lets himself be carried by his senses. He no longer knows where he is or who he is.

He is here. She is there.

He sways between unconsciousness and reality until he falls.

He jolts awake, dizzy and nauseous.

Skyler gags hard, pinned to the ground. His mouth hangs open, propped on shaky arms. His eyes water, an unnatural rush of saliva dripping from his lips, and he feels like something wants to come out. Poison.

The painful contractions stop after a few minutes, and a familiar voice reaches him. Skyler dries his tears of pain and lets himself flop on his side, exhausted.

"Need help?" Skyler would recognize that arrogant voice anywhere. "What are you doing in this hole? Oh, I think I know why. You have company."

"Will you shut up for once, Chris?" Skyler speaks like he's hungover and even Chris notices. His arrogance gives way to concern for a change.

Chris slips something through the opening and Skyler grabs a rubbery-textured mask. He frowns, then sees that Chris is wearing one himself.

"What is this for?" The echo in Skyler's head makes him dizzy.

"The smoke is contaminated," Chris replies in a hollow voice. Skyler puts on the mask and the rubber sucks his face unpleasantly. The air takes on a whole new flavor, and his compressed lungs relax with each cleansing breath.

"I didn't think you'd have company. You'll have to share." Tessa is still unconscious while Skyler struggles to stay awake. "Right now, you need to get out of there, but I'm going to need some time."

"You can't. The slats are welded to the frame." Skyler still feels weak but is slowly coming to.

"I know how. Even if you don't believe me."

"You don't have to." Stupid. Of course, he needs Chris's help.

"Leave it to me. In the meantime, share the mask to detox. I'll be back with Emily."

Crushing the grass in his path, Chris melts into the thick, foul fog.

OVER HALF AN HOUR after Chris's visit, Tessa wakes up. Each time Tessa breathes into the mask, Skyler holds his breath as long as possible, but never longer than a minute. The stress must have something to do with it.

Since his thoughts have become coherent again, the cold has crept into his bones, the artificial climate system still down.

Actually, this is a good thing. The hot winds would probably burn them alive in the vents.

Disturbing flashes from the night before come back to him and he is almost certain that something happened, though he won't admit it.

"He will get us out?" she says once Skyler is done telling her about Chris. He couldn't help but paint an unflattering picture of Chris. At least Tessa will know what kind of guy he is. "How did he find us?"

"He didn't mention it," says Skyler, suspicious. "I was too out of it to ask."

"You said he had left the Medical Bay for another position, right?"

"Yes, why?" He gives her back the mask since it is her turn to speak.

"Do you know what the wristband you have is for exactly?" Skyler runs his fingers over it, suddenly aware of its presence. For as long as he can remember, he has worn it like a second skin.

"They use it to identify us on the Ark. At least that's what I thought."

"The Paragon also uses it to track each passenger."

"You mean Chris is working for the Paragon? He would never agree to help his father. They hate each other."

"He could have borrowed the technology to pinpoint your location." Chris could have been watching his every move. Creepy.

"It doesn't add up. I don't see why he would go to all that trouble."

"Of course, his father would have to invite him into his office to give him access. If what you're telling me is true, then it's unlikely." Chris avoids his father as much as he can, especially since he refused to work for him. That's when their relationship started to go downhill. Chris and Skyler aren't so different in that respect. Skyler's relationship with Dylan isn't flawless either.

"If we leave out that option, all that's left is the Command Center." Tessa moves closer to the light, which calms her down. "They have access to all the technology aboard."

"You mean he works for them?"

"This is the only explanation." The implications are disturbing. What if Chris knew of Skyler's secret ties to the rebel Paragon faction that wants to fulfill the Brotherhood's vision? Would he have the power to take out Skyler?

"We'd better keep him on our side as long as possible."

"Until we carry out the plan," he adds. Tessa nods in agreement.

"It'll be up to him whether he wants to support the Commander or join us." Not the greatest idea, but it would make things easier or else Skyler will have to make things clear between them.

"You know, I wasn't myself yesterday," Tessa says after a while.

"Do you remember what happened?" he asks, his cheeks burning. "I mean, not the details, but—"

"We were both intoxicated. I… I would never—"

"Do you regret it?" he asks, surprised by his own question. She seems taken aback for a few seconds, then becomes serious again.

"Just forget about it." He wants to insist but changes his mind when he hears the grass crack. Two people emerge from the toxic fog: Chris and a smaller figure, Emily.

Chris was telling the truth. She is alive.

Skyler wants to forget what pulled them apart before all this crap happened. He has an irresistible urge to hug her.

"I've got it," says Chris dryly.

"What the hell happened to you, Sky?" says Emily, her voice strange.

"You sound so weird," Skyler says, smiling.

"Don't you dare laugh at me. Look at the mess you got yourself into."

"I'm glad to see you too." Skyler can't hold a grudge against her for what happened. Knowing she's safe is all that matters now.

"The girl," mutters Tessa, who does not join the conversation. Instead, she grabs the extra mask Chris hands her and thanks him.

"It's Emily. Not the girl," points out Emy. "And you're the infamous Tessa." Skyler's gaze shifts from Tessa to Emily.

"I don't want to spoil your reunion," Chris interjects, "but we must hurry."

"How do you plan to get them out of there?" asks Emy, arms crossed.

"With this." He throws a tool to her, and she barely catches it. "We're going to dismantle the gate from the outside. Look, I'll show you."

After a few minutes of shaking the grate back and forth, Chris and Emy clear the opening. They help them out, and Skyler struggles to keep his balance, his legs sleepy. He tells them about Tessa's condition and the fact that she needs to go to Med Bay.

"No," objects Tessa. "It will have to wait. There's no time."

"I agree," Chris immediately adds. "We need to get off the Ark as soon as possible."

"I'm not going back," says Emy. "I think I've made that clear enough."

"You got Sky back like you wanted," Chris retorts, clearly irritated. "As for your family—"

"That's not the point," Emily cuts him off. "I don't see why we should run away with a bunch of cowards who don't even deserve to command the Ark when our families and friends are still here."

"It's not a simple choice, but—"

"Our life is here. Everything is." Skyler recoils at the way these two talk to each other.

"Sky are you coming?" asks Tessa, who can read his mind. "Now's our chance."

"I—"

"If the Command Center detaches from the Ark, this ship will sink to the bottom of the ocean. No one will survive."

"That's why you guys have to follow me now!" Chris sighs as he heads to the trail. "It's the only way."

"Sky, can I talk to you alone first?" asks Emy, who exchanges a furtive glance with Chris. Skyler nods, and they move far enough so that Tessa and Chris are a shadow in the fog, so their voices are a mere whisper that could be mistaken for the rustle of leaves.

"What's the matter, Emy?" His heart speeds up for no reason.

"I … I wanted to apologize for what happened. I shouldn't have said what I said to you. My words went over my head." Emily isn't one to admit when she's wrong, but he never doubted the sincerity of their friendship. He smiles under his mask, relieved.

"I've forgotten already." The next moment, they are in each other's arms, not knowing who made the first move. Both of them say at the same time, "I thought you were dead."

"I thought you would never forgive me." They burst out laughing and finally break their embrace. He had sorely missed this.

"Skyler." A strange emotion crosses Emy's voice and he waits expectantly. "There's something else I need to tell you before you find out for yourself. It's about your parents."

"What do you mean, *my parents*?" The way she looks at him, he knows it's bad.

"I saw them while I was locked up in the warehouse." Locked up? In a warehouse?

"Are they okay?" he says, panic in his throat. "Which warehouse? Where are they now? Why aren't they with you?"

"Sky, I tried, but..." What are they doing here? He must go see them. Mom has probably been off her medication for too long, and her seizures must plague her. Dylan is not fit to take care of her properly.

"I'll go get them. I won't leave them here." He heads into the fog, but Emily grabs his arm and forces him to look at her.

"You can't," she says in a strange voice. "The Paragon will put you in solitary confinement like they did to me."

"Why didn't you bring them with you?"

"They were a mess when they arrived. Chris freed me, but it was already too late for your father. He's ... he died in the warehouse."

"How did you...?" Dead. Dead. Dead? Words fail him.

"I don't have your medical expertise, but he took a big blow to the head. All I could find out was that he got into a violent fight when the Paragon dragged him here."

"And Mom? How is she?"

"Passed out from the gas, but..." Emily lowers her voice into a whisper, "Sky, you can't pretend nothing's happened. Your mother. The Paragon will find out, and they won't spare your family."

"What are you talking about? Her depression is severe, but nothing that can't be undone." Emily stares at him, looking hurt.

"Don't pretend you don't know. You can't hide her pregnancy forever."

"What?" The events of the last few days come flooding back to him. Her nausea. What Dylan wanted to tell him.

Dylan. Dylan is dead.

"How long?" says Skyler, confused.

"What?"

"How long since he died?" he urges her, raising his voice. "I need to know." He needs to focus on the only thing he has left and what he knows for sure: the window of opportunity.

"A little over an hour."

"Wait for me here. I have to go see him."

"Sky, I told you. You can't! You won't come back from there alive, believe me. He's gone. I'm sorry to tell you this, but you have to move on even if it's hard to accept." She doesn't understand. Dylan is dead! His memories, his life, his soul.

"I can't. Not when I know I can preserve a part of him. And Mom." He still has a memory sphere from Mrs. Farrell's transfer. He always brings an extra one just in case. His memories are gradually disintegrating, yet it is still possible to recover something.

"You mean the spheres? Do they really work?" she asks.

"I hope so." Emily nods silently even though he suspects she doesn't approve of the risks involved. She would do the same in his place. That's why Emily is precious to him. She remains genuine, no matter the circumstances, and some misunderstanding won't change that.

"I'll do what I can," she says.

Under her mask, he can hear her smile.

CHRIS HOLDS THE PARAGON SOLDIERS' attention long enough for Emily and Skyler to infiltrate the vast warehouse.

Skyler has walked here so many times to find peace when his world was falling apart, to remember that there are beautiful things—unattainable for now, but maybe not forever.

Life has left this now poisoned place, a decaying tomb. A resting place turned into a sacked sanctuary because of the Brotherhood.

There's that smell again, a mixture of solvent and decay impossible to forget. So many patients have died at the clinic, especially in the last few weeks, but this time it's not a victim he doesn't know about. Dad.

They dumped his remains like an animal carcass, stuck in a corner of the warehouse where the other corpses are piled up. A deep disgust burns in his throat with every blank stare he catches. Chris said that most of them are victims of the explosion that blew up the upper levels, while a fraction died from an overdose of the hallucinogenic gas.

What prompted Duke to take such action? Isn't he supposed to protect the Archeans? It doesn't make sense.

Emily helps Skyler move Dylan's body without a word. He mechanically installs the equipment they picked up in his cabin, to begin the transfer to the memory sphere. A series of worst-case scenarios about his mother having a baby flash before his eyes. How could his parents have kept such a thing from him? They could be convicted for breaking the law.

The sphere is slow to light up. Way too slow. The electric shafts of light expand until they become a small cloud, tiny compared to the other patients Skyler has treated before.

"We have to go," Tessa urges them as she stands in the doorway. "Chris is already on his way."

"Hold on." Skyler stares at the sphere hoping it will light up more, but it doesn't. The rest of his father's memories are lost forever.

29

SKYLER

The sphere is still warm in its case when they emerge from the Gardens' mist. While the others are chatting, Skyler's mind is elsewhere. Why does his misfortune always have something to do with Chris? How can one person bring so much destruction?

It would be so easy to get rid of Chris. He looks so harmless. But would that do Allen and Dylan justice? Truth be told, the more Skyler looks at him, the more he pities him. What is there to hold on to when your bloodline is responsible for the slaughter of a family?

Forgiveness. Is it necessary?

Chris is not his father. Chris rescued them while he didn't have to. Perhaps to redeem himself?

Skyler struggles with the strange feeling that gnaws at his guts, scaring him even—a hodgepodge of contradictions. Should he trust Chris now? He openly decries his father and shows his good will by playing the hero. Isn't that proof enough that he has changed?

The fact remains that Chris let Allen fall when he had a choice.

Chris could have … done what, exactly? He had arrived too late and was just as distraught as Skyler had been. Did Chris really cause Allen's death? That thought alone threatens to send Skyler reeling. They were young, only fifteen, and it wasn't a situation they could have prepared for. Had emotions blinded Skyler? Wouldn't he have toppled over if not for Chris?

As for Dylan, Chris is not the issue. The Paragon is. Duke.

Skyler stares at the overlapping boot prints on the trail that look like a muddy mosaic with sordid charm. Perhaps even the language of an unsuspected beauty: earth, water, angles, and curves that intertwine, solidified by air.

Putting Chris's mistakes behind him is not so simple when the past becomes the present, a frantic race with no way to win.

Skyler tightens his hand around the box. All he has left is his mother, detained by the Paragon. He wanted to go and find her, but the others stopped him for his own good. Skyler obeyed them because of Emily.

"Now what do we do?" she asks once they are out.

"Do you really need to ask?" Chris replies scathingly, glancing at his wristband. "We only have an hour left before the Command Center comes off thanks to Emily for screwing up the internal pressurizer."

"They would have been gone by now, and Sky and Tessa would have died in a ventilation duct."

"The more likely it is for the Brotherhood to break into the Command Center, especially if the door is not airtight."

Tessa sends a subtle smile to Skyler and says, "What are we waiting for?"

"The Mavericks are on the run with rebel soldiers from the Paragon," Emily points out. "What do we do about them?"

Skyler asks them to explain the current situation, but Chris cuts it short.

"The Ark has become hell with the Brotherhood calling the

shots. Even if we all make it out alive, controlling this chaos may be difficult. We expected it to happen, eventually. No matter how a crisis is handled, some people will always be dissatisfied."

"Is that what your new mentor taught you?" Emily says snidely.

"This is the history of our civilization. Justice for some does not equal happiness for everyone."

Skyler is about to say something, but Emily beats him to it, "What do you know about justice? You always got what you wanted from your father. If you were born into a family with less privilege, your definition of justice would take on a whole new meaning."

"Probably," says Chris calmly. "But it's not all about family and privilege."

"What about the explosion?" cuts in Skyler to bring the conversation back. "Who is behind it?" Knowing their identity could turn the tables. What if it was the Paragon and not the Brotherhood?

"I don't have that information. Anyway, what matters is to stay alive. If we die, all will be for nothing."

"It's a detail that could change everything," insists Skyler.

"Is there a way to access the Ark's surveillance cameras?" asks Tessa. "To get to the Command Center safely, we should first make sure the coast is clear, or at least prepare for any run-ins. I know the Paragon, and they are well organized. They must have devised a plan to control the ship."

"They'll let us through, but it'll take time," says Chris.

"I wouldn't count on that. We need to learn more or else it's a suicide mission."

"I agree," adds Emily. "I want to know more about this Brotherhood first."

"Why?" asks Skyler.

"I have my reasons." Chris waves his hands in submission,

clearly annoyed. "We will make a stop at the Archives, but then we won't have time for another detour. Any objections?"

"Since when do you call yourself the leader of this group?" points out Emily. "I hope you realize everyone makes their own choices, whether you like it or not."

"You'll thank me when you live long enough to remember what I did to save us all."

SKYLER AND EMILY walk side by side as Tessa leads the way, gun in hand. Pretty handy to have Tessa who used to work for the Paragon before she switched loyalties. The Brotherhood has planted its seeds in the right places under Duke's scrutinizing gaze, proving that he is not flawless.

Chris also has his weaknesses.

Tessa's condition has improved greatly; her gait is no longer clumsy, so her wound may only be superficial, or this ointment exclusive to the Paragon has powerful healing properties.

As they walk through the corridors barely lit by the Ark's emergency lights, it almost feels like a foray into an alien world. Skyler thought he knew everything about this place, but the secrets are as considerable as the number of Archeans. When Allen introduced him to the in betweens, he should have known that it was just the beginning.

On their way to the Archives, Skyler whispers to Emily.

"What do you really have in mind?" She does not answer immediately, a shadow of melancholy in her face.

"It was during the last simulation. That man on the balcony of that huge building."

The Paragon prepared them for repopulating, sharpening their senses, and fortifying their mental abilities. They warned them that their perceptions and experiences could influence the environment they navigate in the simulation. This is what makes this technology so effective: It has the ability to make them believe.

Isn't it the Paragon who manages the simulations?

"He told me about my mother and the Brotherhood," she explains, her eyes glistening. "The Brotherhood killed her, Sky. Those assholes got her convicted. I can't run away from the Ark until justice is served."

The Paragon and the Brotherhood. The two seem connected, but something is missing. How does the Syndrome fit into all of this?

Skyler feels bad for Emily, but her past is hers only. He knows the pain that comes with it.

"I'm not leaving without you," he says. "I don't even know if I'll be able to see my mother again when this is over. You're all I have left."

"This is not the point, Sky." Emily watches him as if trying to read his mind. "You, of all people, should understand what it's like to know your family's killer is still out there." She says the right thing as usual. Even if he can't stand the methods used by the Brotherhood, their ideal remains the same: what he has always wanted. Some would call it opportunism, but he needs something to keep him going.

He does not care about what happens to the Brotherhood. But Emily…

"You know me," she adds in a lighter tone. "I have to deal with this in my own way. I never intended to run away."

An unspoken agreement. His plans are no secret to her, even if he wanted.

"At least promise me that when you're done, you'll come and join us. I'll try to slow them down on my end so they can't escape, but I'm going to need you for the rest."

When he and Tessa have decision-making power on this ship, Emily will be invaluable to them. She has the charisma he does not have. Although Tessa believes he could lead the Ark to the Promised Land, he knows he's just a pawn in the Brotherhood's plans.

But what will Emily think when she finds out what he is doing? Will she forgive him?

"Anything you want." Emily's tone is so light that Skyler lets out a laugh to hide his discomfort. She squints for a split second, but Chris waves them off as Tessa halts to a stop.

They are not that far from the Archives, far enough from the Gardens to be preserved in case of an accident.

Because of the power outage, it's hard to see if anyone followed them. The gas from the Gardens has seeped out, and the rare bluish lights reflect off it.

Two Paragon agents leap out of the mist, but Tessa is faster and shoots them down with only two shots. Skyler is speechless.

Tessa beckons them forward and steps over the two corpses that lie in a pool of blood without paying them any attention. No one dares say anything until they get into the empty hall of the Archives. Once the automatic doors slide shut behind them, the independent generator starts up and the lights come on and they all take off their masks. A smell of heated plastic hangs in the air and Skyler wipes away the sweat around his mouth, scratching the itch on his face.

"I'll find you a place in the Command Center," Chris says to Tessa. "We need people like you."

"To do what exactly?" asks Tessa, who raises an eyebrow.

"There is a lot to do, believe me." Chris's eyes glint, which turns Skyler's stomach.

"You killed those men as if nothing had happened," Emy says suspiciously. "Is that what the Paragon taught you or is it just you?"

"Emy please," says Skyler. "She saved our lives. You could at least thank her."

"You don't know what the Paragon is capable of," Tessa replies. "Let alone what's going on in their ranks."

"It's you I'm curious about. I was wondering what you were doing with Sky. Shouldn't you be with them? Unless you've deserted."

"My loyalties are none of your concern. I don't share the same vision as Duke, it's true, but I don't want to see the Ark go down either. His methods are anything but commendable."

"What about yours?" Emily glares at her.

"You'll have all the time in the world to settle your accounts in the Command Center," Chris interrupts them. "In less than forty-seven minutes to be precise."

"I was done anyway," replies Emily, who heads down the hallway to a Nave.

"Where are you going?" says Chris.

"Settle my accounts, as you say." Chris unlocks the door for her and slips in. Skyler and Tessa follow them, while Emily's annoyed voice fades as she locks herself in one of the glass cubicles. Tessa does the same and leaves Skyler alone with Chris.

"No more than fifteen minutes," Chris warns him in a vain attempt to control the situation. Skyler does not reply and heads for the sphere room, but Chris stops him.

"Why are you still giving me the cold shoulder?"

"Don't think that I forgave you only because you saved me."

Skyler seals the door in front of Chris's stunned look.

SKYLER SETS his father's sphere in the compartment to scan it and the screen displays an estimated wait time of more than a week. Since when does the process take that long? By then, the Ark will be nothing more than a wreck on the ocean floor.

He sits in the Nave, which purrs at his touch. He browses the Archives as if by instinct, swiping the menus with a wave. The videos of the explosion require a special password.

Even though he hates to admit it, he needs Chris's help. Skyler swallows his pride and calls for him.

"Now you'd like to talk to me?" asks Chris as he steps into the small space.

"Don't make this harder than it is. Your code." Chris could simply refuse, but he taps on the holographic keyboard willingly. Once the access is unlocked, he gives Skyler a smirk before reminding him that time is running out and that they will have to leave quickly.

The smart system has catalogued the videos of the explosion under the same event file from different angles. A preliminary analysis shows significant damage in strategic locations throughout the Ark. The blast blew up a section identified on a real-time map. The Paragon headquarters, the Command Center, and the Gardens and Archives' residential areas are shut off.

Curious to find out what caused the explosion, Skyler watches a re-enactment of the event before the blast. The footage shows gas leaking from a wall leading to an in between. Strange.

He rewinds to make sure nothing contradicts his hypothesis. The in between has no surveillance camera, which means someone who knows the ship's underbelly is responsible.

Suddenly, someone emerges from a corner, tall and very pale, or maybe it's the gas blurring the lens. Something hits the camera and the video cuts. From a different angle, the post-blast images show how extensive the damage is across most of the corridors. All direct means of reaching the Command Center are affected.

How did Chris get to them then? Unless the Paragon cleared up a section, but from the extent of the damage, they would need several days.

Another event appears in the list labeled as evacuation under progress. Survivors of the attack fill the atrium. They brought more to the Gardens, just like they did with Emily and his parents. The news feed shows several checkpoints that the Paragon is using, their symbol prominently displayed on the screen. The explosion has damaged the circuits, and the cameras of the Command Center are offline.

The in betweens could take them there, but with the blackout, they'll have trouble finding their way around as their fall into the air duct evidenced. They will have very little time.

Skyler is about to shut the Nave down, but something holds him back. He pulls himself out and walks over to the control panel. With a wave of his hand, he scans his wristband, which gives him access to the memory spheres directory.

There are more than a hundred of them, shining bright like stars, and a feeling of pride washes over him. Chris knocks on the glass door and urges him to hurry.

Skyler mouths to him he only needs a minute. He chooses a sphere.

There is nothing more personal than someone's memories. He never opened its contents except for the man who had volunteered for the project, even before Skyler used a proper sphere.

This time it's different. Mrs. Farrell was his patient, but also a friend. Her sudden passing is so recent he can still hear her wild stories that would have Emily roll her eyes every ten seconds. Fortunately, Elaine had given him permission to use her sphere for research, even if she hadn't bothered with the jargon, as she said. Mrs. Farrell had trusted him, and he didn't plan to disappoint her now.

Various events are listed, but what interests him most is the label *family*. Video footage of Elaine Farrell's relatives during birthdays and major events follows. Skyler watches intently, though the images don't stay long enough for him to dwell on them. He examines the many faces, which are surprisingly sharp. He was hoping Nathan would finish upgrading the system as he had promised. How strange is it to see through someone's eyes as if wearing a second skin. He cannot imagine what Nathan will be able to accomplish.

Jerky knocks on the glass door startle Skyler, who meets Chris's angry gaze. He turns off Mrs. Farrell's sphere in a hurry as Chris storms in, though the access should be restricted.

"Took you long enough. Thirty-two minutes. We're leaving." Skyler grunts in response and heads for the exit, Chris close behind. They meet Emily and Tessa, waiting for them on either side of the entrance.

Tessa is pacing, deep in her thoughts, and Emily is biting her lower lip, busy looking at her fingernails. Skyler frowns. Something is bothering her.

"The explosion screwed up the cameras," Skyler says to Tessa.

"I still managed to connect to some independent cameras only known to the Paragon," she replies, looking at them in turn. "We'll have to go through the skylight in the dining hall. It's the only shortcut, but first we need to actually get there." Is that how she knew where Skyler was when Clarissa was about to take her life?

"You mean jumping off ten stories?" he says, baffled. Tessa holds back a small laugh as Chris watches them, annoyed. Emily doesn't seem to be paying any attention to them.

"Will the stairs suit you, Doctor?" adds Tessa.

"What's the plan?" says Chris, aggravated.

"We're going to the dining hall, then to the Command Center," Tessa says, unmoved. "Given the way the explosion split the Ark in two, taking a detour would take too long."

Could there be an alternative to the in betweens? Skyler turns to Chris.

"How did you get to us?"

"The same way Emily did. Ask her." Upon hearing her name, she looks up as if they caught her doing something foolish.

"The Strahl," she says, regaining her composure. "It was the fastest way."

"Let's do it that way then," Skyler says, almost relieved. It will be much better. The risks involved in using the in betweens are many, especially since they don't know what lies near the Command Center.

"No," cuts Chris. "We were each able to take a Strahl because Emily screwed up the pressurizer and triggered the evacuation mode. Now that it's fixed and stabilized, there's only one way in and that's from within the Ark, which, let me remind you, will shut off in twenty-nine minutes."

"In that case, we can use the in betweens," says Skyler. "Chris, have you had time to explore the network?"

"A little. Why?" he asks, suspicious.

"You can help me if I ever hesitate. We are all in the same boat." Gunshots, followed by a muffled scream, cut their conversation short.

A limping figure flashes past the corridor, and two civilians march closely behind as they reload their weapons. Skyler recognizes the injured man a split second later.

"Leander!" He rushes out of the archive hall without thinking. The air is much cooler than inside as one civilian turns his back to Skyler. The other marches in the opposite direction, his eyes empty as if his soul has been sucked out. Then, he points his gun at Skyler, who makes a run for it. He loses his balance and falls forward, arm outstretched, as a bullet scratches his back. The gunshot pulses in his eardrums.

Skyler immediately gets back on his feet and forks to the side. Two quick gunshots force him to throw himself on the ground. His forearms absorb the shock as they rub painfully against the metal floor. His skin is already burning, chafed by the friction, and he turns around to glimpse the civilian slumped on the ground.

His ears are still ringing when Tessa walks up to him.

"Are you all right?" One of her braids is loose, and she looks pale.

"I'm fine, thanks," says Skyler as he gets up. "I shouldn't have gotten myself involved."

"Not at all. It gave me a clear shot. They didn't expect me, too busy shooting at you and your friend." Skyler returns a shy smile, still embarrassed by his recklessness, then meets the others gathered in the Archives' hallway. Chris helps Leander stand.

"Let me see that wound," says Skyler, who walks up to him to assess the damage to his flank.

"I can tell you it hurts like hell," he swears through gritted teeth.

"These civilians, are they Mavericks working for the Brotherhood?" asks Emily, frowning. "They looked drugged as if they had lost all sense of reality."

"Unless it's the Syndrome that makes them like that," says Leander. "I have no idea."

"These are not known effects anyway," Skyler replies. "It must be something else."

"We don't have time to argue about what happened to them," Chris interrupts. "Twenty minutes."

"I have to take care of his injury first or he won't be able to keep up," insists Skyler. He digs his fingers into the tender flesh with no warning, and Leander lets out a scream.

"What the hell are you doing to him? You're going to infect his wound and it's going to get worse."

"I'm helping him. Tessa, I need your ointment if you have any left."

"What ointment?" presses Chris.

"It will save him," she answers tersely. Tessa hands over the half-filled tube, and Skyler rushes to open it.

"Just put a little on this time. It'll work just as well." He applies the foamy medicine that fills up the bullet hole. Satisfied, Skyler gets up to give the tube back to Tessa.

"It's anesthetic," she adds. "You should be able to follow."

"I can't," croaks Leander, his eyes bulging as if he hadn't slept in days.

"What are you talking about?" asks Chris, grabbing his shoulders. "I've been looking for you everywhere. Now that you're here, you won't leave us."

"I escaped from the refugee camp. They are killing us all."

"All the more reason to get as far away from them as possible."

"Who?" asks Skyler.

"The Paragon."

"That's nonsense," Chris growls, bewildered. "Why would my father do that?"

"Why don't you tell us," Emily says harshly. "He made you. You share the same blood and the same flesh. You must reason in the same way."

"Emily," Skyler says despite himself. "I don't think Chris knows. That's no reason to go after him."

"But—"

"Chris," resumes Leander. "I have to get to Mira. You know how stubborn she can be."

"If you go now, you'll die with her," Chris retorts, his voice deeper. They both look at each other intently until Leander speaks, his lips pursed.

"I'm willing to take the risk. Mira is at the research center, all alone. She was not with the refugees, which means she might still be alive."

"You don't know that," Chris replies emotionally, his fists clenched. "She is obsessed with her father's illness."

"You won't change my mind."

"Look at you! You won't even make it there." Chris has a bitter smile. He almost looks vulnerable.

"Not if I go with him," Emily offers. Skyler's heart rate quickens, and he grabs her arm.

"You can't be serious. I need you."

"And I need to go there," she says, determined. "I can't tell you why now. You just have to trust me."

Skyler should reason with her, but his throat constricts, and no sound comes out. He drops his arm. When the time comes to command the ship, Emily won't be by his side. Reality hits him hard and his lip quivers. He holds back with all his might, what could overwhelm him if he doesn't keep his mouth shut.

"Once we're done, we'll try to get to you," Emy tells them. "This is the longer detour we talked about."

"You're crazy," says Chris, who raises his arms in exasperation. Tessa approaches Emy and hands her a gun.

"Take this. It will come in handy." They exchange a hesitant look, then Emily accepts. The glint in Tessa's eyes looks like a form of deep respect.

"See you later." Emily tucks the gun into her pocket, stock out, and gives Skyler a hug.

"I'm sorry," she whispers. Something tickles his neck, and he knows it's a tear. Emily joins Leander.

"We'll see you on the other side," says Leander, who moves with Emy's help. Skyler can't believe he's letting them go without doing anything. The feeling of helplessness gnaws at him, the same as when he had to let go of Allen's hand for lack of strength. He can't take his eyes off of Emy until they disappear around the corner.

"Thank you," Chris tells him. "For sticking up for me. For staying."

Skyler hesitates, then walks over to Tessa. They will take control of the Ark and lead the Archeans to the Promised Land for a new beginning. For Emily.

30

EMILY

It's time for answers.

Going with Leander to Delta Labs is just an excuse, it's true. But the wait is over, Mom. Your murderer can't hide forever. He'll be held accountable.

The hard, angular edges of the gun in her hand are charmless. It is too bulky, the burden of a dreaded responsibility. Even though Dad insisted on training her to defend herself following the Paragon's teachings, she has always had misgivings about firearms. There is something horribly wrong with capturing death in a metal device of this size. The spirit of a cold, ruthless judge that has no place on the Ark. Why give it the power to take the lives of survivors? A ghost ship is not the way to start civilization anew.

With her free hand, Emily helps Leander to walk, crippled for his bruised side. The humidity-soaked corridors slowly come one after the other, but time flies. They have less than twenty minutes to find Mira and learn the truth.

"What if we come across armed people?" asks Leander, short of breath.

"We get rid of them," Emily replies flatly. They leave the

seeming comfort of the diffuse lights for a darkness-filled corner.

"This girl... You think you can do what she did? She wasted them without flinching," Leander adds, thoughtfully.

"You can do it if you want." Leander doubts her abilities. She may not be as good as Tessa, but she has guts.

"That's not what I'm saying."

"So shut up and watch." Her false confidence actually makes her feel more confident. Hopefully, it will be enough to get them through the next twenty minutes.

Their shadows stretch on the wall, dimly lit by a stray beam of light.

"She's lucky to have a guy like you," says Emily to lighten the mood. They walk into a new corridor with several perpendicular branches dotted with scattered lights.

"She doesn't know," he says, taking a deep breath.

Emily looks at him in disbelief. He keeps his head down to make sure he doesn't trip over an invisible string.

"You risk your life for a girl who doesn't even know you're in love with her?"

"It's more complicated than that," he says with a grim look on his face. "Especially when this girl has someone else in mind."

"I thought you settled this at the party." She leans against the wall at each intersection to check no one is lurking. Leander seems to stand better on his two legs. This ointment is surprisingly effective.

"Chris," he mumbles. "She loves him." A variation jolts his energy, as if someone had pinched him.

"What did he say?"

"You know him. He doesn't really care about her." Emily pushes Leander to the left and throws herself against the opposite wall. She clutches the butt of her gun and presses it against her chest, her heart pounding.

Damn it. It was just a shadow.

"What the hell?" he breathes out. He helps himself off the wall to get up, but she gestures for him to be quiet. Then she sees the shadow again.

"Someone's coming," she whispers. A headache comes over her at the same time. Exactly what she needed. "Well, I guess so."

Did she see well? Twice, yes, but it happened so fast.

"Are you going to shoot him?" he asks ominously in a low voice.

"You say that like I have a choice."

"If he hasn't shot at us yet, it means he hasn't seen us. We should just run."

"I say it's a bad idea." Her intuition tells her in flashing colors not to.

"Look at the hallway," he adds, pointing a finger ahead. "It's going to take us too long, anyway. If you want to have any chance of reaching Chris and the others, you have to get going." She sighs. Either she shoots or they risk their lives.

Leander raises his eyebrows, "So?"

"If it goes wrong, it will be your fault," she says, immediately regretting her decision.

"You decide and you blame me? For a girl who works in the name of justice—"

"Oh, shut up."

Emily moves on ahead and her fears grow when a figure leaps out to block her path to Delta Labs, the triangular insignia shining tauntingly on the frosted doors. They were almost there!

"Which side?" a young, armed girl around Emily's age asks. Her face shares Reyes's features with her long, dark brown hair, dark eyes, and swarthy complexion.

"Maverick," Leander says while hobbling over to Emily, who stiffens. What game is he playing?

"The coast is clear ahead," adds a middle-aged woman who comes out of the darkness.

Two shadows. Like mother, like daughter. They wear strange colorful clothes tailored from the typical Ark's uniforms emblazoned with the ring of life found in the sanctuary. Their energy is also similar: pinkish hues with drops of red. Emily should have sensed their presence.

"The Paragon scum will go down soon," spits the mother, lowering her weapon, which Emily cannot take her gaze away from.

They are in much trouble if even the Mavericks are armed, which means they broke into the Arsenal, the Paragon's own weapon stash.

"Were the labs damaged?" asks Leander looking ill-at-ease.

"There were skirmishes earlier," answers the mother. "They put up a good fight when we broke in. Fortunately, most of their agents are stationed elsewhere."

"It's safe now," says her daughter. Suddenly, shots ring out, forcing them to seek refuge in the shadows. What a stupid idea! Now that they're allied with the Mavericks, Duke's army will take them down, too.

"Won't they ever give up?" moans the girl.

"A century-old system will hold until it breaks for good," her mother replies. They pretend Leander and Emily are not there and exchange shots with their new attackers.

Emily sneaks towards the labs' entrance, and Leander follows her. Good.

Two, four … no, six Paragon agents swoop in and as the mother and daughter recover, they call for reinforcements through an earpiece. A bullet lodges in a recessed light, and darkness falls over the next two hundred meters.

Emily races until she stumbles, pain shooting through her ankle while her gun flies off several feet in front of her. Leander catches up and grabs the gun. He shoots again and again.

"Run!" he yells at her in a frenzy.

She limp-runs the last two hundred meters and opens the door with her wristband. She shouts at Leander to hurry, which grabs the three remaining agents' attention who run straight for them.

"That was really stupid of me," she says once the doors close behind. She doesn't waste a second to lock them temporarily with her wristband. They are a few steps away from the large empty hall that serves as a reception area for the research center.

They made it.

"At least, we're alive. We are out of ammunition, though." He shows her the empty cartridge and sighs.

Emily's legs are shaking with fatigue, but it won't be for much longer.

"Where is she?" asks Emily, controlling her panting breath.

"Lab 134. This way." Emily could check her wristband to see how much time they have left, but she doesn't, fear gripping her chest.

Leander asks, "Why are you going on this suicide mission with me? We both know we won't get out of here alive." For some reason, Leander's words make her uncomfortable. What has she gotten herself into?

"They convicted my mother for finding out their secret." He leans on the wall, his hand on his wound.

"What will you do once you know?" Emily lets out a sigh.

"Reach the Command Center before it comes off or even better, find who convicted my mother."

"Revenge then."

"Call it what you will. We'd better get going."

The wide doors open quietly onto the research center covered by a bluish film where the pure-white surfaces should be. The group of Mavericks questions them to confirm their loyalty in the same way as the mother and daughter did earlier.

Leander taps his foot, clearly running out of patience and he does not waste a second once the interrogation is over. The wound on his side has mysteriously healed, and Emily struggles to catch up with him. As they walk quickly along, lights flicker on and off a few seconds later.

The long corridor of the research center looks like a horseshoe, with Mira's lab nestled in the middle. Leander gets in, then stops, swearing. His aura takes on a navy-blue hue, definitely something serious.

The door is stuck between two worlds, neither open nor closed. Emily joins him as he crouches. The lab is just like the Bates's cabin: smelly and cluttered with books, notebooks, microscopes, and test tubes. The contents of a counter were tossed on the floor in a jumble of broken glass and splattered solutions. Mira is lying on the floor in a pool of blood mussing her long red hair. Her right fist is closed, as if clenching on for dear life.

Leander is in shock, his eyes bulging. When Emily puts a hand on his shoulder, he jumps and checks Mira's vital signs.

Emily says nothing. There is nothing to say. Leander will curse himself for arriving too late his whole life, or at least for what's left of it.

"Go on," he says, stroking Mira's hair. "I'll stay with her."

Emily nods and slips out of the research center.

SHE HAS TO SLOW DOWN. Her body is beginning to hit its limits, even though she can't afford to rest. Fatigue and stress will have the better of her at any moment, but the atrium is up ahead along with the entrance to the prison. Just a little longer and it will be over.

A dead calm hangs with the ship's hum pulsing like the steady beat of a sleeping heart. When she walks around the atrium's sealed doors to the elevator, muffled screams reach her. She falters.

The Mavericks told them the Paragon controls this area and the refugees. Are Gabrielle and Dad in there as well? Are they in danger?

A powerful swing of energy pulls her out of her thoughts, and she hides in the secret elevator. A group of Paragon agents is marching by the exact spot where she had stood seconds ago. They drag civilians like trash, and a deafening din escapes from the atrium once the doors are open.

"Those lesser men are hiding among them. Keep them locked up and take out every last one of them. They are weaklings." Emily would pound the elevator button harder until it broke if she could. Duke Kay is here. Of course, he's in charge of the attack against the Brotherhood and the Mavericks.

Alone against an army, she has no chance. Dad and Gabrielle must stay in their quarters so Duke cannot go after them in the atrium.

She finds herself reciting an inner prayer to the Creator. When all hope is lost, one can do foolish things.

The elevator stops at the prison level with the bluish glow of emergency lights freezing the place, the air still, as the chaos of the upper level seems to belong to a whole different world.

The infamous detector at the entrance is disabled, though the musty smell remains unchanged, a bitter reminder of a life when she was used unknowingly. They lied to her in so many ways she can't even fathom. Ignorance is such a sweet, devious sin.

The security systems here are top-notch. The Mavericks she questioned that day took advantage of the simulation to get their hands on a prototype or, worse, test their know-how to help the Brotherhood.

Ludo isn't here. Even the sealed door isn't shut any longer. The coast is clear.

The number of the cells scrolls before her eyes: twenty-seven, twenty-six, twenty-five, twenty-four. Reyes's. Of course, it's empty now. No doubt she is leading her own group of Mavericks through the Ark's maze to hunt down the Paragon with the ardor she had when she attacked Emily during her first interrogation.

Eighteen, Milo's. Years seem to have gone by since last time.

The cell looks just as empty. Why would Milo be here when the entire ship is on high alert?

A twinge of disappointment nags at her. Did she believe he would wait for her to come back? That her mother's murderer would, too?

Emily slowly walks back to the entrance, then has a change of mind, overwhelmed by an odd feeling. She opens Milo's cell door with her wristband, just to be sure.

The room is quite empty, except for a minor vibration. She bends over and glimpses a dark yellow glow. Milo is curled up under the table and she whispers his name, afraid to scare him.

His clothes are torn and dirty, his short hair oily and his skin filthy as if the dust from his cell had collected with the force of a magnet. As if it wasn't enough, his irritated wrists are raw. Ludo's mark, of course.

He sees her.

"Oh my God! What did he do to you?" whispers Emily. He is experiencing a severe trauma judging by his aura that swirls into an otherworldly dark spiral. The emotion that had seized Emily when she had abandoned Milo to Ludo's hands chokes her. "I swear I didn't know."

Nothing excuses her from running away. She could have stopped Ludo when she knew what he was going to do.

Tears burn down Emily's cheeks while Milo watches her in silence.

"I barely realized the magnitude of what was going on here. I thought I understood, but I was wrong." He does not answer.

Perhaps he's thinking about the most effective way to kill her. She would do the same.

"I know you're not like them," he finally says. "You wouldn't be here if you were." The unexpected strength in his voice is electrifying. It reignites an impossible hope the suffering he endured couldn't put off. How is this possible?

"Believe in yourself," he says as an answer to her silent question. "That you can make a difference." Milo staggers out of his hole to sit on the corner of the bed bending under his weight, and the white sheets crease around him. He springs up and sits again a little farther, leaving dark stains on the fabric. A thin smile floats on his chapped lips.

Emily feels dirty. She wanted the truth, but this is only part of it. It's no revelation, nor is it a well-phrased proverb. It's a flesh-and-blood person with all his beauty and strength. But there's also suffering and ignorance—her responsibility. She wipes her cheeks.

"You're free now," she says. He gets up and draws near, the whites of his eyes a sharp contrast with his faded ivory skin. Milo's aura embraces Emily's like an electric current where yellows mingle with reds to create a fiery orange which blazes into a flame.

"I am not weak." A shiver runs through her. It's as if Milo transferred his energy to show her how profound his willpower is. Limitless, but also complex in all its beauty.

"I know." Emily was wrong. So wrong.

Milo is just a victim: neglected, oppressed, tortured. No doubt there are others. All these Mavericks, this mother and daughter, Reyes. Their rage is well-founded.

Yasmina and Ludo. Even the Commander's orders. Why this injustice, such sadism? It doesn't make sense.

"You still have five minutes to get to the Command Center," Emily tells him as she reluctantly checks her wristband.

"Don't you want to know what they did to me?" He's so close they almost touch.

"I … I can't." He smiles weakly, a sad glint in his eyes. After what he's been through, how can he find the courage?

Foreign emotions seep into her and spread into her veins as if their auras were in sync while a new energy envelops her: a dream.

"These things will not exist in the Promised Land," he whispers in a warm voice.

"The Promised Land?" Milo takes a few steps towards the door and the surrounding air grows cold. A sense of loss fills her.

"Where the Brotherhood will lead us. Our mission. Today, the leaders will fall to make way for the truth."

"If only it were true. Or even possible." Milo's smile this time looks childish, and the impression is enough to make Emily think they might have been friends in another life.

"They've been preparing for a long time," he says, with his hands on his bony hips. "For the final showdown in the Command Center."

"Does this mean…?" The Brotherhood knew. Have they infiltrated yet? If they do take over the ship, what does that mean for the rest of them?

Milo is about to leave the cell, but his facial features tense up.

"Promise me you will never become like them." He means Yasmina, Ludo, Duke, the Commander, and the others involved in these machinations and lies, illusions they call morality and justice.

"If you can forgive me," she replies, her throat squeezing. Milo's face softens.

"Where we go, everyone will get a second chance." He disappears like a dream, and the traces of his aura leave a glittering rain behind him. Emily remembers the strange electrifying warmth that enveloped her. What was it?

Emily leaves the cell, too, and she locks it behind her.

A second chance? Does she really deserve it?

Milo's blind trust in the Brotherhood is admirable. The temptation is strong, but desires and reality are two very different things. Forgoing the illusions of the Ark and embracing those of the Brotherhood…

Emily must finish what she started. Reconcile herself with reality.

Milo is already on his way to the Command Center. If he runs, he'll probably make it in time. As for Emily … her insides contract. She is aware she is walking towards her own death. Her headache reminds her of her outright madness.

She won't even die with honors for sacrificing herself for a loved one like Leander, or Sky, who wants to stop the Brotherhood, or Chris, who wants to preserve humanity.

Her own curiosity will get the better of her to stop an unalterable past she should have accepted.

The blindfold she wore all these years every time she crossed this hallway has fallen off. She hears the cries of those who have suffered within these walls because of her desire for justice to be done.

So be it.

31

SKYLER

CHRIS AND TESSA ARE ON THE LOOKOUT FOR AN AMBUSH, WITH Skyler following closely behind. What does the future have in store for them?

Each step takes them farther away from Emily but brings them closer to the Promised Land. The hope that she will meet up with them later keeps him going. She is the only friend he trusts, especially since doubt has been eating away at him.

Chris is trying so hard. Skyler can't stop thinking whether it's because he lost his father, or because they risked their lives so many times in such a short time. When this whole mess is over, perhaps he could start anew with Chris who, until proven otherwise, is not like his father Duke.

Skyler himself always hated being compared to Dylan, because he knew it wasn't true, even though it made his mother proud. Chris deserves better treatment from him. The more Skyler replays the fateful day of Allen's fall, the more doubtful he becomes about how it all happened. Did he convince himself of Chris's involvement or, worse, did he reinterpret the events only for his own peace of mind? Wasn't this just an accident? Allen inadvertently slips and Skyler, too young and frail, cannot pull him up. Chris comes across them by chance, not knowing what to do, and reacts instinctively to save his best friend. Nobody pushed Allen to his death. Who is Skyler to put such a burden on Chris?

Skyler isn't ready to see him as a friend, but he might try listening to him rather than picking a fight at every turn. Each time, Emily was right to urge him to talk with Chris. He could have done better, and he accepts the blame for that. How ironic that this is the approach they taught him at the Academy to treat his patients: listening. He never thought he would ever see it this way. This is not his first mistake, an all-too-familiar bitter taste.

"Is everything okay, Sky?" asks Chris, frowning. Skyler nods and, for the first time, believes that Chris is genuinely concerned about him. Maybe it is a way to make it up to him, but with everything that's happened in the last few days, loneliness has been eating away at him. Who will he be able to count on after the Brotherhood's victory? He won't be able to take care of his mother alone, either. Tessa may be there to support him, but he needs to talk to her first.

"Here we are," she says when they arrive at the intersection that Skyler remembers coming to with Allen during their first jaunts. From here, they can go to any main sections of the Ark: The dining hall, the atrium, the Great Gate and, normally, the Command Center, but this section has been cut off from the rest because of the explosion. They will have to make a detour through the dining hall.

Skyler scans the wall for a code showing the entrance to the in between. Nothing has changed. It's in the same place as he remembers. Chris helps him tear open the panel, then they reach in through the opening.

"At this rate, we'll make it to the Command Center in time," says Chris, satisfied.

"How long have we got?" asks Skyler despite himself.

"Just over ten minutes. If you're thinking about Emily, forget about her."

"What do you know about what I think?"

"I'd rather you didn't get your hopes up. She chose to die. You know that very well."

"She will find a way." Or he'll find one for her. He can come back for her when the situation is under control. For once, Chris knows how to keep his mouth shut at the right time. They arrive at a new empty intersection. At least the Paragon is not in their way.

"Do you remember which way we have to go?" asks Tessa, her voice bouncing off the walls. Water is leaking somewhere as Skyler delves into his memories.

Reminiscing about his time with Allen is painful. Skyler can still hear him talking with his infectious energy, which is exactly the problem. What Allen was saying, his expressions, his face, and every single detail are very clear. Even his legendary charisma Skyler didn't get, and his ideas about what the new colony would look like. He was the reason Skyler became so interested in the future and the old Earth.

But this place doesn't speak to him. He accompanied Allen to spend more time with him. The trips to the in between were just an excuse.

"It's been a long time," Skyler says realizing the years that have elapsed since then. "I told you I would need your help, Chris. You kept exploring the in betweens on your own. I stopped when my brother … died."

The echo of these words makes them sound more real, a kind of release.

"I think I know where it is," Chris replies, betraying no emotion. "Wait for me here."

Maybe Chris has moved on. In a way, Skyler has to as well, to stay sane, to keep on living.

Tessa's face is splashed with the still-functional emergency blue lights on the wall. She is looking away, her brow furrowed, but Skyler has a go at it anyway:

"Is there anything you should tell me? We don't have much time left before things change dramatically. We should play fair from now on."

"Those blank-eyed civilians who attacked your friend. I know why they are like that." He did not expect this, but it confirms his doubts: She knows much more than she wants to let on.

"Under Duke's orders, the Paragon performed a series of genetic tests. That's how it started. The Brotherhood knows about it, and that's what made them act faster than expected."

"What kind of tests?" He almost regrets asking the question.

"The Syndrome is an anomaly that arouses interest, especially Duke's. He wanted to test how those infected would react to the different stages of the disease. Trust me, you don't want to know what atrocities he committed." Maybe it's better off that way. Too many horrors already crowd his nights.

"Why was Medical Bay never informed?"

"He is eager to keep his activities secret. Just because the Ark is all that is left of the world does not mean it is transparent. No one on this ship knows more than they should."

"How can we trust each other, then?"

He is stunned. The Commander should keep all Archeans together. He is the pillar on which they all stand. If he can't be trusted, no one can. Why aren't the members of the commanding crew doing anything to stop him? Are they all accomplices? The privileged guard a secret so their survival depends on exploiting other people's ignorance.

"Emily has a point when she says it's human nature to repeat past mistakes," Tessa adds with a sad smile. "The Paragon has exploited the Syndrome to test its limits and find a way to … control."

"Do you mean the Paragon created the Syndrome?" Every

time Skyler is willing to forgive Chris, something comes along to remind him how tainted the Kay lineage is. To think they'll have to repopulate with people like this family.

Do they really have a choice? Do they have to choose who gets to live in this new world?

Chris may be different. He could be with his father right now, but he's not.

"It's beyond our current understanding," says Tessa. "All we know is that it's something much bigger."

"Why did you wait to tell me?" Tessa looks a little confused.

"You would have tracked down Duke by yourself."

"You don't know me very well. That's more like Emily." *As you witnessed*, he wants to add, but he prefers to keep quiet. "How do you know it wasn't the Paragon that designed the Syndrome? With their tests—"

"No." Chris's rushed footsteps end their discussion and Skyler contains his frustration at not being able to find out more. He doesn't trust Chris yet. Perhaps, once he has proof.

Chris's expression is serious. "That's the right way to go. It's not that far to get to the dining hall. Let's go."

THE SEALED DOOR OPENS, and a breath of fresh air similar to an exhale blows at them.

The Command Center. They made it.

Skyler was almost expecting a welcoming committee, the Brotherhood ready to explain the rest of the story to them, but instead they found themselves alone in front of an enormous door with only a dead silence. Thanks to Chris, his new position gives him access to every part of the Ark, including this area.

Chris enters first, then Tessa and Skyler.

A swift movement and Chris collapses.

"What did you just do?" shouts Skyler, panicked. Tessa stands still, her muscles taut, her legs slightly bent. She has knocked Chris out.

"He can't be trusted," she replies evenly. "He is part of the commanding crew." Skyler is speechless. Was this her intention all along? She could have told him before! Aren't they a team?

"Don't tell me you mind, I won't believe you," she resumes as she moves closer to Skyler, close enough for her intoxicating coconut smell to dizzy him.

"What are you talking about? He didn't do anything wrong. In fact, he's the reason we're here!" Skyler has to give him that.

"He and his father do not belong in the Promised Land. We save everyone's precious time by taking care of him now." Tessa pulls Chris out, while Skyler stays still, words failing him. The idea has crossed his mind many times, though—the legitimacy of rescuing the Kays who could turn against them at any moment, their influence too great. Is it really the right thing to do?

Part of him approves of Tessa's actions, but another part tells him it's wrong. They used Chris. Inwardly, Skyler knows it's unfair since Chris has been honest with them. If not, how does that make them different from the atrocities Duke committed? Abusing people's trust is a dangerous step towards immorality.

With a gesture, Skyler slows the closing of the door that will forever separate them from Chris and asks what has been burning in his mind since their visit to the Archives.

"You talk about trust, but I know you're not Tessa Farrell. Who are you?"

"We can't back out now, Skyler."

The door shuts, cutting them off from the Ark.

32

EMILY

EMILY CRACKS THE SECURITY SYSTEM OF YASMINA'S OFFICE. As Chief Warden of this wicked prison, Yasmina really ought to have better security. The secret Emily had coveted for all these years was so close. Every day, she looked at it, listened to it, felt it.

This office and its dull walls suck out all life.

The fake wooden table, adorned with a simple screen, is too clean. But behind is the room where so many uncooperative prisoners suffered from Yasmina's gruesome pleasures to which Emily condemned them. Her accomplice.

If Milo had known what Emily really is... He has faith in the dreams he believes are within his grasp despite all he's been through. Milo has faith in her and believes she is good. How disappointed he would be.

"My agent," Yasmina greets her with a honeyed voice. "You decided to come back while people are saving their skin? Remorse, perhaps?"

"Perhaps," says Emily, who walks into Yasmina's private room where she is waiting patiently.

The sickly smell of disinfectant makes her want to gag. On

the pristine white reflective surfaces, various tools of torture are proudly displayed: whips, obscurely named medical tools, and more. The infamous electric prod used as a last resort has its own stand: an obnoxious imitation of a timeless warrior with waving hands, ready to attack. The marks and permanent pain the prod leaves are irreversible.

This sordid display is the true face of Yasmina, someone Emily had thought was reasonable. But there are more torture tools: glass helmets covered with metal contraptions that can connect.

Yasmina's floral perfume wafts as she stands close.

"People like us don't need a second chance. Human nature is like that: It repeats its mistakes over and over again. Why bother when you already know the outcome?"

Emily moves away from the instruments that seem to pulse with an evil energy. A morbid obsession. An unbridled divine will. Yasmina's heart.

"What if there really was hope?" replies Emily, who stares at the translucent walls of one of the helmets, set on a pedestal as if it were a trophy. "The hope to change."

"An illusion. Like that foolish Promised Land that the Brotherhood and the Mavericks dream about. Do you see where this is going? The Ark is in danger of being sunk forever, a century of effort to safeguard humanity from the destructive forces of nature annihilated. But the real danger was among us all along. You already know the answer."

Yasmina sketches a knowing smile. The artificial lighting blotches her salmon-pink suit that brings out her perfect skin, low-necked enough to distract prisoners. Emily is stronger than her, but Yasmina's aura is overwhelming, a strange golden halo.

"Whether in this life or the next, if there is one, we always end up going back to our roots." Yasmina walks towards the pedestal and climbs the few steps.

"It fascinates you, doesn't it?" continues Yasmina by

brushing it with her hands, then resting her head on it as if to listen to the cries of terror confined in the helmet. "It is still warm and full of life. Reyes's last visit ended more quickly than I would have liked. She confessed everything. It wasn't too difficult."

Yasmina closes her eyes theatrically. Images from Mom's execution at the Archives flash before Emily's eyes. Her terror, her muffled scream, and that sick blue straining her face.

"I don't know why you couldn't get Reyes to confess yourself. I thought you were better at it. I'm meticulous about choosing my talents. Looks like the results of your simulations misinformed me."

"I always did what you asked me to do, even when I didn't agree." Yasmina tilts her head, her mouth half-open, as if she were listening to a sound only she can hear, something funny.

"My agent," she coos with clasped hands. "It is because this will is part of you as much as it is part of me. You can't go against your own nature."

Her voice is soft and maternal.

"You must take it, embrace it. My girl. I've been trying to help you do that for the last seven years."

"You're the one who killed her," Emily articulates in a trembling voice.

"You mean Tyna, your lovely mother?" she asks, looking surprised. "I thought you had forgotten about her."

"You forced me to witness her death, then recruited me. Without me keeping any memory of her executioners."

"You were so young then. A small dose of odorless gas can do a lot of good. Or damage, as you can see."

"We don't have that kind of technology." The gas in the Gardens is the same they use on prisoners, but it does not erase their memory. Her memories of the barn are still crisp.

"What you say is true, but you forget one detail. Short-term memory can easily be affected. That's one advantage of this gas with prisoners: You can torture them and make them forget just enough to stretch the session out as long as necessary."

The way Yasmina talks about it … as if it was the most natural thing in existence. In this room, *her* room.

"The day of your mother's execution was the first time you saw me," Yasmina continues, walking back down to Emily. "A simple piece of information to forget. As for the room…"

Yasmina looks around with a nostalgic expression.

"By coming to work here, your memory has only reconstructed it from scratch." A cool breeze bites into Emily's neck, and she shivers.

"And Gabrielle? She remembers what happened as much as I do."

"The gas has taken its toll. And as for the rest, are you sure you didn't tell her? She was awfully young at the time."

"How could you do that to children? To Gabrielle?"

"Would you have preferred to retain every detail until you thirst for revenge?"

Yasmina's cheeks freeze and her manicured nails dig into her palms.

"Mavericks in the making: the tormented spirit, deprived of their right to be Archeans, their wristbands confiscated."

"So that's what they really are. A product of the system that rules the Ark."

"To a certain extent. But they each have their own tragic story. Some are the descendants of fear-stricken souls who snuck in during the Embarkment, but not all of them."

Yasmina leans against a shelf that immodestly displays some of her torture toys, arms crossed.

"What did you really hope for by coming back here?" she continues in a crystal-clear voice. "That I would ask for your forgiveness?"

The Command Center must have detached by now, and Mom's secret still eludes Emily. Yasmina is cunning. She will do anything to avoid the subject.

It is a game. With her rules.

"I want answers," says Emily, drawing closer to Yasmina. "I've always done what you asked of me with nothing in return. You owe me this, at least."

"That's what the agents do: They execute." Yasmina slides her tongue on her lips. "You know why your mother was convicted, don't you?"

"For treason." The word hurts, rips her apart.

"Her case was interesting, but yes. She had dealings with the Brotherhood." Yasmina talks about it as a mere failed experiment. What kind of relationship did she have with Mom? Did they know each other?

The energy change is barely noticeable. Is Yasmina affected by Mom's death?

"I am sorry to see her daughter followed in her footsteps." Yasmina looks down, as if sorry for her.

"What?" shouts Emily, baffled. "I never consorted with the Brotherhood." Yasmina dislodges the electric prod from the warrior's hands, and Emily takes a step back.

"So, tell me why you released Milo before coming here. I warned you. He is one of their official members."

"I didn't know." Traitor. Traitor.

"So was Reyes, for that matter. You handled their cases differently. I had to deal with Reyes personally."

Silence.

"Ludo also told me about your unusual behavior. You talked to Milo alone while I had allowed Ludo to do his work on our prisoner." Or rather, to satisfy his sadistic desires. Yasmina believes she betrayed her, and this situation is likely to work against her. She will never admit what Mom knew that cost her her life.

Yasmina gets agitated when she catches Emily looking around.

"I know you too well, Emily. You think you have a chance against me because your stupid father illegally trained you to fight."

"If you will answer a simple question, I won't go that far."

It's now or never.

"I know my mother was not convicted only for her ties to the Brotherhood. There was something else. A secret she kept." Yasmina is stone-faced, but the ripple in her aura does not lie.

"Is the Syndrome affecting you too?" sneers Yasmina. "I know your job is to interrogate outlaws to get them to reveal their secrets, but don't overindulge."

"As you say, I have experience. I know when I'm being lied to." The air crackles.

"Believe what you want," Yasmina resumes by shortening the distance that separates them. "If that were the case, her secret drowned with her."

"I know things about you. My visit to the Archives was very informative. I know why you are so adamant about keeping the prison running smoothly, but more importantly, focused on results. When I think about it, coming from you, I want to laugh."

Yasmina's expression changes, "You play the blackmail card with me, but know—"

"You love him." They are on either side of the table. "You wish Commander Hawk would notice you."

"Like mother, like daughter," Yasmina hisses. The blow comes quickly, and Emily grabs the only thing she can get her hands on: a whip. However, the electric prod paralyzes her on the ground almost instantly.

Emily lets out a hoarse howl.

Tingles run over her skin and penetrate her like little

needles, going up to her neck. Her brain slows down and her visual does not keep up with the sound of Yasmina's voice.

"You, of all people, should know what happens to traitors."

33

SKYLER

SKYLER ABANDONED CHRIS. THE ARK. EMILY. HIS MOTHER.

What kind of man would do that? Every time, he could have done better to avoid this senseless situation. Does that make him a monster?

He is trapped in the Command Center that will break away from the Ark forever, leaving the rest of humanity to drown in the abyss. With the damage from the explosion, the temperature dropping by the hour, the electrical circuits failing and the Command Center unable to control the ventilation system, they have no chance of surviving. The lack of oxygen will kill them unless water leaks first.

Did he condemn them because he believed Tessa?

"I trusted you to come all the way here. I could have stayed with Emily and my mother!"

"But you didn't." Tessa's tone is not accusatory, but laden with compassion. Or at least, that's the impression he gets. "You made a better choice to give them a second chance."

"You know they will never survive this long. The Ark will sink."

"That will not happen," she says confidently. "The Brotherhood is here. *We* are here. Once we control the ship, we'll acti-vate emergency procedure, and they will board the twelve auxiliary pods on the Ark."

"Will there be enough for everyone?" She looks away: The answer is clear.

What exactly is going on? The simulation, Leander's words, the memory sphere … their impromptu meetings.

A bitter smile creeps over Skyler's lips.

"The Paragon rebel group never existed. How long have you been a member of the Brotherhood?"

"You are also part of it," she replies without flinching. He ignores her comment.

"You stole the Farrells' identity to get under the radar. I had my doubts when Mrs. Farrell died, which were confirmed when I viewed her memory sphere. She had two grandchildren. But you're not one of them."

"What does it matter?"

"You lied to me from the beginning." Disgust assails him. He distrusted Chris, who did everything to help them reach the Command Center and who is now doomed.

"Besides not being a Farrell, you are the Brotherhood. And don't get me wrong, but I'm not." Tessa opens her mouth to say something, but he interrupts her. "Emily already told me about the Mavericks. You don't exist in the registry. That's how the Brotherhood was born."

A life without identity, worse than living on an Ark. The Mavericks know all about it: stowaways. Desperation has eaten away at their insides so much that they are willing to sacrifice everyone else to save themselves.

"You believe the Archeans have no place in the Promised Land. Only the Mavericks. You sort them into camps: in the atrium, in the Gardens—"

"You don't know what you're talking about." She shakes her head, the beads of her braids knocking.

"If it exists," he adds thoughtfully, and he thinks he's a fool for believing all that gibberish. "Years… No. Over a century of telling yourself stories about what the outside world must look like has distorted your perception of reality." He knows something about it. What seems true at one moment can be so easily different from the next.

"Why are you questioning everything when we are so close? Why do you have to make things complicated?"

"What's worse is that you won't even admit what you've done. What you're about to do." She doesn't answer, but her eyes fill with apprehension.

Skyler turns away to join Emily, but Tessa stops him.

"Without the access code, this door will not open again. Finish what you started."

"Why me? The Brotherhood has nothing to do with me. They have you."

"You are more important than you think. We need you." Tessa extends her hand, but he pushes it away.

"Don't touch me," he says through his teeth. "I want to get out of here." Skyler walks over to the console, determined not to stay with a liar for another second.

"My name is Tessa Auberon." He stops his movement and turns over to say he does not give a damn, but she pushes him against the wall, her body pressed against his. Tessa takes advantage of his surprise to cover his nose with a rag. She looks tormented, as if surprised by what she is doing, and she casts her glance down.

Pain twists Tessa's face while she presses harder, crying silently. He tries to struggle, but her leg and arm locks prevent him from moving. The pervasive smell of alcohol slips into his lungs, and his body gives out.

"I'm sorry."

Total darkness.

34

EMILY

YASMINA DID NOT KILL HER. YET.

Emily is sitting on the floor, her hands securely bound by chains connected to the platform where her jailer was standing earlier. A stabbing pain pulses in her back, but she can bear it. It was not the full power of the prod, though. Yasmina is barely warming up.

"My mother," croaks Emily, her mouth dry. "How do you know my mother?" Yasmina climbs onto the platform briskly, crouches down and grabs Emily's chin. The warden's sharp nails pierce her cheeks, and Emily wants to bite her fingers, but her grip is too stiff.

"Do you still love her?" Her hot breath stings Emily's eyes.

"She is my mother!" she snarls, turning her head away.

"She is dead. Dead. Do you hear me? Dead!" Yasmina's lips exaggeratedly utter each word with a weedy voice. She has completely lost her mind. Her thumbnail flicks back and forth, digging into Emily's cheekbone and does not stop until it is glistening with blood.

"Since you love your dear mother so much..." Yasmina releases her chin abruptly and walks around her. Then she steps off the platform to a section of the room Emily did not notice earlier. Or was it hidden?

Yasmina comes out a few seconds later with a glowing object in her palm.

"Do you know what this is?" she asks as she uncovers a shining sphere, golden like her aura. Curiosity wins Emily over. She has already seen one in the Gardens with Sky.

"A memory sphere."

"Of course, you do. After all, your best friend invented it. With a little help, of course." How did she manage to get one? Wasn't this a recent project?

"Let me enlighten you," continues Yasmina, reading in her mind as if she were an open book. "This marvel would never have seen the light of day without me. My dear friend Valentina Siria from the Archives immediately informed me about the project, so it could become a reality. The project itself was ridiculous, but all it took was a little more imagination. Preserving the memories of humanity for repopulating is an insult to the divine will. Why would the Creator give us such a precious thing? To use it to its full potential, of course."

She stares hungrily at the sphere with a chuckle.

"It only took the little engineer to make it all possible. What people wouldn't do to protect an unborn child." She carefully sets it in a receptacle connected to a machine that is part of another circular platform identical to the one where Emily is chained. The surface of the circle glows a pearly white, and the artificial lighting in the room dims.

"I don't see how memory spheres can have any appeal to you," Emily says aloud, confused.

"Tyna Bates," Yasmina says at a screen that lights up. The embedded golden sphere sparkles and shoots shimmering bubbles on the walls. Yasmina's hand hovers over the screen until she finds what she is looking for.

The bond between Mom and Yasmina cannot be real, and

even if it was, they would have been enemies. Why play this guessing game?

"She must have hated you," whispers Emily, who tries to stand up and then falls back against the platform, exhausted. "Or you're bluffing."

"You don't believe me, do you? My poor child." Blurred forms materialize on the circle in a high-voltage whirring. They become clearer with a disturbing sharpness. Holograms.

Emily hiccups in surprise and covers her mouth, tears burning her eyes. This can't be true!

Mommy! Mom is there, in the flesh. She is younger than she remembers, probably in her early thirties. Her hair only goes down to her shoulders.

"Still in this workshop?" says Yasmina's timeless voice. The small room's mess is worthy of a Bates. Patterns for making clothes are stacked haphazardly in every corner and rolls of fabric are lined up against the opposite wall. A stack of neatly folded uniforms is crammed into a crate that has seen better days.

Mom's tired look turns to Emily.

"They need me." Mom is sitting, and a baggy uniform takes up the entire workspace. The garment resembles the one the Maverick mother and daughter who came across them on their way to Delta Labs wore in every way. Mom meticulously embroiders the finishing touch, that same strange symbol with gold outlines: a wave.

Yasmina's contemptuous voice resumes.

"Where is the woman I admired so much at the Academy? The one who was ready to take over the Ark with her teachings and her power to read others?"

"The Creator wanted it otherwise," Mom replies.

"That's what you want to believe. If we believe his will, then the Flood was an obvious message. Yet here we are today talking about it." Mom keeps calm and casts her a sympathetic glance.

Why does she not feel any hatred towards Yasmina? It's insane!

"There are other ways to be respected," Mom continues as she puts down her needle.

"By helping that crazy old lady?" Mom gets up to move closer to the edge of the platform, her eyes piercing through Emily.

"I'm not asking you to understand my choices. I didn't put you down when you became a prison officer."

"Fine. But I won't protect you anymore." A veil of sadness darkens Mom's features, who stares at the center of the circle, a thin smile over her lips.

"I understand. Promise me you will take care of my little girl, Emily."

"I promised you a long time ago. I will be a good mother." Conflicting emotions churn inside Emily. Tears flow as the vision of the past fades into the darkness. She lets out a sob.

"Five years before she was sentenced," says Yasmina, who shuffles to the center of the circle. "Do you understand now?"

"Mom could never have trusted you," Emily hiccups, horrified.

"These are my raw memories. They can't lie like humans do." Yasmina has softened, her eyes empty. Could they really have been friends at the Academy? Why would Mom ask for Yasmina's protection? Did she know about her future?

"Now, imagine having this technology in a place full of these treacherous liars," adds Yasmina, her colors more vibrant.

"Prisoners," Emily understands. "Did you use the spheres on the prisoners?"

"Their minds open up to me on a level I have never experienced before. I make their lives and their secrets that are so dear to them my own. Because I can. Because I must. The Creator has given me divine power. He made me his goddess." Mom couldn't have entrusted Emily's life to a psychopath.

"If only you knew the whole story," Yasmina replies, anticipating her reasoning. "But that will come with time. The Commander and I will instruct you properly, you can be sure of it. And then, everything will make sense."

"The Commander? What does he have to do with this?"

"See for yourself." Yasmina walks back to the control panel and calls his name. Then she waves her hand like a magic wand.

A new human figure materializes before Emily's astonished eyes. The Commander. He's in his office, judging how organized, clean, and comfortable the space is. He is sitting on a loveseat, a neat work desk in the background.

"Are the tests still negative?" he asks with a look of concern. He seems to be holding Yasmina's hand, but the vision blurs the details.

"I don't know what's going on," she replies in a small voice. "The Creator wants to tell us something."

"What do you think he means?"

"He knows. He knows about Tyna Bates. She entrusted me with her daughter. I already have a daughter." Yasmina seems troubled.

"The time is coming. I'll make sure you two are safe."

"I'll introduce you. You will love her."

Yasmina quickly puts an end to the hologram and joins Emily.

"My daughter. The daughter I always wanted." Her face glows as a shiver of disgust runs through Emily. "I love you as if you were my own daughter. *Our* daughter. The Commander would have wanted that too. He wanted to protect you by inviting you in the Command Center."

Emily's meeting with Commander Hawk comes back to her.

He was courteous and kind and had made her feel good and safe. He hadn't treated her like a Bates.

"How can the Commander love someone like you?" thinks Emily aloud. "He is good. He can't—"

"He knows what is good for us. The Commander saved humanity once before, and he is about to do it again. You have a divine family, my dear." This is pure madness. Did her mother really want to doom her own daughter?

"Will you be a good girl now?"

It doesn't matter what her mother was or won't ever be, Emily is different. She did not betray the Ark, and she certainly wants nothing to do with Yasmina and her eccentric plans.

"What do you want?" Emily's tone is hard, and she stands up with renewed energy.

"To possess you."

"Go to hell. I'd rather die." Yasmina laughs and goes back into her secret room. She comes out with a virgin sphere to set it on the receptacle and puts away the sphere of the Commander in its box.

"No," says Emily, panic rising in her chest. "You have no right to get inside my head."

"We are family now. You came back to me, didn't you?" Emily struggles against her chains, but something pricks her in the arm. A tranquilizer. Yasmina approaches with a glass helmet and clicks her tongue.

"My daughter. Come on, you won't feel a thing." Her limbs are numb while Yasmina puts the helmet on her despite her protests. The cold metal pieces suck her forehead, her cheeks, and her neck. A buzzing sound fills her ears, and an electric current tickles her skin. When Yasmina turns on her infernal device, she feels the nerves of her neck being plucked one by one. Emily gasps with a hoarse cry.

"Look," says Yasmina, obsessed by the sphere that fills with glowing tendrils. "All your sensations, your memories, your life, and your most buried secrets. They are so beautiful. I am so lucky to have such a beautiful daughter."

The procedure takes about ten minutes. Emily is drained, convinced her body is bleeding from the inside. Yasmina grasps the scarlet-glowing sphere and kisses it.

"Let me go," whispers Emily, half-conscious. "You got what you wanted."

"Perhaps if you asked me properly, like a well-behaved girl." Emily swallows a sob. A nightmare like the ones Gabrielle had the first few years after Mom died. It will pass. It will pass. No, it won't.

"I have nothing left," Emily chokes. "You took everything from me."

"That's not true. You have your new family. A mother." Yasmina takes off the sophisticated helmet and puts it back on its pedestal. She looks content with herself.

"I'm sorry," mumbles Emily, desperate. "I'll be good. I'll do whatever you want."

Yasmina brushes her lips against her ringing ears.

"Call me Mom." Emily's eyes bulge, and she swallows a retch.

"I would never. My real mother would never do that."

"But I *am* your mother, Emily." The tranquilizer makes her dizzy. She is confused. Mom? No, that can't be. She's dead. She's been dead for so long.

"You will never be my mother, Yasmina."

"I understand," she says. "Family members don't always get along." Another needle shoots into her arm. "But not mine. A goddess's family is perfect. Divine, and there won't ever be any secrets between us. You'll understand when we are whole with your father, the Commander."

"He is not..." Her throat knots, and her limbs liquefy.

"Don't get too excited. I'll take you to him when you're ready. But until then..."

Yasmina strokes Emily's hair and pulls back her bangs with a smile. Then she glances at the display of her instruments of torture.

"We still have work to do."

35

SKYLER

Skyler is in the Command Center lined with large portholes that offer a glimpse of their destination: the murky waters of the Great Ocean with its dark shades of teal blue that suck in all light. He stands and gazes at their bleak future if they don't make it to land under his command. Tessa is standing with her hands behind her back, smiling. She looks more relaxed, her eyes sparkling. She believes in him, while he gave up on his faith in himself.

The uniform Skyler put on is not his own, but his predecessor's. The rounded hems of the collar trimmed with gold threads run up to his neck in a square-cut navy-blue fabric that falls straight over his shoulders and covers him to the cuffs. Large bronze buttons dot the tightly fastened lapels, and the garment hugs his body as if it had always been his. Yet, there is an unfamiliar weight to it. The fabric is too dense, too thick, but it keeps him warm in the constant cold and damp of the ship that is falling into disuse. His Ark.

Skyler turns around under Tessa's approving glance as she points out the newcomers: The pale man amidst the gas preceding the explosion on the surveillance cameras escorts Chris as a prisoner and shoves him to the ground ruthlessly. Chris kneels and barely avoids hitting the ground face first with his tied hands. Dread fills his eyes as he begs Skyler for mercy.

His judgment has come. Skyler will choose his punishment for being complicit with Duke Kay and the Paragon during the refugees' massacre. What place could someone like him have in the Promised Land?

Someone in the background is gazing at him. He is leaning against the wall, and his features are worn by time. Allen? He shouldn't be allowed to look so real. His dead brother seems to wait for Skyler's judgment. Is this a test? Skyler wants to talk to him first, but Allen's eyes bulge when he realizes his little brother has noticed his presence.

Allen draws closer, but fear overcomes Skyler. Are they all dead? Or is Allen here to take him along?

His brother's hand reaches out to him.

Before he can react, Skyler finds himself in his arms with a strong smell of heat and sweat. Skyler struggles as he gasps for air, but his brother is stronger than he is.

Skyler calms down when Allen grabs his shoulders to have a better look at him.

"Thank God you woke up, little brother." A tattoo peeks out from his uniform sleeve: the blue and curves of the waves crashing on the beaches of yore that fade onto the back of his hand.

Once he breaks their embrace, Skyler understands he was dreaming—the Commander's uniform, Tessa, Chris begging him, Allen: all of it. But why is Allen standing right here in front of him? How is this possible?

"You are dead." Even though he's lying on a comfortable couch, Skyler feels like he's going to fall, so he holds on to the armrest and tucks the blanket wrapped around him. The sudden jump back into reality makes him dizzy. He sits up and his heart beats too fast. Is it because of the drug Tessa gave him or because his dead brother is staring at him?

"Allen is dead, but Neal lives on in his place." Allen adds, his voice deep with emotion. "I missed you so much."

Skyler details each of his features and pulls out a memory of the younger face his brother had before. Allen didn't have stubble, short hair, or even tattoos. He looks so much older than the last time.

"Where have you been?" asks Skyler, still in shock. "During all these years?"

Allen gazes at him as if he was the most beautiful thing he had ever seen, etching every detail in his memory.

"My fall was not … fatal. I ended up in the lower levels, and the Mavericks found me. I didn't fare too badly." His answer comes slowly, overwhelmed by his emotions.

Allen rolls up his sleeve where his tattoo fills his entire arm.

"I had to hide my scars. I fell on this arm, but then I thought it would look better if I had both arms done." The second one doesn't bear the same bright colors whose greens, blues and white are intermingled. Instead, it is inky black, as if seeping out of his veins which make up the long roots of a tree that run to his hand and branches that crisscross his shoulder.

"Why didn't you come back?" Skyler feels conflicting emotions rise in his throat. Sure, he is happy to know he is alive, and yet, he cannot help but blame Allen. "Do you know what happened to Mom after you died?"

Heartbeat … Their mother's teary face twisted with pain … Heartbeat … Their mother screaming in rage at the son who should have not survived.

"I … couldn't." Allen shifts on the sofa, clearly uncomfortable. But Skyler can't stitch his oozing wound, the blood begging to come out and be cleansed.

"She broke down to the point of madness." In a strangled voice, he continues, "I thought it was my fault because I couldn't save you." His vision blurs, but he doesn't care. His brother had a responsibility.

"We both know what happened. Don't blame yourself for an accident." Allen's eyes are downcast. Listening to his now deeper voice should comfort Skyler, but every word slashes at his soul.

"You abandoned us. And all this…" His voice breaks, and he looks around, lost.

The sizable room with its glass desk and portraits of past Commanders must be none other than Commander Hawk's cabin. His brother, who's been *dead* for the last five years and never gave any news, followed his utopian dream of storming the Ark, then sent someone to watch him and drag him into this Brotherhood. Not to mention their wreck of a family, a scar that will never fully heal. This situation is so absurd Skyler doesn't know whether he should laugh or cry.

Skyler says, "Did you know our father died? Not of natural causes. He was beaten to death by one of your agents because I guess the Paragon is under your control just like the Ark now."

"Easy," his brother whispers. "I didn't know about Dad. I don't know what happened."

"Well, maybe it's high time you came back from the dead to see the chaos you've put us all in!" The truth hits him painfully hard: Allen is now the leader of the Mavericks who will lead them to their doom.

"I knew you had twisted ideas, but this…" Skyler says, appalled. "What is going through your mind?"

"I told you about it," says his brother, true to himself. "Don't tell me five years made you forget? Everyone on this Ark has been living a lie for over a century. What did you want me to do? Stand there and do nothing?"

"You could have come back and talked to me. Together we could have worked it out."

"Isn't that what I did when I sent Tessa after you?"

To save his little brother from his anarchic plan.

"I'm not fond of lies, either. It must run in the family, I

guess." Skyler's tone is cutting, and the tears he shed earlier are drying on his now cold cheeks. His insides feel like iron.

"What's up with you?" replies his brother, visibly hurt. "I am not your enemy. I brought you here so we could discuss the plan to reach the Promised Land."

"Did you give me a choice? Who said I would support your ideas?" His expression shifts abruptly and the dark circles under his eyes stand out.

"I know you want the same thing I do," Allen says in a harsher voice. "Tessa knows it too. She's spent the last few weeks watching you."

"I don't want to sacrifice anyone to reach a Promised Land that I have never seen." He almost sounds like Emily, who would be proud. Skyler thought she was pessimistic, but deep down she was right all along.

"I don't know what made you change your mind, but I'm going to give you some time to pull yourself together. Get some sleep until the chloroform wears off."

"I don't need to rest," says Skyler indignantly. Allen seriously thinks he can just walk away! He has a lot to answer for. "Emily and Mom are still on the Ark. We must go get them."

"Nothing and no one will open that door until I get full control of the ship, Sky." Skyler ignores him as the images of his dream become clearer.

"So is Chris. Is that what you really want? To have their deaths on your conscience?"

"Why would you care about him? He'll find his way like his father."

"If it wasn't for him, I would be dead. Just like Tessa, you decide who should live and who should not."

Resentment bubbles in his throat. How can his brother be serious after all he's done?

"Everyone chooses their own path and mine is to set us free. Soon, this will be over. Just trust me."

"Should I?" Trust is a bargaining chip that too many people dangle. The reality is quite different.

"Damn it, we're brothers, Sky!" Allen leaps to his feet, annoyed. "If we can't trust each other, then this whole thing is meaningless."

"Until today, I didn't have a brother. And we don't share the same goals."

"If you knew what I know—"

"What are you waiting for?" says Skyler defiantly. "It's now or never." His brother darts to the desk and taps something on his wristband, and a holographic screen pops up over the table.

Images of the simulation where he and Allen almost crossed paths for the first time show the interior of the building they were in with Emily. The viewpoint shifts from the balcony to an aerial view of a pristine city, where the sun reflects off the white buildings.

"Do you have any idea where this place is?" asks his brother, with eyes fixed on the hologram.

"It looks like a pre-Flood city found in the Archives."

"If I told you that this place still exists, would you believe me?"

"No." Skyler says this with such conviction that his brother recoils. "This is an underwater city. Unless you've been there before—"

"No, but the data in the Archives show there was contact at the same coordinates two months ago." All the cities of the world have sunken, and no other human being could have survived.

"Did you consider that ancient technology could still emit old signals?" argues Skyler to pull him out of his reverie.

"No need. We have the messages they transmitted. Look for yourself." A brief transcript asking the Ark to give its position appears. Excitement fills his brother, but Skyler can't give in that easily.

"Yet the Commander refuses to answer," his brother adds.

"What if they thought it was a hoax?"

"These are protected files. No one can edit them, so they must come from outside, Sky."

"Let's say the message is authentic. Who are these people? Who says they have good intentions?" Allen sighs as he comes closer to the hologram.

"This is how we will survive in the long run no matter the risk. Our scientists will never get us there and if by some miracle they found land, we wouldn't necessarily succeed. Our best option is this message."

"Or rather, give away our location. And then what? Either we meet them, or they do. *If* they really exist. It could be a stray signal that's been looping around for a century."

How can his brother be so naive? If these images had been filmed by a drone of their era, perhaps, but…

"I can't believe you're risking everyone's lives on baseless assumptions."

"What will it take to convince you?" says Allen, raising his voice. "I'm just as much a prisoner of this Ark as you are. But it won't be long now, and you'll be with me." His brother switches the hologram off and stares intently at Skyler like in his dream.

"Why the new name?"

"A new life began when I met the Mavericks," Allen replies more calmly. "I became a new person, and I embraced the potential inside me. I knew I had the power to change things."

Or he wanted to deny his past at his family's expense, a family who worried about him night and day, who would have done anything to have him back or to know he was safe.

"I'll come back later," says his brother. "Get some rest."

The door locks as soon as he steps out, and Skyler feels like smashing it down. He paces around the office, hands behind his head, sighing, leaning against the wall, hiding his face in the fold of his arm. He remembers their reunion, a scenario he would have never imagined. Such illusions can be fatal.

Allen. Neal. One and the same person.

And this supposedly Promised Land.

What will become of them?

Skyler settles down on the couch and slips under the blanket. He lets his gaze wander until he gives in to fatigue, unable to bear the stare of the former Commanders, their lifelike portraits hanging on the wall. Commander Wolfe could have never imagined the Ark would sail the Great Ocean for more than a century, much less that its passengers would one day rebel. What did he think at that moment? Did he really believe they stood a chance to go back to the ground?

THERE'S A KNOCK, and then someone enters. It takes Skyler a moment to recognize him, but it's Allen. Sorry, Neal. What would warrant choosing a different name if not to cut ties with one's family?

"Looks like you have a visitor, little brother."

Neal tries to put on a brotherly face, but it still rings hollow. After all these years, he can't just waltz back into Skyler's life as if nothing had changed.

Skyler blinks to make sure he's awake, that this isn't a poor joke. Still, Neal takes on that big-brotherly look of concern that Skyler craved.

But today is different. His brother is dead.

36

EMILY

EMILY SNAPS OUT OF HER DREAMLESS STATE AS THE COLD BITES her face. The tingling is gone, but her headache has reached new heights, as if the transfer had made it worse.

She's wearing a helmet. Again? Yasmina already has her memories, her brain! There is nothing else for her!

Yet this helmet feels different. It's heavier, much heavier, and older, too. With her hand, she feels it is connected to something big and cylindrical.

Despite her weak legs, she gets up with her chains on and, as if on cue, the golden silhouette of Yasmina comes out of the secret room.

"Is that it?" says Yasmina with a pout. "I thought this helmet would bring back some good memories. You could beg me to take it off, to spare you."

"I won't give you that satisfaction," Emily replies, her voice made hollow by the glass that traps her. She feels hot with this heavy jacket over her shoulders, and her mouth is dry. The light is blinding, and she covers her eyes for a few seconds to give herself a break. Damn it.

"Those headaches again?" Emily frowns at Yasmina's words.

"What do you mean by *again?*"

"Your mother had them too. Despite what you may think, she was not my enemy, even after I sentenced her to death."

"So why didn't you plead her case?"

"It doesn't work like that. She chose her fate."

"Tell me what you have in mind now. I've had enough." Emily is choking as she feels around the helmet to remove it but only ends up scraping her fingertips.

"We have all the time in the world, don't we?" Yasmina's voice is dull against the glass wall. Emily feels like she's been in this room for hours: an endless nightmare. "Though, I must say I am quite disappointed in you. You can't imagine how privileged you are to still be able to breathe. Ever since your actions gave you away, every breath you take could be the last."

"These prisoners, whether or not they are Mavericks, do not deserve to be tortured like this. They are human beings, not animals to play with."

"A threat to everyone's safety on a level you can't even imagine," Yasmina corrects.

"Did you think for a second you were a threat yourself?"

"I thought you and I would have a great time as a family, but I have to face the facts. I will not enjoy teaching you the way I did Reyes."

"My real mother's secret," says Emily firmly. "That's all I want to know." Yasmina looks at her from the corner of her eye, contemplating. She sticks her nose near the glass of the helmet, and Emily reads her lips as she whispers.

"X2O. She knew what it meant."

"What kind of code is that?" snaps Emily, tugging at her chains. "What does it mean?"

"May you find out in the next life, my dear daughter. If the Creator is willing." Yasmina scans her wristband on a console on top of the pedestal and taps something that triggers a whirring sound. Emily steps back with nowhere to run.

"I had high hopes for you," Yasmina says in a hoarse voice as she leaves the platform. "But this is the price to pay for what you did with those Mavericks. I will not let my daughter follow in Tyna Bates's footsteps and challenge me relentlessly. The Commander would never forgive me if I didn't teach you the right way. The Creator will decide whether you live or die."

Icy water gushes out at Emily's cheek with full force, and she lets out a gasp, her body shaking uncontrollably. If she doesn't drown, panic will kill her first.

Oh my God, Mom.

The water rises quickly. Her mouth is already immersed.

Yasmina shuffles around the platform to watch her every move from every angle. A famished beast waiting to bite at its prey just at the right moment.

Think fast. There must be a way out of this. Emily's teeth chatter, and she clenches her jaws to stop it from making her dizzy.

Emily punches the glass to break it, but it's useless. She feels at the back of the helmet and grabs at the pipe. She pulls hard.

Giving up is a sweet temptation. The atrocities she has committed make her no better than Yasmina, but even so, her survival instinct is visceral. It forces her to act. Now she hopes what the Paragon taught her can save her life.

The water reaches her nose, and her breathing becomes labored. She tilts her head back to breathe, and the fog on the glass blurs her vision. She needs something hard and powerful.

The tools. They are all out of reach. Plus, she can't see anything!

No, no!

Had she gone to the Command Center, she would have avoided Yasmina's torture, but she did otherwise.

For a code. A damn code that means absolutely nothing! The secret that had Mom executed.

Emily must find some peace while she still can.

Water is above her nose, and it seeps into her ears as her heart rate slows down.

Drink!

She starts to drink desperately to lower the water level. It's salty and makes her feel sick. If she vomits, it's over.

"Acknowledge me as your legitimate mother and you shall live," says Yasmina, increasing the pressure of the water jets, "or atone for your sins in the Creator's old ways and die."

Emily drinks more and more, holding back the bile that rises in her throat. She can't take it anymore. She can't breathe.

It would be so easy to give Yasmina what she wants, so Emily can survive and maybe have the chance to redeem herself. But no. Yasmina will never leave her alone. She will force her to become a vile person who believes she can control people and break them, who gives up her sense of morality, justice, and love, who denies her own family that has loved and inspired her so much.

Better to die than to live in a lie and follow the shadow of a so-called fallen goddess.

The world around her slows down, and the light refracts into the deadly water that completely submerges her. The images flow in one after the other.

Mom. Daddy. Gabrielle. Chris. Mira. Leander. And prisoners whose names escape her. Sky.

She opens her eyes one last time. It is dark.

Everything is plunged in the most complete darkness. Is the Ark sinking already?

A knock on the glass startles her. She opens her mouth instinctively, and a little water seeps down her throat. She gasps in panic.

Cold. So cold.

Blue lights. A silhouette. Tall.

Control panel. Don't know. Not how. Use.

Emily taps her wristband. Tap. Tap. Tap. Falls to her knees.

Silence.

Arms lift her up.

Blue lights. Everywhere. Close your eyes.

SHE WAKES UP WITH A START.

She is swaddled like a worm. Someone is spooning her.

Normally, Emily wouldn't mind pulling his arm away, but she lacks the strength. The cold is gone, though, which is good. Even her migraine seems to have subsided.

"You're recovering fast," says Milo. He hasn't changed clothes since the last time she saw him.

"What are you doing here?" His familiar aura gives off warmth. "Why did you save me? Why aren't you with the others?"

"I never intended to go." He takes his arm off of Emily's waist. "I wanted to know what you were still doing here."

"It's … personal." She shrugs off the covers, and the cotton slips off her naked skin. She blushes and asks where her uniform is in a reproachful tone.

"I had no choice. You were soaked and your body was freezing," he defends himself, then glances around. "I guess there must be some clothes around."

"Never mind. I'll check out Yasmina's office," she says, pulling the sheet back hard enough for Milo to roll onto his side. At least he doesn't balk at that. "By the way, where is she?"

Yasmina didn't mean to execute her, but she tried anyway, since Emily didn't recognize her as her mother. What twisted mind could imagine such a thing? Yasmina must have been seriously unloved in her childhood to have become what she is. To think that she has been in charge of the prison and Emily's life all this time.

"That bitch will be asleep for a while," he says, propping

himself up from the bed. "While I was watching you, I found a way to cut the power. Afterward, it was quite simple to surprise her, especially with all those toys at my disposal."

Emily is almost disappointed she didn't get to see that. Milo's scarlet aura dazzles her for a moment.

"I know everything she did to Fiona," he murmurs, his eyes widening. "She was doing the same thing to you. It only gave me one more reason to act."

He gives her a compassionate look.

"She was manipulating you, Emily." She would like to believe him, but she has her share of responsibility. How can she ever make amends? Maybe she should start with Milo.

It's so dark that if it weren't for his aura, she wouldn't see him because his skin is so filthy.

"How about you shower while I go get something to wear?" she says in a light tone. "Use one of the water jets in a cell."

"Does it bother you that much? I thought girls liked scruffy men." Emily rolls her eyes. This burst of familiarity is … odd. Just yesterday, he was her prisoner and wrongfully locked up at that.

"I've had mine, as you can see," she says to ease her discomfort. "Don't you want to die clean? I sure do."

She walks out, dragging the too-long sheet before he can answer. The corridor of the Forgotten is just as dark as the rest of the Ark. Soon, when the ship is abandoned by its crew, the emergency lights will go out too.

Emily enters Yasmina's office and blocks out her still painful memories. She half-opens the door to make sure Yasmina is not there, her golden aura easy to spot, even in the semi-darkness. Emily feels ahead until she grabs the desk, and when she feels a handle on the drawer, she pulls.

Yasmina always paid special attention to her appearance in case Commander Hawk would pay her a surprise visit. The relationship between those two is intense, almost desperate. It's nothing but comforting coming from the Commander himself. There must be a better explanation.

Emily's hands find a change of clothes, but the size won't be a match. Yasmina's body is way too small, and her breasts are shapely.

She settles for a department uniform in a clean, bland gray as she rummages through the equipment storage closets. It's pretty wrinkled, but it will do. She slips it on quickly and sorely misses the silky fabric of Mom's dress she wore for *La Orilla*. What she would give to have another one of those magical evenings where her only worry was to get a reservation and pick a fancy dish.

In the doorway, she hesitates. The torture room door is closed, but her curiosity nags at her. What exactly did Milo do to Yasmina? Did he take her out? His aura became so bright when he brought her up. If he ruthlessly killed Yasmina like Tessa did with those officers, it doesn't bode well for Emily.

She opens the door.

The room is swimming in a weak amber light: Yasmina's energy. Her body is hanging off some kind of removable wall, her arms outstretched in a cross. She is a pitiful sight to see.

She is very much alive, though; her fuzzy aura glows as if she were asleep.

Emily quietly draws near, for fear that she will suddenly wake up. Fresh marks from the electric prod have burned her all over in craters of flesh, the skin coming off in shreds. Does it make Milo a good man for sparing her life or worse for beating her up?

Would letting her die from her wounds make Emily an accomplice once again? Emily needs to change now. This masquerade has gone on long enough. Why should she seal people's fates when they should be the masters of their own lives?

Mom must have understood that, too. She also accepted that

Yasmina would never support the Maverick community, even if it meant becoming enemies.

Emily unties the tightly knotted ropes and lays Yasmina's body on the ground. Maybe Yasmina won't wake until the Ark is done for, but if they all survive this mess, she can change as well.

Perhaps.

In the end, Yasmina gave her what Emily wanted: Mom's secrets. Tyna Bates was Yasmina's friend at the Academy, and in the years that followed. Tyna Bates was indeed a traitor by the committee's definition, and its members were unaware of the consequences their discrimination against the Mavericks would bring about, who, after living as outcasts for so long, eventually organized to overthrow the established order of the Ark. A fire fueled over years of injustice, Emily can understand that. Being a Bates also set her apart, and every day of her life she wished she had never been born in this wretched family. But Tyna Bates had struck another chord of the committee: the code.

X2O. Its meaning is still unclear now, but if she stays alive long enough, she will find out what this forbidden knowledge really is, even if it means putting herself in danger.

Emily exits the room to join Milo, who is waiting for her where she left him. She squints, dazzled by his aura.

Oddly, auras are stronger than before, and lights are brighter, even painful. That helmet really messed up her brain. Lack of oxygen, maybe? Sky could give her a diagnosis, but she has to find him first.

"What's on your arm?" asks Milo, clean with his hair still damp. "Does it hurt?"

Emily runs her hand gently over her forearm, where a fresh, tender scar mars her skin, the result of the prod's power, though it's nothing compared to Yasmina's.

"Could be worse," she says with a twinge of envy for Milo's unscarred, freckled skin. "A reminder of Yasmina."

"That bitch," he spits, his hands in his pockets. "Now what do we do?"

Good question. Gabrielle, Dad, and Sky. They're all probably in danger, but the situation on the ship is unpredictable. Her encounter with Duke in the atrium was just a taste of it, not to mention her run of bad luck at the Gardens and with the Mavericks at Delta Labs. There are too many unknowns with all these factions acting independently. A real minefield—the Academy's favorite metaphor for what the Simulation has in store for them—except this time it's for real.

"What was the Brotherhood's original plan?"

"Take control of the Command Center before they run away."

"True," she replies as she covers her mouth thoughtfully. "You told me you knew their plan for leaving us to die."

"The Commander abused his power to weave lies the Brotherhood has been unraveling for years. They came prepared." Milo's aura is adamant, and he doesn't seem worried in the least.

"So, there's more? What kind of lies?"

"You'll find out soon enough, if you believe in the Brotherhood, that is." He draws closer, his fine muscles bulging like those fire dancers at the free party. She has the feeling he might surprise her. It wouldn't be the first time. "Have you decided what you want to do with your new life?"

A heady waft of soap makes her stutter, "What are you talking about? What's changed? We're stuck on a possible ghost Ark."

"I saved you from certain death," he says with a serious look that doesn't match his childish attitude. "You could say that this is your second life, like cats."

"Do I look like a cat to you?" She takes offense. "Careful what you say." Those horrible hairy creatures with their shifty eyes—thank goodness they're not on the ship.

"That's what I'm saying," he says, suppressing a laugh. Even though their situation is dire, Emily smiles.

"I know where I want to go," she says with sudden determination. "Now."

"Where?" he asks, his eyes blazing.

"To the Command Center." He looks at her, disbelieving, then a smirk appears on his golden face.

GOING to the Command Center isn't such a good idea after all. The thought had crossed Emily's mind, yes, but that didn't mean it was the best thing to do for now. And then Milo had to bring up the lies.

Living with the belief that Mom was wrongfully convicted was a horrible experience. Emily convinced herself that there was only one way to follow in her mother's footsteps, in other words, by working for Yasmina and making the Mavericks talk.

As for the Commander and his crew, they must have had good intentions for the Archeans, even if some of their decisions were not unanimous. Why didn't they keep them up to date with what was going on outside? Although the Deltas' research department is fairly big, even if Sky's father works there—used to work there—they would share none of their discoveries. They would only talk about going back to the ground with no other explanation.

But when did they plan to do so?

Behind every lie is a truth. But the only way to find out is to believe in what the Brotherhood offers: their so-called Promised Land. It could be nothing more than a metaphor, but Emily gives them the benefit of the doubt for now.

The corridors of the Ark are plunged into an unrecognizable darkness. No matter where they go, it's the same thing: Bluish emergency lights line the bottom of each wall.

"What makes you think the Command Center hasn't detached yet?" asks Emily, crushed by uncertainty.

"You're the one who wants us to go, by the way," Milo says, his expression unreadable. There's so much more to him than the Maverick. Milo has charm and an infectious likability. Fiona is right to love him for the person he is.

Calling Fiona by her first name seems more accurate now. After listening to Milo talk about her, it's hard to do otherwise. Emily could have been Fiona herself if she had grown up under the same circumstances.

The contrast of Milo's pale blue eyes with his aura is striking. If she looks at him for too long, it rekindles her headache, though she hides her pain from him, knowing it would only worry him needlessly. As long as she can stand, she'll be fine.

"How will we know whether the Commander hasn't already run off?" asks Emily as they slip under a bunch of Paragon officers.

"Easy," he replies, not even looking ahead, as if he had a mental map of the place. "We'll just have to ask. The Brotherhood has already broken in."

How ironic that he can find his way around so easily. The Mavericks were confined to the lower levels of the ship, except for getting food and supplies on occasion. But the darkness is enough to bewilder Emily.

They get to the pressurized door leading to the Command Center, the same she and Chris went through. In the bluish glow of the darkness, it looks like a gate to another world.

Milo taps something on the console and scans his wristband.

"How did you come to know all this?" she asks, curious about his knowledge of the ship. "I mean, you know the Ark almost better than I do."

"You shouldn't believe everything you've been told," says Milo, listening to his wristband. "We each have our own wristbands to blend in with the rest of you which, by the way, are the only thing that sets us apart on the Ark. Getting away with the inspections is a challenge, but not impossible."

"What the hell are you doing? We've been looking for you," says a synthesized voice.

"I have company. Will you let me in?"

The relief she expected knowing the Brotherhood has taken control of the Ark does not come. Nothing will ever be the same again. What do they really know about the Mavericks? What happened to the Commander?

The familiar synthesized voice is unfriendly, and the answer is slow to come, so much that Emily feels as if she had dreamt this moment.

"What the hell is he doing?" mumbles Milo.

"What if they don't come? What do we do?"

"We stay here. They'll have to open at some point if they don't want to rot in there." They finally decide to sit on the floor and with each passing minute, Emily worries about what comes next. What happened to the others?

They could be dead.

The compressed air whistles and ruffles her hair. The door screws open and reveals a tall, well-built man. They get up at the same time.

"You brought her back," welcomes the big bully from the free party.

"She's changed her mind, Dan," says Milo. "How's it going in there?"

"Still some things to work out. Without the access codes, we can't do anything. Walker is working on it."

"Really?"

"You're trying to talk the Commander into giving those codes away, aren't you?" says Emily unflinchingly before Dan's impressive build. He stares at her, and Milo answers in his stead.

"Why do you want to know that?"

"I know someone who could persuade him in her own way." It takes Milo a moment to realize what she's getting at. His eyes widen in disbelief.

"Don't even think about it. That bitch is going to die where I left her."

"Are there any other options? She knows him better than anyone. Hopefully, the Commander will listen to her." Milo purses his lips and scratches the nape of his neck.

"I believe in Walker. He can work miracles. You don't know him yet."

"We'll have to check with him," says the bully as if his brain had just come back to life. "But we're running out of time. There are other problems, too."

He leaves his sentence hanging, thick with innuendo. Milo nods, and Emily asks for an explanation.

"The Brotherhood won't trust you when they're so close to succeeding," Milo replies in a friendly tone.

"I have to show my good will, right?" she asks, exasperated by the turn of events. It's the second end of the world, and she has to prove to a shady group of rebels that she can be trusted. Damn it. Pandering to a terrorist group—her headache is getting worse just thinking about it.

Open for change? Yes. Convert to a cult? No way in hell.

"No one is forcing you to do anything," adds Milo.

"I know what I have to do," she replies dryly. "But thanks anyway."

"As you wish." Then he turns to Dan. "Any news about Fiona?" His dark eyes and thick beard give him the same animal look as those horrible cats. Plus, Milo's aura blends with his, so it's impossible to read either of them.

"Sorry, Lo. Nothing for now." Milo's energy drops a notch, and Emily walks away, eager to make them trust her.

"So, are you coming?" asks Emily, hands on her hips. Milo stares at her in awe.

"Do you really want to go back?"

"Either I go, or your friend here won't let me come with you." She casts a dark glance at the bearded man. "And you need the access codes." Besides, how could Sky and the others get in if the bully was there? Maybe they didn't make it.

"Yeah, well." Milo lets out a sigh. "Are you sure?"

"Absolutely." Emily swallows her concern as she retraces her steps, followed by Milo, who exchanges a few quick words with Dan who stays at the door like a watchdog.

"There's something you need to know," she tells him as they round the corner. The darkness gives them a closeness she never thought she would share with a Maverick, let alone one who would take control of the Ark illegally.

Milo's expression shifts and transfixes her.

"Hey!" An all-too-familiar figure hobbles towards them, Yasmina, who does nothing to hide herself. She hasn't changed clothes since her torture session, and a shiver runs down Emily's spine. Yasmina's wounds are such that it's a miracle she is still standing.

"That's what I wanted to talk to you about," Emily mumbles, concerned about Milo's reaction.

"Don't tell me you…" he says indignantly. "Emily!"

"It's more complicated than you think."

"How do you expect the Brotherhood to trust you?" His aura is blindingly bright, and Emily must look away while Yasmina still has energy to laugh.

"He can't understand us," she says to Emily. "He grew up on the lower levels."

"What difference does it make?" he interrupts. "Do you think that gives you the right to lock us up to control us? To torture us?"

"I do what is expected of me."

"What are you doing here?" asks Milo scornfully.

"I wouldn't miss it for anything in the world," Yasmina

replies as she takes two steps in their direction. If not for her characteristic energy, she would be unrecognizable. Her beauty vanished as quickly as a slap in the face.

"What are you talking about?" Emily says with squinting eyes.

"I know what you are. Coming from you, Emily, this only confirms my suspicions." Not knowing how to read her, Emily decides to play it straight.

"What if you had the power to save Hawk, would you do it?"

"Don't play that card with me," Yasmina hisses through gritted teeth. "You'd rather die than acknowledge your legitimate family. Unless embracing death made you reconsider?" Milo exchanges a worried look with Emily and stops her from moving, as if to pull her closer to him.

The air crackles. Yasmina brought the electric prod. Instinctively, Emily feels her skin burning; the memory of this devil's weapon is forever etched in her flesh.

Milo glares at Emily as she walks towards Yasmina, whose aura falters. He tries to stop her, but she ignores him. This is her problem now.

"Let me take care of this," she says, holding the gaze of the woman who was once her boss. Milo steps back.

"I know you released me," says Yasmina. "Why would you do that? I almost killed you."

"Why wouldn't I?"

Mom is more present than ever, even more so than during her daily prayers. Mom supports her decision. Until today, giving someone a second chance had seemed out of touch with reality. Not anymore.

"You were close to my mother. You didn't want to carry out the orders that day, but you did anyway." Yasmina does not answer, but she lowers the prod, which buzzes off. Her face contorts with tears.

"You can prevent this from happening again," Emily continues. "The Brotherhood has already taken over the Command Center and is looking for the access codes. If they can't get them by conventional means, who knows what they'll do." If the Brotherhood is who they say they are. Yes, Milo saved her life, even though she gave him a hard time. However, he's close to Fiona, who doesn't like her very much. There is also Dan the bully and that Walker. But Neal, the guy from the simulation…

Their leader who knew Mom. The one who has the power to change everything.

"This is your second chance," says Emily, leaving the words hanging. As she says this, she turns to Milo, looking for an answer, but he avoids her gaze. Milo obviously doesn't approve, but Yasmina is their only hope of getting those codes.

"Let's go." Yasmina complies, and Milo takes her prod away with a swift move before walking beside Emily. He scratches his neck and sighs.

"That's what the Brotherhood claims, isn't it?" says Emily, her confidence back. "A second chance, the Promised Land?"

"For those who deserve it, yes," he answers stiffly.

"How are you any better if you think in the way the Commander does? I grew up in a family whose ancestors barely had enough to live off."

"You are different." His eyes soften at that.

"I've tortured prisoners, Milo, more than you can count. Probably several that you know of." His energy wavers ever so quickly that she thinks she's going to lose him. Not now.

"I don't believe you."

"It's true, whether you like it, or not. If you can't accept it, I won't follow you. It's that simple."

"Don't do that." He grabs her shoulder.

"Either we die now, or we die later. You decide." He mumbles a curse, then abruptly veers to the Command Center.

They walk in silence and Yasmina mutters, "You are just like your mother."

An unease creeps up inside Emily, and she pretends she didn't hear anything.

The bully rushes towards them when he sees them coming. He quickly hands something to Milo who gets closer to Emily. Dan takes Yasmina by surprise and binds her hands behind her back using some kind of contraption, a different kind than they normally use at the prison.

Milo takes advantage of Emily's distraction to do the same.

She shouts, "If this is your way to thank me for bringing her back to you—"

"Gag her too," says Milo, who scratches Yasmina's scars deliberately. Emily grimaces, knowing exactly what Yasmina feels. The headache comes back, and Yasmina splits momentarily. Her aura-less doppelganger turns to Emily.

Emily blinks, and the next second it's gone. The fatigue will kill her if this keeps up.

As they enter the Command Center, the door pressurizes behind them.

A strange smell hovers. The air is frozen, electric. Fear. They are stuck.

Milo can't be serious, not after going to all this trouble to save her from Yasmina's clutches. He'll release her once they know she can be trusted. They have a lead to get the codes they need now.

The bully tugs at Yasmina to cause her unbearable pain.

"I haven't forgotten the last time," Emily says to him. "You seem to be enjoying yourself quite a lot."

"Don't make me change my mind about you," he says threateningly. "Seriously, Lo, I can't believe you brought her."

"Come on, Dan. Don't forget why we're here." Milo and Emily branch off from the center aisle and lose Dan and Yasmina at the same time. Something is wrong. Milo leads Emily into a separate room. They are alone and the strange silence makes her uncomfortable.

"Why don't you take us to see the Commander together?"

"That's not the plan. Walker is working on it first, and if it doesn't work out, we'll have to use her."

"What about me? I want to meet the others. You said there was room for everyone."

"Emily. With what you told me earlier, I…" It can't be, after all they've been through.

No need to convince him at this point. He has to see her good intentions by himself.

"At least tell me if Skyler is here," she asks, afraid that desperation will overtake her. "Can you check for me?" He takes a deep breath.

"Sorry." He looks down.

"Milo!"

The door closes. And it is locked.

37

SKYLER

THE SYNTHETIC SMELL OF RECYCLED AIR ENTERS THE ROOM through the open door where Neal stands, his tattoos clearly visible. The time that has elapsed since the last time Skyler saw him is even more striking.

"I want to see her," says Skyler, who leaped off the couch, shaking off the still-warm blanket. According to Neal, Emily reached the Command Center before they sealed it for good. Skyler knew she would succeed unless this was one of Neal's tactics to butter him up.

"Only if you guarantee you will help me reach the Promised Land."

"Are you blackmailing me? Even if it were true, you don't need me for this. You already have your Brotherhood to do it."

"I can't do it without you," his brother insists.

"You've done well so far." The bitter memory of their past run-ins overwhelms him. Old habits die hard, even after death.

"I need your word," Neal continues. "You're the one I trust the most. I know that once you commit, you won't let me down."

"All right," says Skyler, nodding. "I hope I won't regret it."

Neal takes hold of his arm, smiling. He must have showered, because the smell of sweat from the night before is replaced by a pungent aroma of fir.

Skyler returns his smile to hide his uncertainty. Can their trusting relationship ever go back to the way it was? Everything is so … new.

Their wristbands clink and Neal taps something away. Skyler's smile fades just as quickly.

"We're bound now," says Neal, satisfied, as he breaks contact. "You can't take your wristband off anymore. This way, no matter what happens, I'll know where you are. It'll keep us from losing sight of each other again." Blood ties are what truly unite them unless his brother has forgotten over the years. Hopefully, he will keep his promise and that physical bond will be enough to prevent his past mistake from recurring.

Neal explains, "It's the same for every member of the Brotherhood. I can't risk anyone betraying us."

"I didn't know that was your definition of trust."

"Think of it as a symbol of trust." Skyler hopes his brother's madness to command the Ark and conquer the Promised Land won't be a tragic flaw.

"What now?" asks Skyler.

"Welcome to the Brotherhood, little brother," says Neal, who grabs his shoulder to lead him out of the cabin.

THE COMMAND CENTER is bigger than Skyler had imagined, or maybe Neal wants to make sure he can't find his way around. They pass dozens of Mavericks wearing the same uniform that blend in with the other divisions of the Ark. However, there is something different about the way they greet Neal and glance at Skyler, though he can't put his finger on it. Perhaps they share a sense of belonging, a common history, or they feel restless knowing what's coming. His brother is confident as he nods back at every single one of them, as if he had truly been one of them. With all the security the Brotherhood has put in place, the entire crew must be under their control.

"Quite the accomplishment," Skyler whistles after they chat with a pair of Mavericks guarding the entrance to a cabin. "They respect you." His brother gives him an amused look.

"This is just the beginning. Hope I can count on you, little brother." A bloodcurdling shot ricochets through the maze, and Neal's features deepen.

"You stay here. I'll go see what's going on."

"Didn't you say you needed my help?" More shots follow and they press on.

The main command room looks exactly like Skyler's dream with the portholes that look out on the desolate seabed. The metallic smell of blood brings him back to the vision of horror before him. Bloody bodies are slumped over while Mavericks threaten the crew members who, despite their awful appearance, resist with what little strength they can muster. At least two or three guards hold them fast.

"What the hell are you doing?" Neal yells over the din. "Who are these people?" The Commander is among them, his uniform identical to what Skyler imagined. The middle-aged man winces.

"Diana," bellows Commander Hawk as he stares at a lifeless body. The walls are riddled with bullets, and two screens are shattered. Neal looks around and weaves his way to the center of the room where the Mavericks stand off.

"They regrouped here to plot," explains Laurene who struggles to her feet, swats away at a Maverick trying to help her up. "We arrived just in time." Laurene looks dreadful despite the suit she wears. She massages her cheek and Neal waves at two guards posted at the entrance to dispose of the body. He heaves a sigh.

"Commander. Can't you see that it's time to give up your seat?"

"If I gave up every time I faced a challenge, I would be dead by now." Hawk's tone is firm, his face placid.

"It's not just any day," Neal adds, moving closer to him.

"Gunning down my entire crew will only stir the Creator's wrath." Neal has a mirthless laugh and scratches his stubbled cheek.

"We'll see about that."

"Even if you get rid of us and go to that Promised Land of yours, the Creator will punish you. You have no idea what he is capable of."

"I'm listening." Neal crosses his arms, his tattoos glowing in the harsh light.

"I know how to keep our Ark safe. One false move and we are all dead. The Creator is watching." Hawk swallows hard, and his eyes cloud over.

"He stubbornly refuses to give us the code." Laurene's angry face flushes.

"You," swears the Commander who points his finger at her defiantly. "How dare you! I gave you everything! I welcomed you—" The Commander's face turns pale, and he lets out a gasp of pain. His guard catches him just in time to keep his head from smashing to the ground. From the way he's holding his side, Skyler can see he's been hurt.

"What did you do to him?" says Neal, giving Laurene a threatening look. "I won't let you hurt him."

"I didn't do anything," she replies smugly. "Besides, watch your mouth. Remember who made you the next Commander." She storms out with her personal guard, and Neal snorts.

"Lock up the remaining crew members. Search every corner of the Command Center, and make sure they do not talk to each other. Until we get the code, we are vulnerable."

The Mavericks comply, and it is only then that Skyler

notices the dozens of prisoners who look like they haven't slept in a while, a large enough number to pose a threat.

Tessa storms in at the same time, followed by a man wearing a white shirt instead of a uniform. She blatantly ignores Skyler.

"Trouble?" asks Tessa to Neal.

"The usual. Walker, what's going on?" Neal asks, clearly annoyed. The man taps on his tablet and shows him something that makes him raise an eyebrow.

"All access to the server requires the code. The damage to the Ark is more extensive than I thought. On top of that, the gas explosions deployed in the vent badly affected the Sacred Fire."

"How is this possible? Still no trace of the culprit?" Walker nods, looking sorry.

"Without the Fire … damn it. It will all be for nothing."

"What do we do with him?" asks Tessa, crouched down next to Hawk. Skyler feels like he's in the way, so he heads for the exit. They don't need him here. "Laurene is a fool! Now that First Officer Diana is dead, only the Commander knows the code."

"Skyler," Neal calls out to him before he has time to escape. "What are you doing?" The man named Walker puts up his glasses as if seeing him for the first time.

"So that's him." What does that mean exactly? It seems like everyone knows Skyler. Who knows what Neal said about him. They'll be disappointed to find out that Skyler is useless.

"Well…"

"I want you to look after the Commander," Neal says seriously, with a hand on Skyler's shoulder. "We need him alive, no matter what. Can I count on you?" Tessa steals a glance at him as she busies herself giving directions to the guards carrying Hawk, who is still unconscious.

Neal's gaze is insistent.

"Fine."

THE INFIRMARY IS BETTER EQUIPPED than Skyler would have thought. They must have been planning their escape for a long time, as they transferred crates of antibiotics, sanitizer, and medical supplies that would last for months, if not years, if they used them sparingly. These were the stocks cluttering up Med Bay. They had marked them up, thinking the order was a mistake, since they would never need so much.

The room can house two patients simultaneously, and the soundproof walls isolate them from all the hubbub caused by the Mavericks combing the Command Center. Skyler has had to explain why he's here at least three times since entering the infirmary.

The Commander does not seem to be in critical condition. He lost consciousness because his blood pressure dropped too quickly. He's lost a significant amount of blood, but fatigue also has something to do with it. These last days have not been easy on him.

As Hawk dozes, Skyler makes sure his vitals are stable and his blood sugar at the right level. The mechanical gestures and familiar scent of bleach calm him, a rare feeling lately.

The whiteness of the sheets contrasts with the Commander's dark skin. This is not unusual on the Ark. Since survivors of different backgrounds live together, skin color matters little, but for Skyler, it is a testament to an invaluable ancestral heritage necessary for rebuilding their humanity.

Who is this man, really? He wouldn't know. Since Skyler's birth, Hawk has been in command of the Ark: A reign of twenty-one years is now ending. He is the successor of former Commander Herrera, who paved the way for a new era marking the end of the Furies period, at the same time when Ivanka Torres discovered the first signs of the Syndrome. Every Commander has had his share of trials, but never has a group of rebels overthrown one. Is that proof enough of Commander Hawk's shortcomings? To be honest, Skyler doesn't know if he could have done any better. The dream he had the day before was just that, a dream. The burden of leading the last seeds of humanity would petrify him, thinking about how every decision could bear unpredictable consequences. Still, Skyler doesn't support every decision Hawk has made, though he deserves a respect that the Brotherhood denies him.

"Thank you." Skyler turns around sharply, as if the dead had talked. Hawk's eyes are half-open, and he raises his arm connected to the IV drip. He's nothing like a Commander anymore—just another sick man.

"I need to change your dressing." Skyler pulls a little harder than he should, and Hawk groans. The wound isn't healing as well as it should. The damage those electric prods cause needs some serious disinfecting.

"Your group must be proud to have gotten rid of an incompetent old Commander like me," says Hawk in a bitter voice.

"I am not part of the Brotherhood." And yet, his brother officially welcomed him. Skyler needs time, and a wristband won't be enough. Maybe when he meets all the members, and they work together for the Promised Land, or if they show compassion for those who have sacrificed their lives for their survival.

"If they leave you alone with me, then they must trust you," the Commander continues.

"It's more like a … family problem." Is that really what this is, a problem? Whether or not he likes it, his brother leading the Ark is their new reality. Things can never go back to the way they were.

"We are a big family."

"So, why did you ignore the Mavericks?" says Skyler, tossing the soaked dressing away.

"If only it were that simple. There are some things you can't control."

"Even the Commander?" Hawk nods slowly.

"Sometimes, we are forced to make a choice, one that involves a risk we can live with."

"I don't believe this. You have all the power on this ship. You didn't inherit your family's tainted reputation." He thinks about Emily and the hardships her family has had to deal with and about the Mavericks who never had the chance to be born into an influential family. There was a blatant refusal to treat them equally. The Commander must give priority to all the inhabitants of the Ark and not just a few privileged ones. This is common sense, or else what will happen when the time comes to rebuild?

"The Ark's system is over a century old," Hawk explains wearily. "Old habits die hard." Mrs. Farrell used to say that, too. Skyler thought it was because of Hawk.

"Not anymore."

"That's what everyone wants to believe. I don't blame them." Skyler moistens a piece of gauze with alcohol and cleans the wound by dabbing at it gently. "But when we understand all the elements involved, the possibilities close in on us to the point where we wonder if it is not the Creator's will after all. His work goes far beyond our imagination."

"Do you really believe in this Creator?" Skyler asks. Hawk stares at him like it's the most absurd thing he's ever heard.

"The Flood was just the beginning, and it has been testing us every day since. Just because he is invisible does not mean he is absent. We must know how to listen to the signs." Skyler taps a little harder where greenish tendrils abound. He changes the well-soaked gauze for a new one.

"I've never heard his voice."

"He can take many forms, but not everyone is ready to accept it," states Hawk.

"If he really existed, my family would not have been suffering like this." If only he had Tessa's antibiotic ointment.

The foam would be a thousand times better than this simple disinfectant. Why does he always have to work with crap?

"So, that's your family problem," says Hawk, weighing his words. Skyler slows his movement, his hand shaking.

It's much more than that. But how would Hawk know? And what does it matter to him? He hasn't been in Skyler's shoes: dealing with a mother who's ready to disown him; feeling guilty every day for causing the death of a brother who miraculously survived and didn't think for a second about showing any sign of life for five years.

Skyler clenches his jaw. The pus is still lodged deep in Hawk's wound, but Skyler applies a new bandage, anyway. Without the ointment, only a strong antibiotic will do a better job. Hawk winces under the pressure and insists, "I'm sorry, but to deny the Creator's existence is to deny that humans walked the earth."

Skyler shrugs and grabs a vial of antibiotics from the cabinet. A familiar woman ravaged by angry scars enters the infirmary, wheeled by two Mavericks who roughly lay her down on the other bed. More collateral damage of the Paragon.

"I can't believe Neal wants to save this bitch," hisses the long dark-haired Maverick. "Worse, give her proper care."

"I'm not happy about it any more than you are, but there's nothing we can do about it," says her partner. "I trust Neal."

"I should have killed you both when I had the chance," the scarred patient grumbles. The Maverick woman slaps her in the face, and her partner stops her just before she hits again.

"What are you doing?" Skyler says, raising his voice. "Can't you see she's hurt?"

"That's our business," the man replies, spitting at the prisoner. "You should be grateful she freed you. Karma will take care of you." The two Mavericks strap the scarred woman's ankles to the bed's bars. Then the freckled Maverick turns to Skyler.

"Are you Neal's brother?" His expression softens, but Skyler remains tense.

"Am I supposed to know you?"

"I'm Milo, and she's Fiona. We will work together soon enough." Milo gives him a smile that contrasts with his rough attitude from earlier. "Neal wants you to take care of her, too. He says she's vital to the plan."

As soon as they leave, the woman moans in pain. Skyler rushes to administer an antibiotic to the Commander before getting on her case. The scars are deep, and the infection has spread. Neither disinfecting, nor a single antibiotic injection, will be enough. While Skyler prepares a cocktail of painkillers, Hawk croaks, "This is all my fault. I am so sorry, my love."

Skyler freezes and frowns. What?

"She wasn't … fond of the idea," replies the disfigured woman and Hawk grunts. A silence follows while Skyler gives his new patient a first dose of opioids. Hawk's vitals spike as he resumes in a tired voice, "Yasmina, if anything happens to me…"

"Don't say such things. I will not let them touch you, my Commander."

"My sphere?" She sighs and closes her eyes, probably letting herself drown in the painkillers.

"It is safe. I did as you asked." But what are they talking about?

"The sphere?" Skyler can't help but ask. Yasmina blinks and stares at him wearily. Her lips twist unnaturally across the craters on her disfigured face: a smile. Skyler feels nauseous.

"Of course. We are in the presence of its inventor," she finally says, stirring slightly. "I guess I should thank you."

"What did you do with the spheres?"

"You can ask your dearest best friend. She knows all about it." Her voice is now a drowsy whisper. Dr. Siria never told him the other divisions were using his spheres.

"How we meet again." Laurene glides into the infirmary as

Skyler is about to insert the tube for the intravenous antibiotic, obsessed with what he just learned. One of the Second Officer's cheekbones has taken on a purplish hue outlined by a sharp red line.

"You have already taken everything from me!" roars the Commander, who sat up on his bed. His heart rate is skyrocketing.

"What's wrong, Commander?" asks Yasmina, sleepy.

"You're making it far too easy for me," Laurene adds. She clicks her heels on the ground with a sharp thud, the metal whining with each step.

Her face is tense when she glances at Skyler.

"You can wait outside."

"I have to stay," Skyler says, puzzled. "My brother—"

"Your brother…" She seems to be thinking about something and licks her lips. She gets closer to him, way too close. "I don't think you want to take part in our little discussion." She points her gun at Skyler. "It won't be long, I promise."

Skyler clenches his jaws and gets rid of the IV with a sharp tug. He leaves the clinic under Laurene's piercing gaze and heaves a sigh of frustration once outside, her honeyed voice still clear.

"Dear Commander. I hope you understand you must not disclose the code to the Brotherhood."

"The Creator is my witness." Skyler has to do something!

He runs blindly through the maze of corridors until he comes upon a group of armed Mavericks. When he explains the situation to them, they start towards the infirmary.

Once they make it back, they find the Commander kneeling on the floor, his face buried in the hollow of his arm. He is firmly holding Yasmina's hand, which is hanging limply.

Laurene is not around, and a Maverick orders others to search the area.

Skyler takes Yasmina's vitals, but he already knows the

answer. The foul smell of blood mixed with brain fluid stings his nose and soon, the stain on the pillow spreads to the pristine mattress. Skyler pulls the sheet over Yasmina's still face that looks like a wax doll's that has melted in places. In the heavy silence of the infirmary, the Commander sobs in muffled sounds.

Skyler has failed.

SKYLER and his brother walk side by side down the hallway swarming with Mavericks who struggle to contain the crew held hostage. Those who carry meager meals swap roles with their comrades who stand guard. This transition of command can't last forever. Without the code, the Archeans' support, and the Paragon, the Brotherhood will fail. If Duke hasn't stormed the Command Center yet, it's either because he thinks they're already gone, or he's had his hands too full to bother.

"I can't believe she would do this behind my back!"

"I'm sorry I didn't do better," pleads Skyler, who keeps thinking about what he could have done to stop Laurene.

"If she thinks she will get away with this!" Neal clenches his fists and the vein in his neck twitches. Skyler doesn't know what to say to calm him down. After all these years of growing up apart, no words seem fit. Luckily, Neal will let Skyler see Emily, though his brother insisted on coming.

"Only ten minutes," Neal says as he opens the door. Skyler nods and enters. The cabin is significantly smaller than the Commander's, but still looks comfortable, especially the plush mattress in the corner.

"Emily." Under the subdued light, she leaps from the sofa to meet him. Her hair is flattened, and her makeup is smudged all over her face.

"What's going on here?" she asks defensively. The commotion outside is still audible, even though the door is shut. Is Neal eavesdropping?

"Yasmina. I think you know her." Emily looks surprised and starts wiggling her fingers.

"I see you didn't come to get us out of this mess."

"It's up to you," says Skyler.

"What do you mean?"

Skyler shares the conversation he overheard between the Commander and Yasmina, though he deliberately didn't tell his brother, who ignores the implications.

"She used your technology," Emily walks away from him, clearly confused. "Not in the most … honest way, as you can imagine." He is not here to put the dead on trial. All he knows is that no one deserves to be killed.

"Now that she's dead, Hawk won't give away the code," Skyler insists as he tries to shake Yasmina's disfigured face from his mind.

"Do you really support the Brotherhood?" inquires Emily, filled with sadness. If his brother's Brotherhood advocates fair treatment of every Archean while rebuilding civilization, why not? Perhaps they will succeed where Commander Hawk failed.

"That's not the point. They need the code to keep the Ark running and carry out their plan," he replies.

"So why don't they give Commander Hawk his rightful position back?" Emy gives him one of those inquisitive looks that always throws him off guard. When she has an idea in the back of her mind, nothing can stop her.

"You know it doesn't work that way."

"Why not?" Skyler sighs. Emily would normally support him, but something is worrying her. If one of her wonderful ideas involves sabotaging Neal's plans, this is not the time or place to talk about it. If word gets out, Emy could become an obstacle. Allen has changed a lot in five years, and his reactions are unpredictable.

"We don't have much time. My brother only gave us ten minutes." She flinches.

"Yasmina was the Chief Warden, and she found a way to encode the memory of the prisoners."

"Those who died in the prison?"

"No. During her interrogations, while they are alive. From what you are telling me, I have the impression she did the same thing with the Commander." Skyler's eyes widen. The implications are huge. He has never attempted to do this kind of testing on healthy subjects in case it would cause irreversible brain damage. But until proven otherwise, the transfer could work.

"In that case, the code has to be in there somewhere," Skyler concludes. "We need to go there. Now."

"Hold on." Emily grabs his arm, and worry veils her eyes. She is about to speak but shakes her head. "It's no big deal. Let's go."

They explain their idea to Neal, waiting by the door, scratching his cheek. Emily takes the lead, "If the Commander won't give us the code, then we have to get it ourselves. Torture won't make him talk now that he's lost his lover."

Skyler gives her a quizzical look. Wasn't she opposed to the Brotherhood taking over the Ark?

"It doesn't hurt to try," says Neal, who looks at them in turn. "Dan will walk you there."

"The bully?" Emily asks. Neal has a hearty laugh and Skyler smiles. She will never change.

"He'll bristle if you call him that," says Neal once he's regained his composure. "But hey, if you can handle him, it's up to you."

He winks at her, and Emily rolls her eyes.

"I trust you," says Neal, once the tall, bearded man named Dan has arrived.

"You must have been convincing if he let you out of the Command Center," grumbles Dan as they head out.

"We're just doing our job," says Emy casually. Skyler is glad she's chatting him up because Dan doesn't seem trustworthy. The last time Skyler saw him, he was literally spitting fire like a beast. Neal has a knack for surrounding himself with quirky characters. And yet, the Goldbergs have always been known to be rather conventional. Where did his brother learn how to draw them in like a magnet?

They let Dan get a head start and Emily whispers, "If you were wondering, I'm not doing this to help the Brotherhood. I'm doing it to save us all."

Then she catches up with the fire-eater.

DAN DECIDES to wait for them outside Yasmina's office while Skyler and Emily search for the Commander's sphere. Skyler examines the new holographic technology which is beyond anything he could have imagined. Was this what Nathan had in mind?

"I can't believe Yasmina actually kept all those prisoner spheres," Emily shouts from the anteroom. A strange smell of salt water and humidity soaks the room. Skyler doesn't want to think about the torture the inmates within these walls were subjected to. The arsenal is impressive. Besides, what was Yasmina really planning to do with those spheres?

Emily lets out a laugh, "I think I found it."

She returns, all smiles, with a sphere carefully preserved in a shell-shaped box with gold threads from the Commander's uniform. A cloth of the same dark blue covers it, tied with a ribbon, like a gift. An inscription gleams under the loop: forever.

"They loved each other," Skyler says with a serious look at Emily's mocking face.

"I am surprised, that's all. I never imagined Yasmina would be this kind of woman."

Although her body had been severely bruised, she still worried about Hawk. Who deserves this kind of treatment?

"So, you worked with Yasmina?" he asks Emy by the console.

"Right, I never told you about it." Emily hesitates, then lets out a painful sigh, all traces of amusement gone. "Yasmina was … a boss who didn't acknowledge her limits."

Emily sets the sphere on the receptacle and operates the console with jarring ease, "Commander Kevin Hawk." When the machine hums at the sound of her voice, Emily squeals with joy.

"I won't ask you how you learned to use this," comments Skyler.

"Better not to." The hologram comes to life and this marvel of technology thrills Skyler since the details are so much sharper and the experience so vivid. The Naves pale in comparison. However, the mood dampens when Dan notifies them of some last-minute changes.

"We have to get back in less than an hour. Neal's orders."

"Why?" says Emily. "If he wants the damn code, he'll have to wait." Dan shrugs and mumbles that it's not his problem.

They use every minute to find a time when Hawk used the code. The content is rich, and they can't just search randomly. At first, Emily browses the sphere while Skyler tries to spot any clue on the holographic projection. As if that wasn't enough, they also have to juggle Dan's impatience at the five-minute mark.

They witness more than one intimate scene between Yasmina and Hawk, and Emily sweeps them away with an edgy voice command.

"Damn it! We'll never find that godforsaken code!" Emily says as she plays another scene where Hawk was visiting Yasmina on the sly. "These two look like teenagers."

"I think many people would give a lot to have this chance. Wouldn't you?"

"Not the same thing," she stammers, blushing. "I mean, if I was in love, I wouldn't do … that."

"Who would want to fall in love with a bully like you anyway?" he asks nonchalantly.

"This is not the time," she gives him the evil eye and gets back to work.

"Instead of searching through his memories with Yasmina, try to sort out the times when he was alone in his cabin. His computer must be connected to the Ark's central system." Skyler shows her what the office looks like and how to do it. The holographic system is just an augmented version of the Nave, nothing too complicated.

"Here, like this," he instructs her as Emily controls the viewing speed with her hand resting on a half-sphere. "Slow down."

Hawk is at his desk and since they can see through his eyes, the computer screen is in focus. He types in his password, but, of course, it is encrypted.

"Damn, we'll never make it," complains Emily.

"Back up a little. I have an idea." Skyler steps onto the platform and the light jets warm his skin. As he expected, the keys Hawk presses move along with his fingers. They make note of this and double-check three times. Then Dan picks them up to return to the Command Center.

"Remind me next time that this is not the fastest way to find a code." Emily groans and sighs. "My eyes are going to pop out of my head." It's Skyler's turn to laugh this time.

"Amaranth. It's a strange password, don't you think?" he says as they enter the Command Center. "It doesn't sound familiar either."

"Do codes have to make sense?"

"Why not? It makes them easier to remember."

"And easier to hack." Amaranth. Skyler is sure he saw that word somewhere. Unless…

"It's a flower."

"Really?"

"Yes. I think I even saw some in the Gardens." Not just there. He read something about it in the Archives. Does the Commander also have an interest in flowers? Once Dan leaves them alone, Skyler says, "Ready to tell my brother we found the code?"

Emily drags him inside a vacant cabin and glares at him, hands on her hips.

"We need to talk."

38

EMILY

"Your brother is dead, Skyler."

Once the door clicked, she burst out. How could she have thought everything would be settled once they have a moment together? And now Sky is pulling this nonsense on her!

"What's done is done," she adds resolutely. "You can't change the past." A strange stench of death stinks in the empty office.

Sky is staring at her as he says, "Why can't you just accept the fact that he survived?"

"It's been five years. And you said it yourself: a fall from this height is fatal." He remains silent, probably rationalizing. Good. Better weed out the seeds of doubt they've sown before he crosses the point of no return.

"His body was never found," he mutters, his face serious.

"Neal doesn't even look like the Allen that I remember." This Neal looks older and different. Allen was reckless and feisty, a bit of an idealist, but he wouldn't have had tattoos all over his arms. Not to mention his tapered face, especially the jawline, his more ashen, almost brown hair. Even his aura seems different. No, it's too much.

"Emily, you have trust issues, you know that?" Emily's

fingers find a thread protruding from her borrowed uniform, and she coils it around her index finger, again and again. The fiber digs into her now hot-and-throbbing skin.

"Believe what you want. But if this is what you call a brother, the leader of a rebellion, someone who wants you to support their brutal methods…"

"It's my decision, not his," he retorts through clenched teeth. Sparks run between their auras, which expand in abnormal patterns. Calm down. This is Sky, after all. Emily lets out a deep sigh and uncoils the thread that was keeping her busy, then crosses her arms.

"I thought you'd keep a modicum of sanity. This Brotherhood is selling a dream. They make you believe that you are their brother in arms."

"Emily." The way he pronounces her name leaves her speechless. His kindness is gone. The gentle, attentive Skyler, always ready to help or comfort to the point of forgetting himself, is now a thing of the past.

"Neal is my blood brother," he continues without batting an eye. "He spent the last few years with the Mavericks where he joined the Brotherhood. My brother is not dead. Neal is my brother Allen."

There are so many unanswered questions. First, how did Allen recover from his injuries following his fall? How organized were the Mavericks to even have proper medical care? And even if they had been able to heal him, why didn't he simply return to his family? The Goldbergs have an excellent reputation, and they love their children. Sky never complained about any abuse from his parents, unlike Chris, who had to bear his father's whims.

"It is insane!" she concludes, without tempering her annoyance. "Did you think he could manipulate us? All of us. Milo said they know absolutely everything. They know about your brother, and Neal could use that just so you join them. Unless you get a DNA test—"

"Emily, you're overreacting," he says, looking concerned. "Are you sure you're okay? You're not your usual self." She swallows hard. With everything that's happened in the last few days, she doesn't need her best friend questioning her.

"I don't know what to say to knock sense into you," she replies in exasperation. "You don't know anything about them. They are using you to commit horrendous things."

"Just accept reality for once," he says with a flat calm. "I can't be what you want me to be."

Sky doesn't give her time to answer and exits the office.

The feeling of death around her becomes oppressive, but the footsteps and the conversations coming from the corridor remind her she is very much alive. After a while, she settles down on the crisp sofa. The fabric is still dry and stiff under her weight, but oh so much more comfortable than any furniture the Bateses have ever owned. She should be happy about this, but she can't contain her urge to rub the armrest mindlessly until her skin chafes. She would give anything to be able to draw in her sketchbook, Sky's portrait perhaps, but also his so-called brother. To find the differences ... or similarities between the two. Blood brothers, really?

Fatigue eventually gets the better of her, and Skyler's face melds with Neal's in her mind.

Her friend has changed.

YASMINA IS DEAD, but who the Commander really is remains a mystery.

Emily's night's sleep was cut short by the awkward position she slept in. With the many injuries riddling her body, it will take weeks before she can lie on her side without wincing. As if that wasn't enough, snatches of conversations filtered through the walls all night, and then her mind took care of the rest.

At a reasonable, though, very early hour, she got up to carry out her quest for answers. She didn't survive Yasmina's torture simply to toss away the leads her former boss left her.

Happy to have some semblance of freedom, Emily walks out of the cabin that serves as her temporary shelter until the Brotherhood successfully takes over the Ark. Meanwhile, Milo can help her.

The corridor is quiet. The Mavericks who joined the rebellion must have holed up in their new cabins, a luxury they'd never enjoyed. Hopefully, someone hasn't indulged and will give her the right directions. This part of the ship is a maze, or nearly so. Chris would know how to find his way around, but she hasn't seen him. Emily hopes nothing has happened to him.

"The mission was clear."

She slows down, stunned. There is not a living soul around, so it must be coming from the vents, or the insulation is just terrible. The truth is, they might not have been able to sail the Command Center into the ocean without the Ark to power it.

"You can't just change your mind at the last minute and pretend it never happened. I've not worked my ass off all these years so you can do whatever you want."

This voice has a familiar ring to it. It's her, that Tessa. Emily is not sure if she wants to ask her for directions. Besides, she seems like she's in one hell of a state.

"If I lose him, I will never forgive you. Do you hear me? Never!"

Sobs? Did her frozen heart finally melt?

"Give me more time."

Ill-at-ease, Emily hurries on. It's none of her business, and she doesn't want to have to comfort her. Or should she?

A nerd named Walker comes over to show her the way to Milo's cabin. No complications, no explanations. Perfect.

Good thing this Walker was around because Emily was headed in the opposite direction. After a few turns, she knocks. No response, but muffled voices. Perhaps Milo didn't hear her.

"Milo? It's me, I just wanted to—" Her wristband accidentally opened the door, and the scene stops her short. The bed is unmade, and Fiona is standing, clinging to Milo's half-naked body, her tongue stuck in his mouth. Some people have less trouble waking up than others.

Reyes indulges in the moment when she realizes Emily is there. Milo pushes her away, his cheeks flush.

"So, you survived," hisses Fiona Reyes as she adjusts her tank top.

"I was going to say the same thing to you," laughs Emily. It's so hot in this cabin! Just the opposite of the rest of the ship, which might as well be the refrigerated compartment in Violet's kitchen.

"I'll be right back," says Milo, as he puts on a uniform just like the one Mom used to make.

"What's the matter with you?" snaps Reyes, jealous. "We have no business with this bitch."

"She's my problem now." It's hard to tell if this is a pretext or a criticism.

"You will have to explain," commands Reyes who ragingly pulls on the bedsheets. "And you..." Reyes points to her, "... don't hurt him or you'll have a taste of my medicine."

Emily wants to retort, but Milo pushes her out of the cabin and shuts the door abruptly.

"What's up?" He doesn't smell as good as last time. He smells like Reyes, a mixture of sweat and fish.

Emily lifts her head to look into his glazed eyes, as if he hadn't gotten enough sleep. They don't have the same depth they had the night before.

"I want to see Commander Hawk," she says casually. Milo's moods should keep her busy, but instead she is obsessed with their lovemaking. Yet, deep down, she knew they were a couple.

"Is there a reason?" he asks, with a hint of annoyance in his voice.

"I'd rather not talk about it."

"How convincing."

"I know." He looks around as if afraid someone will catch them.

"By the way, I'm sorry." What is he apologizing for? That she will replay his kissing session in her mind for the next few days or that he treated her rudely the night before when he *gently* escorted her into the Command Center? Go for the second one. Less complicated.

"For tying me up?" He hesitates. Does he hope she will add something? She doesn't. He scratches the nape of his neck.

"It was the only way Dan would trust me."

"Fine. We're even." That's the least of her worries right now.

"Is that all?" he asks, tilting his head.

"Yes, that's all." He looks wary.

"Follow me." He leads her to a nondescript cabin in the maze of the Command Center in complete silence. Once they arrive, Milo exchanges a few words with the Maverick guard, who walks away to go on his break. "Are you okay? You seem … weird."

Milo does his little trick from the cell again with his aura flaring up to consume her, which she can hardly resist, but she wants nothing to do with it.

"I have some things to take care of." He pouts, then resigns himself to open the door.

"I'll wait for you here," he insists in a last-ditch effort to coax her.

"It's all right. I'll get back to the cabin I've been so kindly assigned on my own." She avoids his gaze to focus on what comes next.

"Well," he says, disappointed. "In this case, I won't insist." She imagines Milo brushing against her shoulder before leaving—or was it his aura?—and she steps inside.

A new interrogation. She had missed this.

SITTING IN A RICKETY CHAIR, Commander Kevin Hawk is droning while staring at something on his tablet.

The cabin they locked him in is not as luxurious as the one reserved for the Commander. A folded sheet of paper rests on top of the desk, and the chair is pulled out. Hawk barely notices her presence, but eventually his voice fades. His dark purplish aura shrinks so much he looks like he's choking.

"Emily?" he asks in a small voice. She nods, the right words escaping her. This man has just witnessed the death of his loved one. No words seem appropriate.

The same father-loving energy from their first meeting shines through when he speaks to her.

"I'm glad you made it here. For what it's worth now."

"It mustn't be easy." He looks at her, intrigued. The image he was gazing at on his tablet is Laurene's. He has an uneasy smile when he realizes he was caught in the act.

"She was the crew member with the most potential. An unexpected talent." His hands shake slightly, but Emily couldn't say why exactly. Anger? Disappointment? Fear?

"Or was I wrong to trust her?" His voice is hoarse, his words left hanging like a sentence ready to crush him.

"I'm not here to talk to you about the Brotherhood," she says. "What they do is none of my business. They don't know I've come." His fingers are smudged with ink, like Emily after a drawing session. "Do you like to draw?"

"Sometimes, but I was not gifted," he says, calming down a

bit, staring at his fingers. She sits on the armchair in front of him.

"My first portraits were ugly too," she admits, crossing her legs.

"I could never draw anything for an exhibition at the Academy. The artistic side of things didn't work for me. My drawings have always been too organized. When they asked to be original and think outside the box, I wanted to draw the box, not what's outside."

"I'm not an artist either. I draw people I know. Not very imaginative." He has a nervous laugh.

"I enjoyed sketching the ship. I think I would have liked to be an engineer and take care of the design. But we don't always choose our career, do we?"

"I understand," says Emily. She would have traded her job as an agent to be a relic hunter any day, but she wouldn't have become what she is now. She wouldn't be chatting with the Ark's Commander alone. How many people on the ship have that privilege? Despite the dramatic turn of events, he is still the man who sacrificed his entire life to protect them, no matter what his methods were.

"You are Yasmina's best agent." He still speaks of her in the present, which means he hasn't mourned. Emily doesn't know if she could do it differently if Gabrielle, Dad, or Skyler had died.

"We're not always gifted for the things that matter most to us," she says. He nods. They have that in common. "Your children should be proud of your achievements despite everything. This is no small feat."

Kevin Hawk gives her that interested look again, and his features relax.

"I wish my child had lived longer to make him proud."

"Sorry, I didn't know." A proper father at heart.

"It's been a long time, but I keep him close to my heart. I don't know what Yasmina told you about me—"

"I know she had plans. That *you* had plans." Her heart quickens, and she crosses her other leg.

"Losing a baby is difficult, especially for the woman who carried it," he says, rubbing his face. "Yasmina insisted we try again, but her body just couldn't take it."

Are the tests still negative? This is what they were discussing in the hologram.

"She often talked about you, Emily," he adds. "You were almost a mythical figure. The very essence of your mother, her best friend. I tried to reason with her, but..." She had expected anything but that. Did Yasmina idolize her? Was Mom her best friend?

"Yet, you said you would take me as your daughter." He sighs in annoyance.

"I never said that," he replies in a firm but unapologetic voice. "I could offer you the protection necessary to buy her peace of mind. I also know the Bateses and how difficult it was after your mother's sentence."

He sets the tablet on the cushion beside him and clasps his fingertips.

"But lately, Yasmina has had fits of madness. With everything that was going on at the Command Center and the Brotherhood, I didn't give her the time she needed. It shook her up. Please, don't judge her too harshly."

Did he even have an inkling of what this woman was really capable of? Now is not the time to shatter his memories of her. Giving up his ship is hard enough to bear. As if following her train of thought, he looks beaten.

"She needed help, but I let her down," he mumbles. "And I lost her." He lets out a sob, and Emily knows she must let him accept his new reality.

"I'm sorry." The interrogation is over, and she returns to her cabin without running into Milo. A father who lost his baby, the love of his life, and now his ship. Nothing could be more human.

He would have made a good father.

In the middle of the night, the commotion wakes her up. The Commander is dead. Hanged.

WAKING up the next day was even more painful, although she used the hidden Murphy bed. She rummaged around for quite a while, but finding the bed was worth it, at least for falling asleep. It had a sinfully comfortable mattress compared to the one in their family cabin, but not enough to fix her cracked bones and numb her aching muscles.

After a questionable lunch of smelly oatmeal and bread, Neal comes to thank her personally for helping them gain access to the ship's servers.

"Although we do not know what this code means, it allowed us to take control of the Ark." He leans on the edge of the desk and crosses his arms, highlighting his tattoo that glows under the fluorescent light. Emily stays on the sofa, which is softening in the right places.

He continues in earnest, "Without you, we would be at a dead end."

"I don't need your thanks. I did it for myself." He looks better than last time, his complexion a little brighter and his hair waving smartly. Since he's the one in charge of the ship, this bodes well for them all. For now. It's also the perfect time to get to the bottom of things.

"Is there anything you want to tell me?" he asks as he gauges her. At least he is quick-witted.

"I'd like to talk about Tyna Bates. My mother."

"Ah." He nods, as if to himself. "It's a long story."

"I have plenty of time." She crosses her arms in turn. He grins, as if enjoying himself.

"Ask away, and I'll answer them as best I can," he replies, grabbing the edge of the table.

"How did she help with the Brotherhood's plans?"

"She knew of our existence, as well as that of all the Mavericks. She knew the situation was unfair and wanted to have a part."

"By making uniforms?" He looks surprised, but does not let it show, though his aura betrays him.

"Yes, but her contributions go beyond those uniforms. She boosted our morale in a way that made us feel like people, unlike the outcasts the Ark tried to get rid of." The Mavericks' condition did not concern Emily until recently. They were a nuisance to the system, but aren't they a product of it, anyway?

"And she was convicted for helping you," Emily adds bluntly. Neal's face tenses.

Commander Hawk deserved Emily's empathy. The sad reality of his failure to protect his crew and his lover was too much to bear. He had noble intentions in the end. As for Neal, it's a different story. Being a Maverick and having experienced discrimination are abhorrent, but he had been prepared for every step of the way. By founding the Brotherhood and dragging others into this spiral of death, he must bear the consequences, including Mom's death.

"It's more complicated than that," he replies, clearly ill-at-ease. He considers her for a moment. Emily settles into the sofa and fidgets with a pillow in anticipation. "She learned about the X2O that the Commander tried to hide from everyone."

"What does it mean?" That strange code again. The leaders of this ship have made a habit of it, it seems.

"A disease, a direct consequence of the Flood. The fury of God for some. The Paragon was experimenting with their guinea pigs, regardless of their feelings. They wanted to unravel the mystery at any cost. Perhaps even to use it to their advantage." The B-248.

"This disease, is it the Fairy Syndrome? We had prisoners, Griffin and Reed, for example, who had fits of madness and—" Neal raises his hands to stop her.

"This is a conversation you should have with Skyler. I'm not well versed in medicine. All I know is that your mother found out they wanted to use it to control the passengers, possibly the Commander's idea."

What would be the point of controlling the passengers if not to satisfy a perverse desire for manipulation? Someone with very dark plans who would not settle for the control of the ship. Why else?

"I doubt it," she retorts. "The Commander doesn't strike me as that kind of person."

"There is another possibility," he continues, nodding. "Duke Kay, the leader of the Paragon, is known to be ruthless. But he doesn't have the authority to act on his own."

"Now he does. There had to be someone else, with more specific motivations. Someone hungry for power and experience," she says thoughtfully. "And my mother knew these things."

"She was on a solid lead to unmask the mastermind of this plan. Their identity, but also how they were going to use it. The Brotherhood bought her time by providing a cover, but our resources were limited. That changed when Laurene helped us."

"Laurene?" she says, surprised.

"Yes."

"She shot Yasmina ruthlessly."

"She must have had a personal vendetta to settle. Besides, she won't harm anyone else. We arrested her, too." Emily nods. A free mind like her can indeed be dangerous. Yet she really didn't give that impression when they first met. Chris admired her. Had he seen through her game? And if so, why hadn't he done anything to stop her?

"Despite her valuable help, if she turned against the Brotherhood, it would be a mess."

"It can be a double-edged sword," admits Emily, shaking off the cushion. "She would feel resentful for being locked up. That happens a lot with prisoners. They try to befriend the staff, but when they realize they won't get any special treatment, they become aggressive."

Griffin had been the perfect example, along with her poor colleague Iris, who was blinded by his assault. There were other incidents, but fortunately, that was before Emily took office.

"So, that's all my mother did?" she resumes to worm all she can out of him. Neal gets up to stretch his legs.

"Tyna didn't do anything wrong if that's what you're worried about. She reminded us of what makes us human. You probably have what it takes to follow in her footsteps, by the way."

A ringing sound from Neal's wristband makes him frown, and his energy jolts.

"I have to go, but I hope we can work together in the future to set things right on the Ark. With Skyler, of course. I'm sure you'll be able to help the Mavericks fit into the community. You can finish up your mother's work."

A proposal? It would be an opportunity to learn more about the Mavericks and also about Mom's ties to them. Neal doesn't seem like he will tell her anything else. For the rest, she will have to hunt for information.

"I'll think about it," she replies as she gets up.

"And you could even help us find the Promised Land," he adds from the doorway.

"I can't wait to see what it looks like, Allen."

Neal's aura contracts at that, and he leaves her strangely by pressing two fingers to his forehead.

39

EMILY

Now that the Brotherhood has control of the Command Center, it's time to find them.

Emily leaves her cabin after ingesting the horrible fish dish a Maverick left. She makes it to the command room where a heated discussion is raging. Even Milo doesn't notice her.

A huge screen floats in front of the portholes, overlooking the Great Ocean. The sequence shows the atrium in complete chaos. The sound is missing, and she can't make out the cause of all this confusion.

"I told you he was dangerous," Tessa says through her teeth. She is back to her usual self, her crying fit but a forgotten memory.

"That's only one of the two main problems on our plate," says Neal.

"What are they doing?" asks Emily, who sees Duke Kay on the video barking orders to his agents as they herd the Archeans in groups.

Emily's words get lost in the din, but then she catches an answer.

"He gives them some kind of test and those who fail are taken away," says Tessa, troubled.

"I should have stopped them when I had the chance."

What the hell? What if Dad and Gabrielle were among the refugees in the atrium?

Sky is further back, on the same side as Tessa, fists clenched, eyes glued to Chris who is talking to the agents herding people. He looks pissed.

Of course, Duke plotted to control the Ark, and Chris is there to stop him. His father has a habit of using people like soldiers at his beck and call. Dad would talk about it sometimes. Without the officers Diana and Laurene, nothing can stop Duke, now the legitimate contender for becoming the new Commander. He will claim it as soon as he knows Hawk is dead. She is curious to see how the Brotherhood will handle him.

"What about the sound?" asks Emily loudly. "It might help."

"The system was completely fried in the explosion. Only some cameras are still functional," someone replies.

"We need to know what's going on out there," shouts Neal.

Emily can't help but think that with Laurene's help, they could rally the Paragon and free the passengers. But it's not up to her to decide what to do.

"But what are they doing?" mumbles Emily, enthralled by the images.

The people on the video are terrified. They are screaming, crying, but the Paragon officers are grabbing and hitting them with the butts of their guns. Some even threaten them with the tip of their fully charged electric prods, sparks alight. Archeans fall to their knees, hands behind their heads. Children cry. The atrium is crowded with more than half the passengers. Officers drag the prisoners onto the central platform to test them, though the video is too blurry to see what they do to them.

"What's the point of going to the Promised Land if there's no one left? I'm going to take care of him."

"I know Chris. I can try to reason with him," says Sky, stepping towards Neal. Sky has been quiet so far, probably brooding about Chris. Bad idea.

"It's too risky," Neal replies before Emily can get involved. "I can't afford to lose you again."

"Let me handle it," says Tessa, adjusting her bandana. "My contacts in the Paragon can help me get the situation back under control."

"We won't really save them until we fix the Sacred Fire," points out the guy who guided Emily to Milo's cabin.

"What do you suggest, Walker?" Neal urges. The command room is buzzing with people. Fiona and Milo are arguing, unconcerned about what is going on around them, and Emily feels utterly alone in her corner. No one pays her attention, if only for their ghostly auras giving her a migraine. Can't they just control their emotions for once? What she would give to hold Gabrielle in her arms or hear Dad scold her for forgetting to bring back a pastry Skyler gave her during lunch.

Her vision blurs, and the auras split into two.

"Emily! Are you here?" She whispers a weak *yes* as she tries to chase away the vision of horror in her mind. Gabrielle and Dad. If Duke Kay did anything to them…

A hand on her shoulder brings her back amidst the cries of indignation as they recognize faces among the refugees: Tessa's partner in arms, and Leander, who is probably still mourning Mira's death. A familiar-looking tunic catches Emily's eye: Violet and her brother!

No trace of Dad or Gabrielle. They could have been herded like the others. My God, no!

"Emily," shouts Milo whose fiery energy touches hers.

"Milo?" she whispers, still in shock. "What's going on? Where did everyone go?"

"Come with me?"

She nods and lets Milo lead her out of the command room.

THE GROWLING AURAS are not letting up anytime soon. Milo lets go of her hand as soon as they catch up with their group that had a slight lead on them. They haven't been this close since he saved her in the prison.

There are about thirty of them: members of the Brotherhood, well-armed Mavericks, and Laurene who could play a major role in the negotiations with Duke.

"What's the plan?" asks Emily, as everyone's eyes train on her. As for Laurene, she seems to be enjoying herself despite her wrists being bound and the three Mavericks keeping an eye on her. With what she did to Yasmina, they can't be too cautious.

"Not all of us can go. It's too risky," says Neal, a hand on his gun.

Walker's voice echoes through Neal's wristband, "We must reboot the Sacred Fire. If we can't, then we are done for."

"Let's split up," suggests Tessa. "Those who can fight should go to the atrium. As for the others..." Neal accepts, and everyone decides on their group.

"The atrium," Emily says first.

"No," Milo objects, drawing in closer under Fiona's disapproving gaze. Emily glares at him so he would back off. Who does he think he is?

"My family is probably there. I'm going." She steps towards the group designated for the atrium, but Milo grabs her arm.

"You've had too many injuries." Then Milo speaks to Neal directly. "She's coming with me to the Sacred Fire."

"Fine by me." Neal points to four Mavericks and decides that three groups will head to the Sacred Fire separately. The Ark is badly damaged, and it will be hard to reach. There is no room for error.

Once each group is formed, Neal gives his orders. Sky stays

behind a little and advises Emily to be careful. She responds with a grunt.

"Your evil look doesn't scare me," Milo says, laughing at her.

They walk across the same corridor he dropped her in after the free party. Although this place had seemed dark and unwelcoming, the whole ship now swims in this eerie blend of darkness peppered with the blue emergency lights. Emily's headache pounds with the strong smell of humidity. Things couldn't get any better, really.

"It should," says Emily, frowning at Milo's boldness.

"Has anyone told you that you sound like a bully?"

"Mind your own business."

"I knew it." Milo's hard to read. Since they shared that moment in the prison, he's been clearly teasing her. He is in a relationship with Fiona Reyes, so he might just be trying to tempt Emily with insignificant innuendos. Her already touchy situation with her feisty former prisoner would only get worse if Fiona knew. Emily can't drag on past mistakes if she wishes to have a fresh start.

"I wonder how Fiona puts up with you," she quips. "You are unbearable."

"That's my charm."

"Speak for yourself." Enough with the teasing. Duke Kay could shoot down Dad and Gabrielle any time now. The fate of the Ark lies in their hands.

Milo leads them down a hallway she doesn't recognize. They then come to a recess that houses some seemingly unregistered Strahls, whose lining is worn in places as if they hadn't had proper maintenance for ages. For her peace of mind, Emily ignores this peculiar detail.

She slips into the vehicle first, which earns her a whistle from Milo.

"Full of hidden talent, aren't you," he says, taking the passenger seat.

"Shut up and buckle up." She adjusts the fasteners of her safety harness as the Strahl buzzes up to life. A whole range of available options lights up, much better than the last time when the navigation system asked a bunch of useless questions. It must be another model. She looks over the console: manual mode, exploration mode…

Emily has a satisfied smile as she fires it up. This manual mode is great. Milo is pinned in his seat and that's enough to cut out his teasing.

"You don't like being told what to do," says Milo, squirming in his seat as he peers at the copilot's screen showing a detailed map of the surrounding area.

"Who does?" says Emily as she steers the ship out of the recess. The temptation to zip directly to the atrium without stopping by the Sacred Fire is strong, but the others are working on it. She must trust them. She couldn't do much in her condition anyway, and the Ark's beating heart is just as important, so they don't die in a drifting metal carcass.

Milo points in the direction indicated on the map, and Emily zips into the hangar, which—thank God—opens as they approach.

"Can I count on you?" she asks as they get swallowed up by the Ark.

"Are you going to ask me to save you from another ghoul like Yasmina?"

"Actually, she saved us somehow." Milo doesn't seem to understand. "The code. It's all thanks to her." He arches an eyebrow.

"All right. Well, I'm not ready to play the hero again." Emily rolls her eyes and Milo sneers.

"After we have rebooted the Sacred Fire, I'd like to visit the lower levels. To understand the Mavericks."

The Strahl slips through some piping where all the water gets drained. Then they emerge into the hangar where two other vessels are parked. The Strahl's windows quickly fog up, and when they open the doors, the humidity is heavy, almost burning.

"I don't blame you for Yasmina," Milo says slowly, as if weighing his every word. "At first, I did, but then I realized you have a power to forgive that I don't. Not only to forgive, but to see through people, to read their hearts. You are gifted."

Over the years, her gift has become second nature to her. Though it has been useful on occasion, it also has a dark side. Reading people's moods to judge them is wrong. And these unrelenting migraines are exhausting.

Milo's words are refreshing, though, and she does not have the strength to argue with him.

"Thank you." The rust has eaten away at every bit of metal exposed and sprawling cargo of every kind show how much the ship's hull has been neglected. This place could use some serious maintenance.

"This is where they collect the hunters' finds," says Milo, who winds his way through as if he were born here. Wouldn't this be the perfect place for the Mavericks to replenish their supplies?

They meander through several containers without a hint of an exit. Then, a double door appears, nestled between two massive sorting bins.

"You'd be surprised to see how well generations of stowaways have scraped by with so little. I'll show you someday." Sweat tickles Emily's back and she wipes her face off with the sleeve of her stinky uniform, which could use a good washing. She turns to Milo who is drying his face.

"How does the Sacred Fire work?"

"It's complex," he says, sniffing. "I'll explain on the way." The Sacred Fire is a hidden foundry in the heart of the Ark, but that's all the Academy would tell them.

The heat in the corridor is overwhelming, though much better than the foul smell of the ocean. The power outage has severely affected this section and even the emergency lights are flashing, giving a ghostly look to Milo, who is walking up ahead.

"The Sacred Fire is an eternal flame created artificially through collected hydroelectric energy," he teaches her. "Its flame can thrust the Ark forward, but it also spreads throughout the Ark to provide for our every need. The ocean currents are unpredictable, but luckily for us, storms on the surface are common. When a big storm rages, the currents ripple into the abyss and cause seaquakes within the Ark."

In the past, when Emily was young, the shaking had been so intense they had to seek shelter in the Refuge, the safest place in case of emergency. It is the only place they could go if the Sacred Fire died or the Command Center came off, though only for a month. Beyond that, they would run out of food and their end would be inevitable.

"Why does it have to be so hot in here?"

"The timing is out of sync," he replies confidently. "Probably some damage caused by the explosion." The serious look on Milo's face while explaining how this machine works shows how passionate he is about it. Had he not been born a Maverick, what would have become of him?

"If you didn't use your bomb, this never would have happened," Emily grumbles.

"Wait, you think we did this?"

"Well, the ruckus of the last few days... Who else could have done this?"

"We don't know. Walker investigated, but the cameras were damaged. Then there was the problem with the Commander and the code." Who else could have caused the explosion?

Thrown smoke bombs and attacked the Sacred Fire? Duke Kay and the Paragon? Such a waste of resources knowing that the Brotherhood's plans were already underway.

"Chris's father could have orchestrated the whole thing from the beginning," she says. "They bought time while they set up the refugee camps. But why would they just want to kill them?"

"It doesn't make sense." She nods.

"Duke was doing experiments on the X2O. It must have something to do with it. What if the Paragon was sorting Archeans based on whether they have the Syndrome?" Her question remains unanswered. The most massive door she has ever seen is towering in front of them with its tons of compacted metal. Milo struggles to open it and they cover their faces against the blast of hot air until it subsides.

An enormous room, larger than the atrium, occupies nearly half the floor. At its center is a flame, radiating off a series of dark blocks with the green glow of circuitry that Milo calls energy condensers. Emily's breathing becomes shallow as an invisible weight pushes against her chest. It's as if the energy was interfering with hers. She almost feels like throwing up.

"We shouldn't have to stay long," Milo says, with a reassuring hand on Emily's back. "Just what we need to re-synchronize and get the hell out of here." Her nausea gets stronger and stronger as they walk towards the blazing flame, and the constant whirring makes her feel even worse.

They pass row after row of blocks to finally reach a large console. Despite the glow that escapes from the dark matter they are made of, they can only see a few feet away where the light of the Sacred Fire creates a string of stretching shadows.

Milo tells her exactly what to do while he calibrates another kind of machinery, and Emily complies as soon as the screen fills up with a series of senseless codes. According to Milo, they first have to run various tests to make sure the energy levels are sufficient.

She follows his instructions dutifully. She rubs her stomach while waiting for Milo to finish on his side. She can't help but feel this unease creeping up on her, this place clearly interfering with her own energy. As if on cue, Milo's aura has disappeared.

"Are you ready?" he asks. She nods and runs the procedure. An electronic voice guides them as each of the nine hearts are being rebooted.

"You look pale," says Milo, dangerously close to her.

"You're able to see that much?" she scoffs, her throat tight. "I can only see some orange spots all over your face."

"I'm serious," he replies, gently taking her shoulders. "You'd better get Sky to examine you."

"We'll be fine as soon as we leave this place. I don't like it."

The synthetic voice suddenly chimes, "The synchronization has failed."

"What the hell?" shouts Milo, who goes back to the other console.

"What did we do wrong? I followed the instructions exactly as you told me."

"It's not you." He taps something. "There's a problem with the C-24 block. I'll have to check it out myself. Meanwhile, just wait for me. When this turns green, press here."

"Hurry."

"If you feel like throwing up, don't do it on the console," he sneers as he walks away. Emily sighs and closes her eyes to give herself a break.

It has to work. Milo seems confident, but if it goes south, they won't have anywhere to go.

The Ark is their home, the only place on this planet where they can lead a normal life. After getting out of this hell, she will make sure Dad and Gabrielle are treated better. They will move to a bigger cabin and come up with new recipes. Violet's insufferable brother could even join them. Or maybe not since he's so annoying. Sky and his family would be most welcome, though. They've never had a proper family dinner as far as she can remember.

Now free of her obligations with Yasmina, she will try something new. Neal's proposal is enticing. If she can redeem herself by helping the Mavericks, that would make her happy. There might be other Milos out there.

As for her Milo, things might get complicated, especially when it comes to working together and dealing with their odd friendship.

She breathes in deeply and realizes the humming is getting louder. And still no word from Milo. What's taking him so long?

Emily spins around abruptly, convinced she saw a shadow moving. With her pounding headache, her senses are numb. At the same time, the electronic voice confirms that the C-24 block has been reconnected. Hand on her stomach, Emily waits for the icon to turn green, just like Milo instructed her. A jolt of pain sears through her stomach, and she lets out a hiccup of surprise. She bends over and moans, tears in her eyes as the burning sensation spreads like wildfire.

She tries to hold on to the console, the Sacred Fire dancing. As she struggles to get back up with both hands, a hot liquid runs between her fingers.

Panic overwhelms her. She presses her hand back to her stomach to stop the blood from pouring out. She quickly probes for Milo's energy, but the magnetic field is too dense. There is only nothingness.

The dark stain on her uniform is frightening. Was she shot? Was she stabbed?

Emily steps away from the console. Show yourself, you bastard! Is it Milo? Did he want to take her away so he could kill her? On Neal's orders?

Her mind reels as she tries to figure out where the threat might lurk so much that she almost forgets the blood that keeps flowing between her fingers. She was an obstacle to the Brotherhood's plan. Stupid!

"If you have any courage, show your face. Bastard."

Every word is torture and gets lost in her silent hiccups. Tears burn her eyes.

She is going to die.

A brisk movement to her right. She turns around, but her legs give out and she falls hard to her knees. Her veins freeze with fear, and her pulse slows down.

She is about to lose consciousness, but then she hears a familiar voice.

"She didn't even come by herself."

That voice. Every day for two years. Every simulation of the Paragon. That voice…

40

SKYLER

His mother is asleep.

Skyler is unsure whether he should be happy or worried. With all the changes to come, he must make sure everything is perfect. For their future. For the new member who will join their family.

His mother became pregnant when she shouldn't have, especially with her depression. Her recurring symptoms were a red flag, not her worsening illness. Skyler feels like a fool for having missed her pregnancy. Besides, they still don't know whether it will be a boy or a girl. Skyler didn't want to run a genetic test. He wants it to be a surprise.

Neal doesn't know. Skyler will wait until their mother's condition is stable to let him know. Skyler is smiling: There will be a new member in their family. And when Murielle learns Allen is still alive, she will finally heal.

Neal. Skyler still needs time to get used to his new identity. But their days on the Ark are numbered. There is no way to reignite the Sacred Fire. The technology to make the needed components sank along with everything else in the Flood.

The Brotherhood is hard at work preparing to migrate all

the Archeans—those who survived Chris's father's morbid tests at least—to the Refuge. Fortunately, Tessa was swift and skillful at the atrium. With the help of her contacts in the Paragon, they overpowered both father and son, along with the agents in Duke's pay. It is still unclear why Chris was there with him. Skyler hopes he wasn't wrong about him. As for the ventilation system, it's working, thanks to Walker, who reallocated the Sacred Fire's remaining energy supplies, just enough to complete the preparations to move to the Refuge.

Syncing the Sacred Fire could have prevented all of this, but it's too late now. As for Emily…

He exits the room where Murielle lies asleep and drops by next door. He bites his lip, a lump stuck in his throat. He leans against the wall, fighting the emotion which could drown him any second.

Has he done something wrong that cursed everyone he loves? Hasn't he suffered enough already?

He lets himself slide towards the ground, distraught. He stares blankly, unable to move, shaking. No matter what he does, they all end up the same. Death takes them away.

How can anyone believe in the damn Creator? Will there ever be an end to this pain?

SKYLER STANDS there for so long that he loses track of time. His face hurts, his throat hurts. Everything hurts.

A girl he hasn't met before comes out of the room in a rustle of fabric.

"Do you know her?" he asks in a hoarse voice. He swallows the excess saliva that has built up in his mouth. She turns towards him, revealing a face framed by long thick hair. Then, a look of recognition flashes in her eyes. She picks up her long dress and sits beside him.

"The Creator's ways have put us on each other's path." The girl does not look at him directly, but rather stares at the opposite wall. He is grateful for it.

"Thank you for Elaine," she says after a while. "My brother told me about the sphere." The sphere? Yes, now he remembers where he saw this girl's face. When he watched Mrs. Farrell's sphere. Her legitimate granddaughter.

"It's nothing."

"You must not give up hope, even if all seems lost," she says. Skyler remains silent. He doesn't have the strength, anyway. Hope is exhausting. What he thought was the beacon of light that guided him since childhood has slowly faded to nothingness. A wisp of smoke that billows towards the sky.

"The answers are not always where you expect them to be," adds the girl as if in a dream. He turns his head towards her, and even this simple movement is straining. She smiles shyly back at him. He makes out Mrs. Farrell's features in her eyebrows, her forehead, and even the corners of her mouth. The girl's face suddenly lights up, and she dips her hand into a basket at her feet.

"It's not much, but… It was in Grandma's things with a note addressed to you. She must have really liked you."

With a quivering hand, Skyler grasps the old book with the frayed cover. The pages are yellowed with age. He stares numbly as if it were the first book he had ever seen in his life. He opens it, unsure at first, and reads out the title in a hoarse voice, "Amaranth's diary." The girl's smile widens.

"Yes, she was the first Commander of the Ark."

"Wasn't it Commander Wolfe?"

"Everything I know comes from my grandmother, but Amaranth Bellerose was the first person to run this ship. That's why her name lives on even today." Skyler's face freezes.

"What do you mean?" Her confusion turns into amusement, just like a little girl would.

"Didn't you know? Grandma Elaine always taught us that our home is Amaranth. It's the official name of the Ark."

Skyler takes another peek at the old, rough-covered diary. Unintelligible whispers ring his ears as if they were struggling to spring off the aged paper that beats under his throbbing fingers.

Skyler presses the diary against his chest and exhales slowly, his eyes closed.

How many other secrets have been kept from them?

END OF BOOK 1

ACKNOWLEDGMENTS

This debut was beyond anything I could have imagined. The joys, the tears, the frustrations, the hardships, and the steep learning curve made this experience the most valuable of my life. This book is proof that resilience can fulfill any of your heart's desires, however crazy they might seem. In the last six years, I have met many people who have tremendously helped me along my writing and publishing journey.

I would first like to thank Pascal Raud, my awesome developmental editor who is exceptional! Not only is he a mentor, but also a friend who knows how to tap on the potential of a manuscript. It's so handy to have someone who can read my mind and pick the right word to express what I am trying to say. His comments have greatly improved the flow of this book along with my writing skills. It's now my turn to challenge him to write his first novel. Get ready!

My best friend Kim Archambault for all our conversations that rekindle my passion for writing even when self-doubt sets in. She nourishes a deep passion for writing, and she's the best when it comes to brainstorming crazy ideas.

My beta readers Mélissa Lemaire, a fan of the series, and Célia Chalfoun, a friend whose editing skills are unparalleled.

The copyeditor of this book, Heidi Ripplinger, who polished this piece with her insightful comments and clarity.

My parents for their unshakable support. They have always believed in my projects even when I had given up.

My partner who puts up with my blank stares and my hours of silence while I'm busy writing the next novel.

A VERY special thanks to all my Kickstarter backers who helped tremendously crystallize this project:

Sean Willson, Sam Fischbeck, Marty, Janny Lemay-Normand, Tony, Richard Novak, Tim Greenshields, Belinda Crawford, Señor Neo, Niki Coppola, Pauline Baird Jones, Martin Nehmiz, Vicky G, Aspen, Bauman, Gage "oSpaceGhoat" Troy, Jordan G Ritchie, Kate Sheeran Swed, S. B. Tabor, Robert McEvoy, Thomas Schwarz and Sylvie-Lynn.

Thank you, thank you, thank you for being awesome!

I also want to thank you my readers for keeping my passion for writing alive and pushing me to become a better author. Without you, writing wouldn't mean the same.

I can't wait to share more stories with you in the *very* near future.

See you soon!

David M. Snow

ABOUT THE AUTHOR

David M. Snow is a science-fiction and fantasy author for adults. When he is not busy reading with a cup of green tea, running 5km, looking up new words in the dictionary for hours on end, or learning Mandarin, Tagalog, Japanese or Korean, he sits down with his MacBook Pro and types his next novel in a frenzy.

With a Master's in Applied Linguistics and ten years of teaching experience, he is also a linguist, polyglot, entrepreneur and teacher. After living in China for several years, he is in search of new places to explore.

9 781990 368011